Stormswift

Stormswift

by Madeleine Brent

DOUBLEDAY & COMPANY, INC.
GARDEN CITY, NEW YORK

All of the characters in this book are fictitious, and
any resemblance to actual persons, living or dead, is
purely coincidental

Stormswift

I

Soon after dawn on a day in early spring I woke from a dream of the life I had once known. Despite the season, the mornings were still fresh here in the mountains, and I drew the sheepskin blanket up about my shoulders as I lay struggling against the wretchedness of returning to reality.

During my two and a half years in Shul I had rarely dreamed about the time before my captivity, and for this I was thankful. There was little enough pleasure in dreaming of myself as I had been in those days, Jemimah Lawley, daughter of Sir George and Lady Lawley, a vain, arrogant young woman of seventeen, bad-tempered with our native servants, often sickly, and invariably selfish. There was even less pleasure in awakening from such a dream of the past to the primitive and often terrifying life I had known since that hideous day of slaughter in September 1879, the day when Afghan soldiers had run amok in Kabul and attacked the British Mission in the stronghold of the Bala Hissar, massacring almost a hundred souls.

My father and mother had died that day. I had survived only by the loyalty of a native servant, a loyalty I had done nothing to deserve, but in the weeks and months that followed there were times when I wished I had died with the others.

I lifted my head to look across the tiny sleeping chamber to the window—a square hole in the mud brick wall with a wooden shutter on the outside and a curtain of coarsely woven goat's hair within. The pallor of the light showing through a crack in the shutter told me that the sun had not yet risen and I need not get up for a little while yet. My mattress was half a dozen skins laid on the floor. I had not slept in a bed since Deenbur discarded me as his wife some eighteen months ago now. Deenbur called himself *pacha*, which meant king in the tongue of Kafiristan, but he was really no more than a tribal chief. There were other so-called kings like Deenbur in these remote mountains and valleys of the Hindu Kush, each ruling a handful of scattered villages. Sometimes there was fighting between them, so Sandru had told me, and I could well believe it, for the Kafirs were fierce and bloodthirsty men, but Deenbur's little kingdom had not been involved in war during my time here.

The thought I tried never to think flashed into my mind. How long would be my time here? Was I to live and die among primitive strangers in this cruel land? I shivered and closed my eyes. Sandru had told me many times that escape was impossible for me. In winter the passes were blocked with snow, and no man could move through the Hindu Kush. The very name meant "killer of Hindus." In spring and summer travel was possible, but not for a woman alone, especially not for an English-woman who had been seized after escaping the massacre of Kabul and carried off by men who knew where a high price was offered for a young and fair-skinned *feringhee* woman. Deenbur would have no wish for English soldiers to discover that he had held one of their countrywomen enslaved and compelled her to be his wife.

Feringhee was the Moslem word for a European, and in Shul the people often described me in this way, even though they were not Mos-lems and had been known to chop off Moslem heads if a warlike mood took them. Sandru had explained to me that the very word "Kafir" meant "infidel." In their religion they worshiped a variety of gods, prac-ticed animal sacrifice, and had priests or shamans they called *deshtayu*. It was Deenbur's chief *deshtayu* who had made the prophecy that caused me to be brought unharmed on the grueling weeks-long journey from Kabul to the little kingdom of Shul.

The thought came again. How long? How long was my captivity to last? Somewhere in England, in the county of Surrey, stood a fine house in ample grounds on the edge of a forest where the scent of pines was sometimes so strong that it made the eyes heavy with sleep. I barely remembered the house, for I had lived there only intermittently as a child, and had last seen it when I was thirteen. Since then I had lived first in Egypt and then in India, according to my father's duties as a diplomat in the colonial service. But I remembered the scent of the pines. The house and grounds and the substantial fortune my father must have left were my inheritance, for I was an only child, as he had been. But today, only a few weeks before my twentieth birthday, I lived like a slave amid people almost untouched by civilization; people ruled by a man who could have me killed in the next hour if the whim took him. He had chopped off the head of the *deshtayu* whose prophecy about me had not been fulfilled, and I might well have suffered the same fate but for Sandru's intervention.

How long . . . ? The very question suggested hope, yet try as I might I could imagine no way of escape. Sandru had been made captive almost forty years ago and was now content to end his days in Shul. He no longer thought of himself as a prisoner and would have been afraid to return to the world he had known as a young man. Was it inevitable that this would be my destiny also? As a bird flies, Kabul lay little more than a hundred miles away to the southwest, yet my captors, who knew the country well, had taken twenty-seven days to bring me here, by cart, by camel, by pony, and on foot, across desert plains and through high mountain passes where my lungs labored frantically in the thin air, through swollen rivers and across rope bridges over deep ravines. Even though I spoke the language fairly well now and was much hardier than I had been then, I could as easily fly to the moon as make that journey alone.

How long . . . ?

I threw off the sheepskin blanket and stood up. Better to start the day's work now than lie struggling to hold back thoughts that would only make me miserable and depressed. In my old life, when Jemimah Lawley had sulked, thrown tantrums, suffered attacks of the vapors, or screamed in temper, there had always been her gentle mother or her patient nanny to soothe and comfort her with endless concern and sympathy. In Shul I was called Lalla, a corruption of my surname, and nobody cared if Lalla was miserable, nobody would try to coax her into a happier frame of mind, and any tantrum or show of defiance would be promptly rewarded with a severe whipping.

I had learned this on my second night in Shul, following my marriage to Deenbur that day according to tribal custom. When I tried to resist his embraces, not from courage but from sheer terror, he quickly thrashed me into acquiescence. I wish I could claim to have resisted long and bravely, but that night I discovered among other things that I was a coward.

Sandru took me as his servant when Deenbur discarded me, and he had long ago taught me that the best antidote to the misery of depressing thoughts was to be busy. Quickly I stood up and took off the woolen robe I wore at night, a simple garment, just a roughly circular piece of material with a hole for the head and two for the arms. My nightdress was important to me. In winter most people in Shul slept in their clothes, rarely washed, and never bathed. This resulted in a human smell as distinctive as that of goats, sheep, or wet dogs. I had grown used to it by now but had tried desperately to cling to some small standard of cleanliness for myself, perhaps because I felt it was the only way for me to retain something of my own identity and upbringing. Within me was a deep fear of being absorbed by a primitive people, of becoming as one of them. I knew myself too well now to feel any pride in being Jemimah Lawley, but I dreaded becoming Lalla of Shul in fact as well as in name.

Each night I put a pitcher of water on the small fire of dung that smoldered under the vent in the corner of my little sleeping chamber. In the morning the water was still warm. Each day I washed my hands, face, and feet thoroughly, and once each week I contrived to wash my whole body a piece at a time. My hair was short, and I kept it clean by much brushing and by using a shampoo of two eggs every three or four weeks.

I wore my simple nightdress because there were no sheets between my body and the mattress of skins or blanket of sheepskin. This nightdress I washed with some of my other clothes every week in the river. The dress and all else I had been wearing in the hour of my capture two and a half years ago had been taken from me by Deenbur's new wife. I was thankful she had not demanded my head. Now my wardrobe consisted of a few rather shapeless robes of coarse goat's hair, two knee-length shifts with long sleeves, woolen stockings tied below the knee, and sandals. For winter wear I had strong leather boots and a sheepskin coat and hood. Undergarments did not exist in Shul. When it was hot I wore one robe over my shift, and when it grew cold I put on a second or third.

Today, when I had washed myself and brushed my hair, I put on two robes against the morning's freshness before carrying my blanket out and hanging it on a wooden trestle to air. I returned to drag the mattress out, separate the skins, and brush sandy dust over them. Later, when the sun was well up, I would beat the dust away and with it would go any grease and moisture, leaving the skins fresh and clean.

The house where I lived with Sandru stood a hundred yards or so from the river. Like all the houses in Shul it was built of mud brick, but Sandru's was not part of a cluster, as many houses were, and it was larger than most others, which were rarely more than half the size of a single drawing room in England.

To west and east the houses extended in ramshackle fashion for half a mile or more. To the north they thinned out somewhat and became interspersed with tentlike structures called *yurts*, where the poorer people lived. Beyond lay fields of wheat and barley, and there were green pastures for the scrawny cattle of Shul higher up the slope. Much honey was eaten and wine drunk throughout Kafiristan, but we had neither bees nor grapes locally. Our honey and wine came from the village of Chaimee, seven miles to the west.

Ours was the only town in Shul. It was called Kuttar and was the size of a small market town in England. The rest of Deenbur's kingdom consisted of a number of villages spread out over many square miles of hill and valley. At one end of Kuttar stood the temple of the *deshtayu,* where cows and goats were sacrificed during religious festivals to Doghan, Maker of All Things. On a knoll in the center of the town, and not far from Sandru's house, stood the building that Deenbur the *pacha* called his palace. It was a plain square structure, not much of a palace by English or Indian standards, but the only two-story building in the kingdom, and it contained twelve rooms and a large main hall.

I had lived there for many months and knew it well. The exterior was painted with dark red ocher. Inside, the walls of the kitchen and the servants' quarters were bare. The main hall was hung with embossed leather, and in Deenbur's rooms there were rugs on the floors and crude tapestries on the walls. In his sleeping chamber stood a great bed of stout timber, the mattress stuffed with finest wool. Perhaps his new queen slept well there, but I was truly thankful that I no longer shared such luxury with him.

As I finished separating my mattress skins, the edge of the sun broke the distant line of hills to the east. Already Kuttar was beginning to stir, and I was not the only one abroad at this hour. There were goats to be milked, water to be brought from the river, bread to be made, fields to be hoed, sheep to be slaughtered, and all the daily necessities of living to be undertaken.

A gong was sounding in the temple, I did not know why. Probably somebody had paid the *deshtayu* to say special prayers for the dead. There had been a funeral for a rich farmer yesterday. When I looked up to the high stony ridge on the far side of the river I could see a thin column of smoke rising from somewhere on the summit, marking the spot where the coffin had been laid. The Kafirs never buried their dead. The body would be dressed in a fine robe of Cashgar wool, then placed in a box that would be set on the top of a high hill and marked with a smoky fire of green wood and damp leaves.

During my early weeks in Shul I had been too terrified and too turned in upon myself to take notice of anything that did not immediately affect me, but later I was surprised to realize that, though in general the people were of brown complexion, there was a great variety of coloring. Many faces were of a brown so pale they were scarcely darker than mine, now tanned by sun and weather. I had seen Kafirs with hazel eyes and auburn hair, and even some with blue eyes and hair as fair as my own. Sandru claimed they were descendants of Greek soldiers who had penetrated these mountains well over two thousand years ago, when Alexander the Great was marching his armies from Persia to the Indus.

While I was brushing sand over the last of the skins I had laid out, I found myself remembering that Sandru's manner had been a little strange last evening when he returned after being summoned to the palace by Deenbur. I was in his surgery at the time, a square room between the small kitchen and the living room of the house, the latter being also Sandru's bedroom. He had set me to cleaning out the pots in which he kept his medicines, and this was a long task. Some contained dry herbs, others distillations from herbs. Each had to be emptied, washed out and dried, then refilled with whatever it had contained.

The lid of every pot had a wooden label tied to it, and I had to be very careful not to get them mixed up. The names had been burned into the wooden labels with a hot nail, but they were in Greek, and I was still not very good at reading Greek, though Sandru had taught me to speak it fairly well. When he returned from the palace after an hour's absence I had made good progress, so I thought, but he was very testy, snapping at me impatiently and finding fault. This frightened me, for it was quite unlike Sandru, and he was my only friend. If he turned against me, I dreaded to imagine what might become of me in this cruel and primitive land.

As I brought water from the river and set myself to prepare breakfast in the kitchen, that uneasy fear I had felt the night before came back to me, suddenly stronger and more acute, as if some nameless premonition had stirred within me. With an effort I tried to put my fears aside. If they came between me and my work, causing me to make mistakes, Sandru might fly into one of his tempers. He had never yet beaten me, and for the most part he was kind to me, but after living for so long with the Kafirs he had absorbed something of their ways.

I counted Sandru as a friend because I believed he had saved my life when Deenbur discarded me as a wife, and he had since given me the protection that went with my being a servant of Sandru the doctor. Often in private he would talk to me as if we were equals, or even affectionately as if to a granddaughter, but this was at his choice, not mine, and I never dared to be familiar with him. He was nearing seventy now, and quickly became querulous if he felt his dignity or standing was threatened. This was not surprising. He had survived more than half a lifetime in Shul only by retaining the awe and respect of the people.

Before going to bed I had banked the kitchen fire with dung, and it was still alight under the small clay oven. Now I fed it with dry dung, made it burn brightly with bellows, then shoveled some of the fire into the recess on top of the oven and set a pan of water on it to boil. One of Sandru's patients had paid him with plump fresh fish the day before, and I filleted three before putting them in the oven to bake, two for Sandru and one for me.

I had learned much in my long captivity, particularly since being rejected by Deenbur and becoming a servant. Before my capture I would have shuddered and squealed at the very thought of touching raw fish. Now I could wring a chicken's neck or quarter a goat with only a small inward qualm of distaste, and could cook well enough to satisfy Sandru. This was thanks to Meya, a woman who had kept house for him and warmed his bed for many years. She had been dying of a growth when I came to Sandru but lived on for six months in which she schooled me in all the duties of a servant.

Sandru wept when she died, and I wept with him, for Meya had been good to me in her way. I was thankful Sandru had eased her pain and perhaps hastened her end by heavy doses of opium. I helped him attend to her body and followed when she was carried in her coffin to the summit of the funeral ridge. In the days that followed I wondered with sinking heart if Sandru would command me to his bed. When Deenbur had taken me I endured such terror that I thought my sanity would leave me, but I lived through it, and I had not gone mad. I had learned to accept with outward fortitude whatever afflictions might be imposed upon me, for otherwise I could never have survived, but my feelings were not dead, and inwardly I shrank from the thought of lying with seventy-year-old Sandru. I was therefore truly thankful when, as the weeks passed, I realized he had no such plans for me.

When the fish was almost ready I damped the fire under the oven, made some porridge of barley meal sweetened with honey, and went to rouse my master. Usually Sandru was still asleep at this hour, but when I pushed aside the leather curtain forming the door and entered his room I found him sitting up in bed with arms folded, scowling thoughtfully into space. He had a brown wrinkled face, and what little hair remained was cut to no more than half an inch long, standing up in little gray spikes spread evenly over the dome of his skull. His eyes were blue and bright.

He still had good eyesight and good hearing, and although he was not a big man he was strong for his age, with a body that had not yet run to fat.

By Sandru's orders we spoke English, Greek, French, and the Kafir tongue on successive days. I had picked up some knowledge of Kafir speech during my months in the palace, but Sandru insisted that it was important for me to learn the language fluently and also to learn Greek and French, because it would keep my mind occupied and give him a chance to converse in his two native languages. His third European language was English. In this he was a little rusty at first, not having spoken it for so many years, but he soon became quite eloquent in it and seemed to enjoy making conversation. Perhaps his Greek and French were also rusty until he began to teach me, but I had no way of telling.

I remembered that today was a day for speaking English, which was a relief to me since it would allow me to concentrate on my duties. With a little bow I said, "Good morning, master. It is an hour past sunrise, the weather is dry but a little fresh, and breakfast is ready."

"Good morning, Lalla." He looked at me with a vaguely troubled air, then gave a sigh and said, "Very well, bring it to me now, then bring your own. We will eat together, child."

This was not unusual, for Sandru liked talking and made much use of me as a listener. He often referred to our "enjoyable conversations," but in fact they were rather one-sided. For all that, I felt relief to see that he appeared to be kindly disposed toward me this morning. The fact that he had called me "child" was evidence of that.

I said, "Yes, master," and hurried back to the kitchen. There I set out a tray with his bowl of porridge, plate of baked fish, some dark bread with goat's-milk butter, and a beaker of strong tea. On the tray were two knives, a fork, and a spoon, all rather crude pieces of cutlery made by a local craftsman. Few people in Shul used anything but fingers to eat with.

When I had set the tray on Sandru's lap I went back to bring in my own breakfast and sat down cross-legged at the low table to eat. Unless I had something of a domestic nature to say to Sandru I would remain silent and wait for him to address me. It was not for a servant to speak first. As I sat on the coarse rug in the little mud brick house eating my porridge, I did not wonder at the contrast between my life as it had once been and as it was now, or the contrast between the imperious spoiled girl I had once been and the humble creature I had become. All that I had experienced during two and a half years in Shul had burned out of my very being any foolish notion that such things could not possibly happen to *me*. I had learned that anything could happen to me, anything at all, and this was a lesson I had taken to heart.

Sandru laid down his spoon in the bowl and lifted the cover from his plate of baked fish. "I wonder if your generals were any better than mine, Lalla," he said musingly.

"Generals, master?" I looked up. "I'm not quite sure what you mean."

"Military generals," he said a little testily. "Is there any other kind? The generals of my day, in charge of the withdrawal from Kabul forty years ago, were quite stupid. Do you know what they did when the Afghans came swarming across the plain outside Bemaru, firing their *jezails?* Eh? They ordered our troops to *form square!*"

Sandru's voice rose to an indignant squeak. "Form square, if you please! Oh yes, it had been a very successful tactic thirty years before, against Napoleon's cavalry. But for troops confined on a ridge to form square against the distant fire of great numbers of infantry was madness. It simply offered a solid mass into which the enemy could pour their fire."

He was silent for a minute or two, munching his fish, then continued as if there had been no pause. "I often used to wonder what truly happened when the British withdrew from Kabul at that time. I heard many stories here, of course, but I did not know what to believe until you came to Shul. Do they still speak of it in Kabul, so long after?"

"Yes, master. I heard it spoken about often."

He shook his head sorrowfully. "An army of four thousand or more soldiers, and twelve thousand camp followers, including women and children . . . you say they were all destroyed?"

He had asked me this question several times, not because his memory was becoming patchy, but simply because he liked to go over the same subject more than once. I said, "All but a handful died, master. It was very bad."

He nodded, and drank some tea. "So stupid. I do not think your generals, forty years later, were quite as foolish, Lalla. From what I have heard, the British were back in Kabul only six weeks after the massacre you so fortunately escaped." He put down his beaker of tea, frowning slightly as if trying to remember. "How was it that you were saved, child?"

When I spoke I tried to do so without allowing the words to make pictures in my mind. "When the attack on the residency came, master, the Afghans cut holes in the walls and brought up a gun with which they blew down the gates. My father was killed with the British envoy, Sir Louis Cavagnari, while firing down from the roof. My mother died when a group of Afghans broke through the walls. After that I lost my senses for a while. When I came to myself, I found that one of our Afghan servants, a man called Bihzad, had somehow managed to get me through a small gate and across the moat on the south side of the residency . . ."

There was still a gap in my recollection at this point, and the next thing I remembered was lying under filthy sacks in the back of a very small cart, cold and wet, almost demented by shock, fear, and grief. When I lifted my head I saw that a donkey was pulling the cart and Bihzad was leading the animal. He whispered frantically to me in his broken English, telling me to hide and be silent.

I could never judge how much later it was when at last we came to a halt in a gully running off the track leading north from Kabul. Two or three miles away a column of smoke rose from the burning residency. I sat shivering on a low rock, trying to take in what Bihzad was saying to me, something about the need for us to hide until the fighting in the city was over. How we would have survived until then I was never to discover, for it was only an hour later that a little band of Hindu traders, a dozen strong, with a train of mules and camels, halted in the gully.

These men were of different stock from the Afghans and of a different religion. Many Hindus were serving under British officers in the Indian Army, and during the time of my father's appointment in India I had been looked after by Hindu servants and acquired a smattering of Hindustani. My first thought was that these men would help me, but I realized vaguely that Bihzad was apprehensive. His fears were justified. After a few brusque questions the Hindu traders with their mules and camels began talking eagerly among themselves. I could not follow all they said, but gathered that they saw in me the answer to a demand by some king or chief of a distant country.

I shouted at them angrily, threatening them with punishment if they did not aid me. They simply laughed and seized me. When Bihzad tried to help, one of them hit him a fearsome blow with a cudgel which laid him unconscious or lifeless on the ground, and I received an open-handed buffet on the head that made me dizzy and faint.

So began my long journey to the land of Shul, the tiny kingdom ruled by Deenbur. I told the story briefly once more as I sat at breakfast in Sandru's room, and he kept nodding from time to time as my words confirmed his recollection of the tale. During that journey I learned from my captors that they always passed through the country of the Kafirs once each year. From India they brought pepper, cloves, cinnamon, and other spices; matchlock muskets, swords, spectacles, and scissors; beads, mirrors, ivory, and various forms of cloth. They would travel as far north as Bokhara, bringing back with them dried fruits, madder, tobacco, and snuff; wool and raw silk; horses, ponies, and Bactrian camels.

They spoke of a land I had never heard of, called Shul, ruled by a *pacha* whose two wives had failed to give him a child. One of his priests had prophesied that if a fair-skinned *feringhee* girl was brought to bed by him she would surely give him a fine son. This had no doubt seemed a safe prophecy to the priest who made it, since there appeared to be no possibility of a *feringhee* woman ever being available to test the prophecy. The only such women in the whole continent were the wives and daughters of the British in India, and it seemed there could be no hope of securing one from this source. But then, on a September day when the British in Kabul were slaughtered, fate had offered a golden opportunity to the little band of Hindu traders making their way north. Four weeks later they had sold me, unspoiled, to Deenbur in return for three fine ponies and ten bales of best wool.

When I failed to become pregnant as the months went by, Deenbur grew increasingly angry with me until in the end he decided I was barren. He ordered the *deshtayu* to perform a ceremony in the temple to cancel our marriage, and on the same day he had the one who made the prophecy executed. The man's dried head was then used in a game the Kafirs played on horseback, not unlike polo except that normally a sheep's head was used for a ball rather than a human head.

I was not greatly shocked by this. After almost a year in Shul as Deenbur's wife I had witnessed so much savagery that I had grown inured to it. If I had not done so, I would surely have gone mad.

*   *   *

Neither Sandru nor I had spoken for some little time as we sat eating our breakfast. When he gestured with his empty beaker I went into the kitchen to replenish it with more tea. On my return, as I set the beaker down on his tray, he said with a sigh, "It has happened again. Shuma has not conceived, and so Deenbur is having the marriage annulled."

I said respectfully, "But Shuma was married and bore two children before Deenbur bought her to replace me. How is it that she has failed to give Deenbur a child, master?"

"How is it?" Sandru echoed, his voice suddenly waspish. "It is for the same reason that *you* failed, and his two wives before you. The fault does not lie with his women but with Deenbur himself. Active as a stallion he may be, but the truth is, he lacks fertility and I doubt that he will ever bring about conception in a woman." Sandru sat up straight in bed and pointed a finger at me. "And for God's sake never repeat that to a living soul, for if it came to Deenbur's ears he would surely have me shortened by a head."

I said hastily, "Be sure I shall never talk of what you have said, master. But what will happen in the end? When I was his wife he was already obsessed by anger and bitterness because no woman had borne him a son, and as time goes by he will grow more dangerous."

"How the devil do I know what will happen in the end, girl?" snapped Sandru. "All I know for the moment is that he is buying a girl from the *pacha* of Lohstan to be his new wife. There is some old traveler's tale which says that the women of Lohstan are the most fertile in the world." He shrugged gloomily. "What is the use of that when Deenbur is not a fertile man, hey?"

Lohstan was a neighboring kingdom ruled by a man called Akbah. I was surprised to hear that Deenbur was buying a girl from him. In the past there had been wars between Lohstan and Shul, though not for some time. According to Sandru, the men of Shul were good fighters and had given Lohstan's army a bloody nose, but Akbah had attacked and beaten other kingdoms, and they now had to pay him annual tribute in cattle and grain and wool. Akbah's name was a byword for cruelty and violence. Sandru had met him on one occasion and considered the man to be sadistic and quite unstable. Outside his own kingdom he was known as Akbah the Mad.

I was puzzled by Sandru's manner this morning. One moment he was amiable and even quite affectionate, the next he was snapping at me irritably. It was as if something was troubling him deeply, something in which I was concerned. Now he lapsed into a rather doleful silence, his thoughts obviously far away. When he had finished his second beaker of tea I collected our breakfast things on the tray and carried them into the kitchen, once again with the uneasy feeling that something was amiss.

For the next two hours I was busy with domestic duties, heating water for Sandru to make his toilet, washing up, cleaning, fetching fuel for the fires, and riding out to the farms on Sandru's mule, Aristotle, to buy provisions for two or three days. At midmorning Sandru would hold his surgery for those who were able to come to the house, and in the afternoon we would go out on his rounds. On both occasions it was my task to carry out the duties of nurse, and without flattering myself I felt that I now performed these duties quite well. In the beginning I had fainted at the sight of blood and had almost been sick at some of the unpleasant tasks I was called on to do, but under Sandru's brisk and wise instruction I had steadily improved to the point where he was now satisfied with my work.

Sandru had been born in Paris of a French mother and a Greek father. His true name was Georgios Alexandrou. "Sandru" was a Kafir corruption of his surname, just as "Lalla" was a corruption of my own surname, Lawley. He had lived in France until he was ten, then his parents had moved to London, and it was there that he completed his education and went on to study medicine.

When he qualified as a doctor he went into practice in Athens for a time, mainly because his parents had retired there, but within three years both had died. This was a time of great discontent in Greece, and so it was that Dr. Georgios Alexandrou took himself off to Egypt and there secured a commission in the British Army as a battalion doctor in Her Majesty's 44th Regiment of Foot, the Royal Berkshires. Two years later, in 1841, when the 44th Foot were with the British force besieged in Kabul, Captain Alexandrou took part in an abortive sortie to relieve the siege by capturing the fort in the village of Bemaru, which dominated the Kabul cantonments.

The story of the sortie was one I knew, for I had heard it retailed often during the time I was in Kabul almost forty years later. Since becoming Sandru's servant I had learned it was in this action that young Captain Alexandrou had been knocked senseless when his horse was shot from under him during the rout that followed the failure of the sortie. How he escaped slaughter he was at a loss to understand, for he had no memory of the next few hours. When he came to his senses again it was dusk and he was lying beside an injured Afghan soldier in a rocky hollow. The man was grievously wounded in the thigh, but the wound was bandaged with a torn shirt and he had been saved from bleeding to death. The shirt belonged to Captain Alexandrou, but it was some time before the captain was able to comprehend, with his smattering of the language, that he himself had tended the man's wound without having any recollection of doing so.

They were found by a party of Afghans an hour later, and the British officer was thankful then that he had remained with his strange patient, for he would certainly have been put to the sword, and probably tortured first, if the man had not spoken for him. As it was, he was taken prisoner and set to work tending other wounded Afghans in Bemaru.

He still carried the satchel containing his surgical tools and was able to remove bullets, set bones, and clean wounds, all in primitive fashion but one highly regarded by the Afghans, who could normally expect no treatment at all since they had no medical service.

"I doubt that many of my patients survived for very long, Lalla," Sandru told me when recounting the story one evening, "but some of them at least lived long enough to earn me a reputation that was to save my own life. When the British retreat from Kabul began, the head villager sold me to some Ghalzis who were moving north. They traded me for two donkeys in Kohistan, and after that I was sold several times until at last I came to Shul."

Sandru, as he was by then called, had been a prisoner for many months when he was sold in Shul. His uniform had been taken in the first week or two of captivity, and he had become used to living like a native, but he had kept the tools of his trade. As a captive and a piece of merchandise, he had to accept being treated like a slave or suffer brutal beatings, but whenever he was called upon to act as a doctor he immediately adopted a peremptory manner, giving orders as if he had every right to do so.

"It was necessary, Lalla," he told me, holding the beaker of warm milk and honey he liked to drink at night, gazing over it into the glowing fire. "I had to assert the power of my *feringhee* medical skills, for these were all that stood between me and a knife across my throat. Neither the Afghan nor the Kafir respects timidity, and so I had to be boastful and domineering whenever I was needed as a doctor." He chuckled and looked at me sideways, slyly. "The qualities of a successful doctor are one quarter confidence, one quarter fraudulence, one quarter luck, and one quarter skill. Fortunately I was able to exude confidence, and I am an accomplished fraud. I have had reasonable luck, thank heaven, and my skill has proved adequate."

Sandru had been bought by the head of one of the villages in Shul, and during his early weeks there he was in danger from the *deshtayu*. They were medicine men as well as priests and resented a *feringhee* encroaching on their preserves with his alien ways. Then came a stroke of that luck which he claimed was essential to a successful doctor.

The *pacha* in those days, grandfather of Deenbur, had a daughter who had been almost blind from birth. The *deshtayu* had made sacrifices to Doghan, said prayers, and used all their arts of exorcism to drive out the evil spirit causing the blindness, but they had failed. As a last resort, the *pacha* had commanded that the *feringhee* doctor in the village of Chaimee be brought to the palace.

"I was informed," said Sandru with a reminiscent sigh, "that I was to cure his daughter's blindness or have my head chopped off. It was an unusual proposition for a doctor. In civilized countries, doctors usually charge a few guineas for failing to cure their patients. However, I was fortunate. The child was afflicted with a cataract in each eye, neither being progressive. I am never anxious to use the knife, but this case demanded it. I sedated the child with a drug from the hemp plant, much used in these parts, especially by the priests. Here they call it *bhang,* but in India it is called *hashish.* The operation with a sterilized needle was quite simple and took only a minute or two, but I made it more impressive by keeping the child's eyes bandaged for three days."

Sandru paused to wag a finger at me. "Success can bring its own dangers, Lalla. The child's sight was restored, the *pacha* was delighted, and I was raised from a lowly slave to a position of importance as doctor to him and to his family. But I realized that since I had apparently performed one miracle I would surely be expected to perform others, and if I failed . . ."

He rolled up his eyes and drew a finger across his throat. "So I told the *pacha* that although I possessed mighty powers of medicine, these powers were always subject to the will of Doghan, Maker of All Things, and I urged him to sacrifice four goats to Doghan, lest the miracle wrought by my medicine be annulled."

Sandru had served three *pachas* during his life here in Shul. Sometimes his reputation had stood high, sometimes low, but by a combination of skill, cunning, and eloquence he had always managed to survive the dangerous times. He had also long since contrived to come to an understanding with the *deshtayu* by putting his skills at their disposal, so that in time they no longer feared him as a rival or felt the need to destroy him. To a whole generation of Kafirs in Shul, including Deenbur, he had ceased to be a *feringhee* now. He was simply Sandru the doctor, who was more successful than any medicine man in living memory at healing the people's ills and injuries.

When he told me that fraud and confidence were essential to successful doctoring he had spoken the truth. We had a great variety of herbs and potions in impressively painted pots with ornate wooden labels, and some of them would help to ease various symptoms, but few had curative powers.

"The human body either heals itself or it does not," Sandru confided to me one day after a long and difficult surgery. "In many cases the person who is ill becomes well again, regardless of what the doctor may do. But of course the doctor gets the credit. I have come to the conclusion that much depends upon whether or not the patient *believes* he will be made well by the doctor's treatment, so indirectly we are doing the patient some good when we deceive him into believing that the potions in our picturesque pots are effective."

During his early years in Shul he had collected all kinds of herbs and experimented with them in various ways. A few unfortunate animals had died, and possibly one or two human patients, but in the end he had classified a number of herbs and distillations that he knew were at least harmless. Some indeed had the power to ease pain or alleviate distressing symptoms, and quite by chance he had discovered that mildew grown on a certain kind of cheese was remarkably effective in the healing of wounds, though the results were not constant.

"Injuries offer more scope than disease," he claimed. "A broken bone, an open wound, even an abscess—in such matters a doctor can truly help his patient. I am a good bonesetter, thank God, and for injuries of the flesh I believe that to make clean and keep clean is the best way to help Nature to do her own healing."

These were strange things for a doctor to say, but in my time as Sandru's nurse, helping with his patients, I came to believe in his opinions. In some ways he was unfair to himself in making light of his medical skills, especially in his handling of childbirth. Far fewer babies and far fewer mothers died when Sandru was in charge of the birth than when it was in the hands of the grimy midwives of these remote lands.

It was not Sandru who claimed success in this field. I had heard it from the women he attended, and from the mothers of those women, whom he had attended in years gone by. I found it strange now to remember that when I was first brought to Shul I had not known how babies were conceived or how they were born. Since being given to Sandru I had learned quite a lot about the subject, for he always took me with him when a child was to be delivered, and I had provided an extra pair of hands, under his direction, at many difficult moments.

I returned with the mule, Aristotle, well laden about half an hour before Sandru was to begin his surgery. This gave me time to put away my purchases, decide what to offer Sandru for his midday meal, and make sure the room he used as a surgery was clean, with his notebooks, instruments, and dishes set out in the way he liked them. There was no waiting room. The patients sat on a long bench outside the house or stood if the bench was full.

Once or twice during surgery that morning Sandru snapped at me peevishly for some offense so small I was scarcely aware of it. He did not require me to sit with him when I had prepared our noon meal, and so I ate mine in the kitchen. In the afternoon we set out on our rounds. As usual, I walked beside Aristotle carrying one of the two medical bags, while Sandru sat astride the mule with the other bag held in front of him. Normally he would chat about the various patients we visited, thinking aloud about their ills, but today he rode in silence, shoulders hunched a little, and with a moody air that discouraged me from speaking for fear of making him angry again.

Halfway through our rounds, a man came running from one of the *yurts* on the outskirts of Kuttar. His wife had begun to have a baby Sandru had not expected to arrive for another two days, and something was wrong, something beyond the power of the local midwife to deal with. In time past, only women had attended births, but Sandru's coming had gradually changed that in Kuttar as it dawned on the people that mothers and babies were far less likely to die when Sandru attended them.

We hurried to the *yurt*, which consisted of a wooden frame shaped like a beehive and covered with skins, about one third of the size of my bedroom in Kabul. The midwife had gone, and only the girl's mother was there. The husband lit more lamps to give better light, and for the next two hours Sandru fought to save the baby not yet born and entangled in its own cord.

During this time his irritable mood fell away and he became the Sandru I had often known before, kindly and compassionate, gentle and encouraging. I was glad to be helping him as we struggled to bring the baby safely into the world, for the task occupied me so completely that my own fears were forgotten, and there was the added satisfaction of feeling useful. I had never in my life done a useful thing for anybody until Sandru bought me.

It was late in the afternoon when we washed our hands and rested at last on cushions in the dark, smelly *yurt*, drinking tea made for us by the girl's mother. The girl herself sat propped against a leather bolster, the baby held to her breast. It was not yet suckling, but it was perfectly sound and breathing comfortably as it slept. The extra lamps had been put out now, and it was quiet in the *yurt*. Sandru did not believe in bringing a child into a bright and noisy world.

After a little while he said to me softly, "The cord may be cut now. See to it for me, Lalla."

I told the girl's mother to hold the lamp for me, tied ligatures, cut the cord, and made the girl comfortable. "A fine boy," I said to the husband. "Very strong. He will work hard and grow rich."

The man laughed. "May it be so. Tomorrow I will go to the temple and give thanks to Doghan, Maker of All Things."

I wondered vaguely what Mr. Creasey, vicar of the English church in Kabul, would have thought about that. But I had no wish to play the missionary, and so I simply nodded and said, "Give thanks also to my master, Sandru."

That evening as I prepared supper I felt the return of the fears I had known earlier in the day. I tried to overcome them by talking inwardly to myself, demanding to know exactly what I was afraid of. There was no tangible reason for me to be so disturbed, I told myself. I was a good servant who gave no trouble, and because I had a European education I was better able to learn from Sandru and be useful to him than a Kafir girl would be. Also I was a more congenial companion to him than any other person he could find in Shul, because I was the only one of his own kind. So it was foolish of me to be afraid. Sandru had been out of sorts today and snapped at me occasionally, but that was no reason to believe he might sell me. And as long as I remained with Sandru I would be safe.

I did not allow myself to think the thought that had driven me from my bed that morning, to wonder how long would be my time here, for if I did, then I would be forced to realize that Sandru had not many more years to live, and when he died I would indeed have cause to be afraid, for there was no knowing what might become of me without his protection.

He called me in to sup with him that evening, and though he seemed tired and quiet he was very gentle in his manner toward me. When I had cleared away we sat and played chess for a while, using a splendid board of inlaid ivory he had bought from one of the rare trade caravans to pass our way on the route from Bokhara to Peshawar. The chessmen were also of ivory, beautifully carved. Sandru loved the game, though he had been able to play only against himself for many years. I was a beginner, taught by him, but after my early bafflement and confusion at the complexity of the game I had come to like it very much, for it took me away for a brief hour or so from the hard, alien, and sometimes dangerous life I lived as a prisoner in Shul.

Once or twice I had drawn a game against Sandru, but I had never managed to beat him. This evening I won two games within an hour, not by my own skill but because Sandru made simple mistakes. He looked at the position in which I had checkmated him, shook his head slowly, then began to put the chessmen away in the sandalwood box that gave them a subtle fragrance, enhancing the beauty of the carved ivory. When he had closed the box he looked at me across the low table for a few seconds, and I saw pain in his eyes. Then he said quietly, "I'm sorry I have been bad-tempered with you today, Lalla. It was unjust."

I was embarrassed. So far had I come from the world I had known in years gone by that it troubled me to have my master, Sandru, apologize to me, his servant. I muttered, "Please, master . . . don't say such a thing. You are very good to me."

There was silence, then he said in a heavy voice, "I spoke sharply because I dreaded to tell you what I must tell you, child. You know that Deenbur summoned me to the palace yesterday. There he told me that he is buying a new girl to be his wife, a girl from Lohstan. He can do so only by agreement with the *pacha* of Lohstan, and messengers have traveled back and forth over these past few weeks to arrange it."

I thought Sandru must be having one of his absent-minded moments, and I said, "Yes, master. You told me this morning that Deenbur is buying a new wife from Akbah the Mad, but why should that trouble me? If Deenbur cannot father a child on her, and you say that he cannot, then he will blame her for it as he blamed me. Truly, I feel sorry for her, but I am thankful my turn is past."

I glanced up as I spoke and saw that Sandru now sat with head bowed as he said in a whisper, "I have not told you the price, Lalla. The price. That monster Akbah has a fancy for a *feringhee* woman, and Deenbur has agreed to barter you for the Lohstan girl."

II

I was no stranger to fear, for I had lived with it night and day from the time of my capture outside Kabul, through the horrors of my forced mating with Deenbur, to the day when he cast me out of his house in rage for having failed him. But the fear I felt now was more piercing than any I had known. Before, I had been in a stupor of shock, and this had given a kind of unreality to what I had endured. I suffered, but merciful Nature had numbed me in mind and body, so that to some extent my suffering was less acute than it might have been.

But now I was not cushioned by shock. I knew the cold reality of life in Kafiristan and the power of the little kings over their private lands. In two and a half years I had grown up and learned to see with very different eyes from those of the pampered and ignorant child I had once been. To be told now that Deenbur had sold me to Akbah the Mad filled me with raw terror.

I felt the blood drain from my face as I stared at Sandru and said in a shaking voice, "Please . . . please don't let them . . . oh, please, master."

He lifted his head as if with an effort and looked at me with desolate eyes. "My dear, do you think I have not tried? For an hour yesterday I used every argument I could muster, until Deenbur flew into a rage and reminded me that I, too, was a *feringhee* and a prisoner. He said that if I uttered another word it would be my last, since he believed I could be just as good a doctor without a tongue in my head. He meant it, Lalla. I know him well, and he meant it."

"Yes." I could barely hear my own whisper. "I know him well too, master. He meant it."

We sat in silence for a while, and I could feel my heart thumping as if I had carried two heavy buckets of water up the hill from the river.

Entwined with the fear that possessed me was a dreadful feeling of helplessness and loneliness, of being a puppet manipulated by a mindless puppeteer, utterly without power to affect my own destiny in the smallest degree. And nobody on earth cared what became of me except Sandru, who was equally powerless.

If the stories I had heard about Akbah were only half true they were still enough to make me shudder at the thought of what lay in store for me. I could never bear it. I would not bear it. Somewhere deep within my being a tiny spark of anger and determination sprang to life. I said from a dry mouth, "Do you know when I am to be sent to Lohstan, master?"

Without looking up he said in a tired voice, "You are to go when the Lohstan girl arrives. That will be in about eight or nine days."

My voice almost cracked as I said, "I must run away before then, master. I *must!* Please, will you help me?"

Now he looked up, shaking his head sadly. "Lalla, Lalla, do not speak such foolishness. Even as a young man I could never have made such a journey alone. Where will you go? To Kabul? Within a day of your vanishing, Deenbur will send riders all along the route to the south, warning every village to watch for you. And even if by some miracle you journeyed beyond Deenbur's reach, what then? You cannot live off the land. You will have to buy food in the villages. Anywhere in Kafiristan you will be recognized and sent back. Beyond the land of the Kafirs you will be among Moslems, with hardly a word of their language. No Moslem woman travels alone. They will discover you are a *feringhee* and kill you."

"But if I took Aristotle, and a pannier of food, and kept to the hills, away from villages—"

"No, child, no," he broke in with a gesture of impatience, not directed at me but at the hopelessness of my situation. "You are not born to this country, you do not know any secret routes through the mountains. Within a few days you would be lost, and you would either starve or die of exposure. If you follow the known trails you will meet people, and in these lands people do not pass one another without a word. Do you really think a young *feringhee* girl can travel alone without falling prey to rogues or robbers? Believe me, I have thought and thought about your chances of escape, and they simply do not exist, Lalla."

I spoke quickly in my desperation. "But, master, I would be safe if I were hidden among a group of Hindu traders. In England I have inherited a large fortune, and anybody who helped me to safety would be very handsomely rewarded. You could speak for me, explain who I am and how I came to be here. The Hindus have strong ties with the English, so surely they would help?"

"They were Hindus who brought you to Shul and sold you to Deenbur," said Sandru gently. "Besides, we are not expecting any trade caravan to pass this way for several weeks yet. There is nobody for me to speak to on your behalf."

I sat looking down at the chessboard. The first shock had passed. I was still afraid, but for the moment my fear seemed to be frozen, and I felt only a great emptiness. I was almost talking to myself as I said slowly, "All the same, I must run away. I am a coward. I cannot bear to be sold to Akbah the Mad. At this moment, master, I would rather starve, or die of cold, or be killed by a robber, than stay here to serve Akbah's dreadful pleasures. Perhaps when the moment to die comes I shall feel otherwise, but I suppose that is all part of being a coward."

There was a very long silence. I was busy with my own thoughts, deciding how best to accumulate food for my departure, and what kind of food, what clothes, shelter, water. If I traveled west, always keeping the rising sun at my back, Deenbur's riders would not find me because they would be certain I had gone south. I could make my way through Kohistan and find the trail that ran for five hundred miles across Afghanistan to Herat, capital of the province adjoining Persia. There would be British troops and a British Mission in Herat. If I could once reach that ancient city . . .

Five hundred miles. I knew in my heart that I would be lucky to cover fifty miles before I came to my journey's end in one way or another, but that spark of defiance was still alive within me. Come what might, I would go, and if I died trying it would at least mean that I had made one worthwhile effort in an otherwise useless life.

My eyes focused, and I found Sandru looking at me curiously. "You really mean that you will go?" he asked.

"Yes, master. I must try."

He nodded slowly, and his eyes slid past me to stare into space. "Do I wish I had taken the same decision years ago?" he mused. "It is hard to tell. I had acquired patients who needed me, and I was not threatened as you are. But . . ."

His voice trailed to silence. For a moment he was lost in thought, then suddenly he looked sharply at me and lifted a warning finger. "Make me a promise, Lalla," he said. "You have a few days of grace. Promise me you will not go without first telling me. I see no hope for success, but I will help in whatever way I can."

I bowed my head and touched a hand to my heart in the manner of giving thanks I had adopted from the Kafirs. "I promise, master. And I am grateful."

He tugged at his chin. "You must take Aristotle to carry what provisions we can accumulate, but it must appear that you have stolen him, of course. If Deenbur suspects me as an accomplice he will have my tongue, if not my head. You must go by night, and I must be heavily drugged, so that I sleep for a day and a night, and when I wake I will say that you must have put the drug of sleep in my supper."

It was only then I realized that, in helping me, Sandru would be putting himself in danger. I was still digesting this when he picked up the chessboard and got to his feet. "Go to bed, Lalla," he said in a subdued voice, turning away from me as he put the board and box of chessmen in the little cupboard beside his bed. "We will talk again tomorrow, but for both our sakes be sure to behave normally at all times. Let nothing different show in your manner. Go to bed and say your prayers, child. With God's help, all things are possible."

I took his warning to heart, even though we were alone, and as I wished him good night I put my palms together and bowed humbly in the way a good servant should. He still did not look at me, and I knew he was sure I would die on the trail despite any number of prayers for God's help. If I had dared to let myself think about it I would have agreed with him.

During the endless days of nightmare between the massacre in Kabul and my being brought at last to Shul, I had prayed a thousand prayers for rescue, but in vain. After Deenbur made me his wife and whipped me into submission to his desires I did not pray again, for I felt that if there was indeed a God, then He cared not a jot about Jemimah Lawley. It is a measure of my cowardice that, when I went to bed on the night Sandru told me his frightening news, I found that my fear greatly outweighed my sense of grievance, and in very shamefaced fashion I prayed fervently that I might survive the ordeal I would shortly suffer.

I did not sleep very much that night, for I had a great deal to think of, and I rose early to begin my preparations. There was food to be prepared, fish and meat to be smoked and dried so that it could be packed in a small space, would not go bad, yet would provide nourishment out of proportion to its bulk. Sandru had some crude maps bought from traders whose caravans came south from distant Bokhara in summer, and these I copied onto sheets of paper bought from Hindu traders from the south. The maps were on such a small scale and so unreliable that to copy them was more an attempt to encourage myself than a matter of practical use.

My head buzzed with thoughts of food, fodder, clothes, water, blankets, panniers, flint, steel, knife, and the countless small items I would have to acquire for my journey. In the evening we talked in low voices of ways and means to gather all that was needed without exciting comment, but although in a way there was a change in our relationship now that we were conspiring together, I never ceased to speak and behave as Sandru's servant, which I was.

I carried out all my daily duties just as before and assisted Sandru during his morning surgery and afternoon rounds. It was three days later, as we were on our way home from his rounds, that he muttered something in Greek to himself and drew Aristotle to a halt. When I followed his gaze I saw that he was staring at a stranger on a rather shaggy horse moving at a walk up the trail from the river. Behind him came a donkey on a long tether, carrying two large panniers.

Sandru murmured in English under his breath, "Kassim . . . I had forgotten." He sat transfixed for a moment, as if many thoughts were flitting through his head. I wanted to ask who the man was, but it was not for the servant Lalla to ask questions of her master.

Our paths were converging, and as we drew closer the stranger lifted a hand in greeting. He was a tall man, long-legged, wearing a leather hat lined with wool and turned up around the edges, a jacket and trousers of what I took to be yak leather, well-worn boots reaching halfway to his knees, and a topcoat of Kashmir goats' hair with a wide skirt split at the back for riding. A rifle was slung across his back. His face was browner than mine, but not very dark, his eyes blue, his chin bearded, his nose straight and long. It was hard to tell his tribe, for Kafirs were not the only people in whom blue eyes were to be found. The Abdalis, the Ghalzis, the Birduranis, the Kaukars, all had their sprinkling of blue-eyed men and women. Perhaps, as Sandru claimed, the armies of Alexander the Great had left their mark along the march of conquest.

From his dress, this man could have been anything. I thought he would surely not be a Moslem, for the Kafirs would be unlikely to leave his head on his shoulders, but he could have passed for one. He halted his mount a few paces from us and greeted Sandru in the Kafir tongue, but using the accent of the northern lands, which I found hard to follow.

Sandru said, "Greetings, Kassim. Last year you did not visit Kuttar. This year you come earlier than usual."

The man replied something to the effect that the weather had been kind this year, then glanced at me and asked a question. Sandru answered, "This is Lalla, the *feringhee* girl I told you of two years ago, when she was Deenbur's wife. Now she is my servant."

"How is that?" I was able to understand those words, for my ear was becoming attuned to the unfamiliar accent.

"She did not bear him a child," said Sandru, "so Deenbur made her a servant in the palace, and after time had passed I bought her. She assists me well in my work."

The blue eyes studied me without interest or warmth for a moment or two, then Kassim shrugged. "It is the will of Doghan, Maker of All Things."

Sandru gestured toward the well-laden donkey and said, "What do you bring from Bokhara, my friend?"

Kassim grinned suddenly. "The usual goods, but I do not forget you, Sandru. Always you ask for the—," here I missed a word or two—"of the *feringhee* doctor." Kassim patted his saddlebag. "For you I have the small sharp knives, the little saw, the curving needles and gut for sewing, tongs of silvery metal for drawing forth babies, and other strange objects beloved of doctors." His eyes narrowed shrewdly and he leaned forward with the confidential air of the haggler. "All of great value, Sandru. All finely wrought in Muscovy itself."

Sandru wrinkled his nose and turned Aristotle toward our house. "The things wrought in Moscow are less good than those of the English you bring from Peshawar," he said.

Kassim urged his horse alongside, and as we moved slowly forward the two men wrangled happily, rolling eyes in shock, wincing in disbelief, gesturing in reproachful protest. The bargaining was in a mixture of rupees and rubles, for both currencies were used throughout Shul, even though barter was the main form of trade.

As we reached the house, Sandru invited Kassim to sup with him, saying that if Kassim so wished he could sleep in the surgery that night, rather than use the tent he carried or pay for sleeping space in one of the Kuttar houses or *yurts*. Kassim accepted with some flowery words of thanks, but added with a smile and a wagging finger that Sandru must not expect such hospitality to allow him to drive an even harder bargain than usual with a poor traveling peddler.

My heart sank at this, for it meant more work for me, and I already had enough to think about. Kassim unloaded his panniers and carried them into the house with his saddlebag. I led Aristotle and our visitor's two mounts into the small stable at the back of the house, unsaddled them, and gave them forage and water before hurrying to the kitchen to prepare a meal Sandru would consider suitable when a guest was present. It did not matter that Kassim was a simple peddler. The custom of hospitality toward a guest was strong throughout Kafiristan, and Sandru had told me that this applied across the whole of Afghanistan.

I was busy for the next two hours in the kitchen, heating the oven, making some wheatcakes, and preparing a mutton stew with some rice and spices from India, some small beans grown locally, and a kind of dumpling I had learned to make in Deenbur's kitchen. I put a generous measure of walnuts and almonds in a dish with some dried fruit, filled a smaller dish with honey, and uncorked a flask of the wine made from grapes grown in the neighboring village of Chaimee.

While the stew was cooking I heated water and carried two large jugs of it into the big room so that my master and his guest might wash. I could see them through the door leading to the surgery, for the leather curtain was drawn back. Kassim had his saddlebag on the table there and was laying out scalpels and other instruments for Sandru to appraise. Evidently this peddler traded regularly through Shul each year and brought particular items for which Sandru had asked. If I had not been so distracted by my own problems I would have been curious about the man, for he was the first merchant I had known to travel alone. Most of them traveled in groups for safety, but then I reflected that Kassim was scarcely a merchant, for he could carry only a small stock of goods on his donkey and his rather decrepit horse. He was, as I had first thought of him, just a peddler.

It is a measure of how much I had absorbed the ways of Shul that I was pleased to have the supper completely ready at the moment Sandru called me to serve it, for otherwise I would have been the cause of Sandru being shamed before his guest. I carried in the big bowl of stew and set it on the table between them, then brought them a smaller bowl each, beakers, cutlery, and the rest of the food I had prepared, together with the flask of wine.

Both men ignored me, as expected, and as they would have done if I had been Sandru's wife. In Afghanistan women did not sit at table with men. If any in Shul knew that Sandru sometimes commanded me to join him while he ate, they would have been utterly astonished. I had put my own supper aside in the kitchen, and as I sat eating I could hear the two men talking in low voices from the next room but could not distinguish what they were saying. Later I was called to clear away and bring another flask of wine. When I had done so, and washed the dishes and cooking pots, I presented myself to Sandru for further orders.

He seemed a little drunk and gave me a sullen look as he growled in English, "Go to bed, Lalla. We need nothing more tonight."

I bowed to him, then to the stranger, and went to my small sleeping chamber on the far side of the kitchen. It had been a busy day, and this combined with the anxiety that beset me had made me very tired. I could no longer hear the voices of Sandru and his guest, except that just before sleep came upon me I thought I heard Kassim's voice raised in anger. I wondered vaguely if the two men had fallen to quarreling but concluded that if so it was nothing to do with me, and with a mental shrug I allowed sleep to overtake me, not knowing how wrong my conclusion had been.

In the morning, as I went about my usual tasks and then began to make breakfast, I heard Sandru stirring in the big room. Because we had a guest, I made a good breakfast of porridge followed by a dish of partridge cut in small pieces and roasted. The partridge had been given to Sandru in payment for delivery of the baby a few days before.

I reminded myself that today was the day for speaking Greek, and went to ask if he was ready for breakfast. Both men were seated cross-legged at the low table, but they were not speaking, and the atmosphere seemed very strained to me. Sandru ordered me to serve breakfast, and when I had done so I retired to the kitchen to eat my own. Some fifteen minutes later he called my name. I thought he simply wished me to clear away, but as I entered the room he said in English, "Draw the curtain behind you and come close, Lalla." There was anxiety in his face, and I wondered what had happened as I drew the leather curtain across the doorway and moved to stand by the table where both men still sat.

"Speak only in a whisper," Sandru said quietly, and gestured toward Kassim. "This man will take you to Herat. I have arranged it."

I stood dumbfounded, unable to speak for long moments. Herat! Five hundred miles to the west, but with a British garrison. A harsh journey of many weeks, and one I had known in my heart I could never survive alone. But now . . .

I felt a sudden almost painful ache of yearning in my breast at the knowledge that there was now at least a small chance that I might one day be among my own people again, away from the savagery of the mountain tribes and the raw ugliness of their primitive lives. Then I looked at Kassim, and my nerves jumped with alarm. His lips, not hidden by the beard, were set in a thin straight line, and the blue eyes staring at me were cold with hatred.

I almost flinched at his glare, then looked at Sandru, touched my palms together as I bowed, and stammered, "But . . . but master, your guest clearly does not wish to do this."

"It is arranged," Sandru said with a touch of anger. "There is no other way, Lalla. If you go alone, you will die."

I kept my eyes on Sandru and said, still speaking in English, "Yes . . . I know, master. But do you see the way he looks at me? I think he will kill me at the first opportunity." I tried not to let the purport of my words creep into my expression as I spoke.

Sandru lifted a finger to point at me and said in a grim voice, "Listen to me carefully, Lalla. I know this man does not *want* to have you with him on his journeying, but I have bribed him well and he will honor his agreement. As far as lies within his power, he will take you safely to Herat. It will be a slow and wandering journey, for he will be peddling his wares and trading as he goes. But he will *not* harm you, that I promise. I tell you, child, this is the only way, and it is a God-given chance that he came through Shul early this year. An answer to prayer, perhaps. Either you go with Kassim or I give you no further help of any kind. If I seem to speak harshly, it is for your own good. Now . . . what is your answer?"

I hesitated for no more than a second. Without Sandru's help in making preparations and giving me Aristotle I was lost, and if he was sure Kassim would not betray me, then I would have to put my trust in the man. I looked at Kassim now, meeting his hostile gaze, and bowed my thanks to him. Then I looked at Sandru again and said, "Yes, master. I will go with him."

Sandru nodded. "Good. But nobody must suspect that you have gone together, so here is how it must be arranged. This morning Kassim will buy and sell and barter a few things. At noon he will leave by the Anjuman trail to the northwest. Ten miles from Kuttar the trail forks, one branch to the north, the other to the southwest. One mile along the southwest fork there are the ruins of a tomb on the left, set back in a broad cleft. Some of the stones bear Greek markings. Kassim will wait for you there."

I glanced nervously at the peddler again, but now he sat gazing down at the empty bowl in front of him and I could not see his eyes. Sandru went on, "Tonight you will leave with Aristotle and all that he can carry. There should be a clear moon, so you will not find it hard to follow the trail. If you leave an hour after midnight you should reach the tomb before dawn. Kassim will be waiting for you."

Without looking up, Kassim said in the Kafir tongue, "Has the girl understood?"

Sandru said, "Yes. She is very intelligent."

"She knows she is to obey me at all times? Our lives will depend on it."

"She knows. She understands the words you speak now, and she can speak the Kafir tongue well enough herself. Also she knows a little Pushtu, enough to pass as a Durani once you are beyond Kafiristan."

"She does not look like an Afghan."

Sandru made a gesture of contempt. "There are thousands of Afghans who do not look like Afghans. These lands have known conquest by Persians, Greeks, Mongols, Huns, Turks—who can say what an Afghan looks like now? Do not speak stupidities to me, Kassim."

The man got to his feet. "I will wait at the tomb until an hour after sunrise. If she has not come by then, I go."

"She will come."

Kassim shrugged, then went through into the surgery and began to roll up his bedding there. Sandru looked at me with a wan smile. "Kassim will keep his word," he said. "Believe me, he is your best hope, Lalla. Your only hope."

I went through that day in a kind of stupor, full of contradictory fears. I was afraid I would wander from the trail and fail to find the tomb. I was afraid that if I did find it Kassim would not be waiting for me. I was also afraid that he *would* be waiting for me, despite Sandru's reassurance that the man would not harm me. I feared to go and feared to stay, feared to travel alone, feared to travel with Kassim.

Sandru gave out that he was himself unwell that morning and would not be holding his usual surgery. This allowed me time in which to gather food, clothing, bedding, and all I should need for the long slow journey across the rocky hills and narrow valleys, the steppelands and desert, the fierce rivers and dusty plateaus of this harsh country six times the size of England.

At noon we saw Kassim riding slowly off to the northwest with his pack donkey plodding behind. After our midday meal I accompanied Sandru when he went out to visit two urgent cases, and on our return I continued my preparations. Just before dusk Sandru came to me with a small leather case. "I have packed a selection of medical equipment for you, Lalla. Bandages, tweezers, scissors, plaster, disinfectant, and some of my ointments. There can easily be small accidents on a journey such as yours. Please God, there will be no major ones, but in any event it is well to be prepared."

I thanked him and added the leather case to the pile of items I would later be packing in Aristotle's panniers. On Sandru's orders, we supped on soup, cold meats, and fruits, so there was little cooking for me to do. After supper I packed the panniers and set out the clothes I would wear for the start of my journey. Sandru made me take a very small dose of an opiate medicine, then sent me to lie down in my sleeping chamber for a few hours.

I did not expect to sleep, but the opiate had its effect, and the next thing I knew Sandru was shaking me gently by the shoulder and whispering that it was half an hour past midnight. I rose, dressed quickly, shivering a little, then with Sandru's help I saddled Aristotle, muffled his hooves with pieces of blanket, and set the panniers on him.

It was time to go. We stood in Sandru's room in the dim light of the shaded lamp and looked at each other. "May you journey safely and come into your own again," he said softly. "Forgive me for using you as a servant, but in Deenbur's kingdom there was no other way to preserve your safety, Jemimah."

The use of my true name came as a shock, but I understood what he was telling me, and I said, "There is nothing to forgive, dear master. I owe you more than I can ever repay." Forgetting my place as a servant, I put a hand on his arm. "Please remember to take the sleeping drug before dawn, and to shout and rage that I have robbed you when at last you wake."

"I will not forget. Have no fear for me." He patted my hand and sighed. "I shall miss you, child. I had not quite realized . . . but I shall miss you very much."

I felt a sudden loving impulse toward this old man, such as I had never felt in my useless and selfish life before, and I said, "May I kiss you good-bye, master?"

I saw his eyes fill with tears as he opened his arms. I hugged him for a moment, kissed his cheek, whispered my thanks again, and begged him to take good care of himself.

"Yes, yes. Now go, my dear, go quickly, and may God go with you."

Five minutes later I was a hundred yards from the house, leading Aristotle toward the outskirts of Kuttar, my heart in my throat as I prayed that no sleepless soul would chance to see me in the bright moonlight. After another twenty minutes I was on the Anjuman trail and breathing more easily. When Deenbur learned that I had run away, and with luck it might be late in the afternoon before he did so, he would surely believe I had gone southwest in an attempt to reach Kabul, and any pursuit would be in that direction.

To my relief the trail was easy to follow, for it wound between hills that rose steeply, with no side tracks leading off. I took the muffles from Aristotles's hooves and schooled myself to a plodding pace, for I had more than ten miles to go, and no doubt Kassim would expect to push on once we met. If we met. Aristotle could have carried me, but I did not want to add my weight to his panniers, except perhaps for short spells. I was wearing my boots, which were very sound, and I had a spare pair in my baggage. This was by Sandru's foresight. We had called that afternoon at the house of the bootmaker, who owed for past medical treatment, and Sandru had picked out a pair of boots for me in payment, pretending that my own were almost worn out.

The night was cold but, walking steadily, I felt no chill. Under the quiet black sky and bright stars I began to dream that perhaps . . . perhaps I might come into my own again, as Sandru had wished for me. I might succeed in making this hard and dangerous journey. I might not die of cold, or heat, or thirst, or starvation, or at the hands of robbers, Pathans, Tadjiks, Uzbeks, or Turkomen. Or Kassim.

I might one day set foot in England again, where sadly I would have no family, but where I would be mistress of a great house and fortune. The thought of Lalla, slave-wife of a Kafiristan *pacha*, a servant to be sold, a toy to be bartered, a prisoner to be killed at a whim—the thought of this Lalla becoming a gracious lady in England was so unbelievable that it brought from me a small nervous laugh to make Aristotle prick up an ear.

Miss Jemimah Lawley, of Witchwood Hall, Oakhurst, in the county of Surrey, formerly known as Lalla, most humble kitchen maid in the primitive kingdom of Shul, discarded wife of a heathen Kafir . . . if I had not laughed I would have cried. I remembered my father telling me one day that in his will he had appointed his lawyers to be my trustees until I reached the age of twenty-one, but they had discretion to provide funds for any purpose at my request. Walking steadily along the trail on a cold moonlit night through the hills of Kafiristan, leading a mule, in flight from a horror I shuddered to imagine, my face a native brown, my hands work-worn, my body lean and hard and despoiled by a barbarian king, it was impossible to imagine that I might one day put on a fine dress in a fine house and become Jemimah Lawley again. Certainly I would never again become the Jemimah Lawley whose family had been butchered in Kabul. That creature had long ceased to exist.

After four hours I began to panic at the notion that I had missed the fork in the trail. If so, then I must be heading north instead of having turned southwest. I looked at the stars and found Cassiopeia, then the Pole Star. Yes, I was heading west of northwest, so I had not missed the fork. Another mile and I gave a gasp of relief, for here the trail divided plainly enough.

Now as I turned southwest my timorous soul was at once beset by a new fear. Would Kassim be waiting for me? And if he was, would he keep the promise made to Sandru or . . . ? I did not dare to think of the alternative. With sudden alarm I realized that the first light of dawn had crept into the sky behind me. Had Kassim said he would wait until an hour after sunrise or an hour before?

I quickened my pace, and for comfort began whispering to Aristotle. "I'm sure he said an hour after. He was sitting at the master's table, and he got up and said he would wait until an hour after sunrise." Then my old doubt struck again. "But he is an Afghan . . . or a Kafir . . . and whichever he is, he would think nothing of slitting the throat of a *feringhee* . . ."

There was the ruined tomb, a jumble of roughhewn stones set under an overhang of the rocky bluff that curved back in a broad recess on the left of the trail. I halted, staring, but could see no sign of any human or animal nearby. Slowly, not knowing whether I felt alarm or relief, I led Aristotle forward and around the heap of stones.

Nobody.

In the growing light I peered at some of the larger stones and saw roughly carved Greek characters on one of them. There was no mistake. This was the place. I almost jumped clear of the ground as a voice spoke behind me in the Kafir tongue. "You were not followed, woman?"

I spun around, and now I saw that there was a cleft in the face of the bluff, not very wide, but from it came Kassim, his *jezail* in one hand, leading his mangy-looking horse and donkey with the other. I said nervously, "No. I mean, I think not."

He dropped the reins, touched a finger to his lips in a silencing gesture, then stood quite still, listening. Three minutes passed . . . four, five. He gave a nod and said, "We go now. Must go far this first day. Walk one hour, ride one hour. You stay always behind me unless I say different. Understand?"

I nodded, my fears beginning to ease a little, for it seemed that Kassim intended to fulfill whatever bargain he had made with Sandru. He went on, "For six days we will not stop in any village. You will wear veil over face like Moslem woman. If we meet any person, if any person speaks to you, you will make no answer. You do not know Kafir tongue."

He cocked his head in an unspoken question, and again I nodded. "Yes. I understand."

"After six days we will pass from Kafiristan. Then you take off veil and become Kafir woman who knows only a little of the Pushtu tongue of the Moslems. You will be my wife. I will call you Lalla, you will call me Kassim. Is it understood?"

"Yes, Kassim. I will do all things as you say."

He slung his *jezail* across his back, picked up the reins, and moved past me onto the trail. With Aristotle beside me, I fell in behind. Kassim walked with a long, tireless stride, and I was thankful when he halted after an hour, with the sun now risen behind us. In that hour he had spoken no word and neither had I. This was a pattern I would become well accustomed to in the days that followed.

When we stopped, he drank a little water from a goatskin bottle and gestured for me to do the same. I obeyed, and when he mounted his horse I made to mount Aristotle, but even as my weight came on him the mule lurched and sagged. I dropped to the ground at once, swept by new panic, and said, "Oh! I think he's lame!"

Kassim stared for a moment, then dismounted and picked up Aristotle's right forefoot. From under his coat he took out a knife and spent half a minute probing carefully into the hoof and cutting a little of it away. He went to his saddlebag, rummaged in it, and took out a small leather bag in which was a dark brown fibrous substance. He spat on this, rolled it in his hands, then lifted the hoof again and forced a plug of the material into the hole he had cut.

"He will carry the panniers, but not you also," said Kassim, his blue eyes bleak with dislike as he looked at me. "After two days the hoof will be well. Till then, you ride with me." He began to hitch Aristotle to a rein attached to the donkey, and I opened my mouth to protest, for it seemed impossible that his wretched-looking horse could carry us both. Then I closed my mouth again, remembering that I had promised to do all things he might require of me.

He mounted the horse, reached down an arm for me to grasp, and with one easy movement swung me up and astride the saddle behind him. The skirt of the woolen robe I wore was full and flowing, so I was not hampered by it. He said, "Hold well, woman," and set his mount to a walk.

At once, as I locked my arms round his waist, I was aware of several sensations, first that he smelled of leather and stale sweat and dirt-grimed clothes, but this was nothing new for me. In a country such as Afghanistan it was far from easy for people to keep body and clothes clean, nor was it by any means their first concern. I had tried my best in this respect, once I was established in Kuttar, mainly because it was a thread connecting me with civilization, and by clinging to it I could persuade myself that in time I might return to the civilization I had been born to. But I knew now that in the weeks and months to come, if I survived the journey to Herat, I would smell no sweeter than Kassim or any other native.

Another sensation I felt as we rode along the trail came as a surprise to me. Kassim's horse was deceptive. A gelding, it looked a poor and feeble animal, but I could feel the power of it beneath me as it walked, carrying the double burden without effort. Perhaps poor grooming gave the animal its decrepit look, and it crossed my mind that this might be deliberate. Kassim traveled alone, and a good horse was a fine prize. Safer for him to have a seemingly poor creature, perhaps.

The third sensation that came to me was no surprise though very positive. Kassim resented me, not mildly, but bitterly. I could feel it through my arms as they held him. It was not the hardness of his body, for a man who lived a life such as his would inevitably be lean and muscular. The anger he felt came to me by no tangible means, yet I could not have been more aware of it if he had shouted it to my face. I had seen the same thing in his eyes the morning before, when Sandru announced that Kassim would take me on my journey of escape, and the intensity of it baffled me now as then.

What bargain Sandru had made, what he had paid, I did not know, but Kassim must surely have been free to accept or reject it, and if he had agreed to the bargain, then why did he feel such fierce animosity toward me? This was a question I could not answer and dared not ask. Two and a half years ago I had ordered Afghan servants about with a scathing tongue. Since then I had given orders to nobody, and I had learned my place in the world in which I now dwelt. It was not for me to question the man to whom I clung as we rode double on his horse. My life depended on Kassim, and he hated me. Little wonder that as we rode on before the rising sun I quailed to think what might lie in store for me.

III

Seven days later we crossed the main caravan route. This ran south to Kabul, north to Bokhara and Samarkand, beyond the Russian border. Aristotle was no longer lame. We still walked for an hour and rode for an hour unless the terrain prevented us, covering between ten and fifteen miles each day, and I still knew no more of Kassim than I had done on the day our journey began.

The first few miles of trail from Kuttar to the ruined tomb had been easy, but after that the way was grueling for several days as we threaded our way through high mountain passes, sometimes through snow reaching to the tops of my boots. Kassim never spoke except to give an order or utter a warning. Sometimes I could hear the breath sobbing from my lungs as we struggled across a snow-covered ridge where the wind cut like a sword, and I felt my breast would burst with effort, but there was never a word of sympathy or encouragement from Kassim, only an iron hand to drag me on when my legs would no longer obey me.

We always stopped for the night well below the snow line and two hours before dusk, so that there was ample time to make camp, attend to the animals, and cook a good meal for ourselves. Kassim was completely incurious about me. Neither on the march nor when we rested did he ask any question or make any comment. He spoke only to give an instruction. Once or twice I attempted to make conversation, but he either answered with a monosyllable or did not answer at all.

There could be no doubting that he was a skillful and experienced traveler. When to my eyes the trail seemed to have vanished, he did not falter for a moment, and in making or breaking camp he worked with the least possible waste of time or effort. We would halt in a sheltered spot, and at once he would take out flint and steel to start a fire while I began to gather fuel. In no time there would be a good fire of camel'sthorn, wormwood, and alder, banked with dried dung we collected in a sack as we made our way along the trail.

When the fire was going he would help me unload and unsaddle the animals. There was usually sufficient grazing for them, and with the snows melting there were always rivulets to give water. A grunted command would send me off to collect more fuel for the fire, or to refill our water bottles, or to start preparing whatever he had decided he would cook for our evening meal, the main meal of the day. For the first week this was always a stew of goat's meat, made from pieces of smoke-dried meat he carried in a cooking pot strung to one of the panniers. Our breakfast was always chupatty bread, dried fruit, and a kind of sweetmeat made from honey, ground almonds, and pistachios. During the day we would halt for about an hour at noon and rest while we chewed strips of tough dried meat and drank black tea sweetened with honey. At night we ate well of goat's-meat stew with a mixture of vegetables, followed by more dried fruit.

When our meal was finished we banked the fire and slept back to back with our feet toward it, fully clothed, lying on woolly sheepskin groundsheets and wrapped in fleecy blankets woven from the wool of argali sheep. The animals would be hobbled nearby, and Kassim never slept without his *jezail* beside him.

The day before we crossed the main caravan route I discovered that he was an excellent shot when he replenished our provisions by bringing down a wild sheep. It was two hundred yards away on a high crag, and moving, but he dropped it with a single shot from his *jezail*, and then had to make a dangerous climb to reach the carcass and carry it down.

That night we made camp an hour earlier than usual. I guessed why, and as soon as we had attended to the animals I fetched the sharp knife I carried in my saddlebag and began to skin the sheep before quartering it. Kassim had gone down to the tiny stream a long stone's throw away and appeared to be having what I felt sure must be his first bath for several weeks, if not months, in the icy water. I had not been able to take my own clothes off since leaving Kuttar and decided I would follow Kassim's example later, for I was conscious of having acquired a gamy aroma myself.

When Kassim returned I had made good progress with the carcass and had started to cut strips from one of the joints for smoking or part cooking. For once I caught a hint of surprise in those unfriendly blue eyes as he stared at me, then he nodded and grunted, "Good." This was the first comment I had ever heard him make, and it was the equivalent of fulsome flattery from any other person.

I said, "I am glad to do whatever I am able to do, Kassim, and I try not to be a burden to you. I will make our supper tonight, if you permit."

He looked at me for a few moments, then shrugged and turned to sit by the fire. When I had finished my task, when the pot was simmering on the fire, when some fresh meat had been wrapped in the skin for the next day or two, when a good supply of strips lay ready for smoking, and all the remains had been cleared away, I brought a towel from my saddle-bag and said, "I will go to the river to wash now."

Kassim had taken the razor-sharp knife he carried in a sheath at his belt and was peering into a scrap of broken mirror as he began to trim his beard. He did not trouble himself to nod in acknowledgment. I walked to the river, took off my clothes, and stood knee deep in the cold trickling water, teeth chattering, flesh quivering as I lathered myself with a piece of the yellow soap made in Kuttar from goat's tallow and laburnum ash. I did not concern myself about being seen, for I doubted if there was another living soul within miles, apart from Kassim. He was a hundred yards away by the fire, and in any event I had ceased to be nervous of him. It was clear he had no interest in me as a woman, or even as a person, and I was confident that no other traveler would draw near along the trail without Kassim being aware of it.

This watchfulness was something I had noticed from the beginning. I had never known a man as remote as Kassim, neither had I known anyone as wary. Long after we were well beyond reach of pursuit by Deenbur's people, Kassim maintained the vigilance of a wolf through the long hours of our daytime travel, and at night I had only to rouse and stir a little for him to be instantly awake.

When I returned from the river, feeling cleaner in my body but wondering when I would be able to wash some clothes, I found that Kassim had trimmed his beard to a short stubble. With his long chin less hidden and his wary alertness, he seemed more like a wolf than ever. I put away my towel and soap, sat down by the fire, and said, "When may we stop long enough for me to wash and dry some clothes, Kassim?"

He gazed remotely at the jagged mountain horizon to the west, limned with gold a few moments ago but now turning to purple as the rays of the setting sun lifted above it. "After two days," he said at last. "We will stay some days in Qalagah."

"Thank you, Kassim."

My politeness must have caught his attention for a moment. He withdrew his gaze from the horizon to look at me with the barest hint of puzzlement, and I met his look with some of his own impassivity. I did not like Kassim. I had sometimes hated him for the way he had dragged me quite mercilessly through some of the first days of our journey. I savagely resented the lofty manner in which he treated me as if I were no more a living human being than one of the chattels hanging from his donkey, and certainly of far less concern to him than his *jezail* or any of the animals. This was particularly galling when I had struggled so hard to keep up his demanding pace and to help in every way as much as I was able.

On the other hand, I kept trying not to dislike him because I knew that without him I would have been dead by now or in the hands of Akbah the Mad, which would surely have been worse. Kassim was keeping his promise to Sandru; and if, as I suspected, he was a man who hated women in general and myself in particular, then I would simply have to accept that this was his nature and his manner. I was a fool to feel aggrieved, I told myself grimly. God, or perhaps Doghan, the Maker of All Things, well knew that Kassim's hostility was less than a fleabite compared to some of the things I had suffered in the past two and a half years.

One thing about Kassim mystified me. So far we had encountered few other travelers, for it was still early in the year and we were not on a major trail, but when we did meet others, which had happened three times, Kassim was a different person, warm, friendly, talkative. His Pushtu was spoken too rapidly for me to follow, but he seemed to be making jokes and causing laughter, in between asking a number of questions about where the strangers had come from, what they had seen, and whom they had encountered.

At first I thought it was the patter of a peddler trying to sell his wares, but in fact he seemed reluctant to sell, buy, or barter during these casual encounters, for it involved unloading his carefully packed wares for display, perhaps to no profit. Once the other travelers had parted from us he became his usual remote self, though on one occasion I was surprised to see him take a grubby pad of paper from a pocket under his jacket and write on it with a stub of pencil.

In my surprise I forgot my position for a moment and said, "Can you read and write, Kassim?"

The blue eyes fixed upon me with a glare of fury. "It is not for woman to ask man questions!" he almost shouted. "Who are you to ask Kassim questions?"

"I beg that you will pardon me," I said quickly. "I meant no harm. It is a wonderful thing to read and write."

"I cannot," he snapped, still angry, and thrust the pad under my nose to show that it bore little marks and squiggles. "It is for me only, to keep count."

I was unsure what he meant, but since he had just bartered a small looking glass for a bag of meal, albeit without much enthusiasm, I assumed that he had devised some system of his own for keeping a record of his wares on paper.

Two days after coming down from the hills we reached Qalagah, a small native town about half the size of Kuttar. There we took a room in the street of the weavers, and it was evident that this was not Kassim's first visit, for the Pathan who rented him the room greeted him as an old acquaintance, though showing much surprise and amusement at Kassim having a woman with him. For the last three days I had discarded the veil and was traveling as a Kafir woman, barefaced, as Kassim had ordered from the beginning, and I sensed that some bawdy jokes were being exchanged at my expense. I did not care about this. I was no longer a prisoner in Shul, no longer in danger of life or limb from the whims of a *pacha*. I was traveling slowly but surely, and so far safely, with a strong and experienced protector, on a journey of escape to my own world, my own people, and for the first time in thirty long months I could dare to hope that there might be an end to my ordeal.

I was lonely during the days we spent in Qalagah, and if I had not been so thankful to be safe I would have found each day very tedious, for I had no companionship and almost nothing to do. We slept on our own bedding in a small room, but meals were provided by the wife of the man to whom the house belonged. Kassim ate with the husband, and I ate with the wife, her two young children, and their grandmother.

My grasp of Pushtu was only sufficient for the simplest of exchanges, so I could take little part in conversation. During the day Kassim was at the bazaar peddling his wares, but I was not allowed to accompany him, for my bare face drew too many curious stares from the Moslem men, and I could not use a veil since I was supposed to be a Kafir woman. It was quite out of order for me to walk about the village alone, and so I was confined to the house for most of the day, with nothing to do but feed and groom Kassim's horse and donkey, and my mule, Aristotle.

In a labored conversation with our host's wife I learned that Kassim's horse was a Badakhshani from near the borders of Cathay, a breed renowned for speed and endurance. It surprised me that a peddler should own such a creature, and again I wondered if Kassim kept the animal looking unkempt to hide its true qualities.

When he returned in the late afternoon he would sit talking with our host and one or two neighbors until it was time to eat, and this was the other Kassim I had glimpsed before when we encountered strangers, a cheerful, openhearted man, a good talker and a good listener. After supper, when he came to our room and we were alone, he was again a cold and distant man.

On the third day, for something to do, I managed to convey to the grandmother that I would like her to show me how to use the loom on which she was weaving. It was a primitive backstrap loom, the warp threads kept tight by the weaver leaning back against a strap fastened to the long stick with the threads attached. She chuckled, and when she had finished the length of cloth she was making she spent quite a little while showing me how to prepare the warp, then tried to instruct me in the art of using the shuttle. It seemed not too difficult when she demonstrated but proved quite another matter when she allowed me to try, and my hopes of making myself useful proved in vain.

In our room after supper Kassim would crouch by the lamp with his pad and pencil and spend perhaps ten minutes making notes in his own accounting symbols, often pausing to gaze absently in frowning reflection, as if making calculations in his head. When he had finished he would indicate with a word and a gesture that it was time to sleep. Just as on the journey, we would lie down on our bedding back to back, wrapped in our blankets, and then he would blow out the lamp without a word of good night.

On the first evening I was so weary from our journeying that I slept at once. By the third night, having had so little to do, I did not feel sleepy, and when he had finished making his notes I said respectfully, "May we talk for a little while, Kassim?"

"Talk? Why? What do you want to say?"

"Nothing in particular. I would be glad to hear if your business prospered today, or if there is any news you have to tell."

"Why?"

I said despairingly, "Because we are here together, and I grow weary of silence. Often Sandru has talked to me about matters of little importance. I would welcome the gossip of the bazaar, such as you exchange with our host and our neighbors here as you sit in the street or in the courtyard when work is over."

"Sandru is a *feringhee*," growled Kassim with a touch of contempt. "Only a *feringhee* would allow a woman servant to talk with him."

In Shul I had learned total submission, for this was the only alternative to savage beating, perhaps even mutilation or death. But I had known a small measure of freedom for some ten days now, and I was swept with sudden anger such as I had not dared to allow in myself for two years and more. I was too cautious to let my anger show, for my life depended on this man, and I said without expression, "As you please, Kassim," then added in English, for my own satisfaction, "you pig of a man."

With that I went to my bed and began to wrap myself in my blankets.

Qalagah was the first of many such villages we stayed in during the long weeks that followed as we made our slow way along the Bamian River valley to the ancient walled town of Bamian itself, where the vast figure of the Buddha, almost two hundred feet high, had been carved in the rock face of the cliffs more than twelve hundred years before.

Bamian was much larger than Qalagah, and we stayed longer, but the pattern of our daily life remained the same as it had been throughout the two hundred miles we had so far traveled. I was used to it now, used to the silence of my companion and to his almost complete disregard of me. Every mile was a small step nearer to civilization, and my hopes were high now, for Herat, with its British garrison, lay less than three hundred miles to the west.

It was in Bamian that I first saw men who might have been European, a handful of them staying at a small caravanserai, and wearing jackets, shirts, and trousers of Western style. I was hugely excited at seeing them and burst out with my thoughts to Kassim as soon as we were in the room we had taken on the outskirts of the town.

"Those men we saw were *feringhee*, Kassim! I could not hear what tongue they spoke, but they wear the clothes of the *feringhee* countries, and if they are returning to the west they will surely take me with them if I explain that I am English!"

He shook his head and dropped his bedroll on the floor. "They are not from the west. From the north. Muscovy. Russian."

In India and especially in Kabul I had heard enough talk about the threat of the Tsar's armies pushing down through Afghanistan to the Indus. To prevent this was why British politicians had wooed Afghan chiefs and made agreements for British troops to protect the country. Nevertheless I said now, "But even if they are Russian men they will surely take an English girl under their protection and find some way to

send her safely home through their own country. It will save you the
burden of my company, Kassim, and from having to take me all the way
to Herat. Let us speak to them tomorrow—"

"*No!*" Cold anger flared in his eyes as he spoke softly but with fierce
emphasis. "You will not speak to Russian men. It is dangerous."

"Dangerous? That is a foolish thing to say, Kassim. Tomorrow I will
speak to them myself—"

Before I could say more he had taken me by the shoulders and was
shaking me till my teeth rattled and I whimpered for him to stop. In an
instant all the old terrors I had known for so long descended upon me,
and my spark of defiance was extinguished.

He pointed with a long finger held close to my nose, still gripping my
shoulder with one hand, for my head was spinning and I would have
fallen without his support. "I have made a promise to Sandru," he said in
a voice that rasped with anger. "If I do not keep that promise I am
dishonored. I will not allow a woman to bring dishonor upon me. You
have made a promise to Kassim, that you would obey me in all things on
this journey. If you do not keep that promise I will beat you as I would
beat a stupid mule. Is it understood, Lalla?"

I was in fear of him again and I whispered, "It is understood."

"You renew your promise?"

"Yes . . . yes, I do."

He released me. "See that you do not break your word to me, *feringhee* girl, or it will go ill with you." He turned away from me, unstrapped
his bedroll, squatted cross-legged on it, then took out his pad and pencil
and began to write in his own peculiar system of symbols.

I turned to attend to my own bedroll, trembling, and at the same time
condemning myself for having attempted to argue with Kassim. If the
thought of running away to the Russian men touched my mind I rejected it instantly. I knew nothing about them, only that for many years
now Russia had been seeking to acquire influence in Afghanistan at the
expense of the British, who feared this would bring about a thrust into
India. These Muscovites I had seen might well be engaged in matters
they would not wish to be known by any English person, even a young
woman in such a plight as mine. It was foolish of me to have thought of
approaching them. Better to stay with Kassim, the devil I knew. Besides,
I was too much afraid even to think of disobeying him.

We remained for over a week in Bamian, and Kassim was very busy,
though it seemed to me that he had little to show for it. Not that I
cared. In my loneliness the days seemed endless, and I hated him anew

for the way he ignored me utterly. After two days I asked him for a little money, and to my surprise he gave me a few rupees. I spent them on buying some skeins of wool and persuading the coppersmith next door to make me a crochet needle. This he did, once I had drawn a simple picture to show what I wanted, and from then on I was able to occupy myself for a few hours each day crocheting a shawl, as my ayah in Delhi had taught me years ago.

It was a relief to me when we left Bamian to resume our journey. The days of harsh travel were much better than the days of idleness. The long miles, the crude meals, the nights passed sleeping beside a man I detested, all this I had grown used to now, and they were nothing compared to the feeling that I was gradually making progress on my journey to freedom.

The weather grew warmer with the passing days, and once we had descended the pass through the Koh-i-Hisar range it became hot. We no longer wore our thick jackets but walked and rode lightly robed. This was a country of little rain, but a storm broke one evening during our fifth week of travel. Kassim had scented its coming long before the sky grew threatening, and while I cooked our evening meal he set up a shelter of sticks and skins, like a miniature *yurt*, in which we were able to sleep huddled together and remain dry that night.

Each day now we met more travelers on the dusty track that stretched from Persia to Kafiristan, most in groups, a few alone, some on foot, some with donkeys, mules, horses, or the two-humped Bactrian camels. To other travelers Kassim always showed his friendly face and was ever ready to halt for gossip. I found it hard to believe that this was the same remote and wordless man he became when we were alone.

Though the terrain varied, the pattern of our journeying remained the same. We walked, rode, made camp, began a new day, came to a village and stayed for a few days, then moved on again to the same pattern. Once we were safely beyond Deenbur's grasp I had become excited, eager to press on and reach journey's end, but the distance was so great and our movement so slow and leisurely, broken by long halts, that I now schooled myself never to think of the day when we would at last come to the city of Herat and the safety of a British garrison.

The days passed. The weeks passed. I completed my shawl and began another. Kassim bought, sold, bartered, wrote on his writing pad in his secret language, and perhaps exchanged a hundred words with me in a day. I lost track of time, and it came as a shock when he said to me one night as we ate our evening meal, "We will come to Herat in eight days."

I stared at him in the dusk and felt the strangest blend of excitement, joy, and fear. I was almost home among my own people, almost free, almost Jemimah Lawley once more, bereft of family now, but mistress of a fine estate and a large fortune. Yet in my joy there was an element of apprehension. Much had happened to me since I had last been Jemimah Lawley, and I was a different person now. How much of my story would I tell in England? How would I fit into the life that awaited me there? What would people think and say of me if they knew the whole truth of my captivity; of the months when Deenbur possessed me, first as wife, then as servant?

I said, "In only eight days, Kassim?"

"Perhaps seven."

Although I detested the man I had made it a rule always to be polite, and I said, "Thank you for keeping me safe on this long journey. I am truly grateful."

He wiped the gravy from his bowl with a piece of bread and said dourly, "It is not yet finished."

Two of those remaining days we spent in the little village of Janawar, and I was sure Kassim intended to remain one more day, but in the small hours of the second night he roused me from sleep and said we were to leave at once. When I asked why, he snapped at me to be silent, and later, as we rode westward with the first light of dawn touching the sky behind us, he kept glancing back along the trail as it wound its way between rounded hills dotted with pistachio trees. Like the wolf he resembled, he seemed to have hackles raised at the scent of danger, and I wondered what might have happened in Janawar to bring this about but asked no questions.

By midmorning we were weaving our way through a series of low rocky spurs, and I was surprised when Kassim suddenly turned off the track and began to lead his horse and donkey up a dry stony valley that rose steadily to the ridge from which the spurs on the south of the trail descended. It was too early for us to halt for a noonday rest, and in any event Kassim did not halt but increased his pace as we mounted the seamed and riven slope, twisting between tall outcrops of rock.

I found myself falling behind, for Aristotle had decided to sulk. Kassim turned and called in a low voice, "Hurry, Lalla! Hurry!"

I dragged Aristotle on, stumbling and bruising my knees where the red rock formed a steep step. Kassim came scrambling back and pricked the mule's haunches with his knife to goad him on. I gasped in protest but was ignored. When we were a full two hundred yards from the trail Kassim led the way round a towering outcrop and halted.

"Make no sound," he said, wiping sweat from his face. "Keep the animals out of sight from below." With that he drew the *jezail* from its long holster on his saddle and moved to squat close to one side of the outcrop, a position from which he could keep oblique watch along the trail in the direction from which we had come.

I gathered the reins of the animals and whispered, "Do you think some robbers are following us, Kassim?" He made an impatient gesture with one hand but did not answer. Ten minutes passed. There was no movement from Kassim and none on the trail below. I ventured to whisper again, "How long shall we be here?"

"Until I see who follows us." He glanced at me, and for once there was no unfriendliness in his eyes. "There was a man in Janawar who may seek to rob us," he said almost gently. "We will let him pass before we continue. Hobble the animals, Lalla." As I obeyed, he turned and ran his eye along the line of the ridge above us, and when I finished my task he said, "Sit there, your back to the rock, and watch that place on the ridge where the ground dips down a little." He pointed. "You see it? There is a path by which a man might come, if he suspects that we have left the trail. Speak if you see movement, Lalla."

I whispered my understanding and settled down with my back against the outcrop, looking up to the top of the ridge while Kassim returned to keeping watch on the trail below. I felt a little strung up but was not particularly alarmed. On our journey I had many times seen Kassim hunt and fish, and he was skilled at both. I was quite sure that no single robber would succeed against him, for our position was well protected.

Half an hour passed. The sun moved around, beginning to dazzle me a little, for I was facing south. Another half hour. Kassim crouched with endless patience, still as the rock itself. I felt sure now that he had been mistaken in thinking we were followed. Any robber would surely have appeared by now, either above or below us. I relaxed and let my mind drift toward the future. Herat was only five days away . . . perhaps four. There I would find sights and sounds familiar to me, the rows of army tents in perfect lines outside the city, the rhythmic movement of marching men at drill, the voices barking commands, the jingle of harness, thump of hooves, rumble of gun carriages, sound of bugle calls . . .

I came to myself with a start, jerking my eyes open, horrified to realize that I had briefly fallen asleep. Quickly I scanned the ridge. Nothing had changed. Beside me, Kassim still kept watch on the trail below.

Another half hour passed. Kassim sighed and stood up, shaking his head doubtfully. "It seems he did not follow," he muttered, almost to himself. "We will go on now, Lalla."

I rose to my feet, and as I did so a man stood up from behind a boulder eighty paces away up the slope, bringing a long rifle up to the aim. My mouth opened as I tried to shriek a warning, but for an endlessly agonizing instant my throat was numbed by shock. In that instant I knew who was to blame for whatever happened now. Myself, and nobody else. I had allowed myself to doze when Kassim had told me to watch, and so I had failed to see the man who must have shown himself briefly as he crept over the lip of the ridge before going into hiding amid the rocks immediately below it.

My cry of warning broke from me at last, but too late. There came a sharp report, a puff of smoke from the rifle, and a sudden grunt from Kassim. He had risen with his back to the man, and now he staggered as if struck from behind by a club. Because of the sun's heat he was wearing no jacket over his tunic, and I saw clearly the black-rimmed hole in the fabric, midway up his back and to one side, beginning to turn red as he tottered under the bullet's impact, the *jezail* falling from his hand. The ground in front of him fell away almost sheer in a drop of about five feet, for we were on a tiny plateau. Kassim was on the edge, his knees giving way beneath him as he tried to turn, tried to save himself, flinging out an arm across the bare rock, scrabbling for a hold. Then he was gone, and I heard the impact as his body hit the ground, almost a man's height below.

Somehow I managed not to scream, though terror consumed me. I should have snatched up his *jezail* to protect myself, for it was a Snider rifle I had watched him fire several times, and it had been loaded ever since we took up our position here. Whether I could have aimed it properly except at very close range was another matter, but this was not to be put to the test, for I simply ran twenty or thirty paces down the slope by which we had brought up the animals, then turned and ran back along the stretch of rock below to where Kassim lay.

He was on his side, unconscious if not dead, his face bruised and bleeding, blood spreading from the wound in his back, the left shoulder jutting unnaturally beneath his tunic. I had not spent eighteen months as Sandru's assistant without learning something about wounds and injuries, and I knew the shoulder was dislocated. I did not quite break down and weep, but began to pant and shiver with the fear that possessed me as I knelt by Kassim and eased him gently over to lie on his back. There came a brief spark of relief as I found the pulse in his neck and felt his chest move under my hand as he breathed. He was alive, but with that knowledge came the realization that the robber who had shot him would now be coming down the slope to finish what he had begun, and like a fool I had left Kassim's rifle on the ledge above.

I heard a rattle of stones, a slither of booted feet from somewhere above, and the sound brought frost to my veins. There was no clear thought in my head, but I found I had picked up a stone the size of a big orange and was standing between Kassim and the way the robber would come. Then he appeared, thirty paces away, rounding a boulder, a stocky man with the broad Mongol face of the Uzbek tribesmen inhabiting the north of the country. He halted for a moment, staring at me, then came on, one hand holding a rifle of a type I had not seen before.

I cried out in Pushtu, "Go!" and lifted the stone threateningly, knowing with despair that my action was futile. He looked beyond me to where Kassim lay, then drew a long knife from a sheath at his hip and moved forward. I knew then that I was going to die, but there was no room in my being for any increase of terror. As the man drew nearer a curious calm came over me. I waited till he was only five paces from me, the knife held ready for an upward thrust into my body, then I hurled the stone with all my strength.

The man did not even have to evade it, for my throw missed him by almost an arm's length. Without logic or reason, but out of some deep-rooted instinct to protect a helpless fellow creature, I spread my arms wide as if to make a barrier and said to the robber, "No. You cannot. He is badly hurt."

The man did not pause, and now he was close enough for me to see that his eyes were quite without passion. He intended to kill me with no more emotion than if he had been slaughtering a goat.

A double sound. A sharp crack from somewhere near my arm and the simultaneous noise of a cartridge exploding close behind me. The robber stopped as if he had walked into an invisible wall. The rifle dropped from one hand, the knife from the other. His head went back, mouth falling open, eyes widening, then he fell, twisting, and his body hit the ground face down. I saw the big, bloody hole in the back of his leather jacket where a bullet had passed through his chest, making the same gaping exit wound I had seen on the occasional wild goat or wild sheep Kassim had shot during our travels.

I turned, numb with shock and relief at my reprieve. Kassim still lay on his back, but now his head was lifted, and in his sound right hand was a pistol I had never seen before but which he must have carried in a holster strapped to his body under the loose tunic. A wisp of smoke rose from the barrel of the pistol as his hand sank with it to the ground and his head fell back.

I took one swift glance at the robber. No blood came from the great wound, and I knew he must be dead. I ran to Kassim and dropped to my knees beside him. His brown face was a dirty yellow with shock, and his lips were drawn back in a snarl of agony. The blue eyes had closed, but as I knelt beside him they opened again and he stared up at me, blankly at first, then with slow recognition.

"Lalla . . . ," he said slowly, "Lalla . . ."

I rested a hand on his brow and struggled to summon up all I had learned as a servant to Sandru the doctor. He had claimed that to be successful a doctor must have luck, confidence, fraudulence, and skill. I was no doctor, and all I had was a very little skill. I would have to pretend confidence, which in itself would be fraudulent, and as for luck, I could only hope for the greatest possible measure of it to make up for my deficiencies in every other respect.

I said with as much steady confidence as I could muster, "Rest quietly, Kassim. The man is dead. There is no more danger. Your shoulder is out of joint, but I can restore that. Then I will see to the wound in your back. Remember that I was taught by Sandru, the best of doctors, and I have much knowledge and great skill."

He gazed at me from half-closed eyes, and until he spoke I was not sure that he had taken in my words. Then he said softly, "There is something you must do before all else, Lalla. Find the man's horse. He will have left it in the next valley. Find and bring it here. Go now."

He had spoken half those words before realization dawned on me, then fresh shock left me dazed and speechless as I knelt looking down at him, incredulous, unable to believe my ears. The words Kassim had just spoken were in perfect English, and with an accent as English as my own.

IV

Long seconds passed before I was able to say in a thin high voice, "You . . . you're not an Afghan . . . you're *English!*"

He spoke through teeth clenched against pain, and with that spark of anger I had so often seen in him before. "Yes. Had to tell you now in case . . . but never mind that. *Hurry,* girl! Don't just kneel there staring. Fetch his horse before somebody else sees it."

My mind seemed to have collapsed in total confusion, and the first emotion to arise out of that confusion was anger. For weeks I had been traveling with an Englishman, but one who had pretended to be an Afghan and who had treated me accordingly, as if I mattered less than his donkey. That feeling lasted no more than a second, for the man now lay badly wounded before me, perhaps dying, and all the feeling for a patient that I had absorbed from Sandru made me say in English, "I must see to your hurts first, then I'll go and look for the horse—"

Before I could finish he had started trying to struggle up, eyes blazing, voice taut with pain as he ground out, "It's *vital!* Get me up, damn you! I'll go myself."

I was horrified to think what damage he might do to himself if he attempted such madness, and so I chose the lesser of two evils and put my arms around him, holding him for a moment so that he could not move as I said as reassuringly as I could, "All right, all right, *please* don't move. I'll do as you say."

Slowly he allowed me to help him lie back. At once I got to my feet, picked up the pistol and put it close to his hand, then said, "I'll be as quick as I can."

I did not glance at the dead man as I started down the slope, but I was aware that already a cloud of flies had gathered about him. Soon, I knew, the black vultures would come. My mind was still benumbed as I clam-

bered down the rocky slope, slithering on loose talus, hurrying as fast as I
dared to reach the trail and turn back along it, past the first spur to
where the land fell back in a sloping valley similar to the one I had just
descended. Even in his half-conscious state Kassim—or whoever he was
—had worked out that the attacker must have seen or guessed where we
left the trail and climbed to the ridge so that he could come upon us
from behind.

I felt sick with guilt, for Kassim had anticipated this danger and I had
failed him by not keeping proper watch. I was also filled with apprehension that I might not find the horse, for to Kassim it was clearly of
overwhelming importance, and I shivered to think what he might attempt to do if I failed him yet again. But good fortune was with me. I
had climbed no more than fifty paces up the slope when I saw the horse,
a dark bay mare with black points, hobbled in a gully a stone's throw to
my right, still saddled, carrying small panniers and a bedroll.

I talked to her soothingly as I approached and was thankful to find her
a steady creature who showed no nervousness when I began to unfasten
the hobble. I led her down to the trail, back past the spur, then coaxed
her up the difficult steeper slope to where I had left Kassim. As I did so
the paralysis that gripped my mind began to dissolve, so that I was able
to think coherently and to suspect what lay behind the startling mystery
of Kassim's true identity. I remembered how his manner always changed
when we met other travelers or stayed in a village, how he loved to gossip
and ask endless questions. I remembered his thick notepad, which he
carried in a secure pocket inside his tunic, and how he would write in it
after an encounter on the trail, or each night if we were staying in a
village.

I knew, because my father had been a diplomat, that for half a century
a struggle had been taking place in Afghanistan between Britain and
Russia, with the Afghan rulers trying to keep their independence by
favoring first one side, then the other. I knew, too, that this struggle was
not only political, between envoys and missions from both sides. It was a
battle between spies, British and Russian spies who roamed the trails, the
towns, the villages, the bazaars, seeking information, bribing, corrupting,
perhaps assassinating if the truth were known.

A spy. The Englishman calling himself Kassim was a spy, and I
cringed inwardly with revulsion at the thought. Growing up in the Middle East and India, where diplomatic and military circles overlapped, I
knew that among gentlemen the profession of spy was regarded as the
most lowly and contemptible a man could follow. I remembered two

occasions, one in Cairo and one in Lahore, when a messenger had been sent to our home to tell my father that an agent had returned with important information, in one case from the Sudan and in the other from the Northwest Frontier. On both occasions my father had ordered a subordinate to hear the report. "Not part of my duty to sit in the same room as a confounded *spy*," he had declared angrily. "Let me have a report in writing."

When I reached the broad ledge where I had left the injured man I found him sitting up with his back to the rock, eyes closed, his face a poor color and stiff with pain. The body of the other man was no longer in sight. Kassim opened his eyes as we approached, and I glimpsed relief in them as he saw I had brought the horse with me. "Get it up behind the crag with the other mounts," he said in a thin hard voice, "then come back for me. I'll need some help."

I said, "Where is the man?"

He nodded to one side, and I saw a long crevice in the rock with some flies buzzing above it. "Managed to roll him in there with my feet," said the Englishman. "You'll have to cover him with rocks, Lalla."

So this was a spy, a creature of darkness, a thief and assassin, who lived a lie, lurking in shadows to snatch scraps of information as a jackal snatches the leavings of nobler beasts. I did not answer him but led the horse up the slope and back behind the crag, tethering it with the others so that it could not be seen from the road.

When I returned I found the Englishman had started to crawl after me, on his knees but using only one hand. The dislocated shoulder stuck out in a grotesque lump under his tunic. I helped him to his feet, his sound arm about my shoulders, and struggled up the slope with him until we reached the horses, then lowered him to the ground again.

Panting from the effort, I looked down at him and said, "What is your real name?"

His face was running with sweat, and he had difficulty in focusing his gaze on me, but his lips twisted in a kind of grin as he said, "Not so different . . . Caspar."

"Caspar what?"

He shook his head impatiently. "The saddlebag. Give me the Russian's saddlebag, Lalla. I must go through it. He had nothing in his pockets."

It was only then I realized that the man who had shot Kassim (or Caspar as I would now have to think of him), the man who had been about to kill me with a knife, was himself a spy, but from the other side;

a rival in the dark degrading battle being fought underground in Afghanistan. I had hated Kassim and I now despised Caspar, but in my time of working with Sandru I had learned to put aside all such feeling toward a patient and to see only a sick man or woman in need of help.

I went to Aristotle and began to unstrap the pack containing the satchel of medical items Sandru had given me. From where he sat, Caspar called in a weak but angry voice, "Not that, Lalla! Bring me his saddlebag."

I lifted out the satchel and moved to kneel facing the man. Now that I knew he was English, I no longer had to play the part of a humble Afghan woman. "I will do nothing until I have attended to your injuries, sir," I said, and the word "sir" sounded very strange in my ears, for it was in another world that I had last used it.

His blue eyes flared briefly, but the strength was fading in him. "I'm all right," he mumbled, struggling to maintain his anger. "Don't . . . damn well . . . argue."

"I don't intend to argue," I said. "Lie down on your back, please, and chew some of this." Before he could protest I slid a finger in the side of his mouth to open it a little and thrust in a pinch of a fibrous herb, dried after steeping in an opiate made from poppy seeds, and used by Sandru whenever he had to perform a painful operation.

I did not know how much blood Caspar had lost from his wound, and certainly no artery was severed or he would have been long dead, but I think the pain of his shoulder had brought him very close to passing out, and to my relief he did not resist or try to spit the fibrous herb out. I had spoken to him as I had often heard Sandru speak to difficult patients, sharply and with authority, but this manner was a pretense. Inwardly I was terrified of the task that lay before me.

As gently as I could, I helped Caspar to lie flat on his back, placed a blanket under his head, then opened my medical satchel and began to set out what I would need on a clean towel. "Keep chewing," I said, trying to prevent my voice from becoming shrill with the anxiety I felt. "First I'm going to put your shoulder right, then I'll see to your wound."

"Confidence," I told myself, "show confidence!"

"I have been trained in all forms of medicine and surgery by Sandru," I said, watching my hands shake as I wiped the sweat from them, "and I'm perfectly capable of doing all that is necessary."

"Unless the wound is mortal," I thought, "or I fail to prevent it becoming infected. God help me now."

When I turned to look at him he was still chewing slowly, but his half-closed eyes had a vacant look, and when I pushed back an eyelid I saw that the pupil was dilated. I took off my robe, for I was sweating heavily in the heat, then sat down beside the man, facing him, my feet level with his hurt shoulder. Gently I took his wrist in both my hands, lifted the arm a little, and eased my foot into his armpit, my leg slightly bent at the knee. I had seen Sandru do this only once, and I prayed I would do it correctly as I pressed with my foot and drew steadily on his arm until it was taut. Then, summoning all my strength, I leaned back and gave a great heave, thrusting with my foot in his armpit at the same time.

For a moment nothing happened, and I began to feel despair, for it seemed I was not strong enough to restore the joint, but then the sinews yielded and I heard the dull click of bone as the ball slid back into the socket. Tears of relief were on my cheeks as I laid down his arm and got slowly to my knees. Despite the opiate, pain must have taken the spy beyond the limit of his endurance, and I saw that he was unconscious now.

The bullet wound was on the same side as his hurt arm, so I was able to turn him onto his good side, on a blanket, to examine the injury. When I rolled up his tunic, unfastened his belt, and eased down the waistband of his breeches a little way, I saw that the bullet had entered his back from behind, just above the outer curve of the hipbone, but there was no sign of the exit wound I had expected to find. Then I realized what must have happened. On his belt was the holster in which he had hidden the pistol he had used to save both our lives less than half an hour ago. The attacker's bullet must have been slightly deflected by the butt of the pistol and lost much of its impact by passing through the thick leather of the holster and belt, so it was still in his body.

Sickness rose in my throat. The bullet seemed unlikely to have touched any vital organ, but if it remained in his body it would quickly poison his blood, and I was sure I could never summon the courage to cut or probe for it. I held my head in my hands and whispered aloud, "Oh, dear God. What shall I do, Sandru? What shall I do?"

It was almost as if he answered me from far distant Shul, for at once I knew there could be no delay. I had to remove the bullet and cleanse the wound, and the moment to act was now, while the injured man was unconscious. Carefully I felt around his ribs, vaguely aware that the color of his body skin was not that of an Afghan, even the fair type of Afghan, but as pale as my own. Just in front of the hipbone and a little above it I could feel an unnatural lump beneath the flesh; the bullet, which had almost passed through.

I did not give myself a moment to think but pretended I was making preparations for Sandru as I took from my satchel the little case with a scalpel, some thin cord, a quill, disinfectant, strips of cotton bandage, and some plaster. I did not allow myself to hesitate as I swabbed the whole of the wound area with disinfectant, then immediately cut into the flesh above the unnatural lump and eased the bullet out.

Two years before I would have fainted at the sight of blood. Now my hands were red with it. I soaked the cord, a piece of bandage, and a spoon handle in disinfectant, then used the spoon handle to push the cord through the finger-length passage the bullet had made in passing through the man's side. With the cord, I pulled the wad of bandage back and forth several times, soaking it anew with disinfectant.

Make clean. And leave the rest to Nature.

That was Sandru's way with wounds, and it was the only way I knew. With a fresh piece of bandage I drew a liberal amount of Sandru's special ointment made from cheese mold through the wound, put a stitch in the incision I had made in the front, and set a short piece of quill in the entrance hole for drainage, with a stitch each side. I filled one of our pots with water from a goatskin water bottle, washed and dried my hands, then spread ointment-smeared cloth over the two wounds and secured it with plaster. I tied a clean towel around Caspar's waist to form a padding, and with the last of my strength I set up a little awning to give him shade from the sun. Then I squatted down with my head in my hands and wept.

I may have dozed for a little while, but I came to myself at the sound of flapping wings. Three vultures were circling low about the crag. I jumped to my feet, threw a stone to drive them away, then hurried down to the ledge where Caspar had fallen. The body of the man who had tried to kill us lay wedged in a narrowing crevice, a short arm's length down, his back uppermost. For the next hour I collected small rocks and shale to drop down the crevice until his whole body was hidden under a thick layer.

Caspar's pistol lay on the ground. I picked it up and went back up the slope to the place behind the crag, trying to think what I must do next. I had enough food and water for ourselves and for the animals to carry us through the next twenty-four hours, perhaps longer, but then I would need to replenish our water at one of the small lakes or rivulets, and I had no idea how far away the next water point might be.

Caspar was conscious and sitting up with his back to the crag in the shade of the lean-to awning I had set up. Beneath the weathering of sun and wind his face was pallid. I went to sit down beside him in the shade and said, "How do you feel, Mr. Caspar?"

"Just Caspar," he said slowly, and turned his head to look at me. "I feel weak, but I haven't much pain apart from a sore shoulder." He paused, as if making an effort to collect his thoughts. "What did you do about the bullet wound? Is it bad? When can we ride?"

I told him briefly what I had done. "It isn't a bad wound," I said with pretended confidence, "and I don't think it will become infected, but you'll have to rest here for a few days."

He shook his head. "Impossible. Sixty miles to Herat. Under three days, at a steady pace. We'll start in the morning, Lalla."

I opened my mouth to argue, then had second thoughts. It might be dangerous for him to ride, wounded as he was, but if we stayed here and the wound festered, it would be even more dangerous. Better for him if I could get him to Herat, where the Army could give him proper medical attention. Better for me, too, I realized with a touch of panic. Now that I thought about it, I found it difficult to know whether my deep concern for Caspar sprang from natural anxiety for a badly injured man or from the knowledge that if I did not save him I would have little hope of completing the journey myself. No Afghan woman would be traveling alone. My disguise would hold only as long as I was in Caspar's company, and once I was recognized as a *feringhee* I would soon be either dead or a captive once more.

I said, "Very well. We'll start in the morning, but you'll have to ride all the way. If you walk you'll open up the wound. And you must wear your robe to hide the blood on your tunic and breeches. If anybody sees you're wounded . . ."

I had no need to finish the sentence. This was a cruel country and these were cruel times. A traveler unable to defend himself and his woman would not travel far.

Caspar ran his tongue along dry lips and said, "I'm very thirsty. Is it all right for me to drink?"

"Yes, but not too much." I went to fetch water in a beaker and gave it to him. As he sipped slowly I said, "You're a spy, aren't you? And so was that man who shot you."

He looked at me with dull but wary eyes, and after a little silence he said, "Don't ask questions, Lalla. When we move tomorrow, we travel as we have for all these weeks past. You're a Kafir woman and I speak to you in that tongue, but I rarely speak, and you don't speak at all unless invited to. For your own safety and for mine, we have to *think* like the people we're supposed to be. Do you understand?"

I hated him afresh for his words, but I knew, grudgingly, that he was right, and I gave a curt nod. Getting to my feet, I began the long business of setting up camp. Caspar would have little appetite, but if he was to travel he would need strength, and I decided to give him some thick goat's-meat soup followed by bread and honey.

After a little while he said, "Look in the man's saddlebags and bring me any papers you can find, Lalla."

I paused in the act of striking a spark to kindling for a fire. "When we move tomorrow, I shall do everything you say," I informed him, "but for the moment you are an Englishman and I am an Englishwoman, and you might well consider using the word 'please' when you wish me to do something."

He looked at me for a long time with a curiously puzzled air, then said at last in a rather feeble voice, "My apologies, Miss Lawley. Will you oblige me, please, by fetching any papers from the man's saddlebags?"

I went to rummage through the bags and found a wad of papers in a big leather wallet. When I handed them to Caspar he took them eagerly, a spark of excitement showing through the exhaustion in his eyes as he said, "Thank you, Miss Lawley."

I said, "Sandru told you who I am?"

"Yes." He was fumbling through the papers one-handed, resting the shoulder I had reset.

A thought struck me. "Does Sandru know who *you* really are?" I asked.

He glanced up, a grim look in the blue eyes. "He's known that for the last five years. That's how he compelled me to take you with me, by threatening to expose me if I refused."

I said, "You would have left an Englishwoman there in Shul, knowing what was about to happen to her?" I remembered something more and added in horror, "You *did* leave me there when you passed through two years ago!"

He was looking at the papers again and said in a tired voice, "Yes, Miss Lawley. With much regret . . . yes."

I could feel myself trembling with anger as I said, "No doubt that is what I might expect from a *spy!*"

"No doubt, Miss Lawley." He glanced up and touched his shoulder. "Thank you for your very skillful attention to my injuries. I'm most grateful. If for any reason I fail to reach Herat, and you arrive safely, please take all my notes and all these papers to Mr. Arthur Renwick at the British Legation there."

I did not answer but took another pinch of opiate-soaked fiber from my medical stores, held it to his mouth, and said, "Chew this." He hesitated, then obediently opened his mouth for me to put the fiber in. I turned away and crouched to the task of lighting a fire. When it was burning steadily I unloaded and unsaddled the animals, including the rival spy's horse, and began to prepare a meal. For a while I heard the rustle of paper from where the Englishman sat, but at last it ceased and there was silence. I was well used to silence from Kassim and expected little else from Caspar. When I had set the pot on the fire I glanced across at him. He was lying down now, on his good side, head pillowed on a folded blanket, the leather wallet protruding from beneath the blanket, the pistol within reach close to his bare head.

Now that I looked at his fair hair and blue eyes it was hard to believe I could have been deceived through all these long weeks, even though many Afghans had similar features. Hot indignation burned anew within me. The man admitted that he would not have lifted a finger to help me if Sandru had not compelled him. Even so, once on the trail he could have told me he was English, could have treated me as an Englishwoman who had endured an appalling ordeal, instead of treating me like a serf, day after day, week after week. . . . My blood boiled at the memory of it.

The opiate made him very drowsy, and when I had cooked supper I had to hold him in a sitting position to feed him with spoonfuls of soup, for he was barely awake. That night he became feverish, and I feared that despite my efforts an infection from the wound must have entered his blood. There was nothing more I could do now except to give him as much nursing care as possible, which would be little enough, for days of travel lay ahead. The fever would have to run its course, and I could only pray that his bodily constitution would be strong enough to defeat the infection.

In the morning he was less drowsy, but his mind kept wandering from time to time. He spoke to me only in the Kafir tongue, and I responded in the same way. Our lives would depend on maintaining our pretense of being natives when we encountered other travelers on the trail, and the closer we came to Herat the more people we were likely to meet.

When his mind was clear Caspar was desperate to be gone, but I made him drink some more warm soup at dawn while I broke camp and loaded the animals. The worst task of the whole day was getting him down the slope to the trail. His wound had stiffened and he was in great pain, but he wanted to help lead the animals down. There were four now, with the dead man's horse, and Caspar feared I would lose control of them. For my part, I knew I could manage the beasts but was terrified that Caspar would slip on the treacherous scree and open his wound.

It was then, in the face of his stubborn insistence, that I spoke to him in English for the last time. "Listen carefully," I said, putting my face close to his. "The mule is surefooted. You will *ride* him down to the trail. If you refuse, I swear to God I will take your papers and the Russian's papers and *burn* them. Do you hear me?"

He looked at me dazedly for long seconds, and as I glared back at him I felt vague surprise. After two and a half years of total obedience and submission in Shul, I might well have reveled in the pleasure of threatening this man and making him yield to my own demands, but I felt no pleasure, only a curious reluctance to use the whip hand I possessed.

He turned away at last, rested a hand on Aristotle's pommel, and began painfully to lift a foot to the stirrup. "All right, damn you . . . ," he said thickly. In silence I helped him mount, then gathered the reins of his horse and began to lead the other three mounts down the slope, tethered one behind the other. Aristotle, I knew, would do best finding his own way down.

Once on the trail Caspar changed mounts and rode his own horse while I rode the dead man's bay. We traveled at a walk, halting to rest every two hours. Few words passed between us. Caspar rode as if asleep, and I kept fearing he might fall, but it seemed he was one of those horsemen who could indeed sleep in the saddle. Three times we met other groups of travelers that day, and once we were overtaken by traders with a string of well-laden camels. At each encounter, at my warning, Caspar roused himself to call greetings, make jokes, and exchange gossip in his usual fashion.

During the day we replenished our water bottles and found grazing for the animals. In the evening we made camp well off the trail in a flat gully so that we had no need to climb. Caspar's shoulder was no longer sore, but when I examined his dressing I found inflammation on the flesh surrounding the plaster and was thankful I had set a quill in the wound for drainage.

He slept poorly that night, often mumbling incoherently in both Kafir and Pushtu. Because of my anxiety I slept fitfully and tried to keep my spirits up by telling myself that we had covered almost twenty miles that day and Herat was now no more than two days away. But by noon next day, after ten miles, Caspar was having bouts of delirium, muttering and sometimes shouting in a mixture of languages. I so dreaded the attention he might attract that I led the way off the trail into a winding valley, deciding that we must hide for the rest of the day and travel by night.

Even in the shade of the valley it was very hot. Caspar's skin seemed burning to my touch, and he had stopped sweating. I knew his temperature must have soared and that he was in great danger. When I had laid him on his bedding I managed to drag off his tunic, then soaked a towel in water and spread it over his body. This was harsh treatment, but I knew that if I did not bring his temperature down quickly he would die.

Every ten minutes I renewed the wet towel, bathed his face, and lifted his head to coax him to drink. Betweentimes I attended to the animals, lit a fire, and made some soup. I was so frightened, I had little appetite but made myself eat, knowing I would need all my strength. Sometimes Caspar dozed. Sometimes he was conscious and aware, watching me with dull yet curious eyes as I tended him. Sometimes his mind wandered and he talked to some unknown person in Kafir or Pushtu. It was as dusk came, and I began to pack up ready to move, that he spoke in English, though not to me. The words were quiet and clear, with an underlying sadness and spoken as if he were thinking aloud.

"Melanie . . . ," he said. Then, "Stormswift . . . daughter of Electra. Beautiful . . . so beautiful." A pause, then on a fading note, softly and bitterly, "Bitch-goddess."

I found I had stopped short in the act of strapping my bedroll in place, and for long seconds I stood motionless, hearing those strange words again in my head. They had no meaning for me, but they were so out of place and out of character, so completely from another world, that they hung in my mind, sinking slowly into my memory. I waited, but the man lying in the gathering dusk said no more, and after a few moments I went on with my task.

Half an hour later, struggling and panting, I helped him into the saddle of his horse and we began to move once more. For a long time I was terrified of wandering from the trail in the darkness but then realized that it was plain to the animals, for they had the scent of travelers, men and beasts alike, to guide them. I led the way now, with Caspar immediately behind me on a leading rein, followed by Aristotle and the donkey, and my mount plodded steadily on into the darkness without straying from the trail.

It was a long, hard night. I had to let Caspar rest every two hours, but each time this meant an exhausting struggle for me in getting him mounted again. He seemed able to ride even when barely conscious or when delirium gripped him, but his strength was drained, and at three in the morning I wept with despair as I struggled to heave him up into the saddle.

"Trying, Lalla . . . trying," he muttered, his head lolling, one foot in the stirrup.

I could have hit him for being so helpless but retained a few shreds of reason and said as calmly as I could, using Kafir, "You must ride the mule. His back is not so high."

This meant unloading the mule and changing the panniers to Caspar's horse, but at last it was done, and then I was able to get him astride Aristotle without too much difficulty. Shortly before dawn we again hid ourselves away in a valley for the daylight hours. Once we were settled I attended to the animals, chewed some dried meat, coaxed Caspar into letting me feed him with a bowlful of soup, drank some water, then went to sleep, too exhausted to care any more about Caspar, myself, or anything in the world.

A downpour of rain woke me soon after noon, and I rushed to set up the little *yurt*. Caspar woke at the same time and tried to get up and help me, but I almost screamed abuse at him in Kafir, telling him to save his strength for the night's journey. I estimated that we had covered fifteen miles the night before. If we could manage the same distance tonight, we ought to be within sight of Herat by dawn.

Sight of Herat . . . it was a consummation I longed for with such wild dark passion that I dared not let myself dwell upon it. Three days ago, when Caspar had said sixty miles, perhaps he had been wrong. I told myself I must not think of the end, lest it be delayed and my frail spirit break from loss of hope. Lying beside Caspar in the *yurt*, listening to the rain upon the skins, I set up a barrier in my mind against all hopeful expectation; and in the void formed by that barrier I heard words running through my head in a persistent refrain, those strange words I had heard from my companion the night before, "*Melanie . . . Stormswift . . . daughter of Electra . . . beautiful, so beautiful. Bitch-goddess.*"

Caspar slept for a while. When he woke I felt his head and pulse. It seemed to me that his temperature had abated considerably, but when I made him turn over so that I could examine his wound I was alarmed by the inflammation and swelling around it. I told myself that this was to be expected, that I had prevented serious blood poisoning by my cleansing treatment, and that there was bound to be some local infection which his strong constitution could overcome, but I was not convinced by what

I told myself. Although the fever had passed he seemed very weak, not just in his body but in his spirit. Throughout our journeying I had come to regard him as a man of iron spirit and will, but now there was a look in his eyes that troubled me deeply, a kind of acquiescence that seemed alien in such a man.

The day dragged on. We slept, ate cold soup and honey cake, and slept again. The rain ceased an hour before sunset, and I crawled out of the *yurt* to begin making ready to move on. When I had taken down the *yurt* and packed it, Caspar still lay dozing on his bedding, and I had to rouse him before I could complete the task of packing and saddling the animals.

As we stood beside the mule and I braced myself for the effort of heaving him into the saddle, he took my wrist and looked down at me, supporting himself with his other arm across the saddle. "Promise me, Lalla," he said in English, speaking slowly and with an effort, "promise me you will take the papers to Mr. Renwick . . . Mr. Arthur Renwick. At the legation in Herat. Into his own hands. His own hands. Promise me, Lalla."

I said impatiently, "All right, I promise, but we have to get there first. Now keep this leg stiff while I try to lift you by it, and swing your good leg over." He was weaker than the day before, and in the end I found the only way to get him into the saddle was to kneel down on my hands and knees to make a human mounting block for him to step up on. Luckily my time as Sandru's servant, fetching water from the river each day and performing all kinds of heavy duties, had made me quite strong, and I was just able to bear Caspar's weight for long enough.

Once we had turned west on the trail again I let my horse guide us through the darkness by scent, without worrying that we might go astray. Now my fears were renewed that Caspar might fall, and I kept Aristotle close beside me so that I could support my companion when he began to sway in the saddle.

It was a brutally hard night. Sometimes I had a lunatic feeling that I had died and been consigned to hell, where for all eternity I would have to plod through an endless night, responsible for a sick or dying man I detested, constantly afraid and growing ever more exhausted. As before, we began by resting every two hours, but after a while I lost all sense of time. Once I was terrified when a party of other travelers, camped near the trail, called out to us, but when we simply continued on our way they made no attempt to run after us and ask questions.

At some time during the early hours a part of my mind must have retreated into sleep. I continued to do what I had to do but in a remote way, as if the grubby, frightened creature struggling through the night with her burdens was not myself but another person entirely.

An age passed. My right arm ached, and I lifted my head to discover that I was supporting Caspar with it. I could see him clearly now, could see all about me clearly as I blinked in surprise. When I looked back I could see the first light of the rising sun brightening the sky above the eastern horizon.

Perhaps because it had rained the day before there was now a touch of early mist lying low to the ground, but when I looked ahead again and raised my eyes I saw in the distance a city floating on the sea of mist. For a moment I thought it was a mirage, but then I remembered hearing that Herat stood on an artificial mound, almost a mile square and of good height. What I could see was the city wall, the great red fort with its round towers, and the tall minarets rising high above all else, the sun beginning to touch their summits.

I shed no tears. I felt no joy, no relief, for I was now beyond all feeling. "Caspar," I said, my voice hoarse from a dry throat, "Caspar, there is Herat." He did not answer, and when I looked at him I saw no understanding in his half-closed eyes as he sagged in the saddle, leaning toward me.

We plodded on, climbing the gradual slope to the city, and after a little while I began to see scores of small triangular white peaks rising from the dwindling mist. Anyone who had lived in India or Egypt, as I had, was bound to be familiar with the sights and sounds of the military, but it was a full minute before I realized that the white peaks were the tops of tents. The mist was dissolving quickly under the rising sun, and soon I saw the tents of a battalion laid out in immaculate rows, with the horse lines, the wagons, and the big marquees for stabling and for messes. Even as I gazed, the union flag broke from a tall jack-staff, and I heard the brassy notes of a bugler sounding reveille.

There was no response from Caspar. I paused to make sure I had the wallet with his own notes and those of the rival spy tucked in the inner pocket of the robe I wore, then we moved on again. The camp stood outside the city, and the guard tent lay nearest to the point where the trail, now a broad road, met the outskirts. Sections of trestle fencing, painted white, formed the perimeter of the encampment, with the guard tent and point of entry a hundred paces from the city. It was the guard tent that I made for now.

A sentry, standing at ease by the gap in the trestle fencing, lifted his rifle and held it across his body as he strolled forward a little to meet our approach. "Not this way, ducks," he said with a coarse London accent and a jerk of his head toward the crumbling pillars flanking the road where it entered Herat. "Yala. Jildi now." The last words meant, "Clear off. Quick." They were typical of the way the British soldier serving in India managed to pick up a very few words of Urdu or Hindi and mix them with English as a language to use when speaking to natives. But the very sight of this British soldier had brought me out of my mental stupor, and I was suddenly able to think very clearly and decide exactly how to behave. I was no longer the Jemimah Lawley I had once been, a spoiled and petulant child, but neither was I Lalla, slave and servant in the remote land of Shul.

Drawing my mount to a halt, I said quietly but very distinctly, "I am an Englishwoman, and the man with me is an Englishman who has been badly wounded." I put a sudden bite into my voice and snapped, "Stand to attention when I speak to you, young man! Have you no manners?"

He had gaped in surprise when I began to speak, and at my sudden command he jerked to attention instinctively before he had time to consider. I went on quietly again. "That's better. Now call your guard commander, quickly, please."

The man stared, utterly dumbfounded, and I could almost follow his thoughts. This native woman, with her man and train of animals, was speaking with the voice and manner of an English lady, a voice such as he might hear from an officer's wife. Fortunately he did not have to decide whether to believe her appearance or her voice but could safely leave this to a superior.

Turning his head, he shouted, "Sergeant Cooper! Quick!"

A moment or two later a man with a waxed mustache came bustling out of the tent, demanding to know what the trouble was. The sentry gestured toward me with a grimace of incomprehension, and I said at once, "Good morning, Sergeant Cooper. My name is Jemimah Lawley, I am the daughter of Sir George and Lady Lawley. The man with me is English and badly wounded. I have no time to explain further. Please send at once for your orderly officer and your garrison doctor. Be sure to have the messenger say that stretcher-bearers will be needed for my companion, and meantime your men can lift him down and make him comfortable."

I watched a dozen expressions flit across the face of the sergeant as I spoke, but he was a good soldier, quick to decide, and almost as soon as I finished he snapped to attention, saluted, said, "Very good, miss," then

raised his voice in a bellow. "McQueen! Taylor! Reilly! On the double!"
Three men came scurrying out of the tent. The sergeant gave curt orders, sending one off at a brisk trot and supervising the other two as they
lifted Caspar from the mule and laid him gently down.

I slid down from my horse and knelt beside the barely conscious man,
fanning flies away from his face. The sergeant's voice said, "Who is he,
miss? Who's the gentleman, then?"

I shook my head. "I'm not sure, Sergeant. I was abducted to Kafiristan
after the Kabul legation massacre two years ago, and now I've escaped.
This man helped me, but I didn't know he was English until a few days
ago, when he was shot." I looked up. "Not by a tribesman. By a Russian,
I think."

The sergeant stared down at Caspar, twirling one point of his mustache, his nose wrinkling in contempt. "Spies, then," he said. "That's
what they'll be, you mark my words, miss. Him and the Russian, both.
Spies." He made a snorting sound of disgust. Then: "Still, I'm glad you
escaped, miss. Kafiristan, eh? My word, it's a miracle you're alive. A
miracle. Welcome home, miss. Welcome home."

Home. I looked about me, and the realization grew slowly within me.
I had reached Herat and I was alive. My impossible journey was over, my
impossible escape was accomplished. Not quite home, perhaps, but safe
among my own people. Yet still I could not feel the jubilation I would
have expected. There was sorrow in me, and I knew it was because I felt
sure now that Caspar would not live. I had felt quite proud of my
medical knowledge and of the way I had treated his wound, but now I
had to acknowledge that in truth I knew little or nothing of medicine. I
was an ignorant blunderer who had served the wounded man no better
than the most primitive native might have done, and probably worse.

I was sad that I had hated him and been so impatient with him. If I
had been a little more thoughtful, if I had taken a little more care, I
might have saved his life. I was roused from this strange reverie by the
sound of hooves. Two horsemen came up between the lines of tents at a
canter, one in full uniform, a lieutenant, the other in breeches and shirt
sleeves. As they reined to a halt, the latter slipped quickly down from the
saddle, a big black satchel in one hand, and the lieutenant said in a high
nasal voice, "Now what's this extraordinary business about, Sergeant?
Where's this Englishwoman?"

I said, "Here, Lieutenant."

He gaped down at me. "What? You? Good God, what on earth is
going on?"

The man in shirt sleeves was kneeling beside me. He said brusquely, "Shut up, Tony, that can wait." Then, to me: "I'm the doctor. What happened?"

He was a man of about thirty, clean shaven, with short dark hair and quiet eyes set in a lean pleasant face. I felt a huge surge of relief, at both his presence and his manner, and I said, "He was shot from behind four days ago. Through here." I pulled open Caspar's robe, lifted his tunic, and indicated the area of the wound on the now filthy towel that swathed his middle. "I got the bullet out and disinfected the wound as well as I could, then dressed it with a quill for drainage. He ran a high fever for about thirty-six hours, but that seems to have passed now. He's very weak. I wondered if the bullet broke a rib, and perhaps the broken part punctured a lung, but he hasn't brought up any blood."

Caspar lay on his side, and while I spoke the doctor had been cutting away the towel I had used to pad the wound. The plaster beneath was grubby, but it was still firmly adhered, and the droplet of liquid that gathered at the end of the quill was clear. To my surprise and relief, the flesh around the area was no longer inflamed.

A cart came rattling up, and two men with a stretcher jumped down from it. The doctor put his nose close to the wound, sniffed once or twice, then sat back on his haunches and looked at me with interest. "My name is Selby," he said. "Captain Selby. And if ever I get shot in the back I'll send for you, young lady."

He stood up and I rose with him, suddenly feeling very strange, my hands shaking so much that I had to clasp them together. "Will he live?" I asked.

Captain Selby lifted a shoulder. "Can't promise anything," he said, "but if he dies it won't be your fault." He turned to the men with the stretcher. "All right, get him to the Casualty Clearing Station. I'll take a look at him there first, then have him transferred to the British Hospital in Herat." He looked at me again. "We've taken over a suitable building there, and he'll have the best of care."

"Thank you," I said. "Thank you, Captain."

The lieutenant, who I realized must be the orderly officer of the day, had now dismounted and was gazing at me with the same bewilderment I had roused in the sentry and the sergeant. It was hardly surprising. To hear the voice of an educated young Englishwoman issuing from the mouth of a creature with a brown dirty face, the work-worn hands and chipped nails of a scullery maid, wearing the travel-stained and no doubt pungent clothes of an Afghan peasant—this was something almost beyond belief.

The lieutenant said, "We were told a shockingly garbled tale by the messenger. Are you saying that you actually are English? I mean . . . well, dash it all . . ."

Captain Selby said, "Oh, for God's sake, Tony. If you listened to the medical report she gave me you couldn't fail to know she's English." The cart moved slowly off with Caspar and the stretcher-bearers. Captain Selby went on, "Who's your friend, young lady?"

Watching the cart, I said, "He's not really a friend. I only know his name is Caspar. At least, that's what he told me."

The two officers exchanged a glance. The lieutenant said with an air of disgust, "One of those mysterious spy chaps."

Captain Selby shrugged. "They have their uses, Tony." He looked at me again. "And you, young lady? I've pinched myself three times to make sure I'm not dreaming, so perhaps you'll tell us how you come to be here?"

I smiled. It was a moment or two before I realized I had done so, and then I wondered how long it had been since last I smiled. "I'm Jemimah Lawley," I said. "As I've just told your sergeant, I'm the daughter of Sir George and Lady Lawley. They were killed in the massacre at the Kabul legation two and a half years ago, and I was abducted. I've been a prisoner in Kafiristan ever since, but a friend there helped me escape. I mean, he made Caspar take me away, weeks and weeks ago. But I didn't know Caspar was English until four days ago, when he was shot."

There was a silence, then Captain Selby said slowly, "Lawley? Jemimah Lawley?"

I nodded, and smiled again. I was alive. I was free. I was safe. And Caspar might yet survive. "Yes," I said. "That is my name."

"But I thought . . ." The captain hesitated and glanced at his fellow officer.

The lieutenant said uneasily, "I'm sure I read about it in the newspapers."

"Read what?" I asked. I wanted a bath, I wanted to sleep, then to wake up and put on decent clothes, and revel in my return to civilization from a place where I could have lost my tongue or my head at a man's whim.

"Well," said the lieutenant reluctantly, "I'm not actually absolutely sure, of course, but I could have sworn that the Lawley girl turned up safe and sound just a few weeks after the massacre. Some loyal Afghans had been hiding her. At least, that's what it said in the newspapers."

V

I looked from one to the other, but clearly they were not joking.

"That's absurd," I said. "I'm Jemimah Lawley."

"Yes. Yes, of course." The lieutenant scratched his cheek and looked embarrassed. "Stupid of me." He glanced at his companion. "We must have misread something, John. Or perhaps the newspapers got it wrong. They usually do, you know."

I felt little interest in who was responsible for such a silly rumor, and I said, "Can you tell me where to find Mr. Arthur Renwick, please? He's with the legation here, and I promised Caspar I would personally deliver some papers to him." I took from under my robe the fat leather wallet.

The lieutenant said, "Papers?"

"Yes. There are lots of notes that Caspar kept making in some kind of code, and there are also the papers we took from the Russian."

"Russian?" the lieutenant echoed on a rising note.

I said, "Yes. A Turkoman Russian, I think. He was dressed as an Afghan, though, and it was he who shot Caspar after following us when we left Janawar. That was really my fault for not keeping watch properly. Then the man came down from the ridge to kill me with his knife, but Caspar had a hidden pistol and shot him dead. I suppose he was a rival spy, making notes like Caspar. We took a bundle of papers from his saddlebag."

The lieutenant said with contempt, "Spies. What kind of man would do a beastly furtive job like that?"

"They have their uses, Tony," Captain Selby repeated, "and I rather fancy Renwick is a chap who holds a position of some importance in that service. He was a guest in the mess with a few other legation people last week, remember? Little fellow with bright eyes. Reminded me of a squirrel."

"Ah, yes. A civilian," said the lieutenant, giving the word only a shade less contempt than he had put into the word "spies." He held out his hand. "All right, Miss—ah—Lawley. I'll have the papers taken to him."

I would have been glad to hand the wallet over, but to my surprise I found I was clutching it to my chest and saying, "No. I must give this to Mr. Arthur Renwick myself."

The lieutenant looked pained and said, "My dear girl—"

Captain Selby interrupted with a laugh. "Don't waste your time, Tony. Didn't you hear her say she had promised the fellow?" He turned to his horse and swung up into the saddle. "I must go and attend to my patient. You give the young lady an escort to the legation, and let us take pleasure at the thought of rousing them there so early." He drew his horse round and looked down at me with a smile. "It's been a rare pleasure to make your acquaintance, Miss Lawley. I very much hope to see you again shortly." Since he was wearing no cap he could not salute, but he laid a hand on his chest, bowed slightly, and said, "Your servant, ma'am."

The camp was stirring as he cantered away between two long lines of tents in the wake of the cart that had carried Caspar. The lieutenant said, "Well. Yes. I suppose he's right." He lifted his voice to bawl at the sergeant, standing to attention only two paces away. "Sar'nt Cooper! Detail two men for mounted escort!"

"Sir!" The sergeant gave a quivering salute, swung round smartly on his heel, and began to bawl in turn. Five minutes later I was riding slowly through narrow streets on the outskirts of Herat, my string of animals behind me. A soldier rode on each side of me, dressed in pith helmet, khaki jacket and breeches. One of the soldiers was a corporal. They did not speak as we rode, perhaps because they were uncertain how to address me, and no doubt felt that safety lay in silence.

The ancient citadel stood on the highest part of the city, but we skirted this, passed along a broad dusty road, and came at last to a fine building in sand-colored brick. There, after a long wait, the heavy door was opened by a servant. The corporal handed in a message written by the orderly officer, the door was closed, and another wait of seven or eight minutes followed. The soldiers fidgeted uneasily, but I did not mind waiting. After all that had happened to me in the past two and a half years, to wait for a few minutes in peace and safety, without fear, seemed little hardship.

Suddenly the door was flung open and a young man, hastily dressed, hair disheveled, boots not yet laced, came rushing out followed by two native servants. He stopped short at sight of me, gazed incredulously for a moment, then said, "You are Miss—ah—the English lady?" He flapped the message in his hand.

"I am Jemimah Lawley," I said, a little absently, for I was very tired now, "and I have important papers to deliver to Mr. Arthur Renwick from a man I know only as Caspar."

"Of course, of course," said the young man energetically. "Allow me to help you dismount, Miss—ah . . ." He took my hand as I slid from the saddle, then snapped orders at the servants, telling them to take the animals and baggage round to the stables. He dismissed my escort, then guided me toward the open doorway, saying, "I am Forbes, the duty officer, and I roused Mr. Renwick at once with the message from Lieutenant Fowler. Amazing. Quite amazing. Will you come this way, Miss —ah . . . ? Mr. Renwick will attend upon you shortly."

As he shepherded me into a large cool room with English furniture, he kept glancing sideways at me, trying to be unobtrusive as he sniffed the aroma of hard travel I brought with me, and registering complete bewilderment. "How very extraordinary. It is really hard to believe that a young woman could . . . I quite thought Tony Fowler must be pulling my leg with that message. Please be seated. May I take the reports now?"

"No, Mr. Forbes. I will give them only to Mr. Arthur Renwick." I spoke very politely as I sat down on a rush-seated oak chair, but I kept a firm hold on the wallet.

"Oh. I see," said the young man uncertainly, and stood there nonplussed. Quite suddenly I was close to tears, though not of joy and not of weariness. Strangely, very strangely, they came partly from anxiety for Caspar, who might yet die, partly from loneliness, and partly from a new fear I could not name. Yet surely I detested Caspar? And surely I was not alone, but among my own people at last? And surely it was absurd to be afraid of the new and wonderful life that now lay before me?

If it had not been for these strange feelings I might have laughed inwardly now as I watched Mr. Forbes try to adjust to the notion of my presence here. I looked like an Afghan peasant woman, and I smelled like one, yet here I sat in the quiet luxury of the British Legation, a wallet clutched in my grimy hands, having summoned from his bed an important gentleman, a civil servant of the Foreign Office in all probability.

"May I send for some refreshment?" asked Mr. Forbes. "Some tea, perhaps? Lemonade? Ah . . . ? A few biscuits, perhaps?"

"No, thank you, Mr. Forbes. When I have spoken with Mr. Renwick I should very much like a bath, and then I should like to sleep. I have been traveling all night."

"Oh, certainly, I will see what can be arranged. Then there is the matter of clothes. I think perhaps I should speak to Mrs. Dalby. She is the British envoy's wife. There are two or three other English ladies in Herat, wives of senior officers."

He turned as the door opened and a man entered, a small man, freshly shaved, neatly dressed in gray, with bright eyes, like a squirrel. "Miss Lawley?" His voice was deeper than I expected from a man of his stature. He came forward with outstretched hand. "I am Arthur Renwick." He glanced at Mr. Forbes. "Go and speak with Mrs. Dalby's maid, then with Mrs. Dalby herself as soon as she is available, Forbes."

"Very well, sir."

Mr. Renwick bowed over my hand as his subordinate hurried out with a scuffling of loose boots. The small bright eyes were very shrewd as he studied my face. "You have papers for me?" he asked.

"Yes, Mr. Renwick." I handed him the wallet.

"Thank you." He opened it and riffled a thumb across the wad of papers within.

I was angry and said, "Do you not intend to inquire after the man who was shot?"

He smiled, his eyes twinkling, and closed the wallet. "It is a fact greatly to be deplored that the papers are more important to me than the man, Miss Lawley. Equally deplorable, the man is of more importance to me than your estimable self. I mean no offense by that. It is simply a cruel truth. Pray tell me, how is the man who was shot?"

"You mean Caspar?"

He inclined his head. "By all means let us call him Caspar for the moment, while we are alone."

"He was shot four days ago, near Janawar. I treated his wound and brought him here. He seemed very ill when I left him in the hands of Captain Selby, the garrison doctor, an hour ago."

"Thank you. I will speak with Captain Selby myself later." Small teeth, white but uneven, showed in a smile. He moved to sit facing me across a rosewood writing table and continued, "Now I would like to inquire after yourself, Miss Lawley, if you are not too tired to talk for a little while. I fear it will take thirty minutes or so before we can offer you the hospitality of bath and bed. Your arrival here at so early an hour has posed an administrative problem. I do apologize for the irksome delay."

I rubbed my tired eyes with my grubby fingers, then managed to smile. "I have known more irksome problems, Mr. Renwick," I said, and went on to tell my story, as briefly as I could, from the time of the attack on the British Legation in Kabul. I told of the slaughter of my parents, of my escape across the river, my capture by Hindus, and the long journey to Kafiristan. I did not tell him that I had been sold as a wife to the *pacha* of Shul, who had later discarded me, but said that I had first been a palace slave and then become a personal servant to Sandru. When I explained that Sandru was a doctor and had been an officer in the British Army forty years ago, captured during the retreat from Kabul, Mr. Renwick showed no particular surprise, but by now I had come to the conclusion that he was not a man easily surprised by anything.

I did not tell him that Sandru had contrived my escape by compelling Caspar to be my escort under threat of exposing him as an English spy. It seemed impossible that anything I told Mr. Renwick might in time filter back to Shul, but I knew that if Deenbur ever learned the truth he would order Sandru to be killed in horrible fashion, and I could take not the smallest risk of that. Of course, Caspar himself might tell Mr. Renwick what had happened, if Caspar lived, but this was something I had no power to prevent.

When I finished speaking Mr. Renwick gave me an encouraging smile and said, "I feel there are substantial omissions in your account, Miss Lawley."

"Omissions? Of what kind?"

"I cannot understand why the Hindu traders should have taken you all the way to Shul in order to sell you as a slave. A better price, perhaps? But why? And how did they know that? Also, you have said very little of your life there during the past two years and more. I should be surprised if you had not been evilly used by men during that time, yet you make no complaint of this."

I said slowly, "Such omissions from my account are intentional, Mr. Renwick. I am well aware that when I return to England the newspapers and their readers will seek to know every sordid detail of my ordeal, but I do not propose to satisfy their curiosity, or yours. My life in Shul was the very simple, primitive life of a native, and there is little more to tell about it. How soon can you arrange for me to make the journey to England?"

"Oh, quite soon, quite soon," he said amiably. "I take it you know the names of your parents' lawyers there?"

After a moment or two of thought I shook my head. "No, I don't recall the names. I saw very little of my father, and my mother left all such matters for him to deal with, but it will be simple enough to find out once I return. Our family lawyers must have charge of my home, Witchwood Hall, and of my father's financial affairs."

"No doubt," agreed Mr. Renwick. "And I imagine you have relatives in England who will be delighted to learn that you are alive and safe?"

"There are no relatives I know of," I said. "Both my father and mother were the last of their respective lines, and I am their only child." A thought occurred to me. "Do you have in mind that the lawyers will have sought other relatives, presuming me to be dead?"

"Not at all," said Mr. Renwick. "I believe that as the law stands you could not be presumed dead until you had been missing for seven years." He gave me his quick bright smile. "But I must say you seem singularly untroubled by the notion of possible problems, or indeed by all that has happened to you, Miss Lawley."

I thought of Shul, and of the moment when Sandru told me I was to be sold as a bride to Akbah the Mad. I thought of my utter terror then, and of my fears as I crept out onto the trail a few nights later. I thought of the moment when the man who had shot Caspar drew his knife to kill me, and of the many moments of despair I had known during the past four days and nights, struggling to bring the wounded man safely to Herat.

It was little wonder that to the gentleman studying me with his head to one side I appeared singularly untroubled now that all this was behind me. "Mr. Renwick," I said, "I am content to be alive."

Before he could speak again the door opened and a lady entered. She was short and plump, perhaps in her middle forties, with a round and kindly face. She wore a gray dress, but her hair was still in two plaits as if she had risen from her bed too hurriedly to brush it out and pin it up.

"Good heavens alive, Mr. Renwick!" she exclaimed, gazing at me in unbelief. "Is it true? Is this . . . this person really English?"

"She is indeed, Mrs. Dalby," he replied, rising with the wallet tucked under his arm, "and she has suffered a very great deal. I should be most grateful if you would take charge of her now."

"Of course, of course!" Her manner was warm, but she could not help looking doubtful as she approached me. "Your name is Jemimah Lawley, so young Mr. Forbes said. Is that right?"

I had risen with Mr. Renwick, and now I said, "Yes, Mrs. Dalby, how do you do? It's a great pleasure to meet you, and I do apologize for my appearance."

My voice and my words both startled and convinced her. "Good heavens alive!" she repeated. "Oh, you poor child." Gingerly she took my arm, her nose wrinkling involuntarily. "Come along, dear. Karim is preparing a bath, and my little maid is making a room ready for you."

At the door I paused to look back. Mr. Arthur Renwick had seated himself at the writing table again and was already poring over the papers from the wallet. I said, "Will you please keep me informed of Caspar's progress, Mr. Renwick?"

His head came up sharply, and the little eyes held a most penetrating gaze. "You mean Kassim?" he said. "The Afghan?"

I stared, then gave a shrug. "Kassim, if you prefer it."

"I do, Miss Lawley," he said, his eyes still on me, "and I must require you not to discuss this matter with anyone here but myself. I speak as an official of Her Majesty's Government."

For a moment I cringed inwardly before his air of authority, but then reminded myself that I was no longer a slave, and I could speak freely without the slightest danger of suffering a whip laid to my back. Anger rose in me, and I was glad to feel it, glad that I could dare to be angry now. I said, "Be so good as to answer my question, sir."

"Question?"

"I asked if you would keep me informed as to the progress of the wounded man I brought to Herat this morning."

"Ah, yes. I will see that you are informed."

"Thank you. I note that you have spoken as an official of Her Majesty's Government, so let me assure you that I will certainly not discuss this matter further with anyone here, which includes yourself, sir. And *I* speak as one of Her Majesty's subjects, Jemimah Lawley."

I heard Mrs. Dalby give a small gasp at my tone, and I glimpsed something of pity in Mr. Renwick's small bright eyes. Then he turned to the papers, and as he did so I heard him murmur, "That remains to be seen."

*　　*　　*

Two days later I was on my way south to Kandahar, riding in a carriage with two nurses from the Nightingale School for Nurses in London. I had spent most of those two days sleeping and acquiring a small wardrobe of borrowed clothes. These, once I had tried them on, had been altered where necessary by Mrs. Dalby's maid, a young Indian girl I quickly came to like very much for her ready smile and gentle nature.

There could be no doubt that Mr. Arthur Renwick wanted me away from Herat as quickly as possible and without allowing the legation staff or families any opportunity to satisfy their curiosity about me. Meals were brought to my room. Mrs. Dalby produced borrowed clothes from the handful of legation and army wives in Herat. Her maid, Dahira, did what she could with my hair and my nails, and young Mr. Forbes came on the afternoon of the day following my arrival to say I would be leaving next morning.

That evening, before Dahira brought my dinner to the room, Mr. Renwick called, ostensibly to inquire if all was well with me, but in fact to ask several questions about the man who had shot Kassim—he used that name now even though we were alone. Could I describe the man? Had he spoken to me? Could I remember what kind of rifle he had used?

I cut this short by saying I would answer no further questions and that I refused to be involved in anything to do with spying. He sighed but did not seem greatly put out and did not persist. I was thankful for this and said, "Please tell me, Mr. Renwick, do you have any news of,"—I stumbled on the name for a moment—"of Kassim?"

"Yes, Miss Lawley. I am advised that he is now in the hospital here, and his condition has not deteriorated."

This sounded like a very guarded medical opinion. I said, "May I visit him?" I could not imagine why I wanted to visit Caspar. In all the weeks we had been together I had never regarded him as a friend, and he had clearly disliked me heartily from the beginning, yet when I thought of him it was with a curious kind of affection, perhaps arising from the simple cause of our having journeyed long and dangerously together.

Mr. Renwick said, "There will be no opportunity to visit him, Miss Lawley. You leave for Kandahar at an early hour tomorrow."

"I see. Well, I hope Kassim will make a good recovery, and tonight I shall write him a note of thanks for bringing me safely to Herat. Perhaps you will be so kind as to ensure that it is delivered to him?"

"With pleasure, Miss Lawley."

The party leaving Herat consisted of the two nurses and myself, two gentlemen from the legation in another carriage, some twenty soldiers traveling in two carts drawn by pairs of horses, and a mounted escort of soldiers commanded by a lieutenant. The soldiers in the carts were being invalided home to England, some following wounds or injuries, others after malaria or dysentery. There were also a baggage cart and teams of spare horses to take turns in harness.

A long journey lay ahead, for the four hundred miles to Kandahar was only the first stage. There we rested for three days before continuing to the border, through the Khojak Pass into India, and on to Quetta, a short stage of only a hundred and fifty miles.

The two nurses with me were going home on leave in charge of the invalid soldiers. Ruth and Joan were both from Devon and both a few years older than I, country girls of modest education, but capable nurses and very jolly company. They were intensely curious about the mystery of my sudden appearance in Herat, and had heard all kinds of rumors which they retailed to me in the hope that I would respond by giving them the truth of the matter, but I was able to say that I had been forbidden by an important government official to say a word about the subject.

They oohed and ahhed at this and decided between them that we might all be put in prison if they were too nosy, an opinion I encouraged with significant looks and nods. Each night when we halted on the road a tent was set up for us to sleep in, and a soldier was posted on guard. The army food was plain but certainly as good as I had eaten during my journey with Caspar. Throughout the long hot days of travel on the dusty road to the south I became good friends with Ruth and Joan, though I felt ashamed to recall that the Jemimah Lawley of old would have had nothing to do with them and would have felt herself infinitely superior to these truly admirable girls.

Despite this good fortune of getting on well with my companions I found the journey strangely wearisome. Perhaps it was partly because the clothes I now wore seemed so unsuitable for travel, so restricting compared with those I had worn on the journey from Shul. Perhaps, too, I felt uneasy at having nothing useful to do, no responsibilities, no duties to perform. Sometimes I found myself remembering with a kind of pleasure the days I had spent riding Aristotle, following Caspar, with his pack donkey on a leading rein. Then I would come to myself with a start and decide that I must be mad to think so pleasantly of those harsh days. It was a relief when I persuaded Ruth and Joan that under their supervision I could help them look after the invalid soldiers—at least to the extent of providing an extra pair of hands accustomed to such work.

I had needed no money as yet, but in fact I possessed several sovereigns, for Mr. Forbes had sold Aristotle and the horse of the dead Russian on which I had ridden into Herat. The money in my borrowed purse came from the proceeds of that sale.

From Quetta, after a day's rest, we were able to continue by rail to Karachi, where we would await a ship to carry us to England. The five-hundred-mile train journey of this last stage took only two days, and when we reached Karachi we were comfortably accommodated in the married quarters of some barracks. Here we waited for two weeks, and during that time, as instructed by Mr. Renwick, I went to see the District Commissioner. He received me in his office, told me that he had been handed a message from Mr. Arthur Renwick by the lieutenant in charge of our escort, and gave me a check drawn on the Karachi branch of an English bank for the sum of ten pounds.

"This is an emergency grant from government funds in view of your present difficulties, Miss Lawley," he said sympathetically. "I have not been advised as to the nature of these difficulties, in fact I have been required to ask no questions in that respect, simply to provide you with the necessary funds to see you safely home. You will be provided for in Karachi on the same basis as the nurses, and this will also apply when you embark for England. There will be no fare to pay. Also, let me reassure you that the government does not regard this grant as a debt to be repaid."

As I sat listening, my head was still in a whirl from the impact of all the sights and sounds of Karachi, a civilized city teeming with people, its roads thronged with carriages, oxcarts, soldiers, beggars, stray cattle, white and brown and black faces, and every class of person. Great locomotives hissed and whistled at the railhead, tall cranes leaned into the sky above the harbor, while from the river came the hooting of the steamers plying up and down the great waterway of the Indus to Multan, half a thousand miles away.

This was a world I knew, and for the first time since I had seen the minarets of Herat appear through the morning mist, my return from captivity seemed real to me. I was Jemimah Lawley. The long ordeal suffered by a girl called Lalla in the tribal kingdom of Shul was a distant nightmare in whose reality I was scarcely able to believe myself.

Perhaps for this reason I almost laughed when the Commissioner assured me that I would not have to repay the ten pounds. But I did not laugh, for I feared that my laughter might turn unexpectedly to tears, so greatly was I moved by the knowledge that my life could now begin anew. Instead I said politely, "Thank you, sir, but let me assure you that I shall regard this as a debt to be repaid as soon as my affairs in England have been set in order."

"Quite so," he said, and looked down at his hands rather uncomfortably. "We are in telegraphic communication with London, so if you wish me to send a telegram to anybody on your behalf, solicitors or relatives perhaps, you have only to say."

"Thank you," I replied, "but I have no relatives now, and I have yet to discover the name of the firm of solicitors who acted for my father. I imagine this can easily be done at Somerset House from the archives dealing with wills, but in any event I intend to go first to Witchwood Hall, my home in Surrey."

The Commissioner's eyebrows lifted a little. "You think the house will be open?" he asked.

"Oh yes." I had no doubt of that. "My parents always left a staff of three or four living-in servants to look after the house during our long absences abroad. There was Carson the butler, Mrs. Rudge the house-keeper . . . I forget the others. I was barely thirteen when I last saw Witchwood Hall. But Carson will know who the lawyers are, since they must have taken responsibility for the house following my parents' death."

The Commissioner nodded slowly, and I caught a hint of puzzlement in his eyes. "You seem to have thought everything out very thoroughly, Miss Lawley," he said.

I smiled a little wryly. "I have spent the last four weeks traveling from Herat with almost nothing to do all day but think."

"Quite so," he said vaguely, "quite so." Then to my utter surprise he spoke with a very bad accent in the Kafir tongue, almost as if he had learned the phrase parrot fashion: *"Shul oshti kitti wass ka dunnoo-a Herat* [How many days' journey is it from Shul to Herat]?"

I stared at him with rising anger, then said, "My companion and I took many weeks, sir, but clearly it depends on the rate of travel and the length of halts. Are you *testing* what I told Mr. Renwick—that I was a prisoner in Kafiristan for two and a half years? If you or he doubt me, you have only to ask Cas—" I bit back the name. "You have only to ask the man who was my companion on that journey."

"My dear Miss Lawley, you misunderstand me," he said smoothly. "I amuse myself by picking up a smattering of lesser-known Indian lan-guages and thought I would try out my few words of Kafir."

I stood up, putting the check in my borrowed handbag, and the Com-missioner rose with me. I was quite unconvinced by his explanation, but there was no point in pursuing the matter. "I'll wish you good day, sir," I said, and made my way to the door without offering my hand.

He hurried from behind his desk to open the door for me. "Thank you for calling, Miss Lawley, and I trust you have a good journey home."

"Most kind of you." I paused for a moment to look at him and felt a surge of grim delight that I could now speak to a man in a way that would have brought me a painful beating during my years in Shul. "I trust you will shortly find a more competent teacher of Kafir," I said. "Your accent is quite lamentable."

As I went down the wide marble steps to the cool hall and then into the street, I found I was giggling to myself. An open carriage with an Indian driver and the soldier sent with me as an escort were waiting. The soldier sprang to attention and opened the door for me. "All right, miss?"

"Yes, thank you." I gave him a friendly smile and sat back feeling wonderfully content. Jemimah Lawley of old would not have given a private soldier a friendly smile, and Lalla of Shul would have been whipped if she had spoken to a man as I had just spoken to the Commissioner. I was now neither of those persons, and not quite sure what I had become or would become in my new life, but I was very thankful to have left both Jemimah Lawley of old and Lalla of Shul behind me.

* * *

Our ship was called *Bristol Star,* carrying both cargo and passengers. Among the passengers were a hundred or so officers and men from different regiments being returned to England for various reasons, among them the invalid soldiers from Herat. Ruth, Joan, and I shared one of the least expensive of the first-class cabins, and throughout the voyage the two nurses continued their task of looking after the sick. It pleased me greatly that they asked me to lend a hand on one or two occasions when they were exceptionally busy.

We sat at table in the dining room together and were taken little notice of by the civilian passengers, but one or two of the young army officers paid us close attention as *Bristol Star* sailed southwest through the Arabian Sea on the first stage of its journey to Suez. Ruth and Joan had spent enough time in military hospitals to know the ways of young officers and soon showed that they were unlikely to behave foolishly. For myself, I was spared any problems of holding off unwanted advances because on our first day at sea I found to my surprise that Captain John Selby, the battalion doctor I had met at the guard tent outside Herat, was aboard.

I had liked him then, even though our encounter had been brief, and when he sought my company for conversation and walks around the deck

I was well content, because the other officers then left me alone. Captain Selby had traveled down from Herat a week later than the party I had been sent with, but he was able to tell me that the man I had brought wounded to the cantonment—a man we both carefully referred to as Kassim—had begun to recover. I was surprised to find how glad I was at such news but realized this was probably because if my strange companion had died I would have felt that my nightmare struggle of the last four days to Herat had been wasted.

By the time our ship had passed through the Suez Canal into the Mediterranean we had achieved a pleasant friendship, Captain Selby and I. A number of shipboard romances had begun on *Bristol Star*, but to my relief I had no advances from John, as he invited me to call him. He was married, and immensely proud of his young wife, whose photograph he always carried. They had married two years before, when his battalion was in England, but he did not want her to become an army wife in a garrison town of India, Egypt, or some other distant part of the world, and so he had now bought himself out of the Army and was returning to set up a medical practice in England.

Once, and once only, he asked me about my life as a captive in Kafiristan. It was a warm evening and we were strolling around the deck before dinner, with the western sky still streaked with mauve and pink, though it was well after sunset. I hated to talk of those days but did not want to refuse outright, so I briefly told the strange story of Sandru, who had himself been an army doctor, and said that I had been his servant and assistant after the first year of my captivity. John listened while I gave a short account of my daily life in Kuttar, then said, "What about the first year, Jemimah?"

I shook my head. "It was bad," I said. "Very bad. I don't wish to talk about it, John."

"It might help to talk," he said gently. "I am a doctor, and you need not be embarrassed, or fear that I would betray a confidence."

I took his arm as we walked and said, "I'm beyond embarrassment after my time in Shul, and I know you would observe medical confidence, but I simply wish to leave all that behind me. It's strange, but if I had been rescued after only a few weeks, I know I would have been in a dreadful state of mind, a condition of mental collapse, haunted forever by memories. But the long ordeal carried me past that stage. Somehow I learned to accept . . . to adjust. So the memories don't haunt me, and I have no need to talk it out of my system, as Sandru sometimes encouraged a patient to do. I was called Lalla there in Shul, but Lalla was another girl living in another world, and my only wish is to leave that world behind me."

He patted my hand on his arm and smiled. "Very sensible. I thought I might help, but clearly you must be an exceptional girl to have come through such an ordeal so well."

I sighed and spoke reluctantly. "Yes, I was exceptional, John. I was probably the most exceptionally unpleasant young girl you could ever have had the misfortune to meet."

He laughed. "Oh, come now."

"It's true," I said. "When I look back and remember, I almost cringe from shame. Oh dear, that suggests I think I'm vastly improved now, and I don't feel that at all. You know, I spent most of the journey from Shul quite hating Kassim. Isn't that dreadful? No, I just feel I've become another person whom I know hardly at all, and I suppose I shall have to spend some time finding out about myself, discovering who I really am."

He said quietly, "Yes. To discover who you are might prove an ordeal in itself, Jemimah."

"Oh, I realize that." I was about to laugh as I spoke, but suddenly there was no laughter in me, only a chill feeling that, whether John Selby knew it or not, his last words were ill-omened and held a significance infinitely deeper than appeared on the surface. What their significance might be I could not imagine, and next moment the feeling was gone. There came the sound of the great gong calling passengers to dinner, and I saw Ruth and Joan hurrying along the deck, smiling and waving, to claim me as their table companion.

VI

That ominous premonition did not touch me again during the rest of the voyage, but a few days later, as we sailed from Malta after refueling in Grand Harbor, another conversation with John Selby left me greatly chastened.

The ship's crew boasted a small orchestra, and the captain had arranged a ball in the first-class lounge. Since there were more gentlemen than ladies, and since Ruth, Joan, and I were unattached, we were much in demand, but it was a hot night, and toward eleven o'clock, as John Selby and I finished only the second dance we had managed to have together, I asked him to take me out on deck to enjoy some fresh and cooler air.

My wardrobe included no ball gown or evening dress, and I was wearing a light day dress, but the same could be said for the nurses and several other lady passengers. With my shoulders covered, I had no need even of a wrap, and I stood by the rail with John, watching the bright fluorescence foaming along the ship's side. When I looked up at the stars I remembered the many nights in the mountains and on the plains of Afghanistan, when I had lain wrapped in my blanket under the open sky, my silent companion Kassim lying an arm's length away.

"I hope he's well again now," I said, barely aware that I had spoken my thought aloud.

John must have read my mind. "Kassim?" he asked.

I smiled and nodded. "Yes. I suddenly thought of him. Oh dear, when I cut the bullet out and tried to do everything I thought Sandru would have done, I felt quite proud of myself. But pride goes before a fall, doesn't it? He developed a fever and almost died because I tended him wrongly."

In the moonlight I saw John's puzzled stare. "But you didn't treat him wrongly, Jemimah. You cleaned and managed to disinfect that wound. Oh, certainly he had a fever, that was the natural response of the body in fighting whatever small infection you had failed to prevent. Dear girl, before Lister introduced the principle of antisepsis to surgery, only two soldiers in a hundred survived severe wounds. Just two! Now, as many as forty-five in a hundred survive. You applied the principle of antisepsis and saved Kassim's life. What is so extraordinary is that you learned this from a doctor who vanished from the civilized world many years before the medical profession adopted this lifesaving practice."

I was pleased at such praise for Sandru and said, "I think Sandru was a clever man, but he also had a good instinct. Perhaps this told him that cleansing an injury thoroughly and leaving it to Nature was the best way, or perhaps it was because he had no other way to try in a primitive land."

"I would very much like to have met him," John said wistfully.

I was following my own train of thought and said, "But if I treated Kassim properly, why did he almost die? The fever passed, but he just sank into a kind of lethargy."

John was silent for a few moments, then he said, "I knew the man as a patient for only one week, and he was not a communicative fellow, but I think my army experience has given me a special insight into soldiers and men of this kind, and I came to two conclusions about him. First, that he is a man who puts duty before all else, and second, that without realizing it himself he invites death."

I started at the word. "He *invites* death? Whatever can you mean?"

John turned with his back to the rail and moved his shoulders in a shrug. "Men who know great unhappiness, and women too, no doubt, may wish to be freed from it, even at the cost of life itself."

I remembered my early days in Shul. There had been many moments then when I had wished myself dead, but surely the horror of my circumstances made that a very different matter. A thought came to me, and I asked, "Did he ever speak the name Melanie?"

John gave me a puzzled look. "Not in my presence, but why do you ask?"

I remembered the dusk of coming night, and the fevered voice muttering, *"Melanie . . . Stormswift . . . Daughter of Electra. Bitch-goddess."* I remembered the bitter sorrow in those last words and wondered if there might indeed be other kinds of unhappiness just as deep as I had known in Shul, though quite beyond my experience. I had not yet replied to John's question, and now he said, "Who is Melanie?"

I shook my head. "I don't know, and it doesn't matter. But . . . you said you felt that Kassim was a man who put duty before all else. If so, then why did he give up and sink into a lethargy, not caring if he died? We were still three or four days from Herat then, and he was desperate to deliver some papers to the legation there. Surely that was an important duty for him to complete?"

John Selby turned and rested his elbows on the rail, staring out into the darkness. He said, "Kassim asked *you* to deliver those papers in the event of his death, did he not, Jemimah?"

"Yes, several times. It was an obsession with him. But what difference does that make?"

"A considerable difference." John turned his head to look at me, and in his gaze there was a curious kind of respect that astonished me. "If there was one thing I understood clearly from what little conversation I had with Kassim, it was that he had not a shred of doubt but that you would complete his task for him by bringing his papers to the proper quarters in Herat." John smiled suddenly. "And you did indeed. I remember when I first saw you outside the guard tent, you even refused to hand them over to a British officer because you had promised to deliver them to Mr. Renwick yourself."

"I can't think why Kassim was so sure," I said slowly, feeling quite baffled. "After all, I'm female, and not very old, and a terrible coward, and Kassim really didn't think much of me at all."

"Perhaps he changed his mind," said John. "The longest sentence he spoke to me was about you, and I can almost remember his very words. He said something like, 'I didn't think she'd get me here, Selby. Thought she'd have to bury me beside the trail. But she'd have made a good job of it, Lalla would. I knew that. And then she'd have brought my reports safely to Herat. But, by God, she brought me here *too*, didn't she?' Then he laughed in a rather strange way and said, 'That damn girl . . .' I didn't get the impression that he disliked you, Jemimah."

After thinking for a while I said, "I suppose he got used to me, but he really hated me at first. I can understand that now, though. Being what he was, he must have felt horrified when Sandru made him take me with him on a journey right across Afghanistan." John nodded but made no comment, and I went on to voice a feeling I had known several times since discovering the truth about the man I had believed to be a native Afghan. "Toward the end I quite liked Kassim in a way, even though he was doing such a wretched and contemptible job."

Beside me, John Selby stiffened. "Contemptible?" he said softly.

"Well . . . yes." I looked about me to make sure we were not overheard. "You know his profession. Your officer friend at the guard tent spoke of spies doing a beastly furtive job."

My companion exhaled a long sigh of exasperation. "My dear friend Jemimah," he said, "I would not trouble myself to argue with Tony Fowler because, to be frank, he is too stupid to follow a reasoned argument. But I'm sure you are too intelligent to be gulled by popular opinion in this matter."

I was taken aback. In all my life I had never heard anybody refer to spies except in tones of contempt. Before I could say anything John went on, "Tell me now, what is the purpose of an army? Or a navy, for that matter?"

"Oh dear. Is this going to be a reasoned argument?"

"In a way, except I would like you to discover your own line of reasoning by answering questions."

He spoke lightly now, and I fell in with his mood. "Very well, Captain Selby. Now let me think. The purpose of an army is . . . well, either to defend or to conquer, I suppose."

"A fair answer. Now, leaving aside any question of right or wrong, let us consider a campaign by the British Army. Would you prefer to have many dead and wounded, or few?"

"Few, of course."

"And on what would this depend?"

This question called for thought, but after a few moments I said, "Well, I suppose on several things, like weapons and discipline—oh, and morale. I often heard high-up officers speak of that to my father."

"True, but you have missed a vital factor."

I thought again, and remembered being bored at the dinner table by bemedaled men in scarlet tunics discussing long-ago battles in France or the Crimean Peninsula. "You mean the skill of the generals?" I said diffidently.

John gave me an approving look. "Precisely. And on what does that depend?"

I laughed and shook my head. "I'm sorry, John, but I'm not a military expert. I suppose a general's skill depends on how clever he is, but I'm sure that's not the answer you want."

"It's not a bad answer," he said, "but what would you say is the biggest factor of all in enabling a general to exercise his skill?"

"Heaven knows. I give up."

"Then I'll tell you. It lies in knowing his enemy, knowing what forces that enemy has, how they are disposed, *and what they plan to do.*"

I started to speak, to say that this was an obvious fact, but then the full impact of John's argument struck me, and the easy words were silenced in my throat. The information a spy brought to the military could save a thousand lives, ten thousand, perhaps. How many had been slaughtered in the retreat from Kabul forty years ago? Sixteen thousand? And how many would have been saved if just one spy had brought the right information to the general at the right time?

Dirty spy. In popular opinion the two words went naturally together, conjuring up the picture of a skulking sneak thief without honor or courage. Soldiers, in particular, poured scorn on such creatures, yet it was by the work of such creatures that the lives and limbs of soldiers were saved. One man, just one man who brought to a military commander the secrets of the enemy, could be of more value than a whole brigade of soldiers.

The thoughts running through my head now were such a reversal of all I had ever heard or ever thought to myself concerning "dirty spies" that I felt quite breathless. To be a soldier was one thing. You risked wounding and death, but always in the company of comrades, always with their support. How different for the spy, utterly alone in enemy territory, friendless, acting a part with unceasing vigilance, unearthing secrets to save lives and win battles, or perhaps even to prevent battles; and constantly at fearful risk, for in all countries the fate of a caught spy was death.

So if a man such as Kassim succeeded in his lonely task, few would ever know. He would win neither honor nor praise, and his labors in saving the lives of his fellow men would continue to be despised by them. If he failed in his lonely task, then he would die a mean death, would lie in an unmarked grave in foreign soil. Unlike the soldier, he would win no medal and his sacrifice would pass forever unknown to his compatriots, who would continue to hold in contempt the profession of spy.

I was filled with shame now as I recalled how I had hated Kassim when I demanded to know if he would have left me in Shul had not Sandru compelled him to take me. In my mind I could hear again the pain and tiredness in his voice as he replied, "Yes, Miss Lawley. With much regret . . . yes." He had not said that a thousand lives might depend upon his making a safe journey to Herat and that he could not jeopardize them for a single life, but in these last few minutes my eyes had been opened and I understood many things that before had been hidden.

Beside me, John Selby said, "Jemimah?"

I realized that I must have stood in silence for a long time, staring out over the dark sea as my thoughts fell into place. Despite the warmth of the night, I shivered a little as I took John's arm and said, "No need for more questions. I'm sorry I spoke of his work as contemptible. He must be a very brave man."

"They all must be," John said simply. "Not only Kassim, but the Russian who tried to kill him and was himself killed. Theirs and ours alike. But never try to press such an opinion in company, Jemimah, for you'll only be derided."

That I could well imagine. It was an opinion I would have derided myself only ten minutes ago. I said, "Thank you for what you have shown me, John. In spite of everything, Kassim brought me safely through that long and dangerous journey from Kafiristan, and I wanted to respect him. Now I can do so." I hesitated, then added, "Did you ever learn his real name?"

John smiled and shook his head. "In the hospital he was registered as William Smith. I'm sure that was no more true than Kassim."

A few moments later, and with no more said, we returned to the ballroom. As if by tacit consent we did not speak of the man again throughout the rest of our voyage home, but since reaching Herat safely I had begun to say my prayers once more, and in them now I always remembered Kassim, or Caspar, or William Smith.

*   *   *

Early one morning in July our ship carried us up the river Thames to Tilbury, and there we disembarked. I said good-bye to Ruth and Joan, who were remaining with the soldiers until a special train came to take them to London, and made my way down the gangway followed by a porter carrying in one hand my suitcase and on his shoulder the small trunk containing clothes and accessories provided for me by the English ladies in Herat.

To my surprise John Selby came to greet me after I had passed through the customs sheds. I had said good-bye to him the night before, because he had told me that his wife and her parents would be meeting him when we docked, and I thought it prudent for us to avoid disembarking together. Certainly we had nothing to hide or to be ashamed of, but I felt our companionship during the voyage might easily be misconstrued, and I did not want to cast any shadow upon his homecoming.

In the event he insisted on introducing me to his wife and her family, all of whom greeted me in most friendly fashion as he explained that I had brought a wounded Englishman to him in Herat but that he was not allowed to discuss the circumstances. His wife, Margaret, was a year or two older than I, her face too square for beauty, but with the merriest eyes and a warm impulsive manner. It was clear she had no doubts about her husband's behavior. Since they lived in Essex they were making the short journey home by carriage, but she insisted that John should first see me safely aboard the London train and that I should be given their address so that I might write to them if they could be of any service to me.

At the moment of setting foot on English soil I had almost wept, and to find such kindness only a few minutes later left me moist-eyed and with an uncertain voice. I sat in the corner of a first-class compartment waiting for the train to leave and kept telling myself again and again that I was not dreaming.

This was real. I was no longer the discarded wife of a barbarian king in a land where scarcely a civilized foot had ever trod. I was no longer a slave, no longer a servant, and no longer in danger of being beaten, killed, or sold as a bride to a madman. It was true that I wore borrowed clothes, and my purse was light, for I had now spent most of the money I had brought from Herat or been given in Karachi, some on shoes and clothes for myself, some on presents bought in Malta for Joan and Ruth, and the rest on incidentals and shipboard tips. I now had only two sovereigns and some silver left, but I had not troubled to be cautious in my spending as I knew that my situation would soon change.

This train would carry me to Fenchurch Street Station, and there I would cross London to Waterloo and catch a train to reach Haslemere in time to take luncheon there at an inn or at the Station Hotel. Then I would hire a cab to drive me out to the village of Oakhurst, where stone pillars flanked the entrance of a long drive leading to Witchwood Hall, the fine house that was now mine. There would be servants to attend me, and every comfort. A telegram would go to my father's lawyers, and a solicitor would come next day to explain the provisions of my father's will and to name the trustees appointed to have charge of his fortune on my behalf until I came of age. I was sure there would be some charitable provisions but knew myself to be the only child and sole heir.

I sat thinking of my father and mother, not of the manner of their end, but remembering them as they had been during our day-to-day life. I had not known my father very well, for his mind was always on his work, and in fact I had been a little afraid of him, perhaps because of his austere manner. I had loved my mother, at least I supposed I had, but acknowledged to myself that I had often been greatly irritated by her nervous ways.

In the days following their death I had been too shocked and too terrified for myself to mourn them, and by the time I had overcome at least some of my fears, which was not until Deenbur banished me from his bed to become a kitchen slave, too long a time had passed for me to feel true grief. Now, still alone in my compartment on the train, I tried to hold my parents in my mind with humble penitence for my failure to love them as I should have done when they lived, or to mourn them when they died.

When I looked into my soul I found some consolation in knowing that it was not with any sense of avarice that I contemplated my new life as a very rich young woman. Oh, I would enjoy the comforts and the freedom from fear, would enjoy them with a thankfulness and appreciation others could scarcely imagine, for I would ever have the contrast of the recent years in my mind. But after the fears and rigors of my life in Shul there was nothing I coveted, nobody I envied, and I would have been glad beyond words if I had been returning to Witchwood Hall with my living parents there to greet me.

In this mood of reverie I came to London and rode by cab across the bustling city, so different from the cities of the Middle and Far East where I had spent many of my years. It was not until the train from Waterloo drew into the station at Haslemere that I felt a stirring of excitement and a sense of homecoming. It was tempting to drive straight to Oakhurst, but at this hour the small skeleton staff at Witchwood Hall would be having luncheon, and my arrival would throw them into confusion. At one time this would not have mattered a jot to me, for I had given no thought to the feelings of servants. Now I saw all things with different eyes, for I had been a servant myself.

I took luncheon in the dining room of a small residential hotel near the station, attracting curious glances from several people at other tables. No doubt it was unusual for a young woman to be lunching alone there, and my weather-tanned face also set me apart from the regular customers, but I was not embarrassed by their curiosity and amused myself by imagining how shocked they would look if they knew just how unusual my life had been now for almost three years past.

The food was good but my appetite small, and I was glad when two o'clock came and I felt free to pay my bill and set off on the last stage of a journey I had begun in fear almost four months ago amid the mountains of the Hindu Kush. I walked back to the station, where I had left my trunk and suitcase, and ten minutes later I was in a cab on the road running south to Oakhurst. It was seven years since I had last seen the village. We had left in winter, with the trees leafless, the fields bare, and morning frost on the pastures. I was returning now in summer, but apart from the difference of season, nothing seemed to have changed.

Oakhurst was a village of fair size, with shops extending along the high street for a hundred yards or so between the church at one end and the smithy at the other. I thought it likely that the shopkeepers were as unchanged as the shops but could not remember any of them clearly, for I had not had much to do with them during the times my parents and I had spent at home between our sojourns abroad. I remembered the vicar, Mr. Hammond, and his wife. I remembered Dr. Ingram by name, but his appearance was blurred in my memory, and I had only a vague picture of a large and hearty gentleman with graying hair.

There were a few other people I could recall, the constable, the smith, and one or two of the local gentry and their wives with whom we had exchanged morning calls. Some I remembered by name, others by appearance, but I realized that it was unlikely any of them would recognize me on sight, for none had known me well, and I had been barely thirteen when last we left Witchwood Hall.

As the cab rattled through the high street to the village green at the far end I looked from side to side, trying to recognize a familiar face, but saw only one, that of the butcher standing in his shop doorway in a striped apron, fingering his bushy walrus mustache, dark hair sleeked into a quiff over his forehead. I could not remember his name.

The cab slowed as we turned at the green, and I saw a small crowd there, mostly children but with a few adults, perhaps thirty in all, gathered about a painted booth. I caught my breath with pleasure as childhood memories were unlocked by the sight of a Punch and Judy show. Because we slowed almost to a halt for the sharp turn, I was able to catch more than a glimpse of the scene.

Punch was there, bobbing about behind the shelf of the booth, clutching his stick. With the carriage window open I could just hear his squeaky voice but could not make out what he was saying. He appeared to be speaking alternately to the beadle puppet and to a young woman beside the booth who had a small drum hung round her neck. Her hair was dark, tied back with a scarlet ribbon, and she wore a patchwork dress in bright colors. Her face was brown, as brown as my own, and even at a distance I could see the flash of her dark eyes as she answered Punch, the gleam of white teeth as she smiled.

Off the road beyond the green stood a wagon. Between the shafts, a horse tossed its head as it nuzzled in a nosebag. My first thought was that the Punch and Judy girl was a gypsy, but then I doubted it, for as far as I could remember it was the way of gypsies to move in groups. Here there seemed to be no others, apart from the girl I could see and the man hidden in the booth, and in any event I had never heard of gypsies giving Punch and Judy performances.

In a moment or two the scene had passed from my view and we were on our way up the gently sloping lane that led to Witches Wood, a place of dark legend from which my father's grandfather had named the house he had built. On my left now was a high wall of gray stone, buttressed and covered with ivy, the wall encompassing the grounds of Witchwood Hall; but it was not until we turned between the two pillars where the great gates stood open that I saw my home at last. The sight did not move me deeply, for I had lived a rootless life throughout my childhood and felt no strong ties with the place where I had been born, but now that I looked once again upon the broad white architrave and pillars of the portico, the Palladian windows with their arched centers and square flanking sections, I realized how fortunate I was to have such a beautiful home.

As the cab rattled up the long drive I saw that the lawns had been recently cut, the edges trimmed, and the rose beds were full of color. The house itself looked suddenly huge to me. My throat closed for a moment as I remembered the hovel in which I had lived with Sandru, a hovel that would have fitted into Witchwood Hall's scullery, and I suddenly wondered how on earth I would spend my time in a mansion like this, alone except for servants.

Most English ladies had a family to look after, or were at least part of a family. I had none. I could receive and pay calls, go to church, take charge of the household staff, ride, perhaps fend off suitors attracted by my fortune . . . or perhaps have no suitors, since people would surely suspect that I had not spent time as a prisoner of barbaric tribesmen without being dishonored and degraded. But all these ladylike occupations seemed of little account and disturbingly useless. It was startling to think that I might find there had been more satisfaction in the work I had done when helping Sandru with his patients.

As the cab drew up on the cobbled apron before the portico I pushed such thoughts impatiently from my mind. The cabby climbed down to open the door for me, and I added a generous tip to his fare, knowing that the lightness of my purse no longer mattered now that I was home in Witchwood Hall. While he unloaded my trunk and case, I mounted the steps and tugged on the bellpull. Half a minute passed, then the heavy front door swung open to reveal a round-faced man with thinning dark hair, dressed in the tailcoat and black bow tie of a butler.

I was surprised, for I had expected Carson to open the door. The man surveyed me for a moment with a touch of reflected surprise, then said politely, "Yes, madam?"

I said, "Where is Carson?"

"Carson?" He gave me a puzzled look.

"Carson. The butler."

"Oh," he said, and his brow cleared. "You are referring to my predecessor, madam. Mr. Carson left service here well over two years ago now. My name is Hardwick, and I am the butler here at Witchwood Hall."

I said gently, "Then I think you had better invite me in and have somebody carry in my luggage, Hardwick. I am Jemimah Lawley."

He blinked in astonishment, then his eyes narrowed with suspicion as he said stiffly, "I *beg* your pardon?"

I curbed my impatience, realizing that his response was only natural. "Yes, I know this is a shock to you, Hardwick," I said. "No doubt you were told that I died in Kabul with my mother and father, but in fact I was abducted and have been kept prisoner in Afghanistan until I escaped a few months ago. Now please allow me to enter my own house, and send for Mrs. Rudge the housekeeper."

Even at mention of Mrs. Rudge, the man's look of suspicion did not change, nor did he stand aside to let me in, but instead shot a glance past me, to where the cabby had climbed to his seat again in readiness to move off, and called, "Cabby! Wait there!"

Still I kept my temper, understanding the man's predicament. He had never seen Jemimah Lawley before, and my story was strange enough in all conscience. "Please call Mrs. Rudge at once," I said. "She will be able to set your mind at rest."

He shook his head slowly. "The housekeeper here is Mrs. Hallet, and—"

He broke off as a pleasant male voice called from somewhere in the wide entrance hall beyond him, "What is it, Hardwick?"

The butler half turned with a look of relief. "There is a young person here, sir, who says"—he hesitated, then ended apologetically—"who says she is Miss Jemimah Lawley."

The voice gave a chuckle. "Good Lord. Let's have a look at her." The butler stepped back and a man strolled into view, tall, elegantly dressed, in his late forties, with light brown hair and wide-set eyes sparkling with amusement in a humorous face. As he came toward the door I stepped across the threshold and confronted him, annoyed now, and beginning to feel faint stirrings of alarm.

"Who are you, sir?" I demanded.

He raised his eyebrows in mock surprise at my manner and said, "Well, since you ask, I am James Lawley. More to the point, my dear, who are *you?*"

I found myself floundering for words, so great was my shock, and I stammered, "Nonsense! There is no such person as James Lawley!"

The man sighed. "How odd," he murmured. "I have always felt that I existed. It's true that old Matthew Lawley refused to acknowledge my father's existence and disowned him as a son, but that is not to say that Arthur Lawley did not live and breathe and sire a son of his own, and eventually die at a good age . . ."

The man went on to speak a few more words but I did not take them in. A distant chord of memory had been touched deep within me, and I was trying to recall a moment when I was small, listening to a conversation between my father and his father, Edmund Lawley, who died a year or two later while we were abroad. Edmund was the son of old Matthew Lawley, who had built Witchwood Hall, but there had also been a younger son, Edmund's brother Arthur, who had disgraced himself in some way. He had been sent out to one of the colonies in his early twenties with enough money to live for a year and told never to communicate with the family again. As a child of six or seven I had not understood much of the conversation, but some points had remained in my mind.

The tall man in the hall had stopped speaking and was looking at me questioningly. I tried to collect my wits and said uncertainly, "Arthur Lawley? Yes . . . I remember my grandfather speaking of his brother Arthur. But he went abroad, and the family never heard of him again."

"Perfectly true," the tall man agreed amiably. "He settled in Cape Town, and from what he told me and what I have heard from others, my father well deserved his reputation as the black sheep of the family. However, he had the decency to stay abroad and avoid embarrassing them."

"Your . . . your *father?*" I said slowly.

"Certainly." There was a hint of impatience now in the man's amusement. "I am his son, James Lawley, and therefore a cousin to the late Sir George Lawley, which I suppose would make me a second cousin to Miss Jemimah Lawley—or possibly her first cousin once removed. I'm rather vague concerning these terms."

My head was spinning and I felt utterly confused as I said, "But we were never told that my grandfather's brother Arthur had married!"

All humor vanished from the man's face. "I'm quite sure you weren't told, whoever you may be, and neither was the Lawley family told, here at Witchwood Hall. My father had his pride, and they never heard from him again—but that's neither here nor there. I can't imagine who put you up to this or what you hope to gain, but I have now ceased to be entertained by your foolish charade, young lady, and I don't intend to let it continue."

"Charade?" My voice rose sharply on the word, and I was swept by sudden anger. "What do you mean, sir? James Lawley or no, you are now a visitor in my home, and that is something my father's lawyers and any number of people will quickly confirm! I am Jemimah Lawley, and I demand to be received here. As I have told the butler, I was abducted after the Kabul massacre of 1879, and have been a captive in Kafiristan ever since, until I was able to escape a few months ago. I realize you will have thought me dead, but—"

"No," the man broke in dryly, "we did not think Jemimah Lawley was dead. Since you mention lawyers, I take it you have not paid a visit to the firm of Cossey and Wingate?"

"Not yet. I was unable to recall the name of my father's solicitors, but—"

"A pity," he interrupted again. "You would have saved yourself a great deal of trouble."

As he spoke, the butler appeared from behind the door and said, "Do you wish me to send Perkins for the constable, sir?"

The tall man who called himself James Lawley made a brushing gesture with his hand. "Oh, good Lord, no. We don't want the stupid creature prosecuted and sent to prison."

I was drawing breath for a furious response when I heard a new voice and saw a young woman in a pretty pale blue dress coming down the wide staircase into the hall. She was about my own age, perhaps an inch taller, with hair not quite so fair, and as she came down the last few stairs she was saying in a pleasant, mellow voice, "Who is it, Uncle James?"

I saw humor come back into the man's face at her words as he half turned and said, "A most unexpected visitor, my dear."

The girl came forward with a puzzled air, looking at me but addressing the man. "It's rather early in the afternoon to be paying calls," she said, "but should we not invite the young lady in, Uncle James?"

"Oh, I don't think we should encourage her," said the tall man firmly. "You see, Jemimah, she claims to be *you.*"

VII

F or long moments I felt I must be dreaming, and was shaken by the sudden fear that I might wake to find myself huddled on my sheepskin mattress in the tiny sleeping chamber of a mud brick hovel in Shul. Then fragments of memory began to tumble through my mind.

There was the lieutenant by the guard tent outside Herat, who thought he had read of Jemimah Lawley reappearing in Kabul only a few weeks after the massacre. There was Mr. Arthur Renwick in Herat, quizzing me as if he doubted my story, and murmuring, "That remains to be seen," when I referred to myself as Jemimah Lawley. There was the Commissioner in Karachi, who had tried clumsily to test my fluency in the Kafir tongue, as if he too had doubts about the truth of my tale. John Selby had befriended me, and I was sure he had believed me, or at least wanted to believe me, but I had sensed in him an unspoken concern about my homecoming.

The girl in the pale blue dress said incredulously, "She claims to be *me?*" I saw no sign of alarm or guilt in her, only astonishment, then she put her fingers to her mouth to stifle an embarrassed laugh and said, "Oh dear. I'm sorry. Is she a little touched, poor soul?"

I found my voice and cried, "But I *am* Jemimah Lawley! This is ridiculous! Who are you people, and what are you doing here? The whole village must know you are impostors!"

The butler coughed and said diffidently, "I really feel I ought to send for the police, sir. Or perhaps Dr. Ingram?"

The girl took a step forward and said with a look of distress, "Oh no. Please, Uncle James, don't make trouble for her. Just let her go quietly away."

The man calling himself James Lawley said doubtfully, "Well, providing she *will* go quietly away." I groped for words of protest, but my mind seemed paralyzed. He turned to me and his face became stern. "Now listen, young lady. I suspect that you've come here with some pretty little scheme in mind, but if you hoped to take Jemimah Lawley's place you're either sadly out of date or badly misinformed. Jemimah was saved from the Kabul massacre by faithful servants, she was hidden by them for several weeks until the British Army returned, and she has been in residence here in Witchwood Hall, her home, for well over two years now." He paused, and his voice softened. "If, on the other hand, you genuinely believe yourself to be Jemimah Lawley, then I can only suggest that you seek medical advice."

He turned and moved away across the hall, taking the girl's hand and tucking it under his arm so that she accompanied him. I saw her look over her shoulder with an expression of troubled sympathy, then the butler blocked my view. "If you please, miss," he said firmly, and stepped forward so that I had to take a pace back. "We don't want any trouble, do we?" he went on, and moved forward again. Now I had recrossed the threshold and was in the porch. "The cab's still there, miss," he said. "Don't come back."

The door of my home closed in my face with a solid thud. I stood with my trunk and suitcase beside me, dazed and witless as if from the blow of a cudgel. Somewhere in the dark reaches of my mind a terrible doubt was trying to take seed. *Was* I Jemimah Lawley? Or was I some poor creature whose brain had failed? Was it all delusion . . . ? Kabul? The captivity in Shul? Deenbur and the horrors of my wedding night? Sandru the Doctor? The endless journey with Kassim, whose name was Caspar? Captain John Selby and the voyage home?

No, no, no. All this was surely real and true. But even so, *was* I Jemimah Lawley? Might I not be some nameless young woman, abducted by dacoits from anywhere on the vast Indian continent and sold in Kafiristan? Perhaps suffering from loss of memory after the ordeal I had endured? Perhaps imagining myself to be Jemimah Lawley because I had read or heard of her in some way?

The cabby's plaintive voice penetrated my benumbed mind. " 'Scuse me, miss, but do you be wanting to hire me cab or not?"

With a huge effort I pulled myself together. I *was* Jemimah Lawley. I could recall the faces of my mother and father, and of some of the village folk. I had come from London straight to Oakhurst and Witchwood Hall, and I recognized both village and house. The man who claimed to be my father's cousin was an impostor, so was the girl who claimed to be

me. And yet . . . and yet . . . they had not displayed the slightest
hint of dissembling. Every word, every look, had been totally convincing.

I drew a deep breath and beckoned the cabby. "Put my luggage in the
cab, please," I said in a voice that I strove to keep steady, "then take me
back into Oakhurst."

He eyed me doubtfully but climbed down from his seat and mounted
the steps to pick up my trunk. "Anywhere special in Oakhurst, miss?" he
asked, pausing with the trunk on his shoulder.

I was slowly recovering the power to think now, and I said more
firmly, "The police station first. Then the vicarage. Then Dr. Ingram's
house in Willow Lane." These were all places where I would find people
I knew—if the vicar was still Mr. Hammond and if the village constable
was still . . . ? I bit my lip in annoyance, unable to remember his name,
then told myself it was of no importance. He would remember me. He
had known me as the daughter of the titled folk at Witchwood Hall, the
finest house for miles around. So had many other village folk.

I sat back in the carriage as we rolled down the drive, and began to
collect my scattered wits. It seemed possible that "Uncle James" was
indeed that unknown member of the family he claimed to be, and therefore some kind of cousin to me, but how he and the young woman
masquerading as me had contrived to take over Witchwood Hall was a
mystery. I told myself that their pretense would soon be exposed now.
My father's lawyers would be brought into the affair—what had the man
called them? Ah yes, Cossey and Wingate. Evidently they had been
duped in some way by these impostors, but that would quickly be recti-
fied when the truth was known.

The first numbing impact of shock had passed now, and with it the
alarm and confusion I had felt. I shook my head in silent wonder at the
astonishing impudence of the man and the girl in Witchwood Hall.
True, she was of my build and coloring, and in features we were vaguely
similar, but she was certainly not my double, and it was unbelievable that
these two could have succeeded for so long in their deception of so many
people. Yet I had to acknowledge that for a few brief and shattering
moments they had even made me doubt my own identity. Certainly they
must have been immensely plausible.

Suddenly I laughed. In the past few weeks I had often imagined my
homecoming to Witchwood Hall, but I had never dreamed that it might
prove so startling. In all probability the pretenders were now hurrying
frantically to pack a bag or two and be gone, for today the real Jemimah

Lawley had returned as if from the dead, and they must know that their deception was ended.

Now that I could think clearly again I had no doubt that tonight, for the first time, I would sleep under my own roof.

* * *

Two hours later I sat on a bench outside the Royal Oak on the edge of the green, my trunk and case beside me, and watched the cabby drive away with one of my two remaining half sovereigns in his pocket. I felt empty and too tired to think.

What had happened during my encounters that afternoon was almost impossible to accept. As soon as I saw the village constable I had recognized him and remembered that his name was Jim Moss. He listened to me politely at first, then with a deepening frown of disbelief before cutting me short and warning me that if I went about telling silly stories I would soon find myself in trouble.

Yes, he remembered young Miss Lawley from years ago, before she went off abroad with her parents, but she had been back at Witchwood Hall for two years and more now with her uncle—well, her cousin, really, though she called him Uncle James. Everybody knew that, declared Constable Moss with a stern frown, just as everybody knew that her parents had been murdered in foreign parts, poor young lady, and the sooner I took myself off and stopped wasting his time the better for me.

I was irritated by the constable's stupidity and did not stay to argue further but directed the cabby to the vicarage. Mr. Hammond was in his study composing a sermon, so his maid informed me, but when I persisted she asked me to wait in the hall while she spoke with him, and after two or three minutes she showed me in.

The vicar, thin, gray, and somewhat vague, seemed to have changed very little. He received me in kindly fashion, and I waited a few seconds for him to recognize me. When he showed no sign of doing so, I told him who I was and began to recount my story. At once he became wary, pressed the bell for his maid, and sent her to fetch his wife before allowing me to continue. It soon became clear that they did not for one moment believe me.

I dredged my memory for one or two incidents from the past—how I had spilled lemonade down my dress at a vicarage tea party, and fallen off a donkey at one of the church fetes. Neither the vicar nor his wife had any recollection of such trivial happenings, though Mr. Hammond was finally less brusque than the constable had been.

"I can only recommend, Miss—ah—," he said, reminding me of Mr. Forbes in Herat, who had similarly avoided using my name, "that you take your claim to a solicitor and seek his advice, but I fear you cannot call upon me to identify you as—ah—Miss Jemimah Lawley. We knew Sir George and Lady Lawley well, of course, during the periods they spent in England, and young Jemimah also. I had the pleasure of christening her, I recall. But she returned from Afghanistan long ago, with her cousin, Mr. James Lawley, or Uncle James as she calls him in acknowledgment that he is an older person—oh, but of course you dispute this if I understand you correctly. Well, as I say, I can only suggest that you seek legal advice, and I do urge you to act with great caution, young lady. Great caution. Now, if you will excuse me . . ."

My experience with Dr. Ingram was worse. I remembered him as a big jovial man, and no doubt he had shown that manner to Sir George Lawley's daughter, but he was by no means jovial with a young woman who disturbed him at teatime on a matter of urgency, claiming to be Jemimah Lawley.

"Rubbish!" he exclaimed as soon as he understood what I was trying to tell him. "Good God, what makes you think anyone would believe such a cock and bull story?"

"But it's *true*, Doctor!" I said angrily. "You attended my birth, and you must have my medical records. I have a distinguishing mark, a mole on my left hip, not very big, but—"

"Great heavens, are you out of your mind, girl?" He threw himself back in his chair, staring with contempt. "D'ye think a doctor notes such a thing on every baby he delivers? The only one who'd know if Jemimah had a mole would be . . . What's-her-name." He snapped his fingers, frowning in an effort of memory. "Nanny something or other."

"Nanny McWade died of a fever in Khartoum a few years ago," I said. "But—"

"Ah, so you know that, do you?" Dr. Ingram gave me a look of shrewd suspicion. "I rather fancy you must have met her at some time and heard about Jemimah from her, but to imagine you can come here and pretend to *be* Jemimah is too ridiculous for words. Everybody in Oakhurst knows her. She's been back at the hall for a good two years now."

I said desperately, "But nobody here saw her for well over four years before that! I mean, nobody saw *me*, because I was abroad. I was a child when I went away, and naturally I've changed, as anybody would expect, but now this girl who looks only slightly like me has taken my place!"

Dr. Ingram took a watch from his waistcoat pocket and opened it. "Sir George Lawley's solicitors aren't fools," he said briefly, glancing down at the watch. "All right, Miss Whoever-you-are. You've consulted me out of surgery hours to ask my advice, so I'll give it to you." He snapped the watch shut and glared across the desk at me. "Take yourself off. Clear out of Oakhurst before you find yourself hauled into court for attempted fraud. That's my advice, and that will be one shilling, thank you."

I clutched my handbag. "Please Dr. Ingram, you must believe me—"

"One shilling, please."

I sat still for a moment or two, trying to quiet the trembling of my body and hands, knowing at last that no words of mine could begin to make any impression on this man. Slowly I opened my purse. It held two half sovereigns, one florin, two shillings, two sixpences, and three or four coppers. I took out one of the shillings, put it down on the desk, then stood up and moved to the door. I desperately wanted to say something cool, cutting, crushing, but no such words would come, and as I paused after opening the door, all I could manage to say was, "You are wrong, Doctor. Quite wrong."

Later I had only a vague memory of being shown out by a maid who appeared, and walking along the drive to where my cab waited. Shock, outrage, and despair made me feel that my heart was about to burst. In a shaking voice I told the cabby to drive down to the high street, and there I scurried from smithy to grocer to butcher in a frantic and foolish manner, asking startled tradesmen if they did not recognize me as Jemimah Lawley.

Their looks of alarm were an adequate answer, and I quickly recovered sufficient control of my wits to realize that I would be thought mad if I continued in this way. A few minutes later, as the church clock struck five, I was sitting on the bench by the green, my luggage beside me, one half sovereign and four shillings in silver in my purse, spent in body and mind, trying to think what I should do.

My years in Shul had taught me not to deceive myself but to face cold truth, however brutal it might be. Today the truth was that for a long time now there had been in residence at Witchwood Hall a young woman believed to be Jemimah Lawley by our family solicitors, by the local vicar, policeman, tradesmen, and everybody in the village of Oakhurst. I had no doubt that this belief extended to any and all acquaintances beyond the village.

I had last been seen in England when I was thirteen, a thin leggy child with hair in long plaits. There were one or two framed photographs of me in Witchwood Hall at that time, but even the most recent had been taken two years before. If that photograph still existed, it could as easily have been of the girl in the pale blue dress as of me. She had no need to be my double. The natural changes in me between the ages of eleven and twenty meant that she bore as much resemblance to that old photograph now as I did myself. Even if there had been relatives to turn to, I doubted that I would have found support. Memory is easily deceived, and once the young woman had been accepted by my lawyers and trustees as Jemimah Lawley it was out of the question that anyone should doubt her identity. For over two years she had been Jemimah Lawley to all who knew her. Stand us side by side now, and those same people would declare that she was far more like the Jemimah Lawley they remembered than I was myself.

I thought about the firm of lawyers, Cossey and Wingate, so the man calling himself James Lawley had said, and these names struck a positive chord in my memory. Was it possible they could have been corrupted and were party to the deception? I strongly doubted it. My father would have employed a well-established and highly reputable firm, probably with a number of partners, and surely they could not all be suborned?

If the solicitors were innocent, then they must themselves have been deceived, despite the care and caution that would be an essential part of their professional duties. Suppose my faithful servant Bihzad had not lost me to the Hindu traders but had managed to hide me in the hills until the British returned to Kabul a few weeks later . . . how would I have proved my identity? After very little thought I decided that the question would hardly have arisen. Bihzad would have brought me back into Kabul, I would have announced to the military commander that I was Jemimah Lawley, and described how my parents had been killed in the legation massacre. There would have been nobody left to identify me, but I doubted that it would occur to the military commander even to seek confirmation of my identity from Bihzad. Jemimah Lawley was the only girl of seventeen in the legation at that time; she had escaped the slaughter and returned when Kabul was safe. It would not cross the commander's mind to question her identity. It would not cross anybody's mind.

As for the solicitors in London, they would have learned of Jemimah Lawley's safe return from a newspaper report, perhaps the same report the lieutenant by the guard tent at Herat had spoken of. They would seek confirmation through the Colonial Office, and in due time Jemimah Lawley would arrive on a ship from Karachi or Bombay. What proof would she bring? None, for whatever papers and possessions the Lawley family had taken with them to Kabul, all had been destroyed by fire following the massacre.

Perhaps the solicitors would take her to Oakhurst and present her to those who had known her there, the doctor, the vicar, the remaining servants at Witchwood Hall. The servants would know her best, but how reliable would their memories of her be after more than four years? They might feel that Jemimah Lawley had changed, but from thirteen to seventeen were years of major change, and it would hardly occur to them to doubt her identity.

It was more than likely that the solicitors had not even taken this step. The fact that Jemimah Lawley had come out of the hills north of Kabul as soon as it was safe to do so would surely be enough to prevent any shadow of doubt entering their minds. Who else could this young girl be but Jemimah Lawley?

The church clock struck the quarter hour, and one or two people stared at me as they went about their affairs, but I was too preoccupied to care about their curiosity. If what I had been thinking was right, then the girl in the pale blue dress, the girl living in Witchwood Hall as Jemimah Lawley, *must* have come out of the hills and into Kabul as if emerging from weeks of hiding as soon as British soldiers reentered the city. There was no other way in which she could have contrived to be identified as Jemimah Lawley.

Yet how on earth could this have been achieved? Who *was* she? Where did she come from? And how did my long-lost relative, James Lawley, come into the picture—if indeed he was who he claimed to be?

For the moment I had no hope of answering these questions. Perhaps I would never know the answers, I told myself with painful candor. I possessed no shred of proof, and if I went to Messrs. Cossey and Wingate they would regard me as a fraud, just as Constable Moss and Dr. Ingram had done . . . unless I could find somebody to vouch for me. That last thought stirred a small spark of hope in me, but it quickly died. Only one person in the world could truly vouch for me. That was Sandru, for he would know the identity of the girl sold by the Hindu traders. But Sandru was in faraway Shul and might as well have been on another planet.

Mr. Arthur Renwick, whom I had last seen in Herat, might well believe that I spoke the truth, but Mr. Renwick was a man of secrets, a

man who worked in the dark, receiving reports from spies—from men I
had once thought contemptible, until one night on the ship *Bristol Star,*
when Captain John Selby had shown me that they were among the
bravest of the brave. I doubted that Mr. Arthur Renwick would wish to
attract attention to himself by speaking for me. And even if he did, he
could only declare that I had emerged from the harsh deserts of Afghanistan claiming to be Jemimah Lawley.

Captain John Selby could offer no more than that, except I felt certain
John had wanted to believe me and knew I was not deliberately pretending I was another person. But if I tried to look at events through his eyes
I could see how difficult it must be for him to accept that I was not
suffering from some sort of delusion. Jemimah Lawley had returned to
Kabul when the British reentered the city and had now been at her
home in England for over two years, accepted by all. To John Selby, a
doctor, the most likely explanation of my strange tale was that I had
been captured somewhere and at some time by tribesmen; that the shock
of what I had undergone had caused me to lose my memory and identity,
and that in some way I had come to assume the identity of a young
woman I had heard of or read of or perhaps even known, believing that I
was genuinely Jemimah Lawley.

I took from my handbag the card Mrs. Selby had given me with their
address in Essex. Despite what John might think was the truth about
me, there was no doubt that he was sympathetic toward me and had
liked me as a friend. His wife had greeted me kindly, too. I had enough
money left for a night's lodging and my train fare to Essex next day.
Surely they would take me in and give me shelter—

No! I sat up straight, suddenly angry with myself. John Selby and his
wife had been married only two years and he had spent most of that time
abroad. He now had to settle down in England and establish himself in
practice as a doctor. What kind of creature was I to think of burdening
him with responsibility for me at such a time—indeed, at any time? And
what might his wife begin to think? He owed me nothing, and I was
ashamed of myself for even thinking of taking advantage of his kindness.

There was Caspar, though. I had forgotten him for the moment or, if
not forgotten him, had so far not thought of him as somebody who could
vouch for me. Caspar was the one man apart from Sandru who did know
the truth, for he had heard it from Sandru himself. If Caspar had survived, as seemed likely from what John Selby had told me, then he could
speak for me with authority, sufficient authority to make the lawyers
start delving very carefully into my story, seeking confirmation from

people I could tell them of in Egypt and India, testing my memory of those people and places against the memory of the girl in the pale blue dress who lived at Witchwood Hall.

Yes. Caspar was my only hope. But if he lived he was still far away in Afghanistan, well beyond my reach, and I had fourteen shillings to my name. I sat thinking for a little longer, and once I shivered as a wave of terrible doubt swept me. Could it be true that I was indeed a girl whose memory had been destroyed by the shock of being held captive and despoiled by a barbarian in the Hindu Kush? Could it be true that I was not Jemimah Lawley but had perhaps met her briefly at some time during childhood, at school in England, or India, or the Sudan, perhaps? And that, for some reason lodged far down in the dark recesses of a mind robbed of its own memories, I had chosen to become Jemimah Lawley without knowing it?

I shook my head vigorously, as if physical effort would help me to thrust away such doubts, and I looked about me. Thirty yards away, on the edge of the triangular green, Punch and Judy were giving another performance. Punch and the girl with the gypsy looks were arguing, the hook-nosed puppet emphasizing his words with a bang of his stick on the shelf of the booth, and the girl emphasizing hers with a bang on the little drum hung around her neck. I had been vaguely aware of this while so many dismaying thoughts marched grimly through my head, but now that I wanted distraction from such thoughts I could hear clearly what was being said.

With a broad Sussex accent the girl was saying accusingly, "I saw you beat Judy with your stick!" She gave a bang on her drum.

Punch squeaked ferociously, "I'll beat you too!" He banged his stick on the shelf.

"No, you won't. A policeman is coming to lock you up, Mr. Punch!" *Bang!*

"Oh no, he isn't!" *Bang!*

"Oh yes, he is!" Bang!

At the earlier performance there had been a crowd of thirty or forty watching, mostly children. Now there were no more than a dozen, and I could guess that half of them would vanish as soon as the girl began to go around with her collecting bag after the performance. I looked toward the nearby wagon and saw that beside it stood a small covered cart with a donkey between the shafts. In gold letters on the side of the wagon and in smaller letters on the side of the cart, was painted: LORD HENRY BOOT'S WORLD-FAMOUS PUNCH AND JUDY SHOW. Despite my situation I almost smiled at that, wondering if it was legal for a Punch and Judy man to raise himself to the peerage in this way.

In the opening of the brightly colored booth, Punch had just hanged the policeman and was bouncing back and forth, crowing in triumph. The girl gave a roll on her drum and cried, "Now you've done it, Mr. Punch. His *ghost* will come for you!"

Punch stopped short and peered down. "Ghost?" he squeaked.

Was I truly Jemimah Lawley? Or were all my memories of childhood no more than imagination? How could I discover the truth? Sandru alone knew whether the girl brought to Shul long ago was Jemimah Lawley . . . no, not Sandru alone, for he must have told Caspar. But I would never see Sandru again, and how could I ever hope to find Caspar? I did not even know his full name. And what was I to do now, in the next hour, friendless in a land I had not seen since childhood, and with only a few shillings to my name? If I had a name . . .

Something was happening at the Punch and Judy booth. A moment earlier, Punch had been fleeing round and round before the ghost that had come to haunt him, squeaking in terror and protest, but now both puppets had suddenly vanished below and the squeaking had stopped, obviously to the puzzlement of the girl with the drum, who was calling in a tentative fashion, "Mr. Punch? Are you there, Mr. Punch?"

The booth began to shake, then it almost fell over as a figure burst through the canvas curtains at the back and staggered around to the front, a slender man of medium height with curly black hair. He was bareheaded, and wore a shabby black frock coat with equally shabby gray trousers. His arms were flapping, with the ghost puppet on one hand and Punch on the other.

This was a most unexpected phenomenon, and the little crowd of a dozen children and two young men who looked like farm laborers drew back apprehensively from the strange figure. Next moment the Punch and Judy man had fallen to the ground, and the girl had thrown aside her drum and was kneeling beside him, bending over his head, though I could not see what she was doing.

I found myself holding my skirt up to my knees as I ran across the green. What was wrong I did not know, but clearly the poor man was in great distress, and I had a vague notion that he might be in the throes of a fit. The spectators had moved a little closer now and were gazing down with interest as I pushed my way through them and dropped to my knees beside the girl. The man's face had turned reddish purple, his mouth was wide open, his eyes half closed, and though his chest heaved with effort I could hear no breath being drawn. Clearly he was choking.

The girl had her fingers thrust in his mouth, and her face was twisted with fear. I gripped her shoulder and said sharply, "Has he swallowed something? What is it?"

She gave me a terrified glance. "His swazzle," she said in a shaking voice. "Stuck in his throat. It should be on a thread, but—"

"His *what?*"

"Swazzle. Punch-squeaker."

I could only guess that this was something that enabled him to produce the traditional squeaky voice of Punch. Quickly I turned the man's head sideways so that whatever was lodged in his throat would not sink further down, then I lay beside him with my cheek on the ground, holding his mouth open and peering down his throat, glimpsing something deep in his gullet and beyond reach of my fingers. A terrible groaning noise broke from him, and I set my teeth to hold back panic so that I might think what to do for the best. There came a fleeting memory of Sandru and a child with a pebble in his throat. That had been a child, but . . .

I jumped to my feet, pointed to the two laborers, and said with the brisk manner I had always tried to use when acting as Sandru's nurse, "You two. Quick, before he chokes to death. Pick him up by the legs and hold him upside down. Hurry!"

The two men looked at each other, then moved forward doubtfully. I said, "For heaven's sake, be *quick!* Take a leg each and heave him up so that his back is toward me."

Swiftly now they obeyed, hauling the man up so that he hung with his head a few inches above the ground. Still kneeling, I linked my thumbs, raised both arms, and brought my hands down in a sideways sweeping movement to strike flat-handed on his back, just below the shoulder blades. His body jerked, but that was all. With the beginnings of despair I struck again. There came an explosive cough, something wet and gray and oblong in shape flew out of the man's mouth, and next moment came a long wheezing intake of breath as his tormented lungs sucked in air.

I felt weak with relief and said to the laborers, "All right, put him down now, please. On his back. And thank you."

The girl in the patchwork dress gave me a look of mingled amazement and gratitude, then shuffled on her knees to where the man lay with a hand to his throat, his face slowly returning to its normal color, the breath sobbing into his lungs and hissing out as he exhaled.

"God bless you, miss," she said, then glared down at the man. "And damn you for a fool, Henry Boot! I told you last night to let me have the swazzle so I could stitch a new thread on it, but no! You could manage fine, you said! A real Clever Dick you are, and it's a wonder you're alive!"

The man propped himself on his elbows and looked slowly about him. "God help us all," he croaked, "I thought I was a goner for sure." His eyes roved over the little group of spectators who stood watching expectantly as if hoping for more drama, then he patted the girl's arm urgently. "The bag, Paloma. Go round with the bag before they disappear. God knows it'll be a long while before they see better entertainment."

The girl rolled her eyes at me in exasperation but then jumped to her feet. Drawing a small black bag from the skirt pocket of her dress, she began to pass among the children, smiling and coaxing. As I got to my feet the man waved a hand toward me and then toward the two laborers. "Not the beautiful young lady and her muscular assistants, Paloma," he said, his voice still husky and strained. "For them the entertainment is free of charge, and with the grateful compliments of the management."

The children were dispersing rapidly. I bent to pick up the little object the man had choked up and examined it gingerly. It was less than an inch long and a quarter as wide, an oblong that seemed to be made from two thin strips of brass, slightly bent to form an ellipse, and bound round and round lengthwise with a piece of tape, damp and discolored now, with just one thickness of the tape between the brass strips, dividing the ellipse from end to end, somewhat like the reed in a musical instrument.

When I looked up, the Punch and Judy man was standing before me, his ancient frock coat dusty and flecked with pieces of grass. He shrugged, looked sheepish, made a demented grimace of apology, and said, "You're a dandy girl, my lady. Another half minute and there would have been one strolling player less in the world. I'm more than grateful." He spoke in a cultivated voice, and for a moment this surprised me, but then I guessed that he must have taken the trouble to acquire the kind of voice that went with a name like Lord Henry Boot.

I saw now that he was not so slightly built as I had at first thought. His ears stood out rather prominently, his face was long with a square chin and a wide humorous mouth, his nose was broad, and bent slightly as if it might have been broken at some time. I judged the man to be about thirty years of age, or perhaps a little less. In appearance and manner there was something droll, almost comical about him, and I found myself smiling as I said, "I'm glad to have been able to help, my lord." I held up the little instrument between finger and thumb. "Is this really called a swazzle?"

"Indeed it is, my lady." He took it from me and surveyed it with distaste. "When you're using the Punch voice, you press this against the roof of your mouth with your tongue and speak through it, but then you have to shift it to one side for Judy's voice and all the others. It's a great art, my lady, and if you make a mistake you can easily swallow the damn thing—oh, I beg your pardon. There should be a long thread attached to one corner, and you have the thread hanging out of your mouth so that if anything goes wrong you can haul the swazzle out. But the thread broke off this morning, and Paloma didn't stitch another on—"

He broke off and sprang back as the girl came rushing past me from behind and launched a kick at his shin with a sandaled foot. "Liar!" she cried indignantly. " 'Twas me saw the thread gone and wanted to stitch another on, but *you* said not to fuss!" She launched another kick which he dodged as nimbly as the first. "And see what happened just now—you near killed your stupid self!" She was half a head taller than I, a strapping girl, big but not fat, with dark eyes set in a broad face that was almost handsome as she stood glaring at her companion.

"Paloma, my love, my dove, my sweet angel, let us not dispute in front of distinguished visitors," he said placatingly. Then to me, with another eye-rolling grimace: "Pray forgive this unseemly display by my colleague."

I watched Paloma toss her head and turn away to resume her pursuit of the remaining children, shaking her bag. "Her annoyance may be justified," I said, "and I am hardly a distinguished visitor, my lord."

"Oh, there is no need to use that form of address to me," he said earnestly. "Mine is merely a courtesy title, so the address is simply 'Lord Henry.' " He put a hand to his throat and made a small respectful bow. "But since you have saved my life, I should be greatly honored if you would call me Henry, my lady."

For the past few minutes I had been feeling as if I had stepped into a strange but entertaining world of fantasy, and I wanted to cling to it rather than leave it for the real world that had shattered about me in the last two hours. I said, "That is most gracious of you, Henry, especially as I have no title myself and should therefore not be addressed as 'my lady.' "

He smiled. "That was a courtesy title I bestowed on you myself, for services rendered. How do you wish me to address you, please?"

I said, "My name is—" and stopped short. He waited patiently, a comical figure in his shabby and ill-fitting clothes, yet not without a kind of dignity. Some part of my mind had registered that not only did he have a decent accent, but he also spoke grammatically and was more articulate than I would have expected a Punch and Judy man to be. I decided that he must have spent several years in service with gentry and was possessed of enough native intelligence to have educated himself to some extent by imitation.

Henry still awaited an answer to his question. With an inward sigh I allowed myself to be carried back into the real world, of distress and doubt and loneliness, a world where I had either lost my reason or had lost my name and my inheritance to a usurper.

"I am Jemimah Lawley," I said slowly. "At least, I think I am."

He showed no surprise but studied me with sympathy in his gaze as he said, "Yes, the village has been buzzing with gossip about a girl claiming the name of Jemimah Lawley. I thought you might be the one when I saw you sitting across the green with your luggage."

"Saw me?"

"I can see through the strip of gauze set just below the shelf of the booth, you know."

"I hope I didn't distract you and cause you to swallow your—what was it? Your swazzle."

He shook his head and gave me one of his clownish looks. "The blame was entirely mine."

I said a little wearily, "What does village gossip say about me, Henry?"

He sighed but met my gaze frankly as he answered, "I'm afraid the belief is either that you're a fraud or not right in the head."

"I see." By now I had expected nothing else. Something made me add, "And what do you believe, Henry?"

He smiled. "It would be impertinent of me to think of judging a young lady who has saved my life. If you tell me you're the Queen of Sheba I shall believe you, Miss Lawley."

I warmed to the twinkle in his eyes and said, "Perhaps you had better not call me that. It might make the local people stay away from any more performances, Henry."

He stretched his mouth and screwed up his eyes in an exaggerated wince. "There will be no more performances here in Oakhurst. I will not sully my artistic soul by performing for people who speak ill of my friends." He made me a courtly bow as he spoke. "Perhaps you will allow me to address you as Miss Jemimah? After all, nobody can lay exclusive claim to Jemimah as a name."

"Very true, Henry," I said, and dropped him a small curtsy in response to his bow, "but I'm afraid I must take my leave of you now. I have to . . . to decide what I am to do."

The girl called Paloma had now returned and stood looking from one to the other of us as we spoke. Everybody else had disappeared from the green. The horse and donkey stood nose to nose as if in silent communion with each other. Lord Henry waved a hand in an expansive gesture. "Paloma is my cook-housekeeper," he said, "and usually prepares our meals in the wagon, but this evening I intend to dine in style at a suitable tavern. We should be delighted if you would join us, Miss Jemimah."

The girl gave a look that held apology for me and exasperation for Lord Henry. "Dear God," she said, holding out the bag, "what are you thinking of, you daft man? Three ha'pence we got from that performance. Look!"

She held out the bag, but he waved it away and slipped an arm around her waist, smiling down at her. "Unimportant, my angel," he said. "I am of prudent nature and have money in reserve."

Her eyebrows lifted. "Where did you get it?"

"I cracked a crib, my dove." He wrinkled his brow in thought. "Or picked a rich man's pocket when we were at the races. I forget which." He moved away toward the booth.

The girl looked at me wonderingly. "Spring and summer I've been with the man and I still don't know what to make of his jokes. Just when you think he's lying as usual, you find out he's telling the truth."

I did not know what to make of Lord Henry Boot either, but I liked his eccentric ways and outrageous jests. I stood watching as Paloma picked up the two fallen puppets and put them away in a wooden box standing beside the booth. Lord Henry produced a battered top hat from within the booth, clapped it on the back of his head, and wandered back to where I stood. "Will you dine with us, Miss Jemimah? Not here, in Oakhurst. I thought we would drive on for three miles to Little Farrington, which has a pleasant hostel."

I suddenly realized how much I wanted to be away from Oakhurst, away from the scene of the many humiliations I had suffered in the last two or three hours. I needed somewhere to stay for the night, but I could as readily find a room at the King's Head in Little Farrington as at the Royal Oak here in Oakhurst.

How did I know that the hostel in Little Farrington was called the King's Head if I was not Jemimah Lawley, and therefore familiar with the neighboring villages?

I put the thought aside for the moment and said, "Thank you, Henry, I shall be delighted to dine with you and Paloma."

"It will be our pleasure, Miss Jemimah." He raised his broken hat to me. "Excuse me while I fetch your luggage."

"Thank you." I stood watching him, feeling suddenly so tired after all the stress and turmoil of the long day that my mind was empty of thought. I had no employment, no home, and almost no money. I knew only where I was going and what I would be doing for the next few hours. Beyond that, all was darkness.

VIII

I rode out of Oakhurst seated beside Paloma, who held the reins of the horse pulling the wagon. I learned that its name was Benjamin. Ahead of us, Lord Henry Boot drove the small cart pulled by the donkey. In it was the box of puppets, the folded booth, a tin trunk, and a number of bundles tied with string, as well as some pots and pans that clanked noisily as the cart rolled along.

"I'm better with Benjy than his lordship is," said Paloma, flicking her long-handled whip within an inch of Benjamin's ear. "That horse, he don't take to men, see? Do you, ol' darling? He do like to play Henry up something shocking. Pretend you gone deaf and can't hear a word Henry says, don't you, my wicked boy?"

Benjamin twitched his ears enigmatically. My case and trunk were inside the wagon now. It was a neat, orderly wagon, from what I had seen, with a small stove, two chairs and a table, narrow cupboards, a square sink, a wide bed, and several small pictures on the walls. We moved up the curving lane with the mellow brick wall hemming the grounds of Witchwood Hall on my left, and as we passed the open gates of the drive I glimpsed again the great house I had believed to be my home. Then it was gone.

I said to Paloma, "Will it distract you to talk while you drive?"

She laughed, gave me a sideways glance from her fine dark eyes, and shook her head. "Not a bit. We can talk all we want, girl. How was it you stirred up all them folk in Oakhurst? Said you was touched in the head, they did."

I said, "They may be right, but it's a long story."

"Well, tell us, then. Plenty of time."

I began reluctantly, and kept to the bare bones of my story, but almost from the start Paloma seemed gripped and fascinated, her head turning quickly to look at me again and again as she drove, lips parted, eyes wide with wonderment. "Well, there's a story now!" she breathed when I had finished. " 'Tisn't possible *anybody* could make up a story like that if they was touched in the head."

"I don't think I am making it up, Paloma," I said. "I don't think so."

"That's what I meant," she said impatiently. "And you weren't so daft about getting that swazzle out of his gullet."

Ahead of us the Punch and Judy man turned to peer over the covered top of the little cart and waved his ancient top hat to us. I acknowledged the wave. Paloma laughed and said, "He's the one touched in the head, I reckon. You never saw such a mad fellow, the things he does."

I said, "Are you Lord Henry's wife?"

"No. His woman, just." She gave me a challenging stare. "Don't be shocked, young miss."

"I'm not shocked. Please call me Jemimah." After what I had known in Shul, I doubted that anything in England could shock me.

Paloma said, "Jemimah's a funny sort of name. I'll just call you Mim."

"All right." I had answered to Lalla for well over two years, and it would not trouble me to be called Mim for a few hours. "Have you been traveling with Lord Henry for long?" I asked.

"About four months it be now. That's when I run off with him from the *vitsa* during Tillerton Fair."

"The *vitsa?*"

"Romany band. Gypsies. Holy God, Mim, you didn't think I was a *gadje* like you and Henry, did you?"

I could not help laughing. It was easy to guess that a *gadje* was anybody who wasn't a Romany, and Paloma's contempt for such was too honest to be offensive. I said, "Why did you run away?"

She lost her bold manner and looked almost shamefaced. "I was a foundling some other band left by night, so I never had a real family. No brothers to look after me. Big Alex took me for his woman, but then he wouldn't marry me." She cracked her whip angrily. "I showed that big monkey. I ran off, so everyone will laugh at him."

I said, "How did you know that Lord Henry would take you?"

"Because he said so when I asked him, that's how. He needed help with his business, and I'd been lending him a hand during the week of the fair, so he was glad enough to have me join him, for he was without a woman to draw the customers and warm his bed."

I tried to remember what little I had heard about gypsies, and after a few moments I said, "I thought Romany people kept to themselves and didn't go with men or women outside the tribe. Won't they be looking for you, Paloma? And won't—what did you call him? Big Alex? Won't he be jealous?"

"Oh, he'll be looking out for me, sure enough, and I want him to be jealous," she said defiantly.

"But won't it be dangerous for you and Henry if your people find you?"

She shrugged. "Like enough, Mim, but I know the roads they travel and the places they stay, so we keep away from where they might be." She flicked the whip lazily and half smiled. "Besides, they'll not be inquiring after a Punch and Judy man, see? Henry only took to that after we left Tillerton."

I stared in surprise. "You mean he hasn't been doing this very long?"

She laughed. "Not more than ten weeks. Bad enough now, he do be, but the first month I near died of shame, with him using the puppets all wrong and muddling up the voices."

I found myself laughing with her at the thought. "Then what was he doing before he became a Punch and Judy man?" I asked.

We had started down a long hill now, and Paloma was using the brake, which squeaked rhythmically. It seemed that the small cart had no brake, for ahead of us Lord Henry had dismounted and was hanging on to a rope at the back of the cart, bracing himself to act as a human brake.

"He worked in a prize-fighting booth once, before I knew him," said Paloma. "You know what that is? They offer a prize for anyone in the audience who'll go into the ring against one of the booth fighters for five minutes without being knocked down."

"Was that how Henry got his nose broken?" I asked.

"Yes." We were almost on Lord Henry's heels now as he clung to the restraining rope, and Paloma sent the lash of her whip curling out to flick his top hat, but gently, in a kind of caress, it seemed to me. "He tells me he wasn't much good at the prize fighting," she said. "Too often he couldn't knock the other fellow down, see? So they gave him the sack, and he set up on his own with the medicine. That's what he was doing when I ran off with him from Tillerton Fair."

I was thankful to be listening to Paloma's tales of the eccentric man who called himself Lord Henry Boot, for it helped to keep my mind away from the pressing problems of my immediate future. I would have to think about them soon, but too much had happened to me today, and my weary mind needed rest before it was put to the task of finding a way for me to live.

I said, "Medicine? What was Henry doing with medicine?"

"Selling it, he was," said Paloma. "Professor La Botte's World-famous Elixir, he called it."

"La Botte?"

"It's a French word for boot, he says. Lots and lots of labels he had in the wagon, and lots of bottles. The labels had a picture of a tiger's head, all in red, and lots of printing to say all the things this medicine would cure."

"Wherever did he get the medicine from?" I said wonderingly.

"Made it his own self, Mim. I used to help him after Tillerton. Hot water, black treacle, some leaves of feverfew, chamomile, mint, a splash of Friar's Balsam . . . I forget what else."

"Did it ever cure anybody?" I asked.

"Oooh, it did that," my companion said emphatically. "There was folks who'd come back next day and swear their chest or their rheumatics was better."

"Wherever did Lord Henry get the recipe?"

Paloma grinned. "God knows, Mim, and maybe I speak true there, for Henry says a shining angel came to him in a dream and told him the mixture. More likely 'tis one of his old lies he's always telling. Anyway, after a week or two we were over to Leybridge, alongside the circus there with other sideshow folk, and we met this Punch and Judy man who'd had a fall and hurt his wrist so he couldn't work his puppets. Next thing Henry's dancing around, saying 'tis a life ambition of his to be a Punch and Judy man and he's tired of mixing medicine, so in the end they swapped."

I thought I had passed beyond surprise at Lord Henry's antics, but this made me sit up straight in amazement. "You mean . . . he gave this elixir business to the other man and took the Punch and Judy show in exchange?"

She nodded and gave a chuckle. "Said he'd had a sign from heaven."

"Another shining angel?"

"Not that time. But he woke up in the night and heard Lady Jane speaking in a clear voice like the sound of silver bells, saying what he was to do."

"Lady Jane?"

She nodded ahead. "The donkey."

*   *   *

We ate well that night in the small dining room of the King's Head at Little Farrington. There were only four other customers, well-to-do farmers, I guessed, who sat at a table by the window and paid us no attention as they wrangled amiably about crops and taxes and local matters.

Lord Henry Boot was a generous host and an entertaining one, with many amusing stories to tell. Also, despite his ancient clothes and droll face, he had an easy way with him, a way that commanded respect and attention from the landlord and the two girls who served us. There was shoulder of mutton, thick-sliced and tender, with dishes of buttered potatoes, parsnips, carrots, onions, and cabbage. To follow we had a splendid gooseberry pie. During the meal Lord Henry and Paloma drank ale. I tried a sip, disliked it, and contented myself with water. I had occasionally drunk the wine of Shul while I was Deenbur's wife but was unused to alcohol and wished to keep a clear head to cope with the coming hours and days.

As we sat and ate and talked, I kept telling myself how truly strange it was for me to find myself here at this village inn with a gypsy girl and a Punch and Judy man, but I was quite unable to feel any sense of strangeness. Perhaps after my life in Shul, the journey across Afghanistan with Caspar, and the shock of my arrival at Witchwood Hall, nothing would ever seem strange to me again.

Paloma told my story to Lord Henry as she had heard it from me. He listened with interest and asked me one or two questions to flesh out the bones of the tale but was not pressingly inquisitive, for which I was glad. Listening to him talk, I was again struck by the pleasant quality of his voice and his ease with words. He did not sound like an itinerant puppeteer; or a purveyor of patent medicine or a fairground pugilist for that matter.

"Henry," I said as we sat replete at the meal's end, "have you ever been a gentleman's gentleman? A valet?"

"Ah, you're a shrewd young lady, Jemimah." His smile held a glint of admiration. "How did you guess?"

"Well, you have very gentlemanly speech and manners."

"Ah! Did you hear that, Paloma?" he exclaimed with delight. "Jemimah thinks I'm gentlemanly. You see how important it is to imitate your betters? Now if only you will model yourself on me, people will take you for a lady."

"And if you tease me like that," she replied amiably, "I'll fetch you a clout round the ear you'll not forget, Henry Boot."

He grinned and winked at me, then abruptly became serious as he said, "Where will you sleep tonight, Jemimah?"

Reluctantly I made myself face my immediate problems. "I'll ask if they have a room here," I said. "If not, I'm sure they'll know somebody in the village who'll give me a bed and breakfast for a shilling or two."

"You have money?" he asked quietly.

"A few shillings."

"What will you do?"

I managed to smile. "I don't know yet, Henry. I haven't had time to think."

"Would you like a job?"

I was puzzled. "What sort of job?"

"As my assistant in the booth."

I found my mouth was open, and shut it quickly. Paloma showed no surprise but watched him with narrowed eyes. Warily I said, "You're surely not serious, Henry?"

"Oh yes. As you've seen, I'm not a very experienced puppeteer, and part of the problem is handling two puppets at once. If I had a hand free it would be a great help. There's just room for two to sit side by side in the booth, so I thought you could handle Judy and the other puppets while I concentrate on Punch. You could do Judy's voice, too. I think that would be rather good."

Astounded, I groped for words. "But . . . but I don't know how to work a puppet or what they're supposed to do."

"Oh, you'll be a lot better than I was to start with," he said cheerfully. "For one thing, you won't have to worry about a swazzle, and for another we do the same traditional story every time, so you can pick it up with only a few hours of rehearsal."

Paloma drained her pewter pot and weighed it thoughtfully in her powerful hand. "You're not thinking to take Mim as your woman instead of me? Or as well as me, are you, Henry?"

He lifted his hands with splayed fingers, palms toward her, eyes wide in a mime of protest. "God forbid! Ah, Paloma, am I an idiot? Would I invite you to crack my head open by such foolishness? And d'you not see that Jemimah is a lady who'd never dream of behaving in such a disgraceful fashion? Not that I regard you as disgraceful, my sweet, my love, my delicate dove." He looked at me. "Did you know that's what the name Paloma means? It's the Spanish word for dove."

I said to the gypsy girl, "I'm not a rival, Paloma, believe me. But I won't accept Henry's offer if you're against it."

She gave a friendly laugh and set down the pot. "You're welcome, Mim. I wanted to have it straight, just."

Rather dazedly I realized that I had made a decision without quite being aware of it, but there were no second thoughts now. To be part of a traveling Punch and Judy show might seem beyond belief for Jemimah Lawley of Witchwood Hall—if I was Jemimah Lawley—but it would give me the breathing space I so desperately needed, for at this moment I was almost penniless and with nowhere to go; and however poor a life it might have seemed to me once, it was far better than being a *feringhee* girl in Shul.

Paloma was saying, "If we move a few bits and pieces we can make up a bed so she can sleep in the cart. The cover don't let water and she'll be snug enough there."

Henry nodded and looked at me. "The wages will be pitiful," he said. "We do far better at fairs and suchlike than on our own in a village like Oakhurst, but you'll still be lucky to get half a crown a week out of the collection, and it's not often we eat like this. Mostly Paloma cooks for us, so at least your keep will cost you nothing and you won't go hungry."

I looked from one to the other of them and felt tears pricking my eyes. "I don't know how to thank you," I said, "and I promise to be as useful as I can in every way. I'm no stranger to hard work, I assure you."

"That's settled then," said Lord Henry gaily, and offered me his hand across the table. As I took it he said, "Let's throw all notion of thrift to the winds and have a glass of port to celebrate. You'll enjoy that, Jemimah, and it will help you sleep."

I had little need of such help, for now that I did not have to wonder what I should do tomorrow a great lassitude was creeping over me. Later I would have to think about the future, but not tonight, and not tomorrow. "Yes," I said. "Thank you. I would love to try a glass of port."

*   *   *

Two weeks later, at a village fete in Tholebrook, I sat close against Lord Henry Boot on the small bench in the booth, with Judy on my hand, shouting, "What have you done with the baby, Mr. Punch?"

Beside me, with the swazzle in his mouth and a thread hanging from the corner of his lips, Lord Henry squeaked, "It fell out of the window."

"Fell out?" I turned Judy to face our audience. "Did the baby fall out, boys and girls, or did Mr. Punch throw it out?"

There came a roar of response. I was perched on two cushions to bring me level with Henry, and through the strip of gauze hanging below the shelf of the booth I could see that we had a good crowd for this performance. I knew the Punch and Judy story now, knew my lines well, and had been praised by Paloma for handling the puppets better than Henry did, but I was still nervous before each performance.

The first time I had performed before an audience was three days after leaving Oakhurst, and it was a disaster. I was so frightened that I spoke in a whisper and nobody could hear me. Lord Henry was very kind and encouraging about my failure, and in a desperate effort to do better for him at the next performance I shouted my lines so loudly that he said later I had almost deafened him in the booth.

What I had never imagined, and so it came as a surprise, was how severely my arm ached from having it held above my head for the better part of fifteen or twenty minutes. I was quite strong from my hard work in Shul, and my muscles were slowly becoming attuned to this unusual demand, but my arm still felt leaden by the end of a performance. Not that I minded. I was thankful to be hidden in the booth rather than doing Paloma's job of beating the drum, arguing with Mr. Punch, and trying to coax or bully people into dropping a coin in our collecting bag.

We moved every day and gave several performances every day, sometimes alone on a village green or by a school, sometimes at a fete, a fair, or a market. Paloma told me that grown men and women would always gather to watch as long as there were a few children to begin with, so she always tried to collect some children before the performance started, by shouting and beating her drum.

When evening came we would drive a little way out into the country to camp in a field or woods, or perhaps by the roadside. The cart in which I slept was more spacious than Caspar's tent, and the straw palliasse softer than the stony ground of Afghanistan. Each morning we would buy food for the day and fill the wagon's water tank by whatever means was handy—a village pump, a well, a kindly farmer's kitchen tap.

It was no surprise to me to discover that dining out as we had done that evening in Little Farrington was not a regular occurrence. "We just do it sometimes," Paloma informed me, "when his lordship's got a bit o' money to spare." I wondered how Lord Henry contrived ever to have a bit of money to spare, for it seemed impossible to keep the three of us and the two animals on what we managed to collect, but I did not voice this thought.

After my first week with Lord Henry Boot's World-famous Punch and Judy Show I took over the task of cooking from Paloma, who was not very good at it and was glad to be relieved of this duty. I made no claim to be an expert, but what I had learned and taught myself in Shul stood me in good stead now, and after taking a day or two to get used to the stove in the wagon I found I was able to manage very well.

Each morning I woke with sunrise and made my toilet kneeling on the floor of the cart with a bowl of water. When I had dressed, brushed my hair, and hung out my blankets, I would rouse Lord Henry and Paloma in the wagon. While they washed and dressed, I fed and watered Benjamin and Lady Jane, washed some clothes, and began to make breakfast as soon as my companions were clear of the wagon. With the weather fine, we ate outside at a table with folding legs. Only once, when it rained, did we have to eat in the wagon, and even then we were not cramped.

For breakfast we always had a big bowl of porridge each, followed by fried eggs, bacon, bread, and tea. After breakfast we cleared away, packed up, and moved on to wherever Lord Henry had decided was our next destination. We shared the driving. Sometimes I drove the wagon, sometimes I drove the cart with the cover rolled back and Lord Henry lying at ease on my mattress in the back, smoking a clay pipe with a broken stem, and quite often idly teasing Paloma, a few yards behind on the driving seat of the wagon. She enjoyed this, but sometimes pretended to be angry and sent the tip of her long whiplash cracking about his ears, so that he cowered with arms wrapped about his head, laughing, appealing for mercy from his love, his delicate dove, his Romany Cleopatra, his golden-hearted butterfly, his honey-lipped Venus, and similar florid endearments.

Sometimes she would fly into a passion and be genuinely angry with him, usually over something quite trivial. Then she would try to hit him or kick him, as she had done that day in Oakhurst, but he never took her seriously or became angry with her in return. He would only dodge, and duck, and evade her blows, vowing his undying love for her until her wrath was exhausted.

After the morning's drive we would give our first performances, then have a cold meal, usually of bread, cheese, and ale. I was finding ale more to my taste now. It was refreshing after half an hour confined in the booth, with a dry throat from shouting my puppets' words. Sometimes we would move again in the afternoon to the next village, but if we had set up at a fair or fete we would remain for the rest of the day.

Evening was the time for our dinner, and I won praise from both Lord Henry and Paloma for my efforts to make the most of what we could afford to buy. I had feared that Paloma might resent me, but in fact we got on very well together once she realized that I had not the slightest wish to challenge her position as Lord Henry's woman. The longer I knew this singular Punch and Judy man, the more I liked him, but neither he nor I ever gave Paloma a moment's cause for jealousy, and she seemed pleased that we were comfortable with each other. Despite the one-sided quarrels with him that arose from her fiery nature, I became aware as the days went by that she loved this strange man with a passion both strong and deep.

I was so greatly concerned to learn my new tasks, to make myself of use to the man who had come to my aid when I so desperately needed help, that a full three weeks passed before I gave any real thought to my future. When I did so, I could think of nothing I might do to resolve my problems. There seemed no way to be sure in my own mind that I was indeed Jemimah Lawley; or, even if this were so, no way to prove it to the world in general or to my father's lawyers in particular.

When we discussed this over dinner one night as we sat at table outside the wagon, Paloma suggested that we should go back to Oakhurst and seize the young woman who claimed to be Jemimah Lawley. "I got a little knife, Mim," said the gypsy girl, a glint in her dark eyes as she touched her thigh through the bright dress she wore. "If I prick her backside wi' that a few times she'll soon tell the truth."

I said hastily, "No, we can't do that, Paloma."

"Why not?"

Lord Henry winced and rolled his eyes to the heavens. "Because, O gentle Paloma, frail rose of the Romanies, sweet angel of benevolence, if we do that we shall all end up in choky."

She gave a scornful sniff. "All right then, what would *you* do, Mr. Clever?"

Lord Henry cleared his plate of the last morsel of rabbit pie and leaned back in his chair. "Difficult," he admitted. "Let us agree, despite Jemimah's own doubts, that all she has told us is true, and not a concoction of her imagination. Then the key to proving her identity appears to be the mysterious Caspar, with whom she traveled across Afghanistan."

Paloma sucked a rabbit bone clean with surprising grace and said, "How's Mim going to find him, then?"

"A problem, sweet kitten, I agree, but somewhere amid the ministries of Whitehall there is somebody who knows. Mr. Arthur Renwick, perhaps, or his superior. Perhaps Caspar is a soldier, listed in the War Office records. Perhaps he is a civil servant in the Colonial Office. Perhaps he is with some more secret department of government. But if we go to London, and if we say to somebody in the War Office or the Colonial Office that a certain young lady has in mind to tell the newspapers an interesting story about her coming to—what was the place, Mim? Herat. Yes, I remember now—and about her meeting there with Mr. Arthur Renwick . . . Well, I think somebody will be anxious for her *not* to tell this story. So how can she be persuaded? Well, all she wants is to be put in touch with a gentleman named Caspar, surname unknown to her but certainly known to Mr. Arthur Renwick. It's not a large request. Is there any more of that excellent pie, Mim?"

I cut a piece and put it on his plate. Paloma looked at me and said, "D'you think it might work?"

"I've no idea, but I suppose it's worth trying. I mean, if ever I get to London." Strangely, I had no sense of urgency in this, perhaps because I had no illusions. The chances that I would ever prove myself to be Jemimah Lawley were small, however true it might be. Perhaps I could never prove it. If this were so, then it would be foolish to spend the rest of my life in an agony of resentment and frustration. One day I might have to accept defeat and try to build a new life of my own, a life that began only with my time in Shul. Nothing beyond.

I would not give up easily, I told myself, but neither would I let failure destroy me. To be what I was now, homeless, living in a cart, playing a small part in assisting a Punch and Judy man—all this was not much of a life compared with what I had once known, but it was infinitely better than being Deenbur's wife and victim, serving his unloving desires, ever in fear of a whipping, or of death if the mood took him to do away with a *feringhee* girl. As for being sold to Akbah the Mad, I still woke shuddering at night sometimes, dreaming that this was happening.

No . . . even if I could never again be Jemimah Lawley, at least the scars of Shul would always give me a vivid appreciation of how lucky I was to be alive, with food and shelter and friends. I looked at my friends now, very much aware of my feeling for them, and said to Lord Henry, "It would take quite a little time to make any impression on government people in London, I imagine?"

"Very true"—he nodded—"and of course at the moment you haven't any money to go there and take lodgings, which is what you would have to do while trying to make them cough up some information about the mysterious Caspar."

I said quickly, "I wasn't hinting that you might provide the money, Henry."

"Oh, I know that, dear girl. Lord, but you make a splendid pie. No, I was just thinking that in a few weeks we shall be in London, so you might be able to do something then."

I said, "Why shall we be in London?"

He drank some tea and looked at me in surprise. "The days grow shorter, the weather cooler. We can't play the villages in winter, so we go to London and find a spot for the wagon, like Blackheath, or Clapham Common, perhaps. Then we work from there, in parks, playgrounds, street corners, markets—oh, and especially near public houses, that's always a good spot, so Percy told me."

"Percy?"

Paloma said, "Him that Henry took the Punch and Judy from in exchange for all them bottles of elixir medicine."

"Oh, I see." I looked at Lord Henry. "So you've never actually worked London before with the show?"

He wrinkled his slightly bent nose. "Not actually, Mim, but my confidence is absolute."

Paloma chuckled and reached out to stroke his cheek. "I bet it was absolute when you were prize fighting and couldn't knock them other fellers down. I never thought I'd love anyone as daft as you, Henry."

"Ah," he said wisely, "but I obtained a love potion from a pixie, as a reward for saving the wee mite from a ferocious weasel, and I put it in your ale, my sweetheart. That's what makes you love me."

Paloma's eyes grew round. "A *pixie?*" she breathed. "Oh, you never told me, Henry! You never said you'd met one of the Little Folk!"

He winked at me, and she saw it. Next moment she had sprung to her feet with a catch of her breath. Snatching the top hat from his head, she started belaboring him furiously with it. "Tellin' lies again!" she cried. "I'll teach you, Henry Boot! I'll teach you to make fun o' me!"

Choking with laughter, he rolled off the bench where he sat, and fled before her into the woods, all the while exhorting her breathlessly to be calm and ladylike, with his usual great array of flowery endearments. Five minutes later they came back arm in arm, and she wore on her dark head a circlet of small pink flowers he had made for her.

*   *   *

Toward the end of our fifth week together we set up the booth amid the tents and carts of many other itinerant showmen and peddlers at Cranston Races. The weather of late summer was holding well, and there was a good crowd in attendance, some to watch, some to wager, some like ourselves to offer entertainment in the hope of earning a few shillings.

I had never been to a race meeting before and was surprised to see how mixed the spectators were, ranging from ragamuffin children to gentry wearing gray top hats, field glasses hung about their necks, elegantly dressed ladies beside them. A few such as these paused to watch our performances, usually with a bored air of amusement, but most of our audiences consisted of working folk out for the day, with a sprinkling of children.

We took some good collections, and by now I felt reasonably at home sitting beside Lord Henry with a puppet on my hand and others ready on their hooks, shouting Judy's lines or changing to an eerie moaning voice for the ghost. When the last performance ended we emerged from the back of the booth and began to pack up the puppets while Paloma went among the dispersing crowd to make the final collection.

After a moment or two Lord Henry left me to the task and wandered off, his broken top hat perched on the back of his head. I was a little surprised but thought perhaps he had seen an old acquaintance. When I glanced up, I saw him strolling with a faraway manner toward a well-dressed man who stood near a stall where a woman was selling sherbet drinks only a few yards away. The man wore a gray frock coat with striped trousers and a top hat, and he was studying a folded newspaper, or perhaps a race program, I could not quite see clearly.

Henry appeared to stumble as he drew near, and almost fell. The man instinctively put out a hand to steady him. For a moment they were close together, then Henry recovered, spoke a smiling word of thanks, and took off his hat to make a courtly bow. The gentleman nodded in brief acknowledgment, then moved away, once again studying the paper he held. But I had caught my breath in shock, for I was certain I had seen Henry slip something very much like a dark leather wallet into his pocket as he bowed.

I bit my lip and went on putting the puppets away, recalling how on my first evening with Lord Henry he had talked airily to Paloma of having cracked a crib or picked a pocket. I had taken this as being no more than one of his quaint jests, but now I was sure I had seen him pick a man's pocket, and I wanted to weep. A wallet meant paper money, bank notes, five pounds at very least.

My head full of confusion, I began hurriedly to dismantle the booth, fearful that the gentleman might soon discover his loss and suspect the identity of the culprit. After a minute or so Lord Henry strolled across to join me, lighting his clay pipe. "Why all the hurry, Mim?" he said amiably. "We'll only be going a mile or so along the road to Linsford for the night."

"I just thought . . . we might as well get away before the lanes are too crowded with traffic," I said, busy with my task.

He crouched to help me roll up the canvas. "Is anything wrong?"

"Wrong? Of course not," I lied, unable to think what else I could say. "Paloma looks pleased. I think the last collection must have been quite good."

Ten minutes later, when we moved out onto the road, I held the reins of Lady Jane and behind me Paloma was driving the wagon. Lord Henry lay in the cart at my back, as he often did, sometimes calling out to Paloma, sometimes discoursing to me on any subject that took his fancy, ranging from the practical to the fantastic.

After we had driven a few hundred yards I made up my mind and said, "Henry, will you come and sit with me, please? I want to say something."

"All right, Mim." He scrambled onto the seat beside me. "What is it?"

I swallowed hard and said, "You stole a wallet from that tall gentleman with gray hair you stumbled into. I saw you."

After a little silence he said, "So that's why your manner seemed strange just now."

I kept my eyes on the road, and my voice shook as I said, "Why, Henry? What made you do such a thing?"

"Well . . . our funds needed replenishing, Mim."

"That's no reason to steal! Anyway, we're not *starving*, or even hungry. We manage very well."

I felt his finger touch my cheek and heard him say gently, "Why, Mim, there's a teardrop here. Have I made you cry? I'm so sorry."

I tried to squeeze back the tears and sniffed hard to stop my nose running as I quavered, "I'm so upset, Henry. Oh dear, that sounds horribly self-righteous. It's just that . . . well, I realize there must be all kinds of rogues at a race meeting, but you're too nice a person to be one of them, Henry. I've come to respect you very much, and . . . oh, I don't want you to do bad things."

I broke off, taking one hand from the reins to rub my wet eyes with the back of a wrist. As I did so, it occurred to me that by speaking out I might have thrown away the only living I had, for the man beside me could simply stop the cart and leave me at the roadside with my few belongings. Some long seconds passed, then he said thoughtfully, "What do you want me to do, Mim?"

I turned my head to look at him. To my relief he showed no anger but was simply gazing into the distance with placid interest, occasionally sucking at his pipe.

"Do?" I echoed rather stupidly.

He nodded. "Yes. After all, I can't give the wallet back, can I? Even if I were able to find the gentleman, it wouldn't do at all. He might have me thrown in the nearest choky, mightn't he? So what would you like me to do?"

I said hesitantly, "I'd like . . . I'd like to be sure you won't do it again, Henry. I know I'm in no position to ask such a thing of you, for I'm less important to the show than your puppets. But I just hate the thought of you . . . doing such things," I ended lamely.

"You mean pinching people's money?" He was looking at me again with an expression I could not fathom, though I thought there might be laughter in it.

"Yes," I declared almost angrily. "I hate the thought of you pinching people's money."

"All right, Mim. I won't steal in future," he said with cheerful unconcern.

I looked at him warily. "You mean it?"

He put his pipe in his mouth and drew a finger across his chest. "Cross my heart. And I'm sorry I upset you."

I gave a sigh of relief and closed my eyes for a moment. "Oh, Henry, thank you. I'm very glad."

"Well, that's settled then. I'll tell you what we'll do, Mim, we'll celebrate my turning from the ways of wickedness by spending some of my ill-gotten gains on a splendid dinner at the tavern in Linsford tonight. How about that?"

I felt vaguely perplexed and said, "It doesn't seem *quite* right, somehow . . . but I'm not sure why, so we might as well do it. You will keep your promise, though, won't you, Henry?"

"Have no fear," he said, and swung around to drop into the cart again and lie at his ease.

Paloma called out, "What have you two been talking about?"

"Nothing important, queen of my heart," he called back lightly. "Mim was just explaining that she has been seized by an uncontrollable passion for me and is proposing to put deadly nightshade in your porridge tomorrow."

I heard Paloma give one of her full-throated laughs, then came the crack of her whip and a yelp from Lord Henry, just behind me. "Biggest liar in all England, that's you, Henry Boot," she cried.

We dined splendidly that night, just as we had done weeks ago in Little Farrington. Deep within me, I was unsure how much confidence I could place in the promise Lord Henry had so easily given, but for the moment I refused to worry about it. I drank a small tankard of ale and a glass of port, which made me very lighthearted, and the evening passed amid much talk and teasing and laughter. Strangely, there came a moment when I suddenly remembered the silent evenings I had passed in the hills and plains of Afghanistan, in the company of a man calling himself Kassim, with barely a word spoken and never a sound of laughter. How I had hated that man, and how he had hated me.

Once I discovered he was an English spy I could understand his feelings toward me, for I must have been a great burden to him as well as a danger, but I was sad now to feel that I had disliked him so intensely, and I wished I could turn back the clock so that I might have behaved differently toward him. I was explaining this laboriously to Lord Henry and Paloma while finishing my second glass of port, when suddenly the sorrow of it all overwhelmed me and I began to cry. This was the last hazy memory I had of the evening.

My befuddled mind produced some fevered dreams that night, after Paloma had put me to bed. One was of being up in the saddle with Caspar on that deceptively powerful mount of his, riding hard in moonlight across a sandy plain to where a river ran. There stood a *yurt*, far more spacious than ours had been, and with walls of some fine material that allowed a glow of light to show from within.

In my dream, Caspar said, "Wait," and slid from the saddle. As he pushed open the flap of the *yurt* and entered, the light grew brighter, and I saw two shadows on the fabric wall, one of Caspar, the other of a woman. A breeze blew across the plain, carrying their voices away so that I could hear only sounds, not words, yet I knew that Caspar, the grim and unyielding Caspar, was pleading with the woman. The breeze dropped, and one or two of his words came to my ears, appealing, softspoken. *"Melanie . . . Stormswift . . . so beautiful . . . please . . ."*

I heard no word from the woman and could read nothing from her silhouette except that she was tall and elegant. Then the voice of Caspar became harsh, as I remembered it, and the words were flung like stones:

"Bitch-goddess!" His arm moved. From his hand jutted the curving shadow of the long knife he had always worn at his belt. He moved suddenly upon the woman, and my scream of fear and protest woke me in the darkness of the night, sweating and trembling.

IX

Eight days later disaster came to our small company of three. We had
spent the night in woodlands a mile from the village of Thorburn, in a
pleasant grassy clearing a stone's throw from the road, with a handy
stream running through the woods a short distance beyond the clearing.

Rain had fallen during the night, but by midmorning the sky was clear
and the sun warm. Paloma and I decided to do some washing before
moving on. We would have to dry it in stages, as opportunity and the
weather permitted, but we were used to this. Lord Henry produced pots
of green and red paint and announced that he would busy himself refreshing all the curlicues and ornamentation with which the outside of
the wagon was decorated.

Paloma and I took a handle each of our washing basket and made our
way through the woods to the stream. There we took off our shoes and
stockings and began the weekly wash, standing ankle deep on the grav-
elly bottom to soap and rinse the clothes, talking of whatever came into
our heads.

"We'll be going back through Oakhurst on the way to London," said
Paloma, pounding a petticoat on a smooth rock. "You going to try again
wi' them people who stole your house, Mim?"

I wrung out one of Henry's shirts and put it in the basket. "There's
not much point, Paloma. All I can do is to get together enough money
somehow so I can take lodgings in London and pester the War Office, as
Henry suggested. Nobody will believe me unless I can find Caspar and
have him speak for me."

"Getting enough money for that won't be easy," she said, frowning.
"Maybe Henry can help. He's flush sometimes, isn't he? God knows
where he gets it from, unless he has a pile of it hidden away somewhere.
Last time I asked he said he'd met a rich old gentleman coming out of

church, and this man pressed some money on him because he said Henry
reminded him of a favorite dog he used to have, with a bent nose. D'you
think that's likely, Mim?"

I laughed and shook my head. "Not very. But please don't ask Henry
to help me with money, anyway."

"Why not?"

I feared Henry might steal for me but could not voice that fear and
simply said, "It wouldn't be fair. He's done so much for me already."

"And didn't you save his stupid life when he was choking on a swazzle? And haven't you made all the difference, not just with the show but
with the cooking and everything?"

"If I have, I'm glad, but I still don't want Henry to raise money for
me. Where's that other shirt of his? I'm sure there were three."

She looked about her, picking over some of the washed clothes lying
across a boulder close to the bank. "Ah, he didn't put it out, Mim. I told
him to, but it must be lying over the chair by our bed. Will you go and
fetch it while I finish off here?"

"Yes, all right." I could not pull stockings on over my wet feet, and so
I walked carefully barefoot along the little path through the woods. It
was not painful, for my feet were hardened from wearing only open
sandals during the summer months in Shul. As I drew near to our camp
in the clearing I heard some faint sounds I could not identify, a kind of
scuffling, a wordless grunt, a smothered cry.

Next moment I was clear of the trees, my heart clenching with shock
and alarm at the sight before me. Henry was under attack by three men,
one armed with a cudgel. A fourth stranger lay dazed on the ground, a
hand held to his bloody nose. Henry was backing before the onslaught,
his stance like that of the prize fighters I had now seen at one or two
fairs, his fists flying, but even as I screamed, *"Paloma!"* at the top of my
voice, I saw Henry go down before a glancing blow of the cudgel.

Two of the men stepped back. The third stood over Henry, gripping
the cudgel, and said, "Been seekin' you a long time, mister. Us don't like
woman stealers. Us reckon to teach you a lesson."

I was consumed by fear as I found myself running at the man, yet a
small part of my mind must have made an immediate deduction, for I
knew beyond doubt that these men were gypsies and that the man about
to break Henry's bones with the cudgel was Big Alex, who had taken
Paloma as his woman but declined to marry her because she was another
vitsa's foundling. For the sake of her pride and to make him jealous, she

had run away from him with Lord Henry Boot, but now at last Big Alex had found them.

Despite his name, he was only an inch or two taller than Henry, but his body was like a barrel, and not from fat. He wore a faded green shirt, shabby corduroy trousers, and a single large earring. His dark hair was long and hung in curls almost to his shoulders. All this I took in fleetingly as I ran forward, driven by instinct and with no idea what I hoped to do.

I heard myself scream, "No!" and before the cudgel could strike I had the man's wrist gripped in both my hands. He turned his head to look at me with mingled annoyance and surprise, then jerked his muscular arm to shake me off, growling, "Out o' my way, girl."

The strength I could feel in him came as a new shock to me. Two or three full-blooded blows with the cudgel from those powerful arms and shoulders, and Henry would like as not be dead. I was panting, "No! You mustn't! Wait! Please—"

"Get *off!*" he roared, and swung his arm so that I was flung about on the end of it as if I had been one of our puppets. My grip was slipping, and in desperation I lunged forward and set my teeth in his forearm. This brought a bellow of rage and pain, while at the same time I was vaguely aware of Henry's voice from around my feet calling thickly, "Run, Mim . . . for God's sake, run."

Big Alex took a long step to one side, dragging me with him, on my knees now but still holding his wrist with hands and teeth, sick with terror, and struggling inwardly to yield to my terror and run, as Henry was urging. Next moment a big clenched fist came down like a hammer on top of my head, and for long seconds I was in another world, with tiny lights flashing before my eyes through a dark fog, nausea rising within me.

Then the fog cleared, and I was lying on the ground a few paces from Henry, who was struggling to get to his knees, blood running down the side of his face from the first glancing blow he had taken. Big Alex was glowering at his own arm, where blood was also running. From two of his companions came a guffaw of laughter and a comment in a strange tongue, the Romany tongue no doubt.

Big Alex snorted, then hefted the cudgel in his hands and moved toward Henry again. As he did so, Paloma appeared from the woodland path, running hard, stopping short with a startled glance as she took in the scene before her. Big Alex paused, staring. Nobody moved or spoke. Lying propped on an elbow, my head still ringing, I saw a medley of emotions touch Paloma's face in lightning succession, first shock, then bleak understanding, followed by a blend of decision and wry resignation.

"Took you long enough to find me, Alex," she said coolly. "Can't think why you bothered."

He glared and stabbed a finger toward her, then spoke in English, perhaps because she had done so herself. "You're *my* woman!"

She shook her head. "I'm no man's woman who won't marry me."

The gypsy jerked a thumb at Henry, who had managed to get to his knees. "Did *he* marry you, then?"

"Me marry a *gadje?*" Paloma's voice was sharp with contempt. "Don't talk daft!"

Big Alex blinked, uncertain for the first time. "You run off with him," he said aggressively. "You're his woman."

"*Me?*" Her look of incredulity was totally convincing. "You're off your stupid head, Alex." She nodded in my direction. "That's his woman, you great fool."

"Eh?" The gypsy glared from one to the other of us with slow-witted bafflement. "But *you* run off wi' the *gadje!*"

"I ran off with him and his woman, and why not?" Paloma demanded, her big dark eyes flashing angrily. "What's to keep me with the same *vitsa* as you? I'm a foundling, so I don't belong, do I? That's why you said you wouldn't marry me."

Lord Henry had crawled toward me, and now he helped me to sit up, his arm about my shoulders for support. There we stayed, unmoving, watching the scene, knowing that the outcome depended on Paloma. Big Alex twisted the cudgel in his hands and scowled. "Maybe I changed my mind," he said sullenly.

Paloma laughed and said, "Liar!" spitting out the word with scorn.

"It's true, 'Loma," he protested. Then, with sudden suspicion: "Unless *you're* tellin' lies! You swear you never been his woman?" He jerked his head toward Henry.

"Course I swear!" Her eyes blazed with indignation, and before he could speak again she went on: "What's that to you, anyway? I stopped being your woman when I ran off. These two"—she gestured toward us —"they give me a living all spring and summer, now you come spoiling everything. You think they'll keep me on after this?"

"Don't matter about *them!*" he growled. "You're comin' home wi' us, 'Loma."

"I'll not be your woman again, Alex."

He seemed to wrestle inwardly with himself, then said at last, "We'll marry, then."

She jerked her head at the other gypsies. "You're saying that before witnesses?"

He nodded sulkily. "Aye."

"That's settled, then. I'll get my things together." She started to move toward the wagon, not glancing at me or at Henry.

Big Alex gripped his cudgel and turned toward us. "This feller helped you run off, so I'll still teach him a lesson."

Paloma stopped in mid-stride. Part of her skirt flared high for a moment, and then she had a little knife in her hand. I had seen it before, when two drunken yokels pestered us one evening. "*Alex!*" she said, and her voice was like the crack of a whip. He paused, turning his head to her, and she went on in a soft yet frightening voice. "Nobody helped me run off, Alex. They're only *gadjes*, but they been good friends to me. You lay a finger on them and you'll pay dear."

He gave a blustering laugh. "You think Big Alex is afraid of a girl with a bodkin?"

"He'd better be," Paloma said through her teeth, smiling, "if he wants to sleep easy in our bed when we're married." The blade glittered as she twitched the knife in her hand. "A bodkin can do bad things to a sleeping man."

He glared at her in exasperation, then tossed the cudgel aside, muttering under his breath. Paloma said amiably, "There now, that's better surely." She glanced at one of the other men. "Where's the *vitsa* now, and how did you come here, Sam?"

This was the one Lord Henry had knocked down, and he was nursing his nose tenderly with a cupped hand as he answered in a muffled voice, "'Tother side o' Thorburn. Came last night. Farmer's lad said he'd seen you wi' the top-hat feller when we called for milk s'mornin'. We come over wi' Big Alex in a cart."

"Where is it?"

He jerked his head, then winced. "Along the road. Couple o' minutes."

She looked at Big Alex again and said, "Go and wait by the cart while I put my things together. I'll be no more than ten minutes."

He was winding a cotton neck scarf around his bitten forearm and looked up sharply. "We'll wait here. You're too full o' tricks, 'Loma."

She studied him with a half smile. "You used to like my tricks, Alex. Remember? Now make up your mind, d'you want me or not?"

"I've said so, haven't I?"

"Then do as I say. There'll be no tricks. I'll join you at the cart in ten minutes."

He hesitated, then gave a sudden almost angry laugh and turned away, saying something in the Romany tongue to his companions. They followed him out of the clearing, laughing and talking among themselves.

I found I had been holding my breath and let out a long, shaky sigh of relief. Crouched holding me, Lord Henry also heaved a thankful sigh. "God Almighty, that was a close call," he said, and stood up, helping me to my feet.

"It was that," Paloma said, and lifted her skirt to slip the knife into the little sheath above her knee. "If Mim hadn't yelled an' held him till I got here, they'd ha' beaten you senseless, my lad." She came toward me as she spoke and put her hand to my cheek. "You're not hurt, Mim?"

"No." My voice wavered, for I was still trembling in the aftermath of fear. "Thank God you came, Paloma."

"I echo Mim's words, my angel," said Lord Henry, and although he spoke lightly as usual, there was a depth of gratitude in his voice and in the look he gave her. "Now listen, sweet cherub, you don't have to go off with that brute, for I have a shotgun at the bottom of my locker, and—"

"Ah, you're daft as he is, Henry," Paloma broke in with a quick gesture of scorn. "You *gadjes* think we have the second sight when all we have is the good sense to know what has to be. Did you think it could go on forever wi' you an' me?" She turned away. "I must pack my things. Get that cut on his foolish head washed, Mim."

She climbed the steps into the wagon. Lord Henry would have followed, but I held his arm and shook my head, for I knew Paloma had chosen a course from which she would not turn back. I made him sit propped against a wheel of the wagon while I fetched a bowl of water and began to bathe the blood from his face. The place where the skin had been broken was fairly small, but the swelling bruise all about it looked ugly. Henry was pale, but he did not flinch at my touch and sat without speaking, gazing absently into the distance.

When Paloma emerged from the wagon five minutes later I had stopped the bleeding and was dabbing witch hazel on the bruise. She carried her belongings in a blanket tied at the corners, and they did not make a very large bundle. Henry stood up as she came down the steps. She set the bundle down on the grass before turning to look at him, her hands resting low on her hips, head tilted a little to one side, studying him with a wry smile. When she spoke, it was as if they were alone together.

"It was never going to last long," she said, "but for me it was a fine spring and summer, Henry Boot, and you're a good man." He started to say something, but she stopped him with a quick gesture and went on speaking, moving closer to him. "No, don't say anything, for there's nothing to be said. There's a life I was born to, and no changing the way of it. Big Alex is the best I can hope for, I've always known that, but at least I go to him on my own terms now." She put up her hands and drew down the Punch and Judy man's head, looking into his eyes. "Think of me sometimes, Henry. Please?"

She put her mouth to his, kissing him hard on the lips, pressing her body close to him as he put his arms about her. For long seconds they kissed, then she broke almost roughly away and turned to me. "You'll have to beat the drum and take the collections now, but you'll manage all right." She put her hands on my shoulders, leaned forward and pressed her cheek to mine. "Good-bye, Mim," she whispered. "Take care of him."

I was too close to tears to be able to speak, but as she drew back and looked at me I nodded. She gave me a smile, turned, picked up her bundle, swung it over her shoulder, then walked across the clearing and vanished without a backward glance into the path that wound through woods to the road.

Henry leaned against the side of the wagon. "Dear Lord," he said quietly, "I'm going to miss that girl."

After a few moments I swallowed hard and managed to say, "Yes . . . we both will."

*   *   *

During the next few days we discovered just how much we missed Paloma. Without my help in the booth, Henry's performance with the puppets was less than satisfactory, though he practiced hard and was slowly improving. My performance as what Paloma had called a "barker," with the drum and collecting box, was little short of pathetic. I was simply not cut out for the task of banging the drum, shouting, and hectoring the little crowd that gathered to watch the show. I could not begin to match Paloma's natural fire and boldness, and I was miserably aware that my attempts were completely lacking in conviction.

The crowds grew smaller and so did our collections. Henry never complained or attached any blame to me, but constantly apologized for his own shortcomings. Apart from Paloma's work as a barker, we missed her companionship on the road or when we camped each night. This we acknowledged to each other, then tried to accept the fact and put it behind us.

Despite our worries about the poor performances and dwindling collections, we got on well together, Henry and I. At the end of a week, as we were having dinner one evening, Henry said, "Would you like to move into the wagon, Mim?"

If I had never been anyone else but Jemimah Lawley of Witchwood Hall, now aged twenty, his question would no doubt have shocked and outraged me; but, whether or not I had ever been Jemimah Lawley, it was certain I had spent over two years as Lalla of Shul, and many weeks as Mim of Lord Henry Boot's World-famous Punch and Judy Show, and I was no innocent maiden to be shocked.

I finished the last spoonful of soup from my bowl and said, "No, Henry. I like you very much and I know you've been very kind to me, but I don't wish to be your woman. I don't wish to be anybody's woman," I added hastily, for I did not want to hurt or offend him.

We were sitting at our small table outside the wagon, for the evening was mild, and he laughed, shaking his head and leaning back in his chair. "God save us all, Mim, I didn't mean that," he said. "I wasn't asking you to take Paloma's place."

"Oh. I'm sorry, I misunderstood."

"Not that you haven't all the fine looks and attraction any fellow could wish for, of course."

"Thank you." I smiled inwardly, remembering how Paloma had always declared Henry to be the world's greatest liar.

"It was different with Paloma," he went on. "I shall always have the greatest affection and respect for her, but where she was an earthy female who came to me as naturally as breathing, you're a lady, Mim."

I laughed outright at that. "I may have been once, Henry, but it's hardly the word to describe me now." I picked up our empty bowls. "If you weren't asking me to take Paloma's place, what did you mean?"

"Only that the nights will soon be getting cooler, and it would be better if you slept in the wagon and I slept in the cart."

I went up the steps and returned with two enamel plates of pork chops, potatoes, cauliflower, and peas I had put in the little oven to keep warm. As I put Henry's in front of him I said, "Thank you very much for the suggestion, I do appreciate it, but I won't have you turn out of the wagon for me. I'm used to extremely cold winters, and I'm surprisingly hardy, so you needn't worry. Besides, I expect it will be warmer in London than in the country."

"Ah, well . . . we won't be going to London for a week or so," he said vaguely. "I know I said we'd start this week working our way north, but last night I decided we might do well to swing in a loop to the west first."

I stared in surprise. "Do well? We're doing worse every day, Henry. I know it's mostly my fault, but there simply aren't enough people in the small villages. Surely we could do better in London, and we wouldn't have to travel so far from place to place there."

It occurred to me as I spoke that it had been my intention to save money so that I could spend some time in London trying to trace Caspar through one of the government ministries, but at present this was out of the question. There was no money to spare from our dwindling collections; and now that Paloma had gone, Lord Henry could not perform without me to act as barker, so I would have to stay with him until he found somebody to replace me.

"It's quite true, what you say about London," he agreed, cutting into the rather meager chop on his plate, "but I think we'll try looping round through Hampshire first, Mim. We might be lucky there."

My own chop was even smaller, a reflection of our financial situation, but this did not trouble me. We were still far from going hungry, and I had long since learned to take each day as it came. "Why might we be lucky in Hampshire?" I asked.

Lord Henry made one of his despairing grimaces, frowned with intense concentration for a few seconds, then said cheerfully, "Ah yes, I remember now. My fairy godmother lives in Hampshire. I didn't know it, of course, until some years ago when I helped an old crone collecting wood for her fire, and suddenly she threw off her cloak and was revealed as my fairy godmother. You know? Like the one Cinderella had. So if we meet her, she might well cast a spell to bring huge and generous crowds to our performances."

I giggled and said, "Oh, you're quite impossible."

He looked pained. "Don't you believe me?"

"Every word. Now eat your dinner."

He studied me soberly for a moment, then said, "For somebody who's gone through as much as you have, Mim, you're a very nice lady."

His words were so unexpected that I felt suddenly shy, my cheeks warm. "I'm not a lady at all," I said. "When I've got most of the meat off this chop, I'm going to use my fingers for the rest."

In the week that followed we covered longer distances than usual each day, crossing the river Wey into Hampshire, and moving up through Bordon and Alton. Our collections did not improve, and Henry's fairy godmother did not reveal herself. Two days out of Alton, I woke in the night with a feeling of unease. I had no watch but had become good at judging time during my years in Shul, and when I pulled the canvas flap on the cart aside to look at the moon, I knew it was not long past midnight.

I was about to drop the flap when I saw, quite distinctly, the figure of Henry moving off along a path that led into woods from the roadside clearing where we had camped. In the moonlight I could see that he was dressed, and it would have been natural for me to call out to him, but there was something so wary about his manner that a feeling of surprise and disquiet kept me silent. Without making any conscious decision, I threw aside the blankets covering me, reached out for the skirt that hung nearby, and began to pull it on over my nightdress. Two minutes later I dropped from the back of the cart, hastily buttoning a cardigan, bare feet buckled into my black walking shoes, hair still in two plaits.

My throat was dry with anxiety as I hurried along the path Henry had taken. Befuddled by sleep, I did not quite know what I feared, or perhaps I did not want to know. Until this moment I had acted almost without conscious thought, but now reason began to catch up with instinct. We had skirted the village of Granger late that afternoon, making no attempt to give a performance there. This had surprised me a little, and now, with hindsight, I felt that Henry had deliberately chosen to bring us unobtrusively to the spot where we were camped, just off a little-used lane, where woods extended for a hundred yards or so to the walled grounds of a fine manor house I had seen from the crest of a hill as we approached from the south.

My fears began to take shape, and I pressed on as fast as I dared, hoping to catch up. Fragments of memory flickered through my head, memories of Henry lightheartedly saying he had cracked a crib or picked a rich man's pocket; one or two remarks of Paloma's, wondering how Henry managed to produce enough money for our needs; and above all, the moment at the race meeting when I had seen Henry pick a man's pocket. We had dined well that night on the stolen money; no doubt it had helped augment our meager takings for a number of days to come. And now . . . ?

I called in a low voice into the darkness ahead, which was foolish, for I might just as well have called aloud. There was no response. I hurried on and came out of the woods into moonlight again, with a high, ivy-covered wall before me but no sign of Henry. Then I saw an arched gateway, with a narrow but solid oak gate set with iron studs, like a postern gate, standing slightly ajar.

Coldness touched my heart, for now my fears were realized. Henry was about to break the promise he had made me by stealing from the manor house. A brick path led through shrubbery to a wide expanse of lawn, and I almost ran along it, stumbling once but recovering, my heart thumping within me, hoping desperately that I would reach Henry before it was too late.

The path took me past some outhouses, then curved around the wing of the house and became a broad terrace, with mullioned windows set in a gray stone wall on my right. Still no sign of Henry, and now I was distraught, for the house was huge and I had no way of knowing which way he had gone to seek access. I hurried on, turned a corner, and stopped as I saw a faint glow of light coming from one of the windows about thirty paces from me. The sills were on a level well above my head, but when I reached the window I found it open, with a short wooden ladder propped against the wall to offer easy access, and I guessed that Henry had picked this up from one of the outhouses.

Shivering a little from a blend of fear and distress, I mounted the ladder, struggling to keep alive the hope that I might yet manage to prevent my companion from committing burglary. The window gave on to a room furnished as a study, with two doors leading off. The gas was not lit here, but light from an adjoining room came through one of the doors that stood open. I hesitated, my head and shoulders through the window, listening, then screwed up my courage and climbed through. Now I was on the edge of panic, and wondering what madness possessed Henry that he should have lit the gas in the next room to carry out his theft.

Fine rugs covered the study floor, and my feet made no sound as I hurried across the room. Next moment I was in a library. Shelves of books rose from floor to ceiling, a large reading table with two chairs stood in the middle of the room, and to one side were stepladders on casters, for reaching the upper shelves. Of all this I was only vaguely aware, for the whole of my attention was riveted on Henry as he stood by a small safe set in the wall, its door open.

And he was not alone. Beside him stood a man with thin graying hair, wearing a dressing gown, watching Henry count sovereigns into a small drawstring purse. I must have gasped, for both heads turned toward me. The older man at once looked troubled. Henry, after a start of surprise, gave me a rueful smile. "Hallo, Mim," he said. "Didn't you trust me?"

It was hard for me to find words. He showed no sign of shame or alarm, and I was stunned by the presence of the older man. "Henry," I managed to whisper at last, "what are you *doing?*"

"Just getting a little money, Mim."

"But . . . but . . ." Words failed me, and at the same moment I realized that the man in the dressing gown was not entirely a stranger. I had seen him before, but where? When . . . ?

Even as the astonishing answer came to me, a door at the far end of the library opened to admit another figure in a dressing gown, but this was a lady. She was slender, not tall and not young, but her presence was far greater than her physical appearance. In the light of the lamp she carried, her eyes seemed gray. A small straight nose was set between high cheekbones, and her hair, which like my own hung in plaits, was dark and untinged by gray. Only the lines at the corners of her eyes and mouth betrayed her age as being in the middle or late fifties.

The man in the dressing gown seemed to freeze, and his face became quite blank. Henry gave a faint sigh. The lady came forward and set the lamp down on the table. She looked at me without surprise, studying me rather thoughtfully from my face to my stockingless feet in my black shoes, then she turned her gaze upon the two men and spoke in a voice of cool authority.

"You may go, Jackson," she said. The older man gave a bow and mumbled something I did not catch, then moved past the lady and went out through the open door beyond. She kept her eyes on Henry, who had put the drawstring purse down on the other end of the table and stood waiting resignedly. "I suggest you introduce your companion," she said.

"Yes, of course." Henry gave her one of his gentle smiles. He gestured toward me with a courteous bow. "May I present my friend, Miss Jemimah Lawley, of Witchwood Hall in the county of Surrey." He looked at me with apology in his smile. "Jemimah, I present the Most Honorable the Marchioness of Whitchurch . . . my mother."

On his last words my mind stopped working completely, but I managed to make a curtsy and dip my head in acknowledgment. Lady Whitchurch inclined her own head graciously, then looked again at her son.

Her son? My eccentric companion Henry, who after being a pugilist had sold homemade elixir at fairgrounds and had then become a Punch and Judy man with a gypsy girl sharing his wagon and bed? This lady's son?

"What have you been doing since last I saw you, Henry?" she demanded coldly.

"Oh, nothing very special, Mamma," he said politely. "I've been traveling here and there in a wagon, at first selling patent medicine at fairgrounds and race meetings and suchlike, but for the last few months I've been a puppeteer."

"A what?"

"A Punch and Judy man, Mamma."

"Good God," said his mother, but more in sorrow than surprise. "And were you successful?"

"At times, Mamma, but not in an overall sense. I had to wire Jackson to bring me a little cash occasionally when he could manage to get away. I called in tonight because we were running short, I'm afraid."

She nodded and turned her cool gray eyes upon me. "Are you my son's mistress, child?"

I was still so numb with shock, I could not even manage to sound feebly indignant as I said, "No, Lady Whitchurch."

"Very commendable." She glanced at her son. "Though it doesn't say much for you, Henry. She's a remarkably attractive girl."

"I'm well aware of that, Mamma," he said, and he was no longer smiling, "but there are other considerations."

"Really?"

"Yes. For instance, that Jemimah was captured and taken into Kafiristan after her parents had been massacred in Kabul. She was forced to be the wife of a tribal king there, was discarded by him and became a servant, and at last, after more than two years, she contrived to escape by crossing five hundred miles of Afghan wilderness, only to reach England and find that her home, fortune, birthright, and even her name have all been stolen from her. Do you imagine she wants a man pressing his attentions on her after such experiences?"

She turned her head to stare at me with raised eyebrows. "Is this true? You say you are the Lawley girl from Witchwood Hall?"

I said mechanically, "Yes, Lady Whitchurch. I believe myself to be."

After a moment or two she said, "I apologize for the suggestion I made, child." She turned to Henry and went on without pause, "Where is your wagon now?"

"In the woods beyond the lower gate, Mamma, near Friars Lane."

"I see. Well, you had better return there for the night, and I shall expect you to come back in the morning to take up residence here. I mean both of you."

Henry said firmly, "We can't do that, Mamma. You know very well I can't live in the same house as George for half a day without quarrels breaking out."

"I know that only too well," she said, a little bleakly, "but George is no longer living here at Torringtons. Some weeks ago he was appointed to a position in the colonial service, on the staff of the High Commissioner in Cape Town, and he has left England for at least three years." She picked up the lamp and came toward me, halting to study my face quite openly.

After a few moments she gave a little nod. "Yes, it is in the eyes. Life has not been gentle with you, Jemimah. Now pay attention, please. You will bring Henry to me between ten o'clock and noon tomorrow, I rely on you for that, and you will stay here at Torringtons for the time being. Is that understood?"

Again I made a small curtsy and said, "Yes, Lady Whitchurch." The thought of refusing, or arguing, or even asking a question, did not cross my benumbed mind.

For a fleeting moment her austere face was touched by the merest hint of a smile as she said, "Henry is a great tribulation to me, but I must confess that he is never less than interesting, and I shall have many questions to ask you both. Good night, child."

"Good night, Lady Whitchurch."

She turned away and halted again. "Good night, Henry. You may kiss me."

He approached and kissed her cheek. "Good night, Mamma."

She went out, and a moment later Jackson entered. "The butler . . . he must be the butler," I thought vaguely.

"If you are leaving now with the young lady, my lord," he said, "I will attend to the removal of the ladder and the closing of the window."

"Very well, Jackson." Henry had returned the purse with the sovereigns to the safe and was closing the door. "I hope I haven't caused you to be in trouble with Lady Whitchurch."

"She may admonish me, my lord," said Jackson with a dignified air, "but it will be no more than a form of words, as you might say. If I had been disloyal to you by advising her of certain matters, she would have dismissed me."

"Well, that's all right, then. Come along, Mim."

Lord Henry took my hand and led me into the study, then to the open window, where he helped me climb out onto the short ladder. When he joined me at the bottom he took my hand again and we began to walk along the flagged terrace toward the brick path. I was still dazed, still unsure whether or not I was dreaming, and still bereft of words. It was not until we had passed through the iron-studded gate in the wall and were walking along the path through the woods that I found my voice at last, and I said, "In heaven's name, why didn't you *tell* me, Henry? *Why?*"

X

Henry said, "Why didn't I tell you what, Mim?"

"About you being a *lord*, of course!"

"But it's painted on the wagon and the booth. LORD HENRY BOOT'S WORLD-FAMOUS—"

"Oh, I didn't believe that! Nobody believes it. I just thought it was to make people take notice, especially with a funny name like Boot. That can't be real, even if you are a lord."

"Oh, but it is, Mim. It's the family name. An ancestor of mine in the sixteenth century was Henry Boot. He was made a viscount for services to Queen Elizabeth when he was quite old, and later she promoted his son to be a marquess. I'm afraid I inherited my funny name."

I was embarrassed and said, "Oh dear, I'm sorry I said it was a funny name, Henry. I mean, Lord Henry. Or should I call you 'my lord'?"

"God save us all, don't start that sort of rubbish, Mim. You call me Henry."

"Very well." We walked on in silence for a few moments, then I said, "Is a marquess higher than a viscount, then?"

I heard him chuckle. "Oh yes. Marquess is the second grade of the peerage, ranking after a dukedom. Then come earls, viscounts, and barons."

"I don't suppose many of them become Punch and Judy men."

"Well, I haven't heard of any others."

I thought what a silly comment that was for me to have made, but my head was still in something of a whirl after all the anxieties and surprises of the past half hour. In my mind was a confusion of questions I wanted to ask, yet I was beginning to feel shy of Lord Henry. After all, he was in truth a member of the peerage, and it seemed impudent for a girl without a home or name to question him.

But he was still holding my hand, and as we came into the clearing where we had camped for the night he said, "I'm so dry after all that, Mim. Would you come into the wagon and make a cup of tea for us before we go back to bed?"

"Yes . . . yes, of course."

He lit the lamp and sat on the bed at the end of the wagon while I stood a kettle to boil on the spirit stove and set out cups and saucers. After a while he said, "Well, go on, Mim. I'm sure you have questions to ask."

I sat in one of the chairs by the table and said, "You don't mind?"

"Not a bit. I'm rather ashamed at not having been honest with you, for I knew very well you thought the name was a piece of showman's business, and I could easily have told you the truth when you thought I'd stolen that money from Jackson at Cranston Races, but . . . well, I was afraid it might spoil a happy partnership if you knew. You've already changed a little toward me since you found out I'm a genuine lord, and I wish you wouldn't."

I felt relief as I said, "All right, Henry, I'll try not to change. Did Paloma know?"

He shook his head. "I never told her, so I'm sure she didn't know, but it wouldn't have made a scrap of difference to her, except perhaps to make her laugh at the notion of having a lord in her bed."

I smiled and nodded, thinking how true that was. Then I said, "Who is this person George, the one who has gone to Cape Town?"

"And the one I quarrel with?" He smiled wryly. "George is my elder brother, Earl of Fallowfield."

"An earl?"

"Yes, but never *the* Earl of Fallowfield, because it's a courtesy title, like mine."

I put hot water in the teapot to warm it and said, "The peerage seems very complicated, Henry."

"Outrageously so, but I'll try to explain. My father is the Marquess of Whitchurch, but he has lesser titles as well, so he's also *the* Earl of Fallowfield, and also Baron Lynwood. *'The'* represents the prefix Right Honorable, which he's entitled to because he holds the title in his own right. Have you followed me so far?"

"Yes, I think so, but don't test me later, Henry."

"I promise. Now, since my brother George is the eldest son, he gets the highest of our father's lesser titles and becomes Earl of Fallowfield, but without any *'the'* because, as I said, it's a courtesy title."

I put tea in the pot and watched the kettle as it began coming to the boil. "Do you get the next one down of your father's titles, Henry?" I asked. "Are you Baron Lynwood?"

"Ah, no. That title would go to the eldest son of my brother George, if he had one, but he's not married. Any younger sons of a marquess, like me, have the courtesy title of Lord, followed by their Christian name and family name. So I'm Lord Henry Boot. Never just Lord Boot, that would be a title in its own right, you see. And if ever I were to marry, then my wife would be Lady Henry Boot, poor soul, never Lady Boot. Informally she would be addressed as Lady Henry—oh, *unless* she happened to be of higher rank than I am in the peerage, in which case she could keep her own Christian name and be called Lady Jane, or whatever it happened to be."

I made the tea and sat down to let it draw for a few minutes. Henry was lying back across the bed, hands behind his neck, head tilted forward, watching me. After a while I said, "Why did you do it, Henry? I mean, why did you leave your home to be a prize fighter and a quack doctor and a Punch and Judy man?"

He blinked. "Haven't I just told you?"

"Told me? What do you mean?"

"All that rubbish about titles I was explaining. Can you imagine anything more ridiculous? If you had to spend your life paying morning calls and going to hunt balls and having ferocious mothers hurl their simpering daughters at your head in the hope of marriage, wouldn't you run away and become a Punch and Judy man yourself?"

I was shaking with laughter, both at his words and his indignant expression, and I had to steady my hand in order to pour the tea. I said, "I doubt if I would, Henry. I think I might be rather thankful to lead a dull life for a while."

"You'd soon get fed up, Mim. I always do."

"You mean this isn't the first time you've left home?"

"The first?" He made one of his demented grimaces. "Dear Lord, no. I've been doing it ever since I was sent down from Oxford."

I stared. "But you can't have been doing the same thing all the time, Henry. I mean, working the fairgrounds. You'd be better at it if you had, wouldn't you?"

"Oh yes, this was the first time I've tried being a puppeteer. Other times I've tried all sorts of different things, quite a lot of them abroad, tinker-tailor-soldier-sailor—not quite that, but almost everything from breaking in wild horses in the American West to acting as a banker's bodyguard in Hong Kong. Oh, by the way, that was my own money I was stealing from the safe. I have a private income from a trust my grandfather set up. It's not just the awful flatness of life at Torringtons that I keep running away from, you know. There's my brother George, too. Or rather, there was."

"Earl of Fallowfield, without a 'the.' "

Henry grinned. "That's right, you're getting the idea, Mim. And never did a splendid chap like me have a more appalling elder brother. George is such an absolute model of utter rectitude, it makes you want to go out and commit crimes. I don't think he's ever spoken to me without admonishing me for some trivial matter and pointing out the continuing error of my ways. Honestly, Mim, he's the most pompous, stuffy, formal, starchy, self-righteous prig God ever made. I can't imagine where he gets it from. He must be a throwback, I suppose."

I passed a cup of tea to Henry and said as he sat up to take it, "I don't suppose all the faults were on his side, though."

"Far from it. I know I'm quite impossible. Thanks, Mim."

I watched him as he sipped his tea, the lamplight casting shadows to make his face even more quaint and clownish than usual, and I marveled that I should be sitting here in a wagon at this hour of the morning, drinking tea with an English peer; and shortly to become a guest in his mother's house, I suddenly remembered.

A thought came to me, and I said, "You spoke of your father, the marquess, but somehow I had the impression that he wasn't here at the manor house."

Henry nodded. "He's not. Papa vanished from our ken about . . . oh, I don't know, about twelve years ago now. He was carried off by a chariot of fire, like Elijah, or was it Elisha? I get those Old Testament prophets muddled up."

"Chariot of *fire?*" I almost spilled my tea at the words. "Oh, don't be ridiculous, Henry."

"It's almost true, Mim. He wasn't carried off to heaven, though, at least not Elijah's heaven. He was carried off by a chariot of fire called Lucia Carolina Pontieri, a minor opera singer he met in Rome and fell madly in love with. I'm told they now live in a palazzo in Venice, and she sings no more, except for Papa, perhaps. When I refer to her as a chariot of fire, it's just an assumption really, and a thoroughly vulgar one according to my brother George, but I take the view that Lucia Carolina Pontieri must have very potent qualities to have kept my father in Italy all these years."

I said, "Do you mean that he left your mother twelve years ago and has never returned?"

"That's right," Henry said cheerfully, "and I think it suits her very well, Mim. Theirs was an arranged marriage, and Mamma says they weren't at all well suited. He settled heaps of money on her, of course."

I shook my head wonderingly. "You seem to have a very odd family, Henry. Did you like your father?"

"Never had much to do with him, really. He spent most days in London and usually slept at his club. I was off to boarding school at eight, on to public school, then university, and by the time I was sent down, Papa had met La Pontieri and carried her off to the city of gondoliers. He was a pretty eccentric sort of chap, by all accounts. You may not have noticed, but I'm slightly that way myself."

"The thought had crossed my mind," I said. "Would you like another cup of tea?"

"Yes, please."

As I took his cup I said, "Do you think your mother meant it when she invited me to be a guest at Torringtons?"

"Good Lord, yes. Mamma never says anything she doesn't mean."

"But why should she invite me? There's a Jemimah Lawley living at Witchwood Hall, and that makes me a girl from nowhere, without a name."

He said, "Oh, that wouldn't trouble Mamma. She's been something of a recluse since Papa left, and I think she's sometimes lonely. Also, despite her formidable manner, she's interested in her erring son, and she knows she'll learn far more about what we've been doing from you than she would from me."

I wondered how long I might be a guest at Torringtons. No doubt it would be very much more comfortable than living like a gypsy, but I was well used to doing without creature comforts, and I had been looking forward to going to London and trying to trace Caspar. Also, I was somewhat afraid of Lady Whitchurch. I sat attempting to think as I sipped my tea, but it was well past one o'clock in the morning now, and apart from being sleepy I was dazed by all that had happened since I had woken at midnight and followed Henry into the woods, fearful that he was about to commit a burglary. After a little while I realized there was no point in trying to force my sluggish wits, for there was nothing to be decided. Whatever was to happen next, I would be carried along on a tide of events, as I had been ever since the night I had crept out of Sandru's house, full of fear, to escape being sold to Akbah the Mad.

One day, I thought mistily, one day I must really try to take positive control of my life. But not tonight . . . not at this moment.

I smothered a yawn and stood up. "Good night, Henry," I said. "Put your cup and saucer in the bowl before you go to bed, please."

"All right, Mim. Thanks for the tea. Good night, and sleep well."

I had opened the door when something made me pause and turn to look at him as he lounged on the bed, propped on an elbow, sipping his tea. "Henry," I said, "is there anything else you haven't told me?"

"What sort of anything else, Mim?"

"Well, I don't know, do I? But it was a shock to find you were actually a lord, and I'm just asking if there are any more shocks to come."

He frowned in thought for a while, then said with a sigh, "All things are possible."

I stared. "What does that mean? Do you have other secrets?"

He looked at me apologetically. "I have other people's secrets, Mim. They're not mine to tell."

If I had not been so tired I would have been exasperated. As it was I shrugged, managed a half smile, and said, "Well, whatever it is, I hope you'll break it to me more gently next time."

*   *   *

In the days that followed I did not take quickly to a life of sudden ease. Each morning I woke at dawn, only to fidget about with a sense of time wasted until I could reasonably ring for my bath to be filled. Then it was a relief to make a leisurely toilet before going down to breakfast. On the third day Lady Whitchurch took me to London by train and spent a morning buying clothes and accessories for me, brushing aside my protests and becoming formidably stern when I persisted.

"You are Henry's friend," she declared, "and you are my guest. It is therefore proper that I should provide for your present needs. I regret that we are buying ready-made clothes, but at least they are a considerable improvement on the contents of your trunk, and they will do well enough for the moment, since you are fortunately of a size and shape which do not call for skilled dressmaking."

Henry accompanied us on the journey to London, his ancient clothes and appalling top hat replaced by an elegant suit and gleaming topper, a flower in his buttonhole, an ivory-knobbed walking stick in his hand. As soon as we arrived he was dismissed by his mother to spend the morning at his club, and he rejoined us only in time to take us to a very splendid restaurant for luncheon before we caught the train home to Granger. Despite his fine clothes, he still seemed to me to have a comical air about him and appeared to be much amused by the whole expedition.

During my first week at Torringtons I was asked many questions by Lady Whitchurch, but none that went back beyond the moment when Lord Henry had taken me under his wing by offering me the job of assisting him in his Punch and Judy show. From the beginning I had the forethought to ask Henry if I should avoid any mention of Paloma, but he only laughed and said, "Just keep to the truth, Mim. You'll get in a terrible tangle if you try to leave Paloma out of any story you're asked to tell."

It was a relief that I could answer plainly when Lady Whitchurch wanted to know all about the gypsy girl who had shared our travels, and she did not seem shocked to know that Paloma had been her son's mistress. When the fact emerged in response to a direct question she only said, "Did the girl love him, Jemimah?"

I remembered the way Paloma had looked as she kissed him good-bye, and I said, "Yes, I believe she loved him very sincerely, Lady Whitchurch, but she was a fine and generous girl, and she knew that nothing could come of it."

"Poor girl," Lady Whitchurch said softly. "Poor girl." That was the only moment when I saw her show emotion. I was deeply grateful to her for receiving me into her house but found her strangely baffling. She would ask about our travels, about the way we lived in a wagon, and about our experiences in the villages, fetes, fairgrounds, and race meetings, but although she was clearly interested, her manner was always cool and austere, in marked contrast to the kindness of her actions.

On one occasion I said that Henry could tell her far more about his travels than I, but she only gave a delicate sniff of disdain and said, "Henry is utterly hopeless in that respect. He disappears for half a year. On his return I ask him what he has been doing. He says he has been working as a prize fighter, a quack doctor, and a Punch and Judy man. That is his full story, and if I press him he says he can't really remember the details."

I was not quite able to suppress a laugh at this, for it was just what I might have expected of Henry.

During my second week at Torringtons I found myself becoming ever more attracted to the beautiful gardens. This surprised me, for as a child I had felt no interest in the growing of flowers and plants, and I wondered if my years in the bleakness of Kafiristan had given me a yearning for the marvelous variety of flowers and shrubs of my own country. Whatever the cause, I greatly enjoyed spending an hour or so daily in the company of Mr. Wickham, the head gardener, a soft-spoken little old man with a face wrinkled like a walnut, who knew and loved all growing things. He had a lifetime of knowledge to draw upon and was gentle by nature, never too busy to explain or demonstrate or answer the sometimes foolish questions of an ignorant young woman.

I sensed that Lady Whitchurch rather approved this interest of mine. It was not her way to show or declare such approval, but on the occasions when we chatted together she seemed pleased to discuss the gardens with me. It was not until my third week at Torringtons that she made any mention of what had happened to me before I met her son. We were in the drawing room after dinner, and Henry had gone for a half hour's ride in the dusk, another of his eccentric habits. I was reading to her from Mr. Robert Louis Stevenson's book, *Travels with a Donkey*, when suddenly she interrupted to say, "That will do, thank you, Jemimah. Give me a brief account of what happened to you in Afghanistan, please."

I closed the book in surprise. "A brief account?"

"That is what I said, Jemimah."

"Well, I'll try, Lady Whitchurch, but I was lost for well over two years, and a lot of things happened."

She looked up from her embroidery. "Summarize, child, summarize."

I waited a few moments to gather my thoughts, then I said, "I was in Kabul when the legation was attacked. My father and mother were murdered. A servant managed to take me secretly across the river and into the hills, but there some Hindu traders seized me, and I think they left him dead. They took me to a small kingdom far away in Kafiristan, called Shul. The *pacha* was Deenbur, and two wives had failed to bear him a child. A shaman told him that a *feringhee* woman would bear him a son—"

"Explain *feringhee*, if you please, Jemimah."

"It's a word they use to mean a European person."

"Thank you. Please continue."

"The Hindus sold me to Deenbur, and I was forced to be his wife, but when months went by and I didn't become pregnant—"

"You speak in very plain words, Jemimah."

"Oh, I'm sorry. Yes, I suppose I do, but it was a very primitive land, and when Deenbur discarded me I became first a palace servant and then servant to a doctor who—"

"Doctor? You mean a medicine man? A shaman?"

"Oh no. Sandru was a real doctor, and that makes a very interesting story, because he was—"

"Let us not quibble about terms, Jemimah. The man practiced some form of medicine, and you were his servant. I am not interested in his story. I am interested in *your* story."

"Well, I became his assistant, his nurse, and helped him with patients and attended a number of childbirths, so I expect that's why I use plain words. I didn't mean to offend you, Lady Whitchurch."

"I am not offended. My remark was intended as a commendation. I prefer plain words. Please continue."

I said, "There came a time when Deenbur decided to sell me to a neighboring king who was not only very cruel but also mad. I knew I would never live long as Akbah's wife, but it seemed impossible to run away. A young *feringhee* woman alone could never make such a journey. Then a friend of Sandru's passed through, a peddler, making his way five hundred miles across Afghanistan to Herat."

I hesitated just for a moment. I had told Henry about Caspar and later wondered if I had been wrong to do so in view of Caspar's profession. Now I decided that I would not tell Lady Whitchurch. After all, she had asked for a brief account.

I said, "The man's name was Kassim and we spent many weeks on the long trail through high mountains and across desert plains. Three days out of Herat he was wounded by an enemy, but I was able to get him the rest of the way, and I learned later that he survived. Then I came to England and went to Witchwood Hall, my family home, but I found a young woman there who said *she* was Jemimah Lawley. With her was a man she called Uncle James, though he was really a cousin, a long-lost cousin from another line of the family, and he came from Cape Province. He said this girl had been in Kabul and escaped the massacre thanks to some faithful servants, and they had hidden her in the hills for a few weeks until the British returned to Kabul."

Without looking up from her embroidery Lady Whitchurch said, "Do you mean that the same thing happened to both of you?"

"No, that couldn't have been so. There was no other English girl of my age in Kabul."

Now she looked up, her eyes penetrating. "So you are saying that these persons are frauds?"

I nodded slowly. "I think they must be, I really do, Lady Whitchurch. I remember my father and mother, and Oakhurst, where I was born, and

our house, Witchwood Hall, and all that happened in Kabul and after." I
hesitated. "But . . . sometimes I have a strange fear that what happened to me has made something go a little wrong in my head, and that
perhaps I'm imagining myself to be Jemimah Lawley because I once
knew her. I'm not quite sure how or where. There's an area of confusion
and doubt in my head as to exactly what happened or might have happened."

"Did the girl you saw at Witchwood Hall appear to recognize you?"

"No. No, she didn't, now I come to think of it, and I suppose she
would have if we had once known each other."

"She might have." Lady Whitchurch concentrated on a stitch, then
looked up again. "You feel it is distinctly possible that you are not Jemimah Lawley?"

I thought for several moments before answering, then I said, "Deep
down inside myself I don't think it's possible, but at the same time I
can't see how another girl, who is at least something like me, could
appear from the hills north of Kabul a few weeks after the massacre
unless she *was* Jemimah Lawley."

Lady Whitchurch laid down her embroidery and folded her hands in
her lap. "Henry entertains no doubt that you are Jemimah Lawley," she
said, "and he claims that you are the sanest person he has ever known.
But in my view Henry is himself so unpredictable that his opinion on
almost any matter is worthless."

I looked at her in surprise. "Unpredictable? Oh, surely not, Lady
Whitchurch. I know he is unconventional, even eccentric, but I've never
known him other than kind and amiable and"—I was about to say comical but changed my mind at the last moment—"and amusing."

A hint of exasperation appeared in Lady Whitchurch's eyes. "Outrageous would be a more apt description," she said coldly, "but we are not
discussing my son, Jemimah, we are discussing you."

"Oh yes, I beg your pardon."

"I have had my solicitors make discreet inquiries about the people at
Witchwood Hall, and I am bound to tell you that any suggestion of their
being other than the persons they claim to be is regarded as utterly
absurd."

I nodded agreement. "Yes, I'm sure it would be, now that they have
been established at Witchwood Hall for over two years, but did your
solicitors find out what proof or credentials they gave?"

"Credentials? What kind of credentials could be expected of them?
The man, James Lawley, came from Cape Province to India when he

heard of the Kabul affair, seeking news of his family. Shortly after his arrival the girl was brought in from the hills by the servants who had saved her. She was at once recognized as Jemimah Lawley by the British authorities there, and later by her parents' solicitors and all the people who had known her in Oakhurst. There was no question of other credentials."

I said, "That's really what I mean, Lady Whitchurch. Nobody has ever asked any questions."

She frowned. "Why should questions be asked? When my son George returns from southern Africa I shall not ask *him* for credentials."

I said apologetically, "It's not quite the same. After all, you will recognize your son, Lady Whitchurch. You say the British authorities in Kabul recognized Jemimah Lawley, but that isn't so. All the British there who had known her were slaughtered, and the people in Oakhurst had not seen her since she left England at the age of thirteen. They have really accepted her simply because they were *told* she was Jemimah Lawley."

Lady Whitchurch studied me for several seconds with appraising eyes. I felt uncomfortable but continued to meet her gaze. At last she said, quite gently, "I am sure you have no wish to deceive me, or to deceive yourself, and you have said that you do retain some slight fear that you may be imagining you are another person, is that not so?"

I hesitated. Sometimes the fear vanished completely, but sometimes it was quite strong, and I could only answer, "Yes, Lady Whitchurch."

She said, "Then I think it would be wise for you to make up your mind that you are suffering from some form of delusion, Jemimah."

I linked my fingers to stop my hands shaking and said, "But that would mean I don't know who I am."

"Would that trouble you deeply?"

I managed to keep my voice steady as I said, "Yes. Yes, it would, Lady Whitchurch. This is hard to explain, but my name and my identity are almost all I have left. If I give up my belief in them without absolute proof, then I shall feel that in some way I'm betraying myself. As far as I can remember, the only thing in my whole life of which I can feel just a little bit proud is that somehow I fought hard enough to remain alive and sane under conditions and ordeals few people in this country could begin to imagine. If you take away my identity, then you take away even that little scrap of pride with it, leaving me nothing." My words had been coming faster and faster. Now I paused for breath. "I'm sorry, Lady Whitchurch, I didn't mean to speak hotly."

She looked at me with an expression I could not decipher, then picked up her embroidery again and said, "Continue reading, please, Jemimah."

Later, when I was in the billiards room with Henry, he said, "Did Mamma speak to you about those two Witchwood Hall frauds?"

I did not answer at once but marked his score on the board and chalked my cue, studying the lie of the balls, two white and one red. Billiards was hardly a game for a lady to play, but this was not a consideration to trouble either Henry or me. He had nobody else to play against, and I was always glad of an occupation to pass the time. Neither of us was very skilled at the game, but although I had never played before coming to Torringtons I was proving rather better at it than Henry.

"Mim? Did you hear?" he asked.

"Yes," I said absently, "but don't try to put me off, my lord. Wait till it's your turn at the table before you ask questions." He laughed, and after concentrating hard I sent my ball gliding off the red into a top pocket. In the next two or three minutes I made a break of twenty-two before missing a quite difficult cannon.

As Henry marked my score on the board he said, "Well, did she, Mim?"

"Yes. Your mother thinks the Witchwood people must be genuine and that I'm only imagining that I'm Jemimah Lawley. She may be right, Henry."

"Oh, rubbish. You're Jemimah Lawley."

"Well . . . whether I am or not, your mother is still very kind to me in her own rather forbidding way."

He smiled. "I know what you mean. She's always been like that, as if she can't bring herself to show any warmth or emotion. It's rather sad."

"Yes." I watched him as he chalked his cue. "She hasn't told me to leave, even though she thinks I'm a person without a name. I'm not sure what I should do, Henry. I can't stay here as a permanent guest forever, but at the moment I don't know where to go."

"Oh, you haven't been here five minutes, Mim, so stop worrying about what happens next." He crouched to judge the angle of a shot, his bent nose almost resting on the polished edge of the table as he squinted along the baize, and I was reminded of the times we had sat huddled together in the Punch and Judy booth, peering through the strip of gauze below the shelf, trying to judge the size of our audience and their likely generosity.

"When the times comes for something to be done," he said, straightening up, "we shall receive a sign. I may well have a visit from an angel with wings of gold, telling me to go at once to far Cathay, accompanied by Judy, there to find treasure beyond all telling."

"I know you have quite a few acquaintances among the angels," I said, "but who is Judy?"

He paused to stare. "You are, my pet. Who else? Who else has played Judy to my Punch throughout the summer?"

"Oh, I see. Well, I'm not sure about Cathay. I've done rather a lot of traveling this year."

He shrugged. "It's up to the angel, Mim. He may possibly tell me to go at once to Whitehall, there to begin the task of establishing the true identity of Jemimah Lawley. Now don't put me off, there's a good girl." He bent to make his shot, the tip of his tongue protruding from a corner of his mouth.

I kept still and silent, thinking how astonishingly lucky I was to be in such comfortable circumstances. It was sometimes hard to believe that I had once been Lalla of Shul, or even Mim of a rather bad traveling Punch and Judy show. I knew now that I might never be able to establish that I was Jemimah Lawley of Witchwood Hall, and that I might not even be able to attempt the task for some time, but daily I ate at a fine table, nightly I slept between soft sheets, and I was never in danger of injury, assault, or even death, at the hands of a barbarian ruler, as I had once been.

I could stay here at Torringtons until, as Henry put it, some sign was forthcoming to indicate what I should do next. It was a comforting thought, but I would have been startled if I had known how soon that sign would come, and horrified if I had known its nature.

XI

Three days later I returned from an afternoon ride with Henry in time to change and join Lady Whitchurch in the drawing room for tea. He was an excellent horseman, but I was able to keep up with him, for whatever my true name might be I knew I had ridden a great deal as a child, both at home and abroad, and had also spent much time handling horses, mules, and donkeys in Shul.

I had stripped off my riding clothes and had just finished washing my face and hands when there was a tap on the door and a young maid named Ethel entered at my call. "Excuse me, miss," she said, "but her ladyship says to let you know there's a visitor for tea."

I was surprised and said, "Who is it, Ethel? I didn't think her ladyship was at home for calls."

"She's not usually, miss, but this Mrs. Galliard is down from London, not specially to call here, but because she'd been staying the weekend with friends at Longmark, I heard her say, and she thought she'd call and send in her card on the way home."

As I took a dress from the wardrobe I said, "Is Mrs. Galliard an old friend, Ethel?"

"Don't know, miss. I never saw her before, but I've only been here six months anyway."

"All right, button this dress at the back for me, please, then go and thank her ladyship and say I shall join her in just a few minutes. Have you told Lord Henry?"

"Yes, miss. Hold still a minute. There. Yes, I told him and he went all gooey when I said it was Mrs. Galliard."

"Went all what?" I was at the looking glass, tidying my hair.

"Gooey. You know, miss. Sort of soft and romantic in his eyes."

I sat to put on my shoes and said, "I know you haven't been in service long, Ethel, but you ought to know better than to make remarks about your employer to a guest in the house. Or to anyone. I'm sure Mr. Jackson the butler would be very cross if he heard you."

She put a hand to her mouth and looked frightened. "I'm ever so sorry, miss. You won't tell him, will you?"

"No, of course I won't. I only spoke of it to save you getting into trouble in future. Now go and tell her ladyship I'll be joining her very soon."

"Yes, miss, thank you, miss."

I did not have time to think very much about what Ethel had said regarding Henry, for two minutes later I was making my way down the wide stairway that curved from the gallery to the main hall below. When I entered the drawing room Lady Whitchurch had just finished pouring some tea, and she looked up to say, "Ah, there you are Jemimah. That was commendably quick, child. Come and sit down."

I heard her words and answered politely, but my whole attention was on the lady who sat at one end of the chesterfield, a long peacock feather in her elegant hat still bobbing slightly from the movement of her head as she turned to look at me. I had never in my life seen a woman of such beauty. She was, I judged, in her late twenties, with the confidence and maturity of a married woman at that age. Her figure was shapely, her complexion flawless, and if her features were not perfectly regular this only added to her beauty by giving her human charm and distinction. Her hair was reddish gold, her teeth very white, her eyes an extraordinary indigo blue.

This was not all. The warmth and sparkle of her eyes bespoke the most friendly of natures, and there seemed to emanate from her an aura of good will and generosity, completely unforced, touched with light-hearted good humor and a readiness to laugh that was almost impish. Never in my life had any person made such a powerful impression on me. I might have felt gauche and tongue-tied at such an impact, but her direct gaze was so welcoming that I simply felt glad.

Lady Whitchurch was saying as I came forward, "This is our young guest, Jemimah, who joined Henry in his latest series of escapades under most unusual circumstances." She turned her cool gaze on me. "Jemimah, I present Mrs. Anne Galliard."

"My dear, what a pleasure it is to meet you." The lady's voice matched her physical beauty as she smiled and gave me her hand.

I found myself responding to her smile as if to an old friend and said, "How do you do, Mrs. Galliard."

"I am so very glad I ventured to call," she said, glancing at her hostess apologetically, "and equally glad that Lady Whitchurch was kind enough to receive me, particularly now I have learned that dear Henry has returned home after one of his extraordinary adventures." She patted the chesterfield. "Come and sit with me, Jemimah. I am longing to hear what that rascal has been up to this time, if Lady Whitchurch permits."

"Nothing to his credit," said Lady Whitchurch, and poured tea for me. "How is it that you are dressed and down before him, Jemimah? A man has far less to do than a female in making himself presentable."

"I believe he lingered to have a word with the groom," I said. This was untrue, but I was not averse to a white lie if it diverted criticism from Henry. Two things were puzzling me. First, I felt that Lady Whitchurch's manner toward the delightful Mrs. Galliard was perhaps adequate but a little less than gracious, and I could not imagine why. Secondly, I wondered how it was that Mrs. Galliard could refer so familiarly to Henry as a rascal.

Next moment she answered my unspoken question. "My husband was at school with Henry and they went up to Oxford together. He was best man at our wedding seven years ago, and I first met him a year earlier than that, so I am well acquainted with the way in which he flings himself into the most bizarre escapades."

"This year," said Lady Whitchurch a little grimly, "he has been, as he calls it, working the fairgrounds, first as a pugilist, then selling homemade medicine to gullible yokels, and finally becoming a Punch and Judy man."

Mrs. Galliard's eyes were full of laughter and she made no attempt to hide it, for which I warmed toward her. Not everybody would dare to show amusement at something that clearly did not amuse Lady Whitchurch. "But how very exciting!" Mrs. Galliard exclaimed. She looked at me. "I gather that you joined him at Oakhurst. How did that come about, Jemimah?"

"It's rather a long story, Mrs. Galliard. I happened to be there when Henry was giving a performance, and he almost choked on his swazzle. That's the little thing which is held against the roof of the mouth to make Punch's voice squeaky. I was able to help when it happened, and afterward Henry offered me the opportunity to become his assistant." I glanced at Lady Whitchurch, and when I received no warning look from her I continued with the simple truth. "I was in great difficulty at the time, with no home or resources, and so I was very thankful to take up Henry's offer."

Mrs. Galliard nodded slowly, no longer smiling. "Yes," she said gently. "Lady Whitchurch has told me of your dilemma."

If it had been anyone other than Mrs. Galliard I would have felt unhappy that Lady Whitchurch had revealed this part of my story, for she would doubtless have indicated that in her opinion I was suffering from a delusion; but for some reason beyond my own understanding I did not care that Mrs. Galliard had been told. Now she smiled again and said with a roguish widening of her splendid eyes, "Was Henry a very good Punch and Judy man?"

Before I could answer the door opened and Henry himself came in. He had changed into a beautifully cut gray suit and was more elegantly dressed than I had ever seen him. I had also never seen him in his present mood or manner as he came across the room, greeted Mrs. Galliard, shook her hand warmly, and seated himself in an upright chair facing her. Ethel's word "gooey" came to my mind, for it was plain to see that Lord Henry Boot was deeply enamored of Mrs. Anne Galliard.

For a moment I thought such obvious admiration would embarrass her but then realized that with her remarkable beauty and warm personality she no doubt received the same kind of devotion from men both young and old and must be well accustomed to it. I felt my own admiration for her increase with the thought that all this seemed neither to have spoiled her nor made her in the least degree vain.

I took little part in the conversation that followed, except to add a comment here or there to Henry's tales when Mrs. Galliard put a question to me. Once or twice I felt a little sad that he was putting himself out so strenuously to amuse and entertain her, for I knew he was at his most amusing when simply being himself, but apart from this I enjoyed the half hour or so of conversation that followed.

After a little while it struck me as odd that Henry did not ask after Mrs. Galliard's husband, who after all had been a friend of his since boyhood, but then it occurred to me that most men would probably be envious of the man fortunate enough to have Anne Galliard as a wife and would instinctively avoid speaking of him, while she in her wisdom would understand this and therefore make no attempt to bring him into the conversation.

I was disappointed when at last she looked at her wristwatch and said, "I asked for the station cab to be sent for me at half past four o'clock, and it will be here now, so I must say my good-byes." She rose to her feet, and Henry and I rose with her as she said, "Thank you so much,

Lady Whitchurch, and I do hope you will call upon us whenever you come to London."

Lady Whitchurch inclined her head. "Most kind of you, Mrs. Galliard, but I rarely go far from Torringtons. Henry, please ring for Jackson to see Mrs. Galliard out."

"Very well, Mamma."

Henry's usual easy manner was absent, and I knew he was feeling as I felt myself, that his mother might have shown a little more warmth to their guest. Mrs. Galliard seemed quite unruffled, however. As she drew on her gloves she smiled at Lady Whitchurch and said, "If at any time you can spare Jemimah, and if she herself is willing, I should be most grateful to have her come to us at Stanford Square as a companion to me for as long as she may find convenient—and at a suitable remuneration, of course. I am sure we would get along very well together. As you know, my husband is an archaeologist, and his work sometimes takes him away from home, so I should be glad to have a companion as congenial and as interesting as Jemimah."

I was completely taken aback by her words and at the same time greatly flattered. Flushing a little, I said, "Oh, how very kind of you to say so—"

Lady Whitchurch cut in. "Most generous, and I'm sure we shall bear your kind suggestion in mind, Mrs. Galliard."

"That is all I ask, Lady Whitchurch, and please be assured I have no intention of stealing Jemimah from you." As Jackson entered, leaving the doors open, Anne Galliard looked from one to the other of us with her affectionate smile. "Good-bye, Lady Whitchurch, and thank you again for such a happy time with you. Good-bye, Henry dear. Do call upon us in London. Good-bye, Jemimah, I shall pray that your problems may soon be happily resolved."

When Jackson bowed her out and closed the door it seemed to me that the room was a little darker for her going, and I sensed that for Henry this feeling ran even deeper.

After a little silence his mother said, "Now that your friend's wife has gone you can stop making sheep's eyes and play a game of cribbage with me, Henry. The cards are in the bureau."

"Sheep's eyes? Oh, really, Mamma—" he began in quick protest, then shrugged and smiled his old easy smile. "Never mind. Will you join us in a game, Mim? We can make it three-hand crib."

*   *   *

I had been so impressed by Mrs. Anne Galliard that I would have liked to talk about her and ask questions, but since neither Henry nor his mother mentioned her visit again, I thought it better not to refer to her myself. Lady Whitchurch clearly did not share my opinion of her visitor, and I had no wish to debate the question, while Henry on the other hand was obviously so captivated by her that I feared to embarrass him.

A few days later a small incident occurred which I scarcely took notice of at the time, but which I was to recall under strange circumstances in the future. We were sitting at breakfast when Henry turned from the sideboard where he had been serving himself from the chafing dishes there and said, "Why does Wilkinson send a man two days running to wind and adjust the clocks, Mamma?"

I knew that Mr. Wilkinson had a clock-making business in Granger and that he sent a man once a week to wind all the clocks in Torringtons and adjust them where necessary. Lady Whitchurch looked up from her kidney omelet and said, "Two days running? Nonsense, dear. He comes on a Friday morning. It's usually that plump man with the leather waistcoat and red face."

"Yes, I saw him yesterday." Henry sat down at the table, gave me a smile, and went on: "But who was the little dark fellow I saw upstairs on Thursday, doing something to the grandfather clock on the gallery? I've never seen him before."

I said, "Was he wearing a baize apron and carrying a bag of tools, Henry?"

"That's right. Round face with lots of wrinkles, like an elderly cherub."

"Oh, I saw him too, but I didn't know he was from Wilkinson's. He was moving along the passage and wished me good morning very politely. I thought he was a workman I hadn't seen before, a plumber or carpenter, perhaps."

"No, he was seeing to the clocks, Mim. I know, because I stopped and asked him. That's why I was surprised to see the usual clock fellow driving off in his trap yesterday morning."

Lady Whitchurch said rather vaguely, "We did have a different man come one day last year when the regular man was ill, but I can't remember if he looked like an elderly cherub."

Henry shrugged. "It's not important, Mamma. Our goods and chattels appear to be intact, so the cherub can't have been a sneak thief. It was probably a mix-up of some sort at Wilkinson's, with this fellow being given the wrong instructions or the wrong address. Mim, my lamb, my treasure, my angel of mercy, could you possibly pour coffee for me? I long to do it for myself, but my legs refuse to obey me."

I laughed as I got up and went to the sideboard, but Lady Whitchurch stared down the table with some concern. "What is wrong with your legs, Henry?"

"They're just sulking, Mamma. Probably because they're lonely."

"Lonely? What on earth can you mean?"

"Men's legs are trousered, Mamma, each one alone and solitary, confined in its dark cylindrical prison of worsted or barathea. Imagine how lonely they must feel—"

"I shall do no such thing, Henry! Men's legs are not a suitable subject for discussion in female company. Your brother George would never have mentioned such a thing."

Henry grimaced woefully at me as I put down his cup of coffee. "Thanks, Mim," he murmured. My head was turned away from his mother, so I was able to close one eye in a wink of sympathetic understanding. He grinned and said, "You're quite right, Mamma. George wouldn't mention such a thing. I don't think he ever made a joke in his life."

I was used to Henry's wild flights of fancy and enjoyed hearing him play with words, often piling absurd notion upon absurd notion. I regretted that his mother found such humor incomprehensible, but there was nothing I could do to help her find amusement in it, for I had good reason to know that response to humor could never be taught. In Shul it had been considered a great joke to use the head of an executed prisoner for the game similar to polo their horsemen played, but I had never learned to laugh at this, and neither had Sandru, even after all his long years in Shul.

Four days later I woke at sunrise and went to sit by the window in my dressing gown, looking out over the gardens and wishing I did not have to wait at least an hour before I could ring for Ethel to bring hot water for my bath. As usual, I was ashamed of myself for entertaining such a trivial wish and made myself remember the constant fear and hardship of the life I had been living not many months ago.

After a while I decided to read another chapter from my present book, Mr. Thomas Hardy's *Far from the Madding Crowd*, then changed my mind and resolved to tidy the drawers of the cabinet beside my bed.

When I moved to the cabinet I was astonished to see, lying on top of it and half hidden by the base of the candlestick standing there, a gold locket on a chain, oval in shape and with delicate chasing around the rim. I had never seen it before and could not imagine how it came to be in my room.

I examined the chain and clasp. Both were intact, so the locket had not fallen accidentally from its wearer. With a thumbnail I opened it on its tiny hinges. Inside were two exquisite miniature paintings, one each side, the colors glowing like jewels. That on the left was of an attractive young woman, her hair arranged in a style that had gone out of fashion before I was born. I recognized her at once by the forehead and the eyes, the high cheekbones and the small straight nose. This was Henry's mother, the Most Honorable the Marchioness of Whitchurch, painted well over thirty years ago.

The picture on the right was equally perfect in detail and showed a man, a few years older, with enough of his neck and chest showing to reveal that he wore the scarlet jacket of a soldier. This, I realized, must be the Marquess of Whitchurch himself, the husband who had run away to live with a mistress in Venice some twelve years ago now. Henry had not told me that his father was once a soldier, but I knew it was normal practice for one son of any family in the nobility to serve in the Army or Navy.

I guessed that the paintings had been made either during the engagement or soon after the marriage. Henry had said that it was an arranged marriage, but to me as I gazed upon the two faces there seemed a bond of very deep love emanating from each, caught marvelously well by the artist. Sorrow touched my heart at the thought that this love had died with the passing years. The man had turned his back on wife, family, and country. The woman, according to her son, Henry, had not been distressed at her husband's going and simply claimed that they had never been well suited.

Perhaps, I thought, she had made herself appear not to care as a matter of pride. I looked again at the tiny portrait of the man. It was a good face, strong and intelligent, with wide-set eyes and thick brown hair curling back behind the ears. As I gazed, I was suddenly swept by an extraordinary feeling of shock that left me quite bemused for a few moments. It was as if I had been vouchsafed some startling revelation simply by looking at the picture, yet there was nothing new in my mind, no recognition or strange disclosure.

Even as I stood wondering what quirk of imagination had brought this feeling abruptly upon me, my bedroom door was flung open without warning and Lady Whitchurch strode in. She wore a dressing gown and looked much the same as when I had first seen her on the night I had followed Henry from the wagon, but on that occasion she had been calm and composed, whereas now her face was pale, as if with shock. I felt quick alarm, knowing that something serious must have happened for her to burst into my room in this way, and I said, "Lady Whitchurch, whatever is it?"

Her eyes fell on the locket I held, and she stopped short, breathing deeply, her body shaking a little. "Oh, you brazen, ungrateful creature!" she said in a tremulous voice. "How could you do such a thing?"

I was utterly bewildered by her words, and now it dawned on me that the pallor of her face was caused as much by anger as by shock. "Do . . . do what such thing?" I said blankly.

"How could you steal from me?" There was a look almost of hatred in her eyes, underlaid by a blend of sorrow and disappointment. "How could you?"

The accusation left me stunned. I looked down at the locket, then again at Lady Whitchurch, and at last I managed to say, "This? But I don't know where it came from. I found it on my cabinet just a few moments ago."

She moved forward, her eyes stony with contempt, and took the locket carefully from my nerveless hands. "You stole it," she said bitterly, her voice harsh with emotion. "You came to my room like a thief in the night, like the thief that you are, and you stole my most precious possession."

"No," I stammered, shrinking back from the force of her anger. "No, truly . . . I found it—"

She went on speaking as if she had not heard, holding the locket tenderly in one hand, looking down at it. "For many long years I have worn this about my neck, never for the world to see, but always hidden beneath my dress. At night it lies beside me on my cabinet"—her head came up and she fixed me with a gaze of shriveling disgust—"and at some hour of last night, you entered and took it."

"But—"

Her other hand came up, holding a small blue ribbon stitched to form a tiny bow, and I stopped short with sudden fear creeping up my spine, for this was one of a dozen or more similar bows with which my nightdress was decorated. "I found this on the floor near my bedside cabinet," Lady Whitchurch said, her voice steady now but cold as arctic air. "It is from your nightdress, Jemimah. Will you tell me that somebody *else* took my locket last night? That somebody *else* has a garment with just such a ribbon as this missing from it? And that somebody *else* brought the locket to your room while you slept? One of the servants, perhaps? Or my son Henry?"

I moved to the dressing table and opened my dressing gown with trembling hands. In the looking glass I saw that one of the decorative blue bows was missing from the neck of my nightdress, and the fear within me grew deeper yet, for it now seemed that during the night I had committed an act of theft without retaining the slightest recollection of what I had done.

Desperately I sought some other explanation, some other culprit. A servant? But for what reason? I had made no enemies in Torringtons. Henry? Absurd! Lady Whitchurch herself for some obscure reason? Impossible. Her anger and her disappointment were all too real. I stood gazing at myself in the looking glass, seeing myself as a stranger who had committed an act I knew nothing about and wondering if this was all of a piece with my belief that I was Jemimah Lawley.

"Well?" The single word was like a stone hitting a windowpane.

I turned around, forcing myself to meet her gaze, and said, "Lady Whitchurch, I did not steal your locket. Or if . . . if I did take it, I have no memory of doing so."

She made a sound of contemptuous disbelief and turned away to close the door. When she turned back she had gained control of herself, with only the pallor of her cheeks to show the storm of emotion that had swept her. Now she looked past me as she spoke, and her voice was as remote as if we occupied different worlds.

"You realize you cannot remain here?"

At the moment I did not care what happened to me, but I would have given anything to be able to convince her that I was not guilty of stealing from her by intention, or indeed of hurting her in any way after all the kindness she had shown me. But I knew it was hopeless to plead or argue, and I said simply, "Yes, Lady Whitchurch."

She seemed to struggle with herself inwardly for a moment or two, then said stiffly, "I am aware that my son will never believe ill of you. Even if you were to confess to him, he would still not believe it."

I did not understand what was behind her words, and I said, "I have nothing to confess, Lady Whitchurch. I knew nothing of your locket until I found it by my bed this morning. It is as hard for me to believe that I took it without knowing what I did as it is for me to think of any other possible explanation."

She made a small gesture of impatience, and as she did so the blue bow fell from her hand and fluttered to the floor. "My only concern," she said, "is that if I tell Henry that I am sending you away, and why, he will leave Torringtons again and go off on one of his interminable escapades. I should therefore prefer him to believe that you are leaving by your own wish. I imagine you also would prefer this, since it will save you a great deal of embarrassment."

My mind was still dull with shock, and only gradually did it dawn on me that Lady Whitchurch was, in a curious way, asking a favor of me. It was probably true that Henry would not believe I had stolen the locket, despite the evidence, and it was probably true that if she turned me out for this he would not stay long at Torringtons. Her other son was far away, Henry was all she had of close family now, and beneath her cool exterior she was a lonely woman.

After a little silence I said, "What reason can I give for leaving? He will never accept some vague excuse, Lady Whitchurch. He will want to know where I am going, and why."

I caught a hint of relief in her at my acceptance of what she had asked, and she moved across the room to stand gazing out of the window for a few moments. Then she said slowly, "He would accept the notion of your going to London as a companion to Anne Galliard. That was an offer he would consider attractive to you, and there is also the point that you wish to be in London in order to pursue certain matters concerning proof of your identity by way of the War Office, is that not so?"

I said, "Yes. But are you willing for me to go to Mrs. Galliard when you believe me to be a thief?"

"I have only slight acquaintance with Mrs. Galliard," she said coldly, "and it is not for me to bring to her notice what I believe. You claim you are innocent, do you not?"

"Yes, Lady Whitchurch."

She turned from the window. "Then it is not for me to say otherwise. Anne Galliard invited you of her own free will. If you write and accept, I imagine you will have a reply by return of post. She seemed most eager for you to join her. Meanwhile I shall keep to my bed for a few days and let it be known that I have a migraine. This will prevent Henry detecting any estrangement between us." She stared at me with hard eyes. "Is it agreed, then? The matter of the locket is to be forgotten, and you are leaving by your own wish?"

I found I was beginning to shiver a little as I said, "Yes, Lady Whitchurch."

"Very well."

She moved to the door and opened it, then paused to look at me once more. In a low voice she said, "You cannot imagine how cruelly disappointed I am."

I could think of nothing to say, and in any event she did not wait for a reply but went out, closing the door quietly after her. I moved to sit on the bed, shoulders hunched, inwardly chilled, hugging myself, wondering what had truly occurred in the night just past, yet not wanting to think too deeply upon it lest I be driven to accept that there was some part of me that acted without my knowledge or control, for this was a thought too fearful to be borne.

Somehow I contrived to maintain my usual manner with Henry that day, though it meant constant effort that had to be concealed from him. When we drove out to the river to spend the afternoon fishing, I told him that I had written to Mrs. Galliard to say I would like to take up her offer of employment as her companion. I was sitting on a folding stool, the picnic basket beside me, and Henry sat with his rod a few feet from the edge of the bank, under the shade of a sycamore, idly watching his float. By his own admission he was not a serious fisherman, and he was quite content to return home empty-handed. His pleasure, he declared gravely, came from an inward communing with the spirits of field and forest, earth and water, combined with an occasional shout of warning to scare the fish away and so save them from a distressing end.

When I told him what I had done, he sat pondering for a few seconds, then said, "Is that what you want, Mim, to go to Anne Galliard in London?"

"Yes, I really feel I must, Henry." That was mostly true, though it was not really an answer to his question. I opened a bottle of ale, filled a pewter mug, and took it to him, then rested my hand on his shoulder. "You're not cross with me?"

He turned his head so that I could see his face and gave me a smile. "Cross? Good Lord, no, but I'll miss you, Mim."

"Miss me?" I had never considered this.

"Of course I shall. I'm used to you."

I laughed and went back to my seat. "You were used to that dreadful top hat you always wore, but I'm sure you don't miss it."

"Ah, well," he said vaguely. Then, "What made you decide to go to Anne?"

I told the lie I had prepared for this question. "I can't go on indefinitely living as a guest in Torringtons. Both you and your mother have been more than kind, but . . . well, I'm living on your charity, and it dawned on me last night that if I took Mrs. Galliard's offer I would at least be in employment as a companion. That's the main point, but it's also true that if I'm in London I shall have a better chance of making inquiries about Caspar."

"Caspar . . . yes," Henry said thoughtfully. "Well, I'm sure you'll be happy with Anne. She's a wonderful person in every way."

The difficult moment was past, and I breathed an inward sigh of relief as I said, "Yes, I was greatly taken with her. You hardly expect anyone so beautiful to be so kind and unspoiled."

Henry nodded. "I share your feeling," he said. Reeling in his line, he examined the hook, affixed fresh bait, and cast the line again. "I shall probably call at Stanford Square when I'm up in London, so I shall see something of you then, Mim."

"Oh, I shall enjoy that. I mean, if Mrs. Galliard accepts me. I have yet to hear from her."

"I'm sure she didn't make her offer lightly."

We sat quietly for a few minutes, then I said, "Henry, you won't go away on one of your escapades if I leave, will you?"

"Oh . . . I don't know. I might."

"Please don't. It means so much to your mother to have you here."

"What?" He turned to look at me in surprise.

I sighed. "Why are men so dense? You're all she has left of close family, and she wants you here."

"Well . . ." He pushed his cap back on his head and stretched his mouth in a grimace. "I can't stay here doing nothing forever. I even find it difficult just talking to Mamma, because we don't seem to understand each other. It's all right with you here, Mim, but—"

I broke in quickly, letting my anxiety show. "Please, Henry, I know it isn't easy for you, but please remain after I go, even if it's only for a few months. Your mother is a very lonely lady and she has suffered a great hurt by your father leaving. She hides her loneliness and pain very well, but she feels them deeply."

He gave me a baffled look. "I expect you're right, Mim, but in some ways she's always invited loneliness and pain. She's so withdrawn and often so unfriendly. Look how she was with Anne last week."

"Please, Henry."

He sighed and shrugged. "I can't stay forever, but . . . well, I'll stay

at least until Christmas. And I wouldn't do that for anyone other than a
girl who got a swazzle out of my gullet for me."

"I'm truly grateful, Henry. Thank you. And your float's bobbing
about, I believe you've caught a fish."

He turned with a look of consternation. "Oh, damn! Poor little devil.
That's because I forgot to shout."

*   *   *

Four days later I left the great house called Torringtons, making my
farewell to Lady Whitchurch in her bedroom, where she had remained
since the morning when she came to accuse me of stealing her locket. It
was a brief farewell, with little said.

Sitting up in bed with spectacles on her nose and a book on her lap,
she looked at me distantly and said, "I sent for you because Henry would
have thought it most odd if I had not wished to say good-bye."

I made a small curtsy. "Yes, Lady Whitchurch, and I'm glad of the
opportunity to thank you for your hospitality and kindness toward me."

"Fine words," she said dryly.

I bit my lip and struggled to keep my voice steady as I said, "They are
truly meant, Lady Whitchurch, and I am happy to tell you that Henry
has assured me he will certainly remain here at Torringtons at least until
Christmas."

She inclined her head stiffly. "I am obliged to you."

"Well . . . good-bye, Lady Whitchurch."

"Good-bye."

I went from the room and down the stairs, already dressed for the
journey. The landau was waiting on the flagged apron in front of the
portico, my luggage aboard, a coachman and carriage groom sitting up
on the box ready to drive off to the station. Lord Henry was strolling idly
about, hands in his pockets.

"Ah, there you are, Mim."

"Yes, I've seen your mother. Good-bye for now, and thank you again
for everything, Henry."

"I'm coming to see you off at the station."

"There's no need—"

"Oh, rubbish."

He grinned, took my hand, steadied me as I mounted the small step to
the open carriage, then climbed in beside me. We did not talk much on
the twenty-minute drive to the station, but this was not an awkward

silence. We were friends who knew each other well now and had no need to make conversation when there was nothing of importance to be said.

Once he patted my hand and murmured in a voice too low for the coachmen to hear, "What did Anne say she would pay you, Mim?"

His question gave me no embarrassment. We had eagerly counted the pennies and ha'pennies from too many meager collections for that. I mouthed quietly, "Thirty pounds a year."

He nodded. "That's about right. Slightly generous if anything."

"It seems handsome to me."

"Have you anything in your purse to be going on with?"

"Plenty. You paid me half a crown a week, remember? I've hardly spent any of it."

He threw back his head and chuckled. "Rich girl."

When the train came, he saw my luggage safely aboard, tipped the porter, kissed me on the cheek as casually as if I had been his sister, and said, "Don't be angry with me, Mim."

"Angry?" I was puzzled. "Why should I be?"

He rolled his eyes despairingly in an expression familiar to me now. "Just don't be, that's all. Off you go, my angel."

He handed me up into the compartment. The guard waved a flag and blew his whistle. I struggled to open the window and managed it as the train moved off. "Henry!" I called. "What did you mean?" But the distance between us was rapidly increasing, and with cap in hand he was in the process of making an elaborate bow. He straightened up and waved. I waved back, and a few moments later the curve of the rails brought the back of the train between us to hide him from my view.

I half closed the window and sat down, feeling rather strange. I had recovered from the main impact of the shock I had sustained five days before, but I did not want to think about what had happened. It was still deeply painful to know that Lady Whitchurch believed me to be a deliberate thief, and still frightening to wonder if I might have committed a theft unconsciously, walking in my sleep.

I had the compartment to myself at present, and for a while I puzzled over Lord Henry's last curious words, but eventually I put the matter aside with a small inward smile, thinking that with an eccentric person like Henry there was no knowing what he might say or do or mean from one minute to the next.

Watching the fields and hedgerows, the little farms and cottages as they flashed by, I found myself remembering the miniature painting of Henry's father in one side of the gold locket, facing the miniature of his young wife or fiancée. Here were two people who had been deeply in love, and almost forty years later the woman still wore that locket secretly under her dress and kept it beside her bed at night, even though the man had left her for another woman. Yet, according to Henry, his mother had in some way brought this pain and loneliness upon herself by being withdrawn and unfriendly. How could she have been so, I wondered, toward the husband she loved so dearly?

No answer came to me, and a little later, without quite knowing why, I found myself thinking of Sandru. At the same time I felt an extraordinarily deep pang of grief, and my eyes filled with tears. I had often thought of Sandru since that night when I had left him. He had been about to take the strong narcotic drug that would be his only protection against Deenbur's suspicions, while I trod the first anxious steps of a long, strange, and tortuous journey that after so many shocks and alarms had brought me to this present moment; but I had never before thought of Sandru in quite the way that I was thinking of him now, with grief and anxiety.

As the train carried me on to London, as other passengers entered the compartment at stations along the way, I sat visualizing Sandru on his own, without me to serve and help him. I had been his servant for only eighteen months, and he had managed well enough without me through all the years before, but he had been younger then. He would no doubt continue to manage well enough for a few years yet if his health remained good, but in time there must come a day when he would no longer be able to practice his skills, perhaps from failing eyesight, or failing memory, or some other disability of the old.

Then there would be nobody to care for him as I would have cared for him. In the remote and barbaric kingdoms of the Hindu Kush, gratitude was short-lived. The men and women Sandru had healed would care nothing for him when he was of no further use to them. With my eyes closed I said a prayer for Sandru, asking that he might die in peace before that cruel day came. Most people would have thought me wicked, but I had lived in Shul, and I knew I would have prayed the same way for myself.

At Waterloo Station there was much competition for the porters with their trolleys, and I found myself outwitted and outshouted by more experienced passengers, so I was left to wait with my luggage on the platform until one of the porters returned. In less than a minute I saw a man in coachman's uniform coming along the platform toward me with a porter following. As the man drew near he took off his hat and said,

"Excuse me, miss, are you the young lady for number 12 Stanford Square?"

I said, "Yes, I am. Did Mrs. Galliard send you to meet me?"

"That's right, miss."

"How very kind of her. I was intending to take a cab."

"No need for that, miss." He turned to the porter. "All right, m'lad. Get the lady's luggage on your trolley, then follow me."

Three minutes later I was riding out of Waterloo Station in a comfortable town-and-country carriage. For the journey that day I had put on a walking costume of navy serge plain cloth that Lady Whitchurch had bought for me on our shopping expedition, and with it I wore a matching toque hat with the brim edged in white. I felt suitably dressed for taking up employment as a companion, and I was eager to see the beautiful Mrs. Anne Galliard again, but I could not help feeling nervous as we made our way across Waterloo Bridge and along the Strand to Trafalgar Square. Soon we were moving along Piccadilly, with a fine park on our left, but then we turned away from the park and continued through a maze of streets until at last we came to a square enclosing an area of grass and plane trees in the center, with fine houses along each side.

The coachman handed me down and said, "I'll take your luggage round the back to the mews, miss, and Mr. Edge will have it carried up from there. He's the butler, miss."

The man who opened the door to me was short and plump but with an air of dignity, his head bald in the center with wings of thick graying hair on each side.

"Miss Lawley? Ah, come in, please, miss. We have been expecting you. I am Edge the butler. This way, if you please."

He led me across a spacious hall to a pleasant morning room. "If you will be seated, I shall inform Mrs. Galliard of your arrival."

"Thank you, Edge."

He inclined his head and left the room, closing the doors after him. I reflected that he had called me Miss Lawley, which meant that this was the name given him by Mrs. Galliard. I also reflected that if I was not Jemimah Lawley I must at least have been brought up in circumstances where I knew that it was correct for a companion to address a butler simply by his surname, even though both were employees of the family.

No more than a minute passed before the doors opened and Mrs. Galliard entered, her beauty striking me afresh as if I had forgotten how truly handsome she was. Her dress was of primrose-yellow spotted muslin with an underdress of white silk taffeta. The muslin was trimmed with lace, but otherwise there was no ornamentation, and the simple line suited her perfectly. As before, her manner was no less enchanting than her looks, and she greeted me warmly, a smile of welcome in those wide indigo eyes.

"Dear Jemimah, I'm so pleased you have come. How was the journey? Not too tiring, I hope?"

I said, "No, it wasn't at all tiring, Mrs. Galliard, and I'm very happy to be here."

"Oh, that's splendid. I'm sure you will enjoy yourself. London is an exciting city, even though the season is over now, and you will have plenty of spare time to follow your own pursuits if you wish. But we can discuss all that later. First I will show you your room, and by the time you have tidied up after your journey I think we shall be ready to have luncheon served. Come along, my dear."

With the friendliest of gestures she took my hand, and together we moved toward the door. I began to thank her for sending the carriage to meet me at Waterloo, but as we reached the door I heard a man's voice calling across the hall. Next moment we had crossed the threshold and I saw the speaker, a tall figure in a gray morning coat and striped trousers, taking hat, gloves, and a cane which Edge the butler was proffering.

The man had uttered only two or three words, and because I was speaking at the same time I had not been able to distinguish what he said, but something in the timbre of his voice made my every nerve jump with the shock of recognition, though I did not know what I had recognized. Then he spoke again, turning to face us as he did so.

"I shall be taking luncheon at my club, Melanie, so please excuse me —" I did not hear the few remaining words, for they were drowned by the pounding in my ears as my heart raced with new and greater shock.

Melanie? The name came back to me across many months and many thousands of miles, a name muttered by a man in delirium and close to death, lying beside me on the plains of Afghanistan. The same man had just spoken that same name, for the face across the hall was a face I would never forget while I lived; fair hair, blue eyes, lean cheeks, long chin like a wolf; this was the face of Kassim, the Afghan, who had brought me safely from Shul, and who had proved to be Caspar, the Englishman, when he had been shot by an enemy only four days' march from Herat.

XII

For an instant so brief that I could barely be sure of what I had seen, there was a lightning bolt of shock in the blue eyes, then it was gone, and all that remained was blankness touched by no more than a flicker of curiosity.

"I beg your pardon, Melanie," he said to Anne Galliard beside me. "I did not realize you were engaged."

She gave a little laugh. "I'm not engaged, my dear, but I have just engaged a companion to keep me company when you abandon me to dig up old bones in Egypt." There was no reproach in her voice; it was full of affection and she clearly spoke in jest. The butler was moving away now. The man stood holding his gloves, hat, and cane, and Mrs. Galliard continued, "I said nothing because I wished to surprise you, Caspar dear, and I was hoping to keep Jemimah hidden until luncheon, but now you have forestalled me, and you are to be out for luncheon anyway, so it is just as well that I shall have somebody to talk with."

Still holding my hand, she moved forward, saying, "And now I must introduce you. This is Jemimah Lawley, or so we believe, but there is a long story you must hear in that respect." She turned her lovely smile upon me. "Jemimah, this is my dear husband, Caspar Galliard."

He inclined his head, and the familiar eyes looked at me from a face equally familiar, though now without the tan of sun and weather. "Good morning, Jemimah," he said without enthusiasm.

My head felt about to burst with so much bewilderment, but for the moment I could not even formulate any coherent questions to ask myself. Automatically I dropped a small curtsy and responded, "Good morning, sir."

His wife said quickly, "Oh, let us not be formal. It is better that you call us Mr. and Mrs. Galliard, I think."

I said, "Yes, Mrs. Galliard," but I could not take my eyes from the face of the man before me, and I stammered, "Please . . . Mr. Galliard, don't you recognize me?"

Beside me I heard a little sigh as if of compassion. Mr. Galliard's eyebrows lifted in surprise. "You must forgive me if I cannot recall having made your acquaintance, Miss Lawley," he said. The words were polite but his manner was dismissive, and I struggled to hold back a flare of anger.

"But surely you remember our journey across Afghanistan last spring?" I said as calmly as I could.

"I was at a dig in Egypt all last spring and much of summer," he said with a hint of impatience, then spoke to his wife before I could say more. "Do excuse my absence from luncheon, Melanie, my dear. An important business matter to discuss. I shall be with you for dinner."

She said gladly, "Oh, we shall look forward to that, and I do hope your meeting goes well, Caspar. Good-bye, dear." He nodded briefly to me, moved to the front door, and went out.

Mrs. Galliard's hand was resting on my shoulder now, and she said gently, "I know that your experiences have given you rather muddled memories, Jemimah dear. Lady Whitchurch explained this to me, and I shall explain it to my husband. I simply want you to know that you need not worry about these moments when your mind plays little tricks. We shall quite understand, and I am sure the problem will pass with time."

I turned to look at her, about to protest that my mind was not playing tricks and that I had once cut a bullet out of her husband's body before nursing him for four days across sixty harsh miles of Afghanistan. But my protest remained unspoken, for although my mind was a jumble of confused thoughts at this moment, I was able to see that it would be madness for me to claim that Mr. Caspar Galliard was quite simply lying. Nobody would ever believe me, and even if it could be shown that he had scars on his body from a recent bullet wound, this would do little to prove my claim. There had been troubles in Egypt earlier in the year, so I had read, and it would not be out of the question for an archaeologist working there to have become embroiled in some outburst of shooting.

Beneath these thoughts lay others, and they so frightened me that I tried unsuccessfully to smother them. Was I quite, quite sure that Mr. Galliard was lying? Perhaps there were no scars on his body. Could I ever be entirely sure about what had happened to me during the journey from Shul? Was it possible that on seeing Mr. Galliard I had imposed his face on the face of the man with whom I had journeyed across Afghanistan? And how true was my memory of the name Caspar?

It was all too much for me to untangle at this moment, and I tried to smile as I said, "Thank you, Mrs. Galliard, and I'm so sorry if I embarrassed your husband just now."

She laughed and slipped her arm through mine, leading me toward the stairs. "Oh, don't worry about Caspar. He will have forgotten it within a few moments, bless him."

As we mounted the stairs I heard an echo in my mind, the distant sound of a feverish voice muttering, *"Melanie . . . Stormswift . . . daughter of Electra. Beautiful . . . so beautiful."* Then: *"Bitch-goddess."*

I said, "Excuse me, but Lady Whitchurch introduced you to me as Mrs. Anne Galliard, and that is the name Lord Henry used, but I noticed your husband uses a different name."

"Yes, isn't it confusing?" she said lightly. "I have Melanie as a middle name, and from the time we were engaged Caspar always preferred it and always called me by that name."

I said, "Oh, I see." But I did not see. I was wondering if I had remembered or imagined the name I had heard whispered in the Afghan wilderness together with those other puzzling words. There was so much I did not see, but I realized that if I allowed myself to be distracted I would make a very bad impression during my first hours as a companion to Mrs. Anne Melanie Galliard, and with an effort I closed my mind to all speculation until I could be on my own with time to think.

During the next hour I washed my face and hands, tidied my hair, then left my room to be shown over the house and introduced to the small staff of servants while a maid unpacked my luggage. Number 12 Stanford Square was larger than it appeared from the outside, and furnished with great taste. There was a small garden between the back of the house and the mews where the stables and coach house lay. Mrs. Galliard's manner toward the servants was so informal as to be almost friendly, yet this did not bring any hint of familiarity in response, and it was clear to me that they held their mistress in rare affection.

We took luncheon at a small table on the covered terrace outside the dining room, for the air was still mild. Only a light meal was served, and for this I was thankful. After my long captivity in Shul I had no appetite for the quantities of food normally served to English gentry. Even on the ship from India I had barely touched my luncheon and usually left more than a little on my plate at dinner. It had been the same at Torringtons, where I had a companion of similar feeling in Lord Henry. I was able to amuse Mrs. Galliard now by telling her how Lord Henry had declared that constant overeating was a vice of the English upper class and that true happiness lay in nourishing an appetite, encouraging it, tantalizing it, and bringing it to full and hearty development over a long period, then assuaging it by a splendid banquet, as we had done occasionally during our Punch and Judy days.

I was asked many questions about my travels with Lord Henry and answered them all quite truthfully, for so he had told me to answer his mother's questions. It became apparent that Mrs. Galliard was thoroughly familiar with Henry's eccentricities and had imagined that he was on one of his escapades abroad throughout the past months. She was greatly taken by the stories I was able to tell and only wished she might have seen one of our Punch and Judy performances.

Toward the end of luncheon I broached a matter that I felt I had to speak about without delay, and I said, "Mrs. Galliard, I'm not quite sure what Lady Whitchurch told you about me, but I feel bound to tell you that I do believe myself to be Jemimah Lawley, and I don't wish to be called anything else, but I'm beginning to realize that this may cause you and Mr. Galliard embarrassment, since everybody else except Lord Henry believes Jemimah Lawley to have been living at Witchwood Hall for the past two and a half years."

She had a gift for listening intently, and her beautiful indigo eyes did not leave my face as I spoke. Then she gave a small nod of reassurance and smiled at me. "We would never ask you to discard the name you believe to be yours, my dear. I confess I can see no way by which you might persuade the authorities to accept that the young woman in Witchwood Hall is a fraud, but in any event you are perfectly entitled to call yourself Jemimah Lawley, and that is how we shall call you."

That afternoon we went for a drive in Hyde Park, then visited the office of a children's charity in which Mrs. Galliard took a particular interest, and returned to receive calls at four o'clock. Two ladies paid a visit and chatted for about half an hour while they took tea with us, then departed. We spent some time in the sewing room, going over patterns and samples of fabric Mrs. Galliard's dressmaker had sent, then went to our rooms to rest for an hour before getting ready for dinner.

It was a great relief to me to be alone. I took off my dress and shoes, lay on the bed in my petticoat, and began trying to untangle the muddle in my mind. The first decision I made was that for the moment at least I would not doubt my own identity or my own memory, for if I allowed myself to believe that half my memories were imagination, then there could be no point in trying to solve the puzzles that beset me since I could not know if they were real.

Then came the problem of accepting as a coincidence the extraordinary fact that today, by purest chance, I had come to live in the house of the man who had brought me safely out of Shul and who knew from Sandru my true identity. I was aware that life did indeed hold many coincidences, but this was one to strain belief. Suddenly I sat up straight, then lay slowly back as a thought came to me. Perhaps, after all, there was no coincidence here. I had told Lord Henry Boot the whole story of my journey from Shul. I had described Kassim the Afghan, who was in fact Caspar the Englishman. Caspar was a rare enough name in England, and Lord Henry had been Caspar Galliard's friend from boyhood and best man at his wedding. From my description and that Christian name alone, he must surely have guessed at once that the man I sought was his friend, Caspar Galliard.

Why had he not said so? This baffled me, for I had lived long enough with Henry to know that he was my friend. His words came back to me now, the last words he had spoken when he saw me off on the train from Granger this morning: "Don't be angry with me, Mim." And when I had asked what he meant: "Just don't be, that's all."

So Lord Henry had known that I would come to Stanford Square and meet Caspar Galliard, the man I had brought wounded and unconscious to Herat, and he was apologizing in advance for not forewarning me. Then I recalled something else Henry had said, much earlier, and at first I could not quite remember why or when, but then it came to me. On the night I discovered that he was in truth a peer, and we had sat drinking tea in his wagon in the early hours while he told me of his family, I had asked if he had other secrets. His reply was that he had other people's secrets and they were not his to tell.

He could only have meant Caspar Galliard's secrets. Was it possible then that Henry had always known his friend's true profession? And did Mrs. Anne Melanie Galliard know?

A new and disconcerting thought struck me. If my coming to Caspar Galliard's house was not the coincidence it had at first seemed, because there was a strong link between Caspar and Lord Henry, then I was left with an equally great coincidence—that at Oakhurst I had by chance fallen in with one of the few men in England, perhaps the only man, who could have identified my companion of the journey from Shul to Herat. Again this was a coincidence that strained belief.

Unless . . .

A strange possibility occurred to me. I thought about it for a while, then decided that I would test it at the first opportunity. Perhaps, again, what appeared to be coincidence would prove to be something else.

My mind roved on from puzzlement about the past to considerations of the future. Since the day I had been turned away from Witchwood Hall, the one hope I had entertained of proving myself to be Jemimah Lawley was by discovering the identity of Caspar and calling him to witness. That hope now appeared to be vain.

Caspar Galliard had looked upon me and denied me. There was nothing I could do to make him speak. It was hard to resist feeling a tinge of bitterness as I lay gazing up at the ceiling with unfocused eyes, recalling what it had cost me to cut the killing bullet from his body, to cleanse the wound, and to bring him alive to Herat. I did not forget that he had brought me safely across half a thousand miles of the wildest and most dangerous land, but he had done so only because Sandru had compelled him. For his own part, he would have left me in Shul to suffer whatever might befall me.

Still . . . he had kept his word when he could easily have abandoned me in the mountains to die. He had done his duty. Yes . . . what was it Captain John Selby, the army doctor, had said about that? Again sudden recollection made me jump, for it brought both enlightenment and fresh bewilderment.

Speaking of Caspar on the voyage home, John Selby had said, ". . . I came to two conclusions about him. First, that he puts duty before all else, and second, that without realizing it himself he invites death."

Duty before all else. Now I knew why Caspar Galliard had denied knowing me. He was a spy, working in an area of the world where spying was endemic and where a single piece of information secured by one man could decide a battle or save a thousand lives, as John Selby had so forcefully pointed out to me. For several years "Kassim" had passed through Shul, and perhaps he would do so again next year, peddling his wares when the winter snows had gone from the high passes. But if he acknowledged publicly what he had done in bringing me out of captivity, he would destroy the secrecy on which his profession and his life depended. He would fail in his duty, and that he could not do.

My disappointment at realizing that I could expect no help from Caspar Galliard was surprisingly small. Perhaps, deep down, I had never truly believed that finding him would bring me back my home and fortune and birthright. Perhaps, too, after my long ordeal as Deenbur's wife, and the terrors and hardships of Shul, I was so thankful to be safe in my own country that I dared not long for better fortune, for fear that what I had might be taken from me.

I lay thinking about the second thing John Selby had said. How could it be, I wondered, that Caspar Galliard was a man who invited death, even though he might not realize this? If not rich, he was certainly in a very comfortable situation, with an excellent house in London and a staff of servants. Moreover, he was married to a woman whose nature was as warm and glowing as her beauty.

How then could he be a man so deeply unhappy as to invite death? Surely he was greatly to be envied by his fellows.

Melanie . . . bitch-goddess? That was quite impossible. If Caspar Galliard was a man of such unhappiness that life held nothing for him but to risk death, then it seemed the cause must lie deep within himself. It could not stem from his gentle and loving wife. Once I had hated this strange, austere man, so silent and unbending. Now I felt sad for him, but it was quite beyond my power to help, perhaps beyond anybody's power.

I closed my eyes and tried to think what I could do to prove my identity now that I knew Caspar Galliard would never speak for me, but my mind remained blank. Captain John Selby and Lord Henry Boot could say they believed me, but that meant nothing. Mr. Arthur Renwick, that small man with bright eyes like a squirrel, who had questioned me in Herat, might or might not believe me, but in any event he would give no more help than Caspar, and for the same reasons.

The fact was that I could think of nobody who could say with authority that I was Jemimah Lawley. To the world in general, as I had discovered so painfully that day in Oakhurst, the girl who had been living at Witchwood Hall for the past two years and more was firmly established as Jemimah Lawley, and I would be regarded as no more than a pretender to that name. In short, there was no hope of establishing the truth.

Unless . . . unless something were to happen that I could not even begin to envisage, something to prove to the world that my claim was true. Or prove to me that it was false.

*   *   *

Because Mrs. Galliard was so considerate and smoothed my path, it took only a few days for me to settle into a daily routine at Stanford Square.

When she learned that I always woke early, she arranged for my bath water to be brought an hour before the usual time, so that I could take a walk in the park before breakfast. This was an immense pleasure to me, for in Shul I had been accustomed to doing a lot of hard work before preparing breakfast, and the walk made something of a substitute for this. I always thought it the best part of the morning and returned with a good appetite.

My life in Shul, and later on the road with Henry and Paloma, had made it almost painful for me to be idle; I would quickly feel uneasy and begin to fidget, so I was happy to find that my days as a companion to Mrs. Galliard were quite full. She had an interest in a number of charities, and on most mornings this would occupy some of our time, either in visiting one of the offices or dealing with correspondence.

In the afternoons we might spend an hour chatting in the sewing room, or perhaps pay or receive "morning" calls, as they were so strangely termed. In Shul I had learned to stitch sheepskin or goatskin, but at neat or decorative sewing I was really very bad. Fortunately Mrs. Galliard sewed beautifully, and under her guidance I struggled to improve.

When we made or received calls, she always introduced me simply as "Jemimah Lawley, my companion." If anybody privately questioned that name, I never came to hear of it. We did not by any means go everywhere together, sometimes she would go off on her own, perhaps paying calls or to one of her charity offices; at other times she would sit reading in the library while I labored over my sewing, or she might herself settle down to some sewing, telling me with that endearing smile of hers to do as I pleased for the afternoon. I thought this practice wise, for it gave us fresh matters to talk about when we came together again.

A man called Johnson came twice a week to cut the grass in the small walled garden and to tidy the flower beds, but he was not a true gardener, as old Mr. Wickham at Torringtons had been, and there was little to show for his efforts except a few rather sad dahlias, asters, Michaelmas daisies, and some climbing roses that were rapidly getting out of hand. When I mentioned to Mrs. Galliard my talks with Mr. Wickham her eyes lit up.

"My dear, whyever don't you take charge of our little garden here? I believe there are several books upstairs in the library to guide you, and it would be so pleasant for Caspar to have a beautiful garden, for he looks out upon it from his study window when he is at his desk."

The outcome of this was that I took charge of Johnson on the two half

days that he came, and on other days would happily spend an hour with
gloves and secateurs, hoe and hand fork, pruning, planting bulbs for
spring, and working to prepare a better garden for next year, constantly
referring to notes I had made while reading up the subject.

By this time I had long since come to an unspoken understanding
with Caspar Galliard. On only the second occasion of my walking in the
park before breakfast I had been somewhat taken aback to encounter
him walking with long strides, cane tucked under his arm, hat in hand.
We happened to meet on paths that converged from either side of a
shrubbery, and we both stopped short in surprise. Until then I had
exchanged only a few words with Mr. Galliard since my arrival at Stanford Square, mainly at breakfast and dinner, for he appeared to spend
most of his time either out of the house or in his study, and on no
occasion had we been alone together. At table his manner had been
polite, but he had said little, and that mainly in response to remarks from
his wife, who smilingly apologized to me on his behalf, saying that he
was always rather quiet and distrait when engaged in writing.

It was then I discovered that Caspar Galliard was indeed an archaeologist, as his wife had said at Torringtons. He had written two books and
had several papers published by learned societies. "I feel he is as much an
explorer as an archaeologist," said Mrs. Galliard, her lovely eyes resting
on him affectionately, "for sometimes he goes off quite alone to the most
remote places, seeking for traces of ancient cities and the like. I am
sometimes quite worried about his health and safety in these uncivilized
parts."

I thought how much greater cause she would have to worry about his
health and safety if she had known the truth, which I was sure now she
did not, and I also thought that the work Caspar Galliard purported to
do, and no doubt had genuinely done from time to time, made the most
excellent concealment for his activities as a spy.

Apart from that brief instant when he had first set eyes on me in the
hall of number 12, he had never shown so much as a flicker of recognition, and even when we met in the park his surprise was no more than
seemed natural at an unexpected encounter with his wife's companion.

He gave a slight bow and said, "Good morning, Jemimah."

"Good morning, Mr. Galliard."

He was a man who hid his feelings well, but I sensed tension in him as
he stared just over the top of my head with a remote gaze. Since it would
have seemed stupid for either of us to turn back, we began to walk on

together, slowly at first, then more briskly, as we had both been doing when we met.

"You are abroad early," he said.

"Yes, Mr. Galliard, I am an early riser." As you well know, I added in my thoughts, remembering the times I had risen at dawn to start breakfast when we were journeying together. Aloud I added, "Mrs. Galliard was kind enough to arrange that I might take a walk before breakfast, if I wished."

"Yes," he said flatly. "I see." There was heaviness in the words that quite baffled me.

I said, "I hope I am not intruding upon you, Mr. Galliard?"

"Not at all," he replied without conviction, "not at all."

With an innocent air I said, "I feared you might be composing some lines for the book or paper you are writing about your recent archaeological expedition."

"No," he said slowly, and I almost thought I caught a distant note of humor in his voice. "No, I don't think I shall be doing that."

Since we were walking side by side, I could only see something of his face by turning my head to look up at him, and there was no more to be read in his austere expression now than there had been during those long days in the wilderness, but I sensed a gradual relaxation of the tension within him, and it dawned on me that since this was our first meeting alone he would of course be apprehensive, expecting me to challenge his denial of having known me before, but now he was relieved because I had not done as he expected.

Indeed, I had no intention of doing so, for I knew it would serve no purpose. Nevertheless, I believed that I had traveled across a huge and dangerous country with this man, I had slept beside him for half a hundred nights, I had seen him shot down, had cut a bullet out of his body, had sick-nursed him through fever, delirium, and unconsciousness; and now, if my belief was true, I could not resist letting him know that I was not so stupid as to accept his denial, or to accept that he had spent spring and summer in Egypt, as his wife believed.

"Mrs. Galliard is anxious about your health when you are traveling in foreign lands," I said. "I trust you suffered no ill health on your recent expedition to Egypt?"

We walked on in silence for a few seconds, then he said, "I was somewhat incapacitated by a fever following a severe mosquito bite."

After a few paces I said, "You encountered an uncommonly large mosquito, perhaps?"

He nodded stiffly. "Remarkably large. Fortunately my companion's medical knowledge proved invaluable."

I said, "I am glad to hear it, Mr. Galliard. You must forgive me for imagining, when we first met, that I had made your acquaintance before, somewhere abroad. I now realize that this is quite impossible."

Another pause, then he said slowly, "I was much distressed to have to contradict you, Jemimah."

We walked on in silence, and after a while it was strangely like being once again on the snowy passes or dusty trails of Afghanistan, where we had walked or ridden for hours without a word between us; but now it was surprisingly pleasant, and I was amused to think that no ordinary English lady and gentleman could possibly have walked together as we were doing without making conversation.

Five minutes later I said, "Has Mrs. Galliard explained to you how very kind your friend, Lord Henry Boot, has been to me?"

"Yes." Now there was fresh strain in his voice, and I wondered why. "Yes, I've heard about Henry's fairground escapades and his tour with a Punch and Judy show. I had no idea that he was spending the summer in such a fashion. He really is the most outrageous fellow."

I thought this was probably the longest speech I had ever heard from Caspar Galliard. It occurred to me that, having made my point and received an oblique acknowledgment from him, it would be wrong of me on any future occasion to speak as I had just spoken in veiled terms of our time together in the past. This was the last occasion that I might do so, and therefore it would be the best opportunity to test the notion I had conceived on that first afternoon at number 12, the possibility that perhaps my encounter with Lord Henry at Oakhurst had not been a wild coincidence.

"May I put a hypothetical question to you, Mr. Galliard?" I asked.

He gave me an impassive look. "I am not enamored of hypothetical questions, Jemimah, so I will not promise an answer, but please ask your question."

I said slowly, looking straight ahead, "If there was a person to whom you felt you were in debt for some reason—let us say, for example, the companion with medical knowledge you spoke of just now; and if you had cause to be somewhat concerned for that person's future but could not offer any help or protection yourself—let us say because you were recovering from illness in a distant land, or perhaps also because your profession forbade you to give open help . . ." I paused and drew a breath. "Under such hypothetical conditions, Mr. Galliard, into whose hands would you be most likely to entrust the care of that person to whom you felt you were in debt?"

I glanced at him as we walked on. He was swinging his cane, and his lips were pursed judicially as he considered my question. When he looked at me briefly I again caught the ghost of an amused smile in his eyes, and something else that seemed almost like a touch of affection, though it could not possibly have been that. Then his face was once more the face I had known as Kassim's: hard, unyielding, almost cruel.

"It is not easy to conceive of the circumstances you have described," he said coldly, "but under such conditions I would get in touch with my oldest friend, Lord Henry Boot, by telegram if I were in a distant land, and ask him to take care of the person on my behalf."

I looked soberly ahead and said, "Thank you, Mr. Galliard."

So now I knew it was not by coincidence that I had encountered Lord Henry in Oakhurst after being turned away from Witchwood Hall and then failing to secure recognition from anyone in the village. Caspar Galliard had sent a wire to his old friend at Torringtons, telling him to look for me in Oakhurst on the day *Bristol Star* docked at Tilbury. No doubt Jackson the butler had brought the message to Lord Henry, just as he had brought money from time to time; and Henry had then arranged to be in Oakhurst on the day of my arrival, to contrive in some fashion to take me under his wing.

For a brief moment I wondered if his choking on the swazzle had been playacting, but at once put the notion aside. There had been no pretense about that, for I had seen the swazzle stuck deep in his throat, and in any event he could not have known that I had some nursing experience that would bring me to his aid. The incident had given him a good opportunity to offer me work and shelter but, failing this, he could easily have approached me in other ways, using Paloma to allay any fears of his intentions toward me. My case had been so desperate, I would have been glad to accept.

Twenty minutes later Mr. Galliard and I were back at number 12, having indulged in no more than half a dozen quite amiable conversational exchanges in that time, which was a great deal more than we had ever spoken in a whole day on our Afghanistan travels, I reflected.

After that first encounter in the park, Caspar Galliard sometimes accompanied me on my morning walks, sometimes not. I found his manner strange, for when he joined me he would usually be as pleasant and as seemingly content as he was capable of being, but as the walk went on he would become more dour and impassive, almost as if he was suppressing anger. Once I asked if I had said or done anything to offend him, but he brushed the idea aside impatiently. I could only conclude that he became angry with himself as we walked but could not fathom why.

It was much the same with my work in the little garden. I was in full view from the window when he sat at his desk in the study, and often I felt he was watching me. Sometimes he came out to chat for a while, rather stiffly and awkwardly, but soon the dourness and inward anger would come upon him, so that at last he would turn abruptly and walk away. Twice he came out, hard of eye and tight-lipped, to ask coldly that I should leave the garden alone that day, as I was distracting him.

I did not take offense at this. His manner toward his wife was often equally cold, but she always responded with smiling affection. The better I knew Anne Galliard, the more I admired her, and I was not alone in this. It is rare for other women to like a truly beautiful woman, yet she was clearly well liked by those in her circle of acquaintances, perhaps because she was so utterly without vanity and so outgoing in her friendship.

If my childhood recollections were correct, when calls were made it was unusual for the men of the house to appear, for they preferred to keep out of the way and leave the ladies to gossip; so I was amused to note how often men of all ages would join us when Anne Galliard visited. Husbands, brothers, fathers, all were anxious to bask in the glow of her presence, just as Lord Henry had been when she called at Torringtons. Yet her manner with them all was such that I never saw a hint of resentment toward her in any of her women friends. Annoyed with their menfolk, especially their husbands, they might well be, but not with Anne Melanie Galliard.

All this made it impossible for me to understand Caspar Galliard's manner toward her: never impolite, but always cool and distant. I noticed that they occupied separate bedrooms and tried not to wonder about this since it was none of my business. In the library I looked up in an encyclopedia the names Caspar Galliard had muttered in a delirium of fever as I bathed his face and laid wet cloths on his fiery body to keep his temperature down. *"Melanie . . ."* that was the name he alone used for his wife, then: *"Stormswift . . . daughter of Electra . . ."*

The first reference I found to Electra, a name I recalled vaguely from lessons in Greek mythology, seemed to have no significance. Electra, daughter of Agamemnon, sent her brother Orestes to kill their mother because their mother had killed their father—a familiar Greek story of blood and murder. Then I discovered another Electra, this one a nereid, which meant daughter of a sea god, Nereus. She had given birth to the dreaded Harpies, from a Greek word meaning "snatchers," monstrous birds with the faces of women, who devoured human prey. Some of the Harpies, daughters of Electra, had been named by the ancient Greek writers. There was Swiftfoot, and Swiftwing, and—

I stared in shock at the printed word. *Stormswift!*

XIII

Anne Melanie Galliard . . . *Stormswift?*

How could that possibly be? Even in a mind confused by delirium, how could Caspar Galliard speak of his wife by the name of a Harpy, a devourer of human prey? And it could not be that I had misheard, for he had spoken another word, equally cruel and bitter. I had never heard the word "bitch-goddess" before, but there could be no doubt as to its meaning.

It baffled and saddened me that a woman of such fine qualities should be seen as if through some horribly distorting mirror by her husband. I felt sure she was too sensitive a person to be unaware of this, which made it all the more astonishing that she remained so serenely affectionate in her manner toward him. It was as if she were able to forgive him and take no hurt because she knew that his mind was flawed.

I thought I had discovered something of the secret of Anne Galliard's serenity when I learned that she had a retreat she called the Sanctuary, to which she repaired for a day or sometimes two days at a time. The Sanctuary was a very small house on the south bank of the Thames, in Southwark. This was not a district where gentry lived, but that was as Anne Galliard wished.

"It is my very own, very private retreat," she told me one morning, just before leaving to spend a day at the Sanctuary for the first time since I had become her companion. "It was once a tiny private chapel, and I have converted it to a refuge where I alone may go." There was no solemnity about her as she told me this. I had never yet seen her solemn. On the contrary, those startling indigo eyes were filled with laughter and deprecation, as if she were gently mocking her own peculiarity in having such a retreat.

"I use it only for three or four days in each month, unless I am in particular need, and betweentimes it is looked after by a caretaker who lives across the road"—her eyes sparkled—"a reformed burglar from our Ex-Prisoners Charity, and such a dear little man. It is something quite away from the rest of my life, Jemimah. I take no servants with me and receive no visitors. Even Caspar has never been inside the Sanctuary." She made a wry face. "I confess it is immensely selfish, but I wish to have the Sanctuary for myself alone."

I said, "It doesn't seem selfish to me, Mrs. Galliard. I'm sure it must be the sense of total privacy that helps you to restore yourself. That is why you go there, isn't it?"

She smiled approval and patted my hand. "You're a perceptive girl, Jemimah. I go there to find"—she hesitated, then with a little gesture of apology—"well, to find spiritual peace. Oh dear, I'm sorry that sounds so pretentious."

I shook my head. "No, I can understand, at least a little. But I'm intrigued to know if you do anything in particular to . . . to calm the soul."

"That's a very good phrase, dear," she said gently. "Well, I don't think I do anything in particular. By day I often sit looking out on the river, and by night on the lights of London, and I think about all kinds of things, but in a rather faraway fashion. I suppose you could say I meditate, as Caspar tells me the holy men in India do. I also have my Bible and some books on religious subjects, so I read quite a lot. I drink only water, and eat only one simple meal each day, provided by the wife of my dear little reformed burglar, and"—she paused and spread her hands, laughing—"then I come home completely refreshed."

I laid down the clumsy piece of embroidery I was working on and said, "I think it's a quite wonderful thing to do, Mrs. Galliard." I felt a rueful twinge of envy as I spoke. My words were true, but I knew that even if I had possessed a sanctuary of my own it would never have done for me what Anne Galliard's did for her, because I quite simply lacked her qualities of mind and spirit.

*　　*　　*

I had been just over four weeks at Stanford Square when Caspar Galliard said at breakfast one morning, "Henry Boot is in town, Melanie, staying at the club. I ran into him there yesterday, and he asked to call this afternoon if that is convenient to you. If not, I'll leave a message for him."

Anne Galliard clapped her hands gently together and said, "But of course he must come and see us today, my darling, and we won't be at home to anybody else. Henry is such a dear, and I'm longing to ask about his adventures as a Punch and Judy man. Jemimah has told me quite a lot, but I'm sure there must be more, and it's such an exciting story. Did you know he had a beautiful gypsy girl with him until her tribe came and took her away by force?"

"I didn't know," said her husband dryly, "but it sounds exactly like our Henry."

I felt very happy at the thought of seeing Henry again and had to restrain myself from jumping up to greet him when he was shown into the drawing room next day a little before four o'clock. With his slim body he looked very elegant in a fine gray suit as he bent to kiss Anne Galliard's fingers, but then he ruined the effect by putting his hand to his mouth for a moment and greeting me in the squeaky voice of Punch. "Hello, Judy! Hello, Judy! What a pretty dress, what a pretty dress!"

As he bent over my hand I struggled to look severe and said, "Henry! Behave yourself!"

At that moment Caspar Galliard entered, to be greeted in the same ridiculous fashion, and for the first time I saw that impassive face break into an involuntary grin. "My God, is that really how you spent the summer, Henry?" he said, and glanced at me. "Did Jemimah have to sit beside you in the booth with that appalling voice inches from her ear?"

Henry took the swazzle from his mouth and slipped it into his pocket. "It's a splendid voice," he protested. "Jemimah never complained. Besides, she was bawling her Judy lines in *my* ear. You should hear her. Go on, Mim, do that part when you find I've thrown the baby out of the window."

I said, "Henry, please!"

Voice shaking with laughter, Anne Galliard said, "Oh, but we would love to hear an excerpt while Henry is here. You shall do it for us later, Jemimah, when we have had tea."

Because the day was mild, we took tea on the small terrace. Henry studied me carefully and asked how I was, and I said truthfully that I was very happy at Stanford Square. In turn I inquired after Lady Whitchurch and asked him to carry her my best regards, then took no further part in the conversation except when brought into it, for despite my friendship with Lord Henry I did not think it my place to initiate conversation with my employers' guest.

An hour passed very pleasantly, even including the five minutes when

Henry and I enacted a brief scene from Punch and Judy, pretending we were working puppets on our hands. I had never known Caspar Galliard so at ease, and in one way this was most strange, for Henry's adoration of his wife was plain, just as it had been when she visited Torringtons. I could only suppose that Caspar Galliard was well used to other men adoring his wife. Either that, or he did not care.

After tea Anne Galliard insisted that I take Henry around the small garden and show him the work I had been doing. This offered us our first opportunity to speak privately, and as soon as we were out of earshot of the terrace Henry said quietly, "Not cross with me, Mim?"

"No, of course not. But it was quite a shock, suddenly finding Mr. Galliard was Caspar."

"I know, but I couldn't warn you. It wasn't my secret. I thought perhaps Caspar had arranged for Anne to invite you here, but I still couldn't speak."

"No, he didn't arrange it. But he arranged for you to find me at Oakhurst and look after me, didn't he, Henry?"

"Yes, by wire from India. Is he going to help establish that you really are Jemimah Lawley?"

I shook my head. "He doesn't acknowledge what happened in Afghanistan."

Henry said, "Oh, damn. I was afraid of that. But if the story was made public, it could cost him his life to go back to Afghanistan as Kassim." He shrugged a little sadly. "Not that he's likely to be much concerned about that."

I said, "Does he intend to go back?"

"Lord knows, Mim. He'll go where his masters send him, but he knows Afghanistan intimately and has the language, so that's the most likely place."

As we turned the corner of the path at the bottom of the garden I said, "Why do you say that losing his life is of no great concern to him?"

"Well . . . because I believe it to be true."

"Yes, but *why?*"

He turned to look at me with one of his despairing grimaces. "I can't imagine, Mim. He used to be such an outgoing chap, with a great zest for life, but now . . . well, you've seen for yourself, he's a grim and sorrowing man. Yet he's married to the most marvelous woman, and he should be happy as a king. I don't understand. Perhaps it's the work he does that has changed him so."

"Perhaps." I nodded, but I did not think so myself.

194   MADELEINE BRENT

After a little silence Henry said, "What are you going to do about proving who you are?"

I stopped to pinch off some dying blooms from a climbing rose, as I had seen the gardeners at Torringtons do to encourage fresh blooms. "There isn't anything I can do for the moment," I said. "I don't know if I ever shall be able to do anything. Sometimes I feel angry, but I try not to, because if I let it become an obsession I shall have a very unhappy life. After what happened in Shul, even our life on the road was like paradise, and for myself I'm really quite content. It's just that sometimes I feel I'm betraying my mother and father by allowing my name and birthright to be stolen . . . I mean, if the people I remember as my mother and father really were Sir George and Lady Lawley."

"Oh, for heaven's sake, Mim, you're no fraud."

"Not a deliberate one, but all the evidence is against me, Henry."

He wrinkled his nose and gazed pensively at a rather feeble dahlia I was trying to encourage. "I must give it some thought, Mim," he said vaguely.

*   *   *

As autumn gave way to winter and the days grew short, I became even more at home in the Galliard household, but my puzzlement over Caspar Galliard's strangeness was in no way diminished. I reflected that if Lord Henry, who had known him from boyhood, could not understand him, then there was little chance of my doing so.

At Anne Galliard's suggestion I began to spend a few hours each week helping Caspar Galliard with his work. This involved going through numerous well-thumbed notebooks, deciphering handwriting and abbreviations, and writing out a copy in a fair hand. I was also able to look up particular references he gave me in books written by other men, and to mark the relevant pages in readiness for him to read.

There could be no doubt that as an archaeologist he was widely informed, but few of the notebooks were in his writing, and I suspected that much of his raw material was provided by others, under an arrangement by somebody like Mr. Arthur Renwick, to maintain the notion that Caspar Galliard's travels abroad were solely concerned with exploration of ancient cities.

Sometimes it seemed that he was pleased to have my help, and sometimes he was as cold and unfriendly as his other self, Kassim, had been. Most baffling of all was his manner on the occasions when his wife was away for a day or perhaps two at the Sanctuary, and we were on our own, for then I never knew what to expect. Sometimes he seemed to be filled with relief and even happy in my company as we worked together or sat at table together. On other occasions he would spend most of his time away from the house and would barely exchange a word with me when we did chance to encounter each other.

I learned, as I had learned in the wilderness, to accept Caspar Galliard as he was at any given time, and to expect nothing. In this way I had the occasional pleasant surprise of an hour or two when this puzzling man was quite human and companionable.

There were some matters which had not particularly struck me during my early days at Stanford Square but which occurred to me as time went by. It seemed, for example, that Caspar Galliard must have a handsome private income, for he followed no paid profession—except the secret profession of a spy, and I could not imagine that this was a source of much income. Then again, he and Anne Galliard had been married for seven years, so she had said, yet there were no children, and never any mention of the possibility. I realized that the cause of this could be medical—as it had been with Deenbur, thank God. Such failure, as I had learned from Sandru, could lie with either the man or the woman, but I did not think this applied to Caspar and Anne Galliard. A simpler explanation was that they slept in separate bedrooms.

Another point that occurred to me after my first week or two at Stanford Square was that neither he nor she appeared to have any close family, for no reference was made to fathers or mothers, sisters or brothers, on either side. Later I discovered that Caspar was in fact an only child who had lost both parents when he was at university, but I was wrong concerning Anne Galliard's parents, who were still living in Suffolk, where she had been born. Her father was a solicitor, her maiden name was Grant, and there had been a sister two years older who had died when only seventeen, I did not know from what cause.

In early December we paid a visit to these parents and stayed for the weekend, traveling up by train to the village of Saxmundham. It was the most depressing weekend I had spent in England. The house was comfortable, the servants attentive, Anne Galliard was her usual warm and happy self, and I had never seen Caspar Galliard make such an effort to be a pleasant and cheerful companion. But Mr. and Mrs. Grant were like husks, empty of life, gray of spirit, and unresponsive. They were vaguely courteous to us all but seemed to have no energy for anything further. They did not show any particular pleasure at seeing their daughter, and I

196 MADELEINE BRENT

had the feeling that they were simply waiting patiently for us all to go away and leave them alone.

Certainly I found it a relief to be on the train returning to London, and I sensed that Caspar Galliard felt the same, but no word was said.

Lord Henry called every three or four weeks. We did not always have an opportunity to speak privately, and indeed had nothing private to say to each other, but on one occasion he called unexpectedly when Anne Galliard was away at the Sanctuary and Caspar Galliard out at a meeting of some archaeological society. I gave Henry tea, we exchanged pieces of news, laughed over some reminiscences of our Punch and Judy days, and wondered rather wistfully how Paloma was faring.

At one time I was greatly tempted to tell him the truth about my reason for leaving Torringtons—that I had found his mother's locket in my room one morning, and she was convinced I had stolen it because a ribbon from my nightdress had been left in her bedroom. I felt it likely that Henry would be more certain of my innocence than I was myself, and I would have been grateful to have such support and encouragement, for although I tried to shut the incident out of my mind it was frightening to wonder if I might have done such a thing without knowing it.

In the end I held my tongue and said nothing, though I could not have given any clear reason for my decision. Later I found it hard to decide whether I was glad or sorry not to have spoken. That night I dreamed of Sandru, as I had done once or twice since coming to London. This dream was curiously different from those I had dreamed earlier, for although it took place in Shul, and in the way of most dreams had little rhyme or reason to it, Sandru was not as I had known him but was a young man of about the same age as Caspar Galliard and was wearing the uniform of a soldier.

In the dream I was once again Lalla the servant, bringing breakfast to my master, but this was not the elderly and sometimes querulous Sandru I knew, sitting up in bed to have his breakfast. It was a much younger Sandru, an army officer, sitting at a small table beautifully set with silver cutlery and fine china. There was something I had to tell him, and I knew it to be important, but I could not think what it was, and I stood trying to speak but finding no words, becoming ever more worried at my loss of memory until I broke into a sweat of panic and woke up in my bed at Stanford Square, trembling and breathless, my nightdress clinging to my damp body.

*   *   *

Christmas was drawing near. I helped Anne Galliard and the servants to make the house look festive with decorations, bought a small present for her and another for Caspar Galliard, and remembered with a stab of grief that Sandru would be spending something approaching his fortieth Christmas in a cruel land of barbaric tribes.

On Christmas Eve, well wrapped up against the cold, Anne Galliard and I joined a carol-singing party from our local church, St. John's. On Christmas morning, after breakfast, we exchanged presents. From Anne Galliard I received a slim silver bracelet, and from her husband, much to my surprise, a quaint little china ornament for my bedroom, a beautifully made and rather comical mule, with legs splayed, looking over its shoulder with a stubborn air. I was at once reminded of Aristotle, who had carried me from Shul to Herat, but made no mention of this since Caspar Galliard's wife was present. When I thanked him, he wished me a happy Christmas and bent to kiss me awkwardly on the cheek, but there was not the slightest hint in his expression that the mule had any particular significance.

I also had a present that had arrived by post two days before, from Lord Henry. This was a gold chain bracelet with a tiny gold charm attached, and the charm was a miniature drum with two drumsticks laid across it. I had sent him a Christmas card but no present for fear of annoying his mother, and I was shocked at his extravagance in having this gold charm especially made for me. With it was a card saying, *With love from Punch to Judy.*

I had to explain the significance of the drum to Caspar and Anne Galliard, recounting how first Paloma and then I had worked as "barker," banging a drum and shouting to attract an audience, and as I told my tale I heard Caspar Galliard laugh for the first time.

The old year died, and as I lay in bed on the last night of the year I recalled with awe and gratitude all that had happened to me since the coming of spring had melted the snows in the high passes of Kafiristan. I wondered, too, with a shiver of fear, whether I would still have been alive and in my right mind now if I had been sent as a bride to Akbah the Mad.

Since the beginning of December there had been two or three small dinner parties given by Anne Galliard, with never more than six or seven guests, and I understood that this was her custom during the winter months. Her husband always attended as a matter of courtesy and performed his duties as a host, but he had no interest in these occasions, and it was his wife who made all arrangements and chose the guests. Often neither Caspar Galliard nor I would know who was coming until they arrived, for it was in her character to delight in giving surprises, just as she had done when first bringing me to number 12.

It was toward the end of January that she gave a dinner party at which I was to receive a shock that turned my whole world upside down. There were six guests, and the first four to arrive proved to be two middle-aged couples I had met before on committees of the various charities Anne Galliard supported. One couple was named Winslow, the other Mortimer, all very amiable people, the two husbands trying hard, as husbands usually did, not to look continually at their beautiful hostess.

We sat in the drawing room, exchanging pleasantries, the men taking a glass of sherry. I felt, most immodestly, that I had become quite good at striking the right note on these occasions, not being too forward in making conversation since I was an employed companion, but trying to respond brightly, and in particular to pay special attention to any guest who seemed difficult to draw out.

A few minutes later we heard the doorbell sound. I guessed that this would be the last of our guests. Edge, the butler, would receive them in the hall, a footman would take hats and coats, gloves and muffs, then Edge would announce them. Anne Galliard was saying to the Winslows and Mortimers, "I think you may not be acquainted with my other guests, I met them myself only recently. They live mainly in the country but have a house in Belgrave Square where they are staying for a few weeks."

Belgrave Square . . . I had distant memories of a house there, forgotten till now, a house my father had owned and which we had used occasionally when I was very small. The memory faded as quickly as it had appeared. I could remember no details of the house, form no picture in my mind. Perhaps I had been too young, or perhaps it was a false memory.

Edge opened the doors of the drawing room and stood to one side. "Miss Jemimah Lawley and Mr. James Lawley," he announced, his face quite expressionless. As he spoke there entered the man and the young woman I had last seen as I stood on the threshold of Witchwood Hall, shaken to the very marrow of my being as I watched the door of the home I had believed my own close firmly in my face.

Like the other men, James Lawley wore an evening dress suit. His companion wore a dress of shell-pink satin and ninon, with bows of velvet in a darker shade decorating both shoulders and one hip. Her hair was dressed in a chignon. Long sleeves of white kid reached to her elbows, and in one hand she carried an ivory fan.

I sat frozen and felt the blood leaving my face with shock. They were smiling politely as their host and hostess moved to greet them, and as if from a great distance I heard Anne Galliard's voice saying warmly, "Miss Lawley, how delightful of you to join us. May I present my husband, Caspar? Caspar, my dear, I present Miss Jemimah Lawley of Witchwood Hall and her cousin, Mr. James Lawley, who is also in a manner of speaking her guardian, I understand."

For a moment I felt I must be experiencing a nightmare. I could not believe that Anne Galliard would bring to her house the two people who had stolen from me my name and my birthright . . . or who might have done. Even if she felt I was deluded, this was still beyond all comprehension.

Mr. Winslow and Mr. Mortimer had risen to their feet. Both they and their wives looked puzzled and uneasy, darting glances at me. I knew I should have risen too, for I ranked only as a companion, but my head was swimming and I had to wait a moment or two before I dared force myself to stand. Anne Galliard was introducing her new guests to the others, eyes sparkling, a radiant hostess. Just beyond her I saw Caspar Galliard looking at me, his gaze intense but his eyes without expression.

The new guests reached me at last, and I saw the girl blink in astonishment as she recognized me an instant before Anne Galliard spoke my name: "This is my companion, and by strange chance a namesake of yours, another Jemimah Lawley." She gave an amused laugh. "We must try not to become confused, mustn't we?"

The girl look startled, then embarrassed, but recovered quickly, inclining her head politely and murmuring, "How do you do?"

Then I was being presented to the man she called Uncle James. Amid the confusion of thoughts in my head, I wondered if at sight of me he might decide to withdraw with his young cousin, declaring that I had tried to usurp her place and that he could not therefore remain under the same roof. He studied me quizzically, then said in a dry tone, "Good evening, Miss Lawley." His manner said more than his words. He had been given a few moments longer than his cousin to absorb the shock of seeing me and to make up his mind as to how he should act, and his look told me plainly that he did not intend to upset his host and hostess, but that if I caused a scene by renewing my ridiculous claim he would deal

with me very sharply. What he read in my face I could not know, I only
knew that I must keep silent, that it would be folly to do otherwise at
this time, for I would be more likely to be thought mad than to be
believed. I dropped an automatic curtsy and with a dry mouth managed
to say, "How do you do, Mr. Lawley."

He passed on, and Anne Galliard was nodding at me with smiling
approval as I sank into my seat and braced myself to face the ordeal of
sitting at table and spending the evening with two people believed by all
the world to be Jemimah Lawley and her cousin, James Lawley, of
Witchwood Hall. I set my teeth and began to breathe deeply, trying to
restore color to my cheeks; and at the back of my mind I heard the voice
of Lalla of Shul whispering to me, encouraging me, saying, *"Better than
Deenbur . . . better than the whip and the violation . . . better than
Akbah the Mad . . . far better, far better . . ."*

                    *   *   *

I came through the evening without making a fool of myself, though I
was distrait and sometimes lost the thread of the conversation. At the
back of my mind was the thought that I must ask Anne Galliard how she
could do such a thing, but by the time the evening was over and the door
had closed on the departing guests I felt too limp even to string a few
words together.

Anne Galliard seemed quite unaware of anything amiss. She made no
reference to the matter and simply spoke brightly of what a pleasant
evening it had been. I stood with my hands resting on the back of a
chair, numb and listless. Caspar Galliard was watching me, his back to
the drawing-room fire, hands tucked under his coattails. "You look tired,
Jemimah," he said in a voice that held no note of sympathy. "Go to bed
now."

"Yes, Mr. Galliard. Thank you. Good night, Mrs. Galliard."

I turned to the door, and she called after me in a warm voice, "Good
night, Jemimah dear. Sleep well."

It was a great effort to undress, put away my clothes, put on my
nightdress, and brush and plait my hair. I felt exhausted but at the same
time knew that the thoughts churning uselessly in my mind would prevent me from sleeping. I needed something to distract me and hoped
that if I read for half an hour or so I would feel calmer and be able to put
off thinking about the events of the evening until tomorrow.

I had just finished reading *The Adventures of Tom Sawyer*, a book by an American author, Mr. Mark Twain, and had not yet chosen a new book for bedtime reading, so I put on my dressing gown and slippers, lit my bedside candle, and made my way along the passage to the library. I was there no more than a minute or two and selected Mr. Swinburne's *Poems and Ballads* to read. On my way back I saw that the door of Anne Galliard's bedroom stood slightly ajar, with a narrow strip of light showing from within as I approached along the passage. I halted for a moment to tuck the book under my arm, leaving a hand free to shield the candle, for I did not want to be noticed as I passed the door.

Then I froze, for suddenly I heard the voice of Caspar Galliard from within the room, harsh with anger. "It was cruel, Melanie! Wickedly cruel!"

I heard her speak but could not discern her words. On tiptoe I moved forward, anxious to pass the door and reach my own room on the far side of the gallery, but then I heard Caspar Galliard pacing close to the door, and I stopped again, wondering if I should go back and hide myself in the library for a time. I had no wish to overhear a dispute between Caspar Galliard and his wife.

He spoke again. "To bring the so-called Lawleys here and confront Jemimah with them was unforgivable! I cannot imagine how you could torment her so!"

I caught my breath, alarmed to realize that I was the subject of the dispute. I was nearer the door now, and when Anne Galliard replied in a voice both gentle and without reproach, I heard her clearly. "Dearest Caspar, the very last thing I would wish is to hurt Jemimah in any way, surely you know that? My only purpose was to help her."

"Oh yes!" There was grim irony in Caspar Galliard's tone. "I'm familiar with your ways of helping people, Melanie."

"Please don't be unkind, my darling. I thought about it very carefully and acted only for the best."

"Best? What the devil do you mean? Whose best?"

"Jemimah's best, my dear." Her voice was as patient as ever. "Don't you see? I reasoned that if her belief was right, and the Lawleys were frauds, then they would show every sign of guilt when unexpectedly confronted by her. On the other hand, if the poor child is imagining herself to be Jemimah Lawley, then I felt that such a confrontation would shock her into reality and perhaps restore her true memory."

"A case of being cruel to be kind?" His voice was savage.

"Please don't accuse me of cruelty, Caspar. It is deeply hurtful."

"Was your purpose served? Did the Lawleys display guilt?"

"To be honest, I did not detect any sign of guilt."

"And do you imagine that as a consequence Jemimah no longer believes she is the true Jemimah Lawley?"

"I don't know, Caspar dear. But I may have sown a seed, and even if I failed in my purpose, I acted with the best of intentions."

There was silence, and when Caspar Galliard spoke again his voice was low, but in it there was a quality that made me shiver. "Don't do it again, Melanie," he said, and every word seemed to carry a red flare of danger. "Don't subject Jemimah to torment again. I warn you, I will not allow it."

On the last phrase his voice became louder and I knew he must be approaching the door. In panic I realized that it would seem I had been deliberately eavesdropping, which was inexcusable, and in an instant I had blown out the candle and was pressing myself back against the wall.

The door opened and a panel of light fell across the hall. Caspar Galliard closed the door with a slam, turning away from me to stride along the passage to his own bedroom. Without looking back he threw open the door and closed it behind him. From within Anne Galliard's room I heard a faint sound of sobbing, as if the final words flung at her had at last broken down her serenity and brought her to tears. But as I tiptoed past her door in the darkness of the passage, there came the startling thought that the sound I heard might be the sound of laughter.

XIV

An inch of snow fell during the night, and when I went for my morning walk before breakfast, mine were the only footmarks to appear in the thin blanket of snow in the park, until I encountered Caspar Galliard. I had not expected to do so on such a morning, and I doubt that he had expected to find me abroad in the wintry weather, but we should both have known better, for we were well used to walking in snow far worse than this.

We greeted each other politely, talked even a little less than usual, and did not refer to our dinner guests of the evening before. At breakfast, with Anne Galliard present, there was still no mention made, and I began to have a feeling of unreality, as if I might have dreamed or imagined that two guests calling themselves James Lawley and Jemimah Lawley had dined with us last night.

Caspar Galliard was his usual self, remote and taciturn. Anne Galliard was also her usual self, happy and sparkling, seemingly untouched by her husband's anger of the night before, and unaware that I might be distressed by the ordeal she had subjected me to. I did not feel able to raise the matter myself. As an employed companion it was not for me to question my mistress's choice of dinner guests. Nevertheless, I now found myself feeling not quite at ease in Anne Galliard's company. To me the atmosphere was subtly different, but she did not appear to feel this herself, and her manner toward me continued to be as warm and kindly as ever.

Three days after the dinner party she announced that she would spend the weekend at the Sanctuary. I was glad, for I felt that if we were apart for a day or two I might be able to rid myself of the unease I had been feeling. She left Stanford Square after breakfast on the Saturday morning, and Caspar Galliard left the house only an hour later, saying that he had been invited to his publisher's house in the country for the weekend and would not return until the Monday.

I looked forward to two quiet days alone, when I could try to sort out my thoughts and feelings, write a letter to Lord Henry, and plan the work to be done in the garden once winter was past. At six o'clock that evening I was sitting in the library writing my letter when Edge entered with a tray on which lay a buff envelope.

"Excuse me, Miss Jemimah," he said with a worried air, "but a telegraph boy just brought this wire for Mrs. Galliard, and I don't rightly know what to do about it."

I put down my pen and picked up the telegram, staring at it as if it might tell me something. Edge watched me hopefully. "Hadn't you better send it on by messenger to the Sanctuary?" I said at last.

He drew in his breath. "Oh no, miss, I daren't do that. There's very strict orders that no servant must ever go to the Sanctuary. It's Mrs. Galliard's special private place—"

"I know, Edge, but a telegram is bound to be important."

He shook his head regretfully. "I can't take the responsibility, Miss Jemimah. I really can't. I mean, even the master himself never goes there."

I nodded, turning the telegram over in my hands and beginning to feel at a loss. I knew the Sanctuary stood in Ardley Road, Southwark, but by now all post offices would be closed and I could not send a message by telegram. For the same reason I could not wire Caspar Galliard to ask for instructions, even if Edge knew the address where his master was staying. I bit my lip, increasingly worried, and said, "Well, we can't just leave a telegram here unopened till Monday morning, Edge. That's out of the question."

"I wonder how important it is, miss," he said diffidently. "Perhaps you might take it upon yourself to open it, seeing that you're Mrs. Galliard's companion. Then if it's something serious . . ." His voice trailed away.

I said, "Then what?"

"Well, Mrs. Galliard would *have* to be told, and you'd have a good enough reason to go to the Sanctuary."

"*I* would?"

"Yes, miss. Please."

I stood up. Whether I liked it or not, I was the only authority left in the house for Edge to appeal to, and I could not possibly expect him to make a decision like this by himself. "Since it will probably have to be taken to the Sanctuary anyway, I prefer to take it unopened," I said. "Call a cab for me, please. I shall be ready in five minutes."

Some light snow was falling and the night was dark as the hansom clattered along the length of the Victoria Embankment and turned to cross the river at Blackfriars Bridge. Soon we were winding our way through a warren of streets on the south bank, coming at last to a halt at one end of a short narrow street where the houses backed onto the river. The coachman opened the trap in the roof and called down, "This is Ardley Street, miss. What number d'you want?"

I said, "The house is called the Sanctuary, and I don't think it has a number, but it was once a small private chapel."

"Ah, well, I can see an 'ouse just a few steps along by the lamp, and it's got a sort of little spire on it, miss."

"I expect that's the one. Wait here for me, please." I opened the door and climbed down, turning to move along the pavement to a street lamp only a few yards away, where I could see the shape of a tiny spire rising from a building not quite like the other houses. In a few seconds I was at the front door, peering to see if there was a knocker or bellpull. I was quite startled when the door suddenly opened and a man emerged, almost bumping into me as I stepped back. Surprisingly, he wore no hat or topcoat and was carrying a tray under one arm. The lamp shone full upon us as we stood staring at each other, and I saw a look of sudden recognition and alarm leap into his eyes. In the same instant I knew I had seen this man before, this small dark man with a round and wrinkled face, like . . . *like an elderly cherub!*

Lord Henry's words flashed into my mind. This was how he had described the man we had both seen at Torringtons, who had claimed to be attending to the clocks. Now the same man stood before me in the doorway of the Sanctuary. I was too startled and confused even to begin to understand how this could be so, but from the man's look of alarm I knew that something was badly amiss, and I said sharply, "What are you doing in Mrs. Galliard's house? I saw you at Torringtons! You said you were from the clockmaker, but—"

Before I could say more the man darted past me, jostling me so that I staggered. He ran across the road, dropping the tray in his haste, and disappeared into a dark alley. A chill of apprehension touched my spine. Deep in my mind was the thought that the elderly cherub had been up to no good at Torringtons. I had yet to discover in what way, but I was quite sure now that he was no clock mechanic, and I feared what he might have been doing in the Sanctuary, for Anne Galliard was there.

The front door stood open, as he had left it, and after a moment's hesitation I stepped into the passage, the telegram clutched in my hand but forgotten now. To my right a door stood ajar, but no light showed from the room beyond it. Ahead of me a passage led to the back of the house, and beside it were stairs running up to a landing. The far end of the passage was all in darkness, but at the top of the stairs I could make out a faint glow of light.

I called, "Mrs. Galliard . . . ?" but my throat was dry and my voice emerged with little power to carry. Nervously I mounted the stairs, and as I reached the top I saw that the glimmer of light came from under a door to the right, which would give onto a room at the back of the house, overlooking the river. Again I hesitated. This was Anne Galliard's retreat. She might be at her prayers, might be lost in meditation . . . but she might be lying hurt, for I had just seen a man I suspected of being a criminal run away from the house. In any event, I suddenly remembered that I still had the telegram, so I could not turn away now.

Holding my breath, I rapped with my knuckles on the door. For a moment or two there was silence, then I heard movement, and finally Anne Galliard's voice called, "Yes? Come in."

Relief swept me as I turned the handle and pushed open the door, then I stopped short, utterly dumbfounded. This was a large room, well lit by gas lamps, with a fire burning in the grate, golden velvet curtains at the window, fine rugs on the floor. It was furnished with two lyre-back chairs and an oval table in mahogany, a lady's dressing table and pier glass, a wardrobe, two easy chairs covered in Cherwell velvet, and a large bed upholstered in white silk, with draperies at the head. The bed was unmade, with the sheets and blankets flung carelessly back.

On the oval table a light meal of cold meats had been set out, with fine cutlery and an open bottle of white wine standing on a silver coaster. Two people occupied the lyre-back chairs at the table. One was Anne Galliard, half turned away from me, her magnificent hair hanging loose down her back over the froth and frills of the peach-colored negligee she wore. The other person at the table was a man I had seen only once before. He was in his forties, well built and quite handsome, wearing a long, dark red dressing gown. I could not remember his name, but I had been introduced to him some weeks ago when paying a morning call with Anne Galliard, and I knew only that he was the husband of the lady on whom we had called.

He was so placed as to be able to see me the moment I opened the door, and now he sat frozen with a glass of wine half raised to his lips, staring at me in alarm. Anne Galliard said as she turned, "What is it, Cromer? You've brought everything we need—"

Then she saw me, and there was utter silence. The indigo eyes did not blink, and no muscle of her beautiful face moved, but something strange and quite horrible happened as I stared at her. It was as if the person within, who normally looked out of those eyes, was steadily withdrawn to leave only a husk or shell and was then replaced by something quite alien, something remote yet malevolent, that sent a shudder through my body.

The lips moved in the blank face, and the voice said without expression, "Out. Get out."

My cheeks felt bloodless, and I was in such a state of paralysis that for long moments I could not move but simply stood there, hearing the noise of my breath hissing through my lips as I panted with shock. The strange entity with Anne Galliard's face and body did not speak again but continued to stare at me with that empty, shriveling gaze. I took a step back, then a hesitant step forward, holding out the telegram.

Through chattering teeth I said, "I came . . . to bring a t-telegram." Neither she nor the man stirred. There was nowhere for me to put the telegram down, and nothing could have made me go further into that room. With an effort I opened my fingers and let the buff envelope flutter to the floor, then I turned and fled, slamming the door behind me and almost falling as I stumbled down the dark stairs.

Moments later I was out in the night and the falling snow, hurrying toward the cab waiting a little way along the street, shaken by horror and revulsion, hearing once again in my mind the words I had never before understood. *"Melanie . . . Stormswift . . . Bitch-goddess."*

* * *

I remembered little of the journey back to Stanford Square. My mind was in turmoil, and so much was still beyond my comprehension. I did not have to be told that the man I had seen in that bedroom was no solitary lover; there had surely been others before him, for the furnishing and adornments of the room told their own tale. I knew now that beneath the surface Anne Melanie Galliard was utterly different from the woman so greatly loved and admired by all who came in contact with her, myself among them. There were some few who had seen behind the mask. The men who had known that room in the Sanctuary must know the truth. And I suspected that Caspar Galliard knew.

I wondered how many she had entertained in that boudoir of velvet curtains and silken bed, and I wondered above all how she had contrived to keep her secrets and avoid all gossip. That no man had let slip an unwary word, that no breath of scandal had touched her, was quite astonishing.

I realized that the small dark man with the round wrinkled face must be the caretaker who looked after the Sanctuary in her absence, and no doubt acted as servant while she was there. She had spoken of him as a dear little man, a reformed burglar who lived across the road. I knew now that his name was Cromer. When we met at the front door he had been leaving after serving the meal, and when I tapped on the bedroom door Anne Galliard had thought it was Cromer returning for some reason. She had called to him to enter and addressed him by that name before seeing that it was I who stood in the doorway.

But what in heaven's name had Cromer been doing at Torringtons? He had entered the house and gained the run of it by presenting himself as the clock mechanic from Wilkinson's, but even if he was an unreformed burglar he had stolen nothing as far as I knew.

I was still greatly shaken when the cab reached Stanford Square, and made a great effort to pull myself together as I mounted the steps. Edge must have been looking out for me, for the door opened as I reached the porch. "Ah, you're back, Miss Jemimah," he said, anxiety breaking through his usual calm manner. "Is everything all right? Mrs. Galliard wasn't put out on account of you going there?"

I had no idea what would happen when Anne Galliard returned to Stanford Square, but I could not tell Edge the truth of what I had seen. "I didn't intrude on her," I said. "I put the telegram through the letter box and rang the bell."

"I expect that was the best thing, miss," he said, taking my coat. "I just hope she got it safely."

"I'm sure she did, Edge. Will you tell Mrs. Pentland not to bother about dinner for me tonight? I haven't much appetite, and I'd just like a boiled egg with some bread and butter, please, on a tray in the library. I'm going there to finish writing a letter now."

"Very good, miss."

An hour and a half later I was in the sewing room trying to concentrate when Edge entered with an envelope on a tray. "A messenger just brought this from Mrs. Galliard by hand, Miss Jemimah," he said. "There was also a note for the master, to await his return, and I've put that in his study. This one is for you."

It was addressed in Anne Galliard's firm round writing, and I tried to hide my apprehension as I opened the flap and drew out the note. Astonishment swept me as I read it.

Dearest Jemimah,

The telegram was sent by my father and gives the sad news that my dear mother died suddenly and without warning earlier today. My father wishes to have no mourners but myself with him at the funeral, and I am writing to tell Mr. Galliard this. I shall go up to Saxmundham by the ten-fifteen train tomorrow, and return on Wednesday after the funeral. Please have Daisy pack a case for me, and tell Edge to bring it to me at Liverpool Street Station tomorrow at ten o'clock. I shall go there direct from the Sanctuary.

Affectionately,
Anne Galliard

It was as if I had never stood in the doorway of that ornate bedroom in the Sanctuary, to gaze on the scene within and to see another person behind those indigo eyes. I tried to make sure that bewilderment would not show in my face as I looked up and said, "I'm afraid Mrs. Galliard's mother has died suddenly, Edge."

He became grave. "Oh, I'm deeply sorry, miss. Are there any instructions for me?"

"Yes."

I read the last half of the letter to him, and he said that he would make all necessary arrangements. When he had gone I looked at the subscription again . . . *Affectionately, Anne Galliard.* It was almost enough to make me wonder if I had dreamed my nightmare experience at the Sanctuary.

I slept poorly that night and found it hard to settle to anything next day, which was Sunday. Caspar Galliard did not return from his weekend away until noon on the Monday and was at once given the message from his wife by Edge. He stood reading it in the hall, still wearing his overcoat, which was lightly flecked with snow, for there had been another fall in the last hour.

I had come to the hall to greet him on his return and to ask if there was anything he wished me to do. Watching him as he read, I saw his mouth tighten for a moment. He lowered the paper slowly, as if his thoughts were busy, then turned for Edge to help him off with his coat and said, "When did the telegram come, Jemimah?"

"Shortly after six o'clock on Saturday, Mr. Galliard," I replied.

"While Mrs. Galliard was at the Sanctuary?"

"Yes."

"How was she advised of its contents?"

Rather nervously I said, "I didn't feel I could open it, Mr. Galliard, but neither could I let it wait for her return, so I took it to her at the Sanctuary."

"You went there? Yourself?"

"Yes, Mr. Galliard."

He stood very still, and there was no expression on his face, yet I felt this was because he was rigidly schooling himself to reveal nothing of his thoughts. At last he said, "You delivered the telegram into Mrs. Galliard's hands?"

I looked down as I answered with a lie. "No, I was unwilling to intrude, so I slipped it through the letter box."

He drew in a long breath, then said slowly, "I see. Yes. Well, thank you, Jemimah." He looked again at the note he held. "I regret not attending the funeral, for I was very fond of Mrs. Grant, but I must of course observe my father-in-law's wishes. I shall write him a letter of condolence at once." He turned to Edge. "Have one of the maids come to my study for it in ten minutes, to take it to the post."

"Very good, sir."

I said, "Will you be having luncheon at home, Mr. Galliard? I should like to tell Mrs. Pentland."

He started to shake his head, then seemed to change his mind, and after a brief hesitation he said, "Yes, I shall be here for luncheon." My heart sank. I was already ill at ease because I had just lied to Caspar Galliard, and I did not relish sitting at table in his company today, knowing what I knew of his wife.

In the event, luncheon was less of an ordeal than I had feared. It was as if Caspar Galliard had set himself to make easy conversation, and for most of the time we talked about the many notes I had been sorting and collating, and about the references I had been looking up and writing out for a book he was planning on methods of interpreting prehistoric artifacts.

Toward the end of the meal, when Edge had served coffee and left the dining room, Caspar Galliard said, "I propose to take a good walk this afternoon, Jemimah, and I should be grateful to have your company if it is not inconvenient for you."

I was taken aback but said, "Oh. Yes, certainly, Mr. Galliard. I would enjoy that."

"The park lies under two or three inches of snow. Do you have adequate boots for such walking?"

"I have stout laced walking shoes and galoshes," I replied.

"Then let us meet in the hall twenty minutes from now, if that is agreeable to you."

"I shall be ready, Mr. Galliard."

No snow was falling as we left the house, and the sky was blue with a few wispy clouds, yet it was cold still, with no hint of a thaw. I found the air and the exercise bracing as we made our way to the park and entered by the great iron gateway. A few children were romping and making a snowman, but there were hardly any strollers.

I waited for Mr. Galliard to open the conversation and had a shock when he did so. "I wish to speak about your visit to the Sanctuary," he said bluntly. "It is not a subject to be discussed in the house, where one of the servants might overhear."

Feeling greatly disconcerted, I said, "Oh, there really isn't anything more I can say about my visit there, Mr. Galliard. As I told you, I simply—"

"Yes," he broke in curtly. "As you told me, Jemimah. And I hope you will not be upset when I say that I know you did not tell me the truth about your visit. I realize you acted from the best of motives, but I am quite certain you did not simply go to the Sanctuary and put the telegram through the letter box there. I am quite certain you delivered it into my wife's hands."

With a feeble attempt to brave out my lie, I said with unconvincing indignation, "How can you know such a thing, Mr. Galliard? You were not there!"

We walked on through the soft snow for several moments before he said quietly, "I once had a traveling companion to whom I entrusted important papers to be delivered to a certain man. Despite untold dangers and hardship, and despite the fact that when all such problems were over the final delivery could have been left to another to complete, my traveling companion steadfastly insisted on keeping the promise given to me—by delivering those papers in person, from hand to hand . . ."

I remembered the guard tent outside Herat, the officer holding out his hand and announcing that he would take the papers to Mr. Arthur Renwick for me. And I remembered how I had refused.

Caspar Galliard was saying, ". . . and you are so much like that traveling companion, Jemimah, that I know beyond all doubt you could *not* have risked possible delay in the delivery of that telegram. If you had not concocted a story about putting it through the letter box, looking guilty as you told the story, I might have assumed that my wife opened the door to you and took the telegram, whereupon you left at once. That would have been quite possible. But because you did not tell me the truth, I know that something else happened, something you were deeply afraid to speak of. I wish you to tell me now exactly what did happen at the Sanctuary when you went there on Saturday evening."

An urchin was approaching, pulling a smaller urchin on a homemade sled, and I was thankful to have a few moments to collect myself as I waited for them to pass out of earshot. One thing I knew, denial was useless, and at last I said in a low voice, "Please don't ask me, Mr. Galliard. I am your wife's paid companion, and it places me in an impossible situation."

"I admire loyalty, Jemimah," he said in a dry, rather weary voice, "but you need have no fear that you are giving away secrets. I am well aware of the real use to which my wife puts the Sanctuary. She entertains her lovers there, and I suspect that by some mischance you stumbled upon this fact on Saturday night."

I turned my head to look up at him and said, "So you do know, Mr. Galliard?"

"I have known for years," he said bleakly, "in fact from soon after our marriage. Melanie made sure of that."

"Made sure?" I was aghast. "But why? And why haven't you . . . well, done something about it, Mr. Galliard? Oh, I beg your pardon, it's none of my business—"

"It is very much your business," he broke in sharply, and increased his already brisk pace. "The time has come for the truth to be told, for otherwise you may well become one of her victims. She has already made a beginning."

I did not grasp his meaning, or rather I had only a nebulous sense of what lay behind his words. Though the air was cold, my body was glowing with warmth from the exercise of walking at such a pace, yet despite that warmth I felt a chill in the marrow of my bones as I said, "What do you mean when you speak of my becoming a victim, Mr. Galliard?"

Our feet made no sound in the snow, and I heard him give a small sigh. Then he said, "What I shall tell you now is disloyal to my wife, and I have never before been guilty of that. But it must be said." He paused for a moment as if choosing his words, then continued: "I beg you not to think I exaggerate when I say that Melanie, my wife, is a destroyer. She is, I fear, a profoundly wicked woman. Evil is not too strong a word to use, I think, for her pleasures have an almost satanic quality."

I remembered the horrifying moment in the Sanctuary boudoir when it seemed that another entity had stared at me from behind Anne Galliard's eyes. Beside me, her husband made a brief dismissive gesture and said, "I am not speaking of the men she seduces in the Sanctuary. That is disloyal to me, and a betrayal of her vows and her duty, but it is not essentially evil. The evil lies in her purpose, which is to destroy their happiness, to destroy *anyone's* happiness." He turned to look at me, for I had fallen a pace behind. "That is the sole purpose in all she does, Jemimah, to bring misery to others. I think you know I am not a man to indulge in melodrama, but I say to you now that, as a vampire feeds on blood, so does Melanie feed on the pain and misery of others."

I wanted to protest, to beg him not to make such wild accusations, but within me was the sickening knowledge that he was not speaking wildly at all. I said a little breathlessly, "Could you please walk more slowly, Mr. Galliard? It's difficult for me to keep up with you."

Behind the disarray in my mind I recalled how I had sometimes fallen behind Kassim in the knee-deep snow of the high mountains, and how he had turned to haul me onward without a word. Now Caspar Galliard said, "Oh, my dear, I beg your pardon. I failed to realize I was walking so quickly. Perhaps you would take my arm?" At another time I would have been astonished by the endearment and by the notion of his offering me his arm, but at the moment such thoughts were overwhelmed by other emotions. As we moved on at a slower pace, my arm linked with his, he said soberly, "You saw something very distressing at the Sanctuary, did you not?"

There was no longer any reason for me to lie or to keep silent. Hesitantly, unhappily, I gave the briefest possible account of what had happened after the man named Cromer fled from the open front door when I recognized him. As I stopped speaking, Caspar Galliard nodded. "I believe Charles Hutton is the present incumbent at the Sanctuary," he said without animosity. "Poor devil. I wonder what torment she plans for him."

I remembered the man now. With Anne Galliard I had twice paid calls on Mrs. Hutton, and her husband Charles had been present. He was a Harley Street doctor of considerable repute and had been called in as a consultant by physicians treating members of the royal family.

"You have glimpsed only a small part of Melanie's secret self," said

Caspar Galliard in a controlled voice, staring ahead at the white land-
scape, "so I must try to justify the appalling things I have just said about
her and leave you to decide for yourself whether what I say is to be
believed, Jemimah. First let me ask, do you recall forming any particular
impression of her parents, Mr. and Mrs. Grant, when we visited them in
December?"

"Well . . . yes." I thought for a moment, then went on: "They
seemed to have no life in them. Not from illness, but as if from being
drained of all spirit. They were like husks, empty inside. I'm sorry if that
sounds impertinent, but—"

"No, no. It is a true description. You will remember they had an elder
daughter who died when only seventeen. The terrible truth is that she
took her own life. That was of course an abiding sorrow to her parents,
but it was made worse by their belief that she was driven to suicide by
her younger sister, Anne Melanie, inflicting a hundred subtle torments
upon her."

I jumped with shock and said, "Oh, surely not! How could that be
possible?"

Caspar Galliard shrugged. "I can only tell you what her father, Andrew Grant, let slip to me with a few unguarded words a year or two
after our marriage. We were paying one of our rare visits, and he had
taken an extra glass of port after dinner. Melanie and her mother had
left us at table together, and he mumbled, almost as if thinking aloud,
'Don't let her destroy you, Caspar. She drove poor Emily to her death,
and she's sucked the life out of Martha and me.' Then he shook his head
and said, 'Can't help it, you know . . . any more than Lucifer can help
being a fallen angel. She bears a damaged soul. But fear her, Caspar. She
is . . . Stormswift.' "

The man whose arm I held glanced down. "That was a classical reference, Jemimah. In Greek mythology Stormswift was one of the Harpies
who—"

"I know, Mr. Galliard," I broke in. "I heard the name many months
ago from a man delirious with fever, and I've since looked up the reference in your library."

"Ah," he said, "well, that is the name Andrew Grant applied to his
daughter. I greatly doubt that his telegram asked for her to be present at
her mother's funeral, or that he required me not to attend, as she declared. Most likely it simply informed her of her mother's death, as was
proper. However, we shall see how he replies to my letter."

We had been walking for ten minutes since entering the park, and now we turned to cross Broad Walk just short of the Zoological Gardens. "Your unhappy experience with Deenbur," said Caspar Galliard, "means that you are not an ignorant or easily embarrassed maiden. I feel I can therefore speak plainly in saying that my marriage to Melanie has never been consummated."

I shook my head slowly. "I'm not embarrassed . . . but I'm astonished, Mr. Galliard."

"You must realize that I did not know the real Melanie before we were married. I loved to distraction the wonderful creature I believed her to be. At first I was denied the marriage bed on one pretext or another, always made with great apparent affection. I was understanding and did not protest. Her torments are slow, Jemimah, perhaps to give them more savor. Only gradually did it dawn on me that I was forever to be denied, and that in any event I would have been far from the first man to enjoy her favors." He gave a short hard laugh. "Her favors? I doubt that any man has known Melanie in that way without suffering a hundredfold for whatever pleasure he has taken in her."

I said diffidently, "But if she denies you as her husband, is that not grounds for an annulment of the marriage?"

We walked on a little way before he spoke, and at first it did not seem that he was answering my question as he said, "I am the last of a family which has given steadfast service to our country over several generations, Jemimah. My father and his father were soldiers. My father's brother commanded a ship of the line. My elder brother was a naval lieutenant. All but my grandfather died on active service. I will not drag the name they bore through the courts and the press with a story so sordid. Besides, I made vows to my wife at our marriage, and I shall strive to keep those vows till death us do part. Whatever she may do, it gives me no license to break my given word."

I remembered Captain John Selby describing this man as one who would put duty before all else, and I thought how true that diagnosis of his patient had been. Caspar Galliard said dryly, "In any event, it would be impossible to prove that Melanie withholds herself from me if she chooses to deny it. Not that I have the smallest desire for her now. The very thought repels me."

I said, "Isn't there anything you can do to . . . to restrain her, Mr. Galliard?"

"Not without a monstrous scandal. I cannot expose her to the world without bringing contempt upon myself and shame upon my family name. I cannot lock her up away from the world." He pressed my arm gently. "As you know, I am often away from England for long periods, and to keep incessant watch on her is out of the question." He was silent for a little while, then continued slowly: "It is so difficult to convey to you how a pattern of behavior gradually comes into being, and then becomes impossible to change. Can you believe that the Sanctuary was my wedding present to her—at her request? I thought it was for the purpose she announces to the rest of the world, but within a few months of our marriage I knew there had been lovers in her life, because in some way she contrived to convey this to me, and in time I came to know how she used the Sanctuary. By then it was no great shock or surprise. I already knew too much about the real Melanie to be surprised by any act of hers, however infamous."

I said, "How has she managed to avoid a scandal in all this time?"

"That is her most astonishing power," he said very quietly, and I caught a breath of awe, perhaps of fear, in the voice of a man I knew to possess infinite courage. "Of course, she chooses her lovers, her victims, with great skill. They are always men of reputation with much to lose, always family men, husbands and never bachelors, always men of good character who have never before indulged in such behavior. The seduction is slow and very subtle. They are gradually drawn in, their resistance steadily weakened without their realizing it, until the time comes when they fall to her, and the Sanctuary is opened to them, a place of assignment they can visit unseen. The man you saw, Cromer, brings them by boat after dark to steps leading up from the river to the back of the house. He is Melanie's slave, no doubt because she has some powerful hold over him to ensure obedience."

A question about Cromer touched my mind, but this was not the moment to ask it. Instead I said, "You spoke of her lovers as victims, Mr. Galliard. What did you mean?"

"They are basically good and decent men," he said with a hint of bitterness. "She destroys their sense of honor, then seduces them, then discards them, with apparent remorse at having betrayed me and with the constantly implied threat that she will tell all, confess to me, confess to their wives. As a skilled tormentor, she no doubt varies her procedure according to the circumstances and nature of the victim, but I know that over the years she must have driven many a man, many of my acquaintances, almost insane with fear of discovery and ruin, for, as I have said, she chooses only men of reputation who would be made social outcasts if the truth were known."

After a few moments I said nervously, "May I ask a question that may seem to show disbelief, Mr. Galliard? It won't be meant that way."

"Ask any question you like, Jemimah."

"Well . . . how can you *know* this procedure she goes through with her lovers? I can't imagine she has ever told you herself."

When I looked at him I saw no anger in his face, only resignation. "You're quite right," he said. "Melanie has never told me these things, but I learned them from one of her lovers, an architect, some years ago now. By chance this man discovered while at the Sanctuary that a predecessor had been there before him—a great shock, for these men are so besotted with her that they all think they are the first and only ones. He happened to be acquainted with his predecessor and to know that the man had suffered a mental breakdown and made an unsuccessful attempt to commit suicide. Then came the time when the architect himself was discarded and was made to believe from week to week and month to month that Melanie would confess to their liaison, confess to me and to his wife. Unlike the others, he had cause to suspect that the torment was deliberate. He therefore arranged to emigrate with his wife and family to Canada and start a new life there; and on the day before they left he came to me in shame and told me the whole story. That is how I knew at last what I had before only surmised."

We walked on without speaking for several minutes, turning along Outer Circle to walk by Grand Union Canal. "The servants think highly of her," I said at last.

"Oh yes, she does not make victims of servants. On the contrary, she always wins their affection. But you are not a servant, Jemimah, and she has now begun to practice her craft on you."

"On *me?*" I turned my head to look up at him in surprise.

"Certainly. Inviting the so-called Lawleys from Witchwood Hall was her first move. God knows that must have been a difficult evening for you."

"Yes," I said slowly, "it was. I expected Mrs. Galliard to say something to me afterward, to explain why she had done it, but she said no word. She simply acted as if nothing had happened."

Again Caspar Galliard gave that short, humorless laugh. "Such is her method," he said. "Sometimes it seems so incredible that you begin to doubt your own sanity. You may be sure that when she returns from Saxmundham she will say nothing to you about what you saw at the Sanctuary. Do you know, she has never, never quarreled with me? In the early months of our marriage, when I came upon some outrage she had engaged in, I would challenge her about it, reprimand her, attack her in words, but to no effect. She responds with gentle patience, she tells blatant lies with apparent affection, and offers such devious explanations as to cause me to despair of making her comprehend the viciousness of whatever it is she may have done. For you, sitting at table with the Lawleys was your first and not too painful experience of the rack on which she torments her victims, but there will be more, Jemimah."

My head felt so crammed with all I had been told in the past twenty minutes that I found it hard to disentangle any coherent chain of thought, but I knew that in reaches of my mind beyond conscious thought I believed all Caspar Galliard had said. With that belief came a particular fear, and I voiced it uneasily. "I would hate to think that Lord Henry might become a victim, Mr. Galliard. He is greatly enamored of her, you know."

"Most men are, Jemimah, and to seduce my best friend would give her enormous pleasure, but I think he is safe. Melanie has an extraordinary understanding of men, especially their weaknesses, and this gives her immense power over them. But Henry, I believe, is an exception. He is an oddity among men, an eccentric, and she does not quite understand him. In my opinion she fears to try her powers on him because the first essential is to destroy the man's sense of honor, and she is aware that she might well fail in this, which would leave her revealed to him in her true colors. There is also the point that he is a bachelor, with nothing to lose but my friendship, as she would see it."

"I'm truly thankful," I said with feeling. "I have a great regard for Lord Henry." We walked on in silence for a little while, then I came to a decision and began to tell the true story of why I had left Torringtons, explaining that it was because Lady Whitchurch believed I had tried to steal her locket. My companion listened intently, darting me an occasional look of astonishment. "I even wondered if I might have walked in my sleep and taken the locket," I concluded, "but now I feel that Cromer's presence in the house a few days earlier must have some bearing on what happened. The trouble is, I can't work out how that could be so."

After a few moments Caspar Galliard said softly, "It's really very simple, once you know the true Melanie. She wanted you to come to Stanford Square as her companion, but Henry's mother declined fairly sharply on your behalf. I rather think she is one of the few women who suspect that Melanie is not all she seems. However that may be, when Melanie wants something she is not easily deterred and will go to any lengths to gain her ends. Cromer is a criminal, supposedly reformed. I don't doubt that she instructed him to do whatever was necessary to ensure that you would be turned out of Torringtons. For this he would have to obtain a plan of the house, discover who occupied which rooms, and decide how best to gain access by night without leaving any trace; so he presented himself one day as the regular man from the clockmaker's and was able to roam the house more or less at will, even to the extent of snipping one of the small bows from your nightdress in preparation for the plan he had formed."

"Oh!" I exclaimed as light dawned. "Lady Whitchurch kept the locket beside her bed when she slept, so if Cromer secretly broke in a few nights later, he was able to throw suspicion on me by putting the locket in my room and leaving the blue bow in Lady Whitchurch's room."

Caspar Gilliard nodded. "I have investigated the man's prison record," he said. "There have been no convictions for six years now, but before that time he was renowned among the police for his skill as a cat burglar, so he would not have found it difficult to move like a ghost from room to room without waking either you or Lady Whitchurch."

I felt a huge sense of relief at knowing that this mystery was at last deciphered and that I was not subject to some mental defect that could cause me to commit a crime without knowing it. But, as before, this emotion was quickly overtaken by fresh bafflement.

"Mr. Galliard," I said, "I'm sure you're right about the way Cromer tricked Lady Whitchurch into believing me to be a thief so that she would send me away. But what I cannot for the life of me understand is *why* your wife went to such extraordinary lengths to secure me as her companion."

We had left the canal and were approaching York Gate, where we would leave the park. For discretion's sake I would have withdrawn my hand from Caspar Galliard's arm, but he held it tightly by pressing with his elbow. "Melanie wants you in our home as a means of tormenting me," he said. "That is why I have had to speak out at last."

I said, "Tormenting you? But how, Mr. Galliard?"

"It is not easy for me to explain. Melanie has long since guessed that my journeys abroad are not exclusively concerned with exploration or archaeology. She knew, when I returned from my last trip, that I had been injured and in hospital for a time, though she did not know the nature of the injury. She also knew something more, Jemimah, for she is diabolically perceptive. She knew I had undergone an experience that affected me profoundly, and this aroused her curiosity. I told her my injury had been treated by a most excellent doctor, and made the error of letting slip the name of John Selby, whom you will no doubt remember."

I said, "Yes. We traveled home on the same ship, and he was very kind."

"A good man indeed. Unknown to me, Melanie wrote him a letter of thanks, care of the War Office, which was sent on to him at his private address. I believe she must also have included some seemingly innocent questions with her thanks, for he replied with a letter in which he spoke glowingly of the part played in saving my life by a young woman calling herself Jemimah Lawley, of Witchwood Hall. This letter she showed me, but I confirmed no part of it and responded noncommittally, as I was duty bound to do, you understand."

I recalled what John Selby had said about the brave men who followed Caspar Galliard's dangerous, lonely, and despised profession, and I said, "Yes, I understand."

"The rest is surmise, but I am certain that Melanie determined to seek you out, and I have no doubt she began by paying a visit to Witchwood Hall, where she would have discovered a most intriguing situation. A few inquiries in the village would reveal that you had left with Lord Henry Boot's World-famous Punch and Judy Show many weeks earlier—for of course my return to England was long after yours. She would at once know that I had wired Henry to take care of you, and she had only to arrange for somebody in Granger to inform her when Henry eventually brought you to Torringtons. Then she was free to pay a visit and make her first attempt to bring you to Stanford Square."

I realized that now, for the first time, the man beside me had acknowledged in plain terms that he was Kassim, my guardian and companion on the long harsh journey from Shul, but for the moment this was of no importance. I said, "Being badly wounded as you were, and coming so close to death, was of course an experience that must have affected you deeply, but why should that make Mrs. Galliard take such an interest in me? I really don't understand."

Caspar Galliard said gently, "It was not the wounding or the nearness of death that made such a lasting impression upon me. It was you, Jemimah. As I said a moment ago, Melanie is diabolically perceptive, and the first word is well chosen. When I came home, she knew something had changed me radically. When she read John Selby's letter, she knew it was you who had affected me so deeply. She knew that I loved you."

XV

For two or three seconds Caspar Galliard's words failed to register in my mind, for their meaning was so wildly beyond any conception I had ever entertained of his feelings toward me. Then came a moment of blank disbelief, followed at once by the alarming certainty that he could not possibly be lying to me and had spoken the plain truth.

I might have felt embarrassed, I might have felt flattered, but in fact my only emotion was one of dismay. "Oh, dear God," I said shakily when I at last found my tongue. "What a dreadful situation for you, Mr. Galliard. I'm so sorry. But are you quite sure? Is it possible that you think of me fondly because we were companions in danger and I was able to help you at the end?"

"That alters nothing, Jemimah," he said with measured emphasis. "Certainly I came to love you on that journey, but only because it enabled me to know you through and through. I did not suddenly fall in love with you romantically, as I and a hundred others have fallen in love with Melanie. I came to love you for what I saw in you day by day, for your courage, your determination, your spirit, and for the way you never once complained but set your hand to whatever task lay before you. From loving you, I could so easily have come to falling in love with you, but I could not allow myself this, for I am not free. It is wrong of me to have spoken to you as I have done today, but the greater wrong was to remain silent and let you become ever more deeply entrapped in the webs of misery that Melanie will spin for you. That I could not do."

My skirt was wet around the hem now and plucked at my ankles with each step, but I was hardly aware of it. "Do you mean that Mrs. Galliard brought me here to hurt me?" I asked.

"Yes. Because by so doing she can hurt me. I am always her chief victim, and that is why she has contrived to throw us together, encouraging our morning walks, urging you to work in the garden, where you are constantly in my view, and suggesting that you help me in secretarial ways. She knows me, Jemimah. She knew all this would torment me with both frustration and guilt. Now she has begun to twist the knife in me by turning her attention to ways of playing cat and mouse with you, as she did by inviting those impostors from Witchwood Hall."

We were out of the park now, waiting to cross the road. A few cabs were passing, but from where we stood I could see no more than half a dozen people on foot, and all were out of earshot. I was still confused and found myself groping for words as I said haltingly, "I'm deeply honored to know your feelings toward me, Mr. Galliard. I . . . I do understand why you have revealed them now, but I think we should not refer to them again. Please tell me what you wish me to do. Would it be best if I went away at once, before Mrs. Galliard returns?"

"Away? Where?" There was such strain in his voice that I turned my head to peer at him and saw that his face seemed almost gray with an emotion I could not fathom. It was surely not fear, I told myself. I had seen this man less moved when lying on a rocky hill in Afghanistan with a bullet in his body and a dislocated shoulder.

"Where?" he repeated.

"I hadn't thought, Mr. Galliard, and it doesn't matter where." That was true. Once such things had been all-important, but I had lived so long now without knowing my future from one day to the next that I had learned not to be greatly troubled by uncertainty. The whimsical thought touched me briefly that Lord Henry would probably take me on the road again with him if I asked.

We walked in silence for a minute, then I said, "A little while ago you spoke of the Lawleys as impostors, Mr. Galliard. Is that what you believe?"

"Of course it is what I believe." He sounded startled. "Sandru told me your story. Why should you think I might doubt him?"

"It wasn't that," I said. "I've been in doubt about what to believe myself, wondering if I was suffering from a delusion, as everyone but Lord Henry seems to think. After all, it's so hard to imagine how that man and the young woman could have achieved the imposture."

"I agree," he said, and there was anger in his voice, underlying a note of bitter regret, "but achieve it they did, and only Sandru or I can refute them, for we alone know exactly how and when Jemimah Lawley was brought captive from Kabul to Shul. But, my dear, though I would give my right arm to help you, I am debarred from speaking in your cause. My duty to my country will not allow it."

I said, "Yes. I know." I was surprised to feel no resentment; it would have been natural enough, but I could feel only pity for this strange, tortured man at my side, whose pride in his family name made him a prisoner of a wife who was destroying him; whose rigid sense of honor compelled him to keep the vows he had made to a woman who dishonored him time and time again; and whose overwhelming devotion to duty would not allow him to help a woman he loved . . . myself.

Many would have found such behavior a cause for mockery, but not I, who had known a world of savagery such as few Englishmen or women could imagine. I respected and admired Caspar Galliard as a man of principle, even when his principles were to my detriment, for I had never forgotten how he had given his promise to Sandru, under duress, to do all in his power to take me safely across Afghanistan to Herat. In the cold harsh world of the spy, another man would quickly have defaulted on that burdensome promise and left me to die in the mountains, but not Caspar Galliard. Only a near fatal bullet had taken the burden from him, and then at the very close of our long journey.

He said, "You have every right to be deeply angry, Jemimah."

I pressed his arm and answered, "But I'm not, Mr. Galliard." Then I took my hand away, and after a little pause I went on: "You haven't yet told me what you wish me to do."

We were within a hundred yards or so of Stanford Square now, and he said in a strained voice, "For God's sake, don't go away, Jemimah. I had to speak, to warn you against the vicious games Melanie will play, so that perhaps you can avoid some of the pain she will try to inflict. But please don't leave me yet, for without your presence and support I don't know what I might be driven to do."

I looked at him sharply, recalling with alarm the ominous dream I had dreamed about him, and I said, "You mustn't think such thoughts, Mr. Galliard."

"I cannot help myself!" He spoke through his teeth, and his voice held desperation. "I am afraid of myself, Jemimah. Please stay and help me, just for a little longer, for soon I must go back to the land where I found you. I may leave suddenly, without warning, for from the moment I am called to duty I travel secretly, not under my own name. And when I go, you must go also. Go to Henry for help. I shall never be able to rest if I carry with me the knowledge that you are left alone with Melanie. She knows I love you, and I fear the lengths she will go to in contriving to hurt me through you. Can I count on you to do as I ask, Jemimah? Please?"

I imagined what might happen to Caspar Galliard during one of his secret and dangerous missions if he was distracted by anxiety for me, and I shivered inwardly. "Yes, Mr. Galliard," I said. "I promise."

"Thank God," he murmured, and held the iron gate open for me. As we mounted the steps he drew a deep breath, then said in his normal cool voice, "Your skirt is wet, Jemimah. Be sure to change at once."

*   *   *

Anne Melanie Galliard returned from Saxmundham two days later, preceded in the morning by a letter for Caspar Galliard from her father, which he showed me. It read:

Dear Caspar,
*   Thank you for your kind letter.*
*   For my dear wife's sake I have continued to receive Anne's visits since her marriage to you. Now my wife has passed on, and I am free to say that I never wish to see my daughter again. You will assuredly know why, and you have my respect and gratitude for all you have done to protect my wife from further sorrow.*
*   My telegram invited your attendance at the funeral. Anne tells me you declined, but as I surmised and as your letter shows, this was a lie.*
*   During your visit in December I thought well of the very pleasant young woman who is now Anne's companion. Please try to safeguard her from unhappiness or harm, Caspar, for she is in a singularly vulnerable position, as I am sure you realize.*

*   With kindest regards,*
*   Andrew Grant*

We were in the study, and I felt pale as I looked up from reading the letter. Caspar Galliard said as he took it from me, "My only purpose in letting you see this is to show that I have neither imagined nor exaggerated Melanie's true nature. These are the words of her father." He slowly tore the letter to shreds. "Now please let me see the references you have been gathering on the use of stratigraphy in dating prehistoric artifacts."

Apart from Caspar Galliard's comment on the letter, nothing more was said between us concerning all that had been revealed during the extraordinary hour when we walked alone in the silent park. As he had predicted, when his wife returned to Stanford Square her manner was as warmly affectionate as ever. She now wore mourning, and about her there was an air of quiet serenity that seemed to enhance the aura of inner beauty she had always possessed. No word was spoken about my visit to the Sanctuary, and so totally convincing was her manner that it would have been easy to believe I had dreamed the whole incident, except that I was no longer disposed to doubt my memory or sanity now.

I knew I was Jemimah Lawley; I had heard Caspar Galliard reveal the truth about his wife; I had seen the dreadful letter from her father; and above all I would forever recall with horrifying clarity that moment in the Sanctuary boudoir when the dark soul of Anne Melanie Galliard had looked at me nakedly from those beautiful eyes, chilling my blood with revulsion.

In the days following her return I did my best to behave normally. Perhaps I was not very successful, for I could claim no skill as an actress, but I reasoned that this mattered little, for Anne Galliard would expect me to be ill at ease after what I had seen and was probably finding pleasure in my discomfiture.

I came to believe that my presence was indeed a help to Caspar Galliard, for I noticed that now he had opened his heart to me he no longer had those swift changes of mood, amiable at one moment, dour and remote the next. His wife noticed it too, for once or twice I caught a momentary glimmer of curiosity in her gaze as she smiled upon him. Each day when I woke I warned myself to be alert for her next attempt to distress me. I realized that it would probably be something as totally unexpected as the visit from the Lawley impostors had been and that, since I could not hope to anticipate her subtle contrivance, I would simply have to brace myself to withstand whatever ordeal awaited me.

If I was not particularly apprehensive, it was because I had the comfort of knowing that I was very different from most English girls of my age, or of any age. I had been a captive in Shul, and I doubted that Anne Melanie Galliard could inflict on me any ordeal to match the terrors of that.

A few days after her return Lord Henry called to offer his condolences. Out of consideration for her feelings, he did not remain long. Caspar Galliard and I saw him to the door when he left and listened soberly as he said how sad this bereavement was for Anne, how wonderful she was, and how bravely she was bearing her loss. I felt heavy-hearted that a man as kind and decent as Henry should be so deceived, and I was sure

Caspar Galliard felt the same, for we were both careful not to look at each other when the door closed and we returned to the drawing room.

That night I dreamed again of Sandru as a young man, wearing the scarlet jacket of a soldier. As in the earlier dream, I was Lalla of Shul, his servant, but attending him under conditions of great luxury, in the paneled dining room of a fine house where he sat at the head of the table and a young woman sat at the foot. In my dream I poured wine for Sandru, then moved to take up my waiting position by the sideboard. To my astonishment, Henry was standing there in the livery of a footman.

I said in a fierce whisper, "What on earth are you up to? A Punch and Judy man can't be a footman! Go away before you get me into trouble!" Henry smiled at me. "But I live here, Mim," he said. "I live here."

Then I was awake, propped on an elbow, panting with shock. I groped for matches and lit my candle. The small clock on the cabinet beside me told me that it was almost six o'clock. I lay back, my heart still thumping from the revelation my dream had brought me, for I had suddenly been vouchsafed knowledge possessed by no other living soul, and there was not a shadow of doubt in my mind as to its truth.

As I lay staring up at the candlelit ceiling of my bedroom at number 12 Stanford Square, I knew why a woman in a great house called Torringtons wore a locket containing two miniature paintings hidden beneath her dress. I knew why Lady Whitchurch treasured that locket even though her husband had left her for another woman years ago. I knew why she was a recluse, and why her son Henry had said that she was so often withdrawn and unfriendly. And I knew why her firstborn son had been christened George.

Later, when I went on my morning walk and met Caspar Galliard, I was tempted to tell him of my extraordinary discovery, but I held my tongue. This was not my secret to tell. Besides, since the day we had walked and talked in the snow, we had both been careful not to exchange confidences that might take us beyond the formal relationship between the master of the house and his wife's companion.

I was now very anxious to visit Torringtons and speak with Lady Whitchurch. She might refuse to receive me, but I did not think this likely, for she could not do so without explaining to Henry, and this would cause a breach between them. I did not want to ask Anne Galliard for a day's leave to go down into Hampshire, for if she suspected I had a special reason for wishing to go she might well find some plausible way of thwarting me, though of course with her usual display of affection.

After long thought I decided to be patient and await an opportunity I knew would not be long in coming. In fact it came a week later, when she announced at luncheon that she would spend the next day at the Sanctuary, as she felt the need of going into retreat for a full day to meditate and pray. As she said this, there was not the slightest hint, even in the very depths of her eyes, of her being aware that I well knew how she spent her time at the Sanctuary.

I tried to keep my own expression blank as I murmured some reply. Caspar Galliard said nothing. I was careful not to look at him, but I could imagine, could almost feel with him, the sickness of heart his wife's words must bring. The knowledge of what she intended was somehow made worse on this occasion, for she wore a black dress with a mourning brooch pinned to the breast and looked almost angelic in her grave yet serene beauty. I shivered inwardly, feeling that her deception went far beyond hypocrisy; it was blasphemous, and I had the chilling sensation of sitting at table with a monster in the guise of a goddess.

A few minutes later, following a plan I had decided on, I said, "When Lord Henry was last here he asked me to go down to Torringtons and visit his mother one day soon. I suppose tomorrow would provide an opportunity if you are to be at the Sanctuary and have no need of me, Mrs. Galliard, but . . . oh dear, I do find Lady Whitchurch a rather formidable hostess. Perhaps I could leave it for a few weeks."

"Oh, Jemimah, no, that would be unkind. You must go tomorrow," said Anne Galliard, gently smiling. "Lady Whitchurch has a somewhat forbidding manner, I know, but that is just on the surface. Underneath, she is the most sympathetic of women. Do please convey my warmest regards to her."

I said meekly, "Very well, Mrs. Galliard," and tried to look as if I were trying not to look unhappy. I had guessed correctly. Anne Galliard would think I dreaded an encounter with Lady Whitchurch, who had turned me out of her house as a thief. It would therefore feed her loathsome appetites to make me endure such misery, innocently brought about by Henry.

That afternoon I wrote to Henry, asking if he would please meet me off the train at Granger and take me to have luncheon there, but saying I had a particular reason for asking him not to speak of this to his mother for the time being. At nine o'clock next morning Anne Galliard went off in a cab to the Sanctuary, and at a quarter past came a telegram from Henry to say he would meet me as arranged. A few minutes later I went to the study to ask Caspar Galliard if he wished me to work with him for half an hour before leaving to catch the train for Granger. There were a few footnotes to be prepared for a paper he had written, and I felt he might be able to deal with them before I left.

He was standing by the window, looking out on the garden when I entered, and he shook his head when I asked if he wished to work on the footnotes. "Not today, Jemimah."

"The publisher wrote to say that he hoped the paper would be ready by tomorrow, Mr. Galliard," I ventured.

"Out of the question," Caspar Galliard said, and turned to look at me. I could hear a note of stress in his voice, and the expression on his face took me back to those moments on the rocky slope in Afghanistan, when he had squatted with his *jezail* cocked and ready to fire, waiting with bleak patience for sight of the enemy who sought to kill him.

"I want you to tell Henry," he said abruptly. "Tell him the truth about Melanie."

I could feel my eyes widening with shock. "About your wife?" I faltered. "Oh, but I couldn't, Mr. Galliard. It's not my place to do so, and anyway he would never believe me."

"Do you care for Henry?"

"Yes, of course. He was a wonderful friend and companion to me."

"Then do it for his sake. Tell him of Melanie."

"His sake?" I found I was wringing my hands in dismay at the prospect. "I don't understand what you mean."

"I can't explain," he said quietly. "Do you trust me, Jemimah?"

"Yes." The answer came automatically. "Yes, I can't help but trust you, Mr. Galliard, but—"

"Then do as I say, for the sake of a friend and a good man."

I stood gazing at him stupidly, trying to find a way of escape and knowing there was none. At last I whispered, "I shall never be able to make him believe me. He thinks the world of her."

"Tell him what you have seen with your own eyes. You are the one person he will believe. Promise me, Jemimah."

Slowly, sick at heart, I bowed my head in acquiescence. I had enough anxieties already about my visit to Torringtons without this, but once Caspar Galliard had made Lord Henry's welfare the issue it was impossible for me to refuse. He said, "Thank you, my dear," and came toward me, holding out his hand for mine. I hesitated, then gave it to him. He bowed over it, barely brushing the knuckles with his lips, and said, "I'm deeply grateful."

He turned away to the window and stood looking out again, hands clasped behind his back. "You had better run along now. Good-bye, Jemimah."

"Good-bye, Mr. Galliard. I expect to return by seven o'clock, in time for dinner."

"Very well."

I waited for a moment or two, but when he said no more and did not turn, I went out quietly, closing the study door behind me.

* * *

When the train steamed into Granger at a few minutes past twelve that day, Lord Henry was waiting on the platform to greet me with a smile, a hug, and a kiss on both cheeks. "By God, it's good to see you, Mim," he said, tucking my arm through his as we made our way along the platform. "Life here has been sapping my confidence since you left. Everything is desperately formal, nobody laughs at my jokes, and a lot of hopeful mothers are hurling their depressing daughters at my head again. They won't believe it when I keep saying I'm unworthy of them."

On another occasion I would have laughed and relaxed completely at being in Henry's company again, but now I was too tense at the prospect of the ordeal ahead. A cab was waiting outside the station, and as he helped me into it Henry said, "I didn't bring one of the carriages from Torringtons because you said in your letter that I mustn't mention your visit. What's all the mystery, Mim, and why are you so jumpy? It's not like you."

I said, "Oh dear. Does it show? I'm sorry, but I have so much to tell you, and most of it you won't want to hear, but I've promised Mr. Galliard."

He sat back in the cab, turning to look at me curiously. "Lord, it does sound serious," he said, "but don't upset yourself. Just try to unwind, and once we're settled you can tell me all about it."

I gave a sigh and said, "Well, thank goodness it's you. I'm hardly going to know where to begin. I've two things to tell you, Henry, one quite awful, and then there's something else, entirely different, that I have to tell your mother." I looked out of the cab window. "Did you arrange something for luncheon? Oh, I wish it was summer so we could have a picnic by the river and be quite on our own."

Henry scratched his jaw doubtfully. "I told Jack Whittle at the White Hart that I'd be bringing a lady along for luncheon. I could easily have him serve us in his private room, but I don't want to harm your reputation."

"Oh, for heaven's sake," I said impatiently, "we traveled the road for weeks on end, just the two of us. What difference does it make if we have luncheon in a private room at an inn?"

"None to me, my little angel," said Henry, "but I'd be a miserable knave if I didn't think of you."

"Well, now you've thought, and thank you very much, I do appreciate it, but please let us take Jack Whittle's private room."

This proved to be a pleasant upstairs room of a tavern between Granger and the next village. Lord Henry was evidently well known by the innkeeper, and I suspected that he had brought ladies here before on occasion, but he managed to make clear to our host and his wife that I was a lady in a different category.

A fire burned in the grate, and as soon as I had taken off my hat and coat a light but excellent meal was served. "I'm agog to hear this quite awful news you have to tell me," Henry announced, "but serious matters hinder digestion, so first we'll eat, limiting ourselves to one half pint of ale each, to keep our heads clear. Then Jack's wench shall bring us a large pot of coffee on a spirit stove and close the door on us while you tell your story."

I had little appetite but made a fair effort to do justice to the meal as we talked of unimportant matters. Then came the moment when we sat on either side of the fireplace with our coffee, and Henry said, "Well, go on, Mim. Tell me the worst part first."

Throughout the train journey from London I had devoted all my thoughts to devising the best way of saying what had to be said, and I had come to the conclusion that it would be best simply to recount what I had discovered in the sequence that it had occurred. "This concerns Mrs. Galliard," I said. "Mr. Galliard made me promise to tell you, and I want you to be prepared for a great shock, Henry."

I began my tale with the arrival of the telegram, which had been the beginning of the whole affair. Henry looked baffled when I spoke of my encounter at the door of the Sanctuary with the man he had described as an elderly cherub. Then, with the words sticking in my throat, I came to the moment when I stood gazing on the scene in the boudoir, and as I spoke I saw the color fade from his face. He set down his coffee cup with a shaking hand and said, "No, Mim, no. That can't be so, there's some mistake—"

I broke in on him, greatly agitated. "For God's sake, let me say it all without interruption or I'll never get through, Henry dear. What you believe in the end is a matter for you, but please let me keep my promise to Caspar Galliard."

He got to his feet and paced across the room, wiping a hand across his lips. "All right, Mim," he muttered. "Go on."

I told what I had seen in the boudoir and tried to describe what I had felt when it seemed some alien creature stared at me with basilisk gaze from behind Anne Melanie Galliard's beautiful eyes. I went on to recount, as faithfully as I could recall, all that Caspar Galliard had said to me as we walked alone through the park in the snow, about his unconsummated marriage, about the suicide of his wife's sister at seventeen, about Anne Galliard's own father speaking of her as Stormswift, a Harpy. I told how even in delirium in Afghanistan, muttering in fever, Caspar Galliard had called her Stormswift and bitch-goddess. I told of the spine-chilling letter her father, Andrew Grant, had written to Caspar Galliard after the funeral, and how only this morning Caspar Galliard had made me promise to tell all this to his friend, Lord Henry, though I did not know why.

As I spoke, Henry sometimes paced the room, sometimes stood quite still, staring at me with eyes that seemed to have sunk deeper into his head. He poured fresh coffee, gulped it down, sat for a few seconds, then began to pace again. When all was told my throat had become dry and my voice flat with a kind of weariness. Finally I said, "I know you worship Anne Galliard, and I don't expect you to believe me, Henry. I can only say, whatever I've told you that I saw with my own eyes or felt in my own heart, those things are true. The rest is what Caspar Galliard told me, and I cannot disbelieve him."

Lord Henry moved to the table, sat down, and held his bowed head in his hands, elbows resting on the table. I did not speak, for I had nothing more to say; I could only feel thankful that my worst ordeal of the day was behind me now. A full three minutes passed, then Henry sighed, lifted his head, folded his arms, and looked at me with an attempt to smile.

"I've been trying not to believe you, Mim," he said in a tired voice. "I've worshiped Anne for years, and I've been telling myself that if I could be so hugely mistaken about her, then I could just as easily be mistaken about you. I mean, leaving Caspar aside for the moment, why should I believe that Anne Galliard's beauty of form and nature conceals a monster of cruelty, any more than I should believe that *she* is what she

seems to be and *you* are secretly a cruel and wicked creature to slander
her so . . ."

He shook his head, lifted a shoulder, and made a vague gesture with
his hand, still trying to smile. "But it's no use. The fact is, I only know
the outward Anne Galliard, and I've only ever been in her company
formally. But I know you inside out, Mim. We've lived together in the
closest intimacy short of sharing the same bed. I also know how well
Paloma liked you, and there was no fooling that girl, bless her. I've sat
huddled beside you in the booth while we worked the puppets together,
and I've seen you make the best of every difficulty."

He shook his head again. "I *know* you, Mim, so whether I want to or
not, I'm compelled to believe you, damn it. And on top of that, there's
all that Caspar says, backed up by the extraordinary way he changed
after his marriage. Dear God, it's little wonder your friend John Selby
felt Caspar was a man who invited death." Henry gave a shaky, humorless laugh. "I could weep for him. I could weep for myself, for the years
of adoring a monster. What a fool. I'm a born clown, I suppose, but even
a clown feels pain. A beautiful dream has just become a hideous nightmare, and I'm brokenhearted, Mim, honest to God I am."

I got up and went to stand beside him as he sat at the table, then I
slipped my arms about his neck and stooped a little so that I could hold
his head against my shoulder. "You weren't a fool, and you're not a born
clown, Henry," I whispered. "You're a kind and honorable man, and I'm
desperately sorry you've been so hurt, for I owe you more than I can ever
repay."

I gave him a little kiss on the temple, then went back to my easy chair
by the fire, surprised at what I had just done, but in no way regretting it.
"Thanks, Mim," he said slowly, staring down at the table. Then he
looked up and gave me a smile that was something like his old smile.
"Would you like some more coffee?"

"Yes, please, Henry. I'm so dry."

He poured a fresh cup, brought it to me, and stood looking down at
me curiously. "You said you had two things to tell me. I hope the other
isn't anything like the first."

"Oh no," I said with a feeling of relief, "it's quite minor and it won't
take long to tell." I paused to think for a moment, then went on: "But
you might become angry, so promise not to speak till I've finished."

"Angry?" He looked surprised. "All right, I shall remain mute."

"Well . . . I have to tell you the true reason why I left Torringtons.
It was because your mother believed I had stolen a locket of hers—"

"What?"

"Henry, please!" He got up and began tramping around the table, lips set. I told of discovering the locket beside my bed and how Lady Whitchurch had accused me of its theft because she had found a bow from my nightdress in her room. "I couldn't even argue," I said, "because I thought I might have done it without knowing. It was impossible for me to stay on, but I knew you would make a fuss if you were told, and your mother suggested I should go to Anne Galliard, who had said she wanted a companion. After I saw Cromer, your elderly cherub, at the Sanctuary, I was sure he must have been involved, but it was Caspar Galliard who immediately guessed how and why—"

I broke off sharply, putting a hand to my mouth in sudden alarm. Lord Henry stopped his pacing to stare at me, and when I simply stared back without speaking he said, "Well, go on. You can't stop there. Obviously Cromer had a good look around when he pretended to be from the clockmakers, and later he broke in and did something you would be blamed for. But *why?* If Caspar guessed why, tell me what he said."

I pressed my hands to my cheeks and muttered, "I'm so stupid. I've only just realized I would have to explain why, and that means I have to betray a confidence. At least, I think it does, though he didn't say I mustn't speak of it."

Henry ran a hand through his hair and said with one of his eye-rolling grimaces, "God save us all, Mim, who didn't say you mustn't speak of what? And why did Cromer do what he did?"

I said reluctantly, not meeting his eyes, "Anne Galliard made Cromer do it so that I would have to leave Torringtons and become her companion. I know this sounds foolish, but she thought . . . well, she knew, really, that her husband loved me, and she wanted me there as a means of tormenting him because she knew he was bound to behave honorably. I don't think I quite explained that before when I was telling you about her, did I?"

"You didn't explain it at all," he said soberly, and dropped into the chair facing mine. "How did Anne know Caspar was in love with you? He's hardly a man to wear his heart on his sleeve."

"I know. But when he returned from abroad she was aware that something had affected him very deeply, and then, by mischance, she discovered through Captain John Selby that I had played a part in bringing him to safety when he was wounded. She is very perceptive—diabolically perceptive, Caspar Galliard says—and she was quite certain he had come to love the young woman who had helped him." I looked up to meet

Henry's eyes. "I expect it seems foolish to you, but Caspar Galliard really does believe that he loves me."

"It doesn't seem at all foolish to me," said Henry, studying me with an air of exasperation. "Confound it, Mim, you always manage to disarm me. I was just about to be extremely angry with you, but then you turned my anger aside by distracting me with something else. When I think of it, when I think that Caspar's wife could actually contrive to bring you into the home as a means of tormenting him . . ." He broke off with a shudder. "Yes . . . that's the act of a Harpy."

I said, "Why were you going to be angry with me?"

He slapped the arm of the chair and glared. "Need you ask? Damn it, Mim, how could you treat me so badly? How could you let yourself be turfed out of Torringtons without telling me you had been falsely accused?"

"I wasn't sure, Henry," I said patiently. "I wasn't even sure of my own identity at the time, and I was so afraid that I had started doing bad things without knowing what I'd done. So I just acted in the way I thought best and would cause least trouble. It's no use your glaring at me, you simply haven't the right face for looking stern, you just look comical."

He leaned back in his chair and laughed. "Ah, Mim, I've truly missed you. Listen now, I've been thinking it would be great fun this summer to go to America and sail all the way down the Mississippi River from Minneapolis to New Orleans. That's almost the whole of its two-thousand-mile length. Why not come with me, Mim?" He slapped his knee. "We could take the Punch and Judy show with us!"

I was laughing myself as I said, "Oh, stop talking such nonsense."

"I'll even include you in the billing. Lord Henry Boot and Miss Jemimah Lawley's World-famous Punch and—"

"Henry!"

"All right, I'll stop," he said mildly. "But I do mean it, Mim." He took out his watch and looked at it. "You said you wanted to see my mother this afternoon. Is that to tell her about the elderly cherub and the locket?"

"Partly," I said, "but there's something much more important. Quite by chance I've discovered . . . well, a secret of hers, and by a very strange coincidence I know something that I'm certain she will wish to know, but I can't tell you about it because it's not my secret."

He nodded slowly, a look of amused resignation on his mobile face. "Highly mysterious," he commented. "I'll say one thing for you, Mim. When you come to visit a chap, there's no boring small talk."

XVI

I was unable to prevent Henry taking charge of my arrival at Torringtons. Without allowing Jackson to announce me, he marched into the drawing room with me on his arm. Lady Whitchurch looked up from a book she was reading, and I saw her shocked surprise at sight of me, but her son spoke before she could utter a word, his manner kindly but very firm.

"Good afternoon, Mamma. I now know exactly why Jemimah left this house, and I also know beyond any doubt whatsoever that she was falsely accused, as you will be compelled to admit when you have listened to what I have to say. She has *not* returned to protest her innocence, however, but to tell you of something she believes to be of great importance to you. If you refuse to listen to what we have to say, then with much regret I shall leave this house at once and I shall not return."

Lady Whitchurch studied him in silence for a few moments before transferring her gaze to me. I could read nothing in her expression, but then she laid her book aside and said, "Very well, Henry. You and Jemimah may sit down."

"Thank you, Mamma," he said politely. Making sure I was comfortably seated, he took a chair for himself, then went on briskly: "To understand what I am about to tell you, it will be necessary for you to accept the astonishing fact that Anne Galliard is not at all what she appears to be."

His mother sniffed. "That does not astonish *me*," she said coldly. "How the rest of the world can be taken in by a woman with a heart so ugly I have never understood. It would have been quite pointless for me to tell you she was dangerous, so I am very glad you have discovered it for yourself."

Both Henry and I were taken aback. For a moment he looked at me openmouthed, then with an effort he pulled himself together and plunged on. "The fact is, Mamma, that Anne Galliard was determined to have Jemimah in her house for very wicked reasons of her own, but reasons which are no concern of ours."

"To plague her husband, I imagine," said Lady Whitchurch dryly. "Is he in love with the girl, perhaps?"

Henry breathed hard through his nose and said tautly, "That is not our concern, and please stop interrupting me, Mamma. What does concern us is that, in order to get her way, Anne Galliard sent a man in her employ to carry out an act designed to make you believe Jemimah is a thief."

Lady Whitchurch's manner changed, and she looked at me sharply. "What man?" she demanded.

Henry answered for me. "The man who purported to have come from Wilkinson's to attend to the clocks, Mamma. The little dark man with a round face like an elderly cherub. Do you remember now?"

There was silence for almost a minute. Lady Whitchurch gazed with unfocused eyes, and I could almost follow the sequence of her thoughts. "Yes," she said at last, very slowly, then looked at me. "My sincere apologies, Jemimah. I will not say I was stupid, for the thing was so cunningly contrived that I think it would have deceived anybody. But I am mortified that I did not follow my instinct rather than my reason."

She looked at Henry, and her eyes flared with anger. "This was a criminal act. Can it be proved? I don't mean proved to me, I mean can it be proved in a court of law? I will *not* allow that woman to go unpunished—"

"Wait, Mamma, wait," Henry broke in gently. "There is Caspar to consider, and there are other aspects to this matter that you don't yet know about."

"What other aspects?"

I spoke for the first time. "I have made a discovery I believe to be of great importance to you, Lady Whitchurch. If Henry will leave us now, I shall be glad to tell you about it."

She studied me with a puzzled, almost wary gaze, then replied with a brief nod. "Very well."

Henry had already risen. He gave me a smile, moved past me to the door, and went out. For a moment I was tongue-tied, then I drew in a long breath and said, "When I found the locket at my bedside, I looked very carefully at the two miniatures in it, Lady Whitchurch. I recognized you as the young woman, and I thought the young man must be your husband, but now I'm quite sure he wasn't."

She looked down at her hands and said, "What makes you say that?"

"Because I recognized the man, Lady Whitchurch. Oh, not at that moment. In fact, not until much later, after I had twice had strange dreams about him. The second time was a few days ago, and I woke up with the shock of sudden recognition—"

Lady Whitchurch broke in upon me with a gesture of agitation. "Impossible," she snapped. "It is quite impossible for you to have recognized the young man. He died many years before you were born."

I said, "Forgive me, but you are wrong, Lady Whitchurch. His name is Georgios Alexandrou, formerly captain and battalion doctor in the 44th Regiment of Foot. I last spoke with him less than a year ago, in spring, the night I escaped from Shul."

Lady Whitchurch swayed in her chair, eyes half closed, face white and drawn. I jumped to my feet and caught her by the shoulders, afraid she might fall, but after a moment or two she said in a surprisingly steady voice, "Thank you, Jemimah, thank you. Just give me a moment to recover, child." She reached for my hand, and I stood holding hers, patting it gently and watching the slow return of color to her cheeks as she breathed deeply.

At last she nodded and waved me to my chair, then sat gazing at me with wondering eyes as she said slowly, "He was reported as having been killed in action during the retreat from Kabul in '42."

I said, "He was taken prisoner, but they spared his life because he had saved the life of a badly wounded Afghan. Eventually he was taken up into Kafiristan, to the little kingdom of Shul, and he has been there ever since. I was his servant for well over a year . . ."

I went on to tell Lady Whitchurch all I knew of Sandru's story, and of his life spent as a doctor in Shul. It was a tale that took almost half an hour in the telling, and not once did she interrupt me, but sat erect, hands clasped tightly in her lap, completely in control of herself, except that from time to time she would close her eyes and tears would trickle down her cheeks, to be brushed away with a lace handkerchief.

When at last I fell silent she said nothing for a while, then gave a great sigh and whispered, "We were so deeply in love, my Georgios and I, but he had foreign blood and no great wealth, so my family would not hear of my marrying him. I would have eloped, but Georgios would not let me do that. He was a soldier, standing by to go overseas . . ."

She dabbed her eyes with the handkerchief and drew in a quivering breath. "In all these years I have never ceased to love him. When he was reported killed, I no longer cared what happened to me. A marriage was arranged. I became a dutiful wife but not a loving one. Neither my husband nor I was happy. The fault was mostly mine, for I have always carried Georgios in my heart." She shook her head slowly, her eyes full of pain. "Now I learn that he did not die. Oh, the waste of it all, the lifetime of waste. I am old now, and he will be older still, a captive living in primitive squalor in a barbarian land. Oh, my poor Georgios. How was he when you left him, Jemimah?"

I said, "For a man of almost seventy, he was in very good health, Lady Whitchurch. He made me his nursing assistant, and we held surgery and went out on rounds every day. He was still vigorous and doing splendid work, for he is a very fine doctor, but—"

I stopped short and would have bitten off that last word if I could. Lady Whitchurch pounced. "But what, child? What?"

I shook my head, angry with myself for such stupidity. "It's nothing really."

She said gently, "You have no gift for hiding the truth, my dear. For pity's sake tell me what you were about to say. I realize you are withholding something that will distress me, but I would rather know what it is."

I found my own eyes were suddenly moist as I said, "I worry about what will happen in a few years' time, when Sandru can no longer continue working. He has no family to look after him, and neither Deenbur the *pacha* nor the *deshtayu*, the priests, will have any regard for him when he is no longer of use to them."

Lady Whitchurch bowed her head and sat very still. "Oh, dear God," she murmured. "My poor Georgios, my poor darling."

I said anxiously, "I'm so sorry. Perhaps I shouldn't have come here today, shouldn't have spoken at all."

"Oh no!" Lady Whitchurch's head came up. "Whatever sorrow I may feel, I shall always be deeply in your debt for what you have told me today." She paused as if a new thought had struck her. "Of course, you *are* Jemimah Lawley. There can be no imagination or delusion about what I have just heard."

I said, "Yes, I have no doubts about my identity now."

"So the people at Witchwood Hall are criminals who have usurped your position, Jemimah?"

"Yes, but I'm afraid it's unlikely that I can ever prove that now. They are too well established."

"Does this not distress you?"

"I don't let myself dwell on it, Lady Whitchurch. I shall do what I can when I can, but Sandru taught me the wisdom of not wasting my energies in bitterness and grievance."

She stared into the flames of the logs burning in the great fireplace. "Sandru . . ." she murmured, as if trying the name on her tongue. "I wish there had been time for him to teach me as much."

There was a long silence, but it was a strangely companionable one. At last she looked up and braced her shoulders back. "I should like to be alone now, child," she said quietly. "I have much to think about. I am deeply sorry for having misjudged you so cruelly, and I hope you will forgive me. It would be a great pleasure for me if you would return to Torringtons."

I said, "Thank you, and I would like to do so as soon as Caspar Galliard goes away again, but I must stay at Stanford Square till then. He has asked me to and says he needs me badly."

She nodded. "That I can understand, my dear. Well, come as soon as you are free. Now go and find my son, and tell him all that has been said between us. I want him to know." She reached out her arms. "God bless you, child. Come, give me a kiss, if you will."

I found Henry in the billiards room, idly practicing, and we sat together on the long oak bench while I told him about the locket containing the miniature paintings of his mother and Sandru. There was no long tale to tell, for Henry already knew Sandru's story. He sat looking at me in astonishment when I stopped speaking, then said wonderingly, "So that's what blighted poor Mamma's life. It's awfully sad, Mim. I mean, sad that she's nourished her grief all these years instead of trying to put it behind her. God knows, you've suffered enough, but you don't let it govern your life."

I shook my head. "No, but I had one great advantage, Henry. Strange though it seems, it was truly a blessing for me that I was simply forced to come to terms with fear and suffering. But for that, I would be long dead by now."

"A blessing?" he echoed, then laughed and patted my hand. "Come on, I'll play you a hundred up for a shilling, Mim." He stood up and moved to the rack to pick out the short cue I used, but I did not immediately follow. I sat with my hands in my lap, staring toward the expanse of green baize, aghast at what my own mind had revealed to me without warning in the few seconds that it took Henry to speak the casual words he had just spoken.

The revelation was totally unexpected, thoroughly disconcerting, and quite absurd, but in those few seconds I realized that I did not simply feel fondness and affection for Lord Henry Boot. If suddenly wishing him to hold me, to kiss me, to cherish me . . . if wishing to cherish him in return, to give myself gladly to him, and to spend my life in his company . . . if all this was no less than love, then most surely I loved this droll, eccentric, and irrepressible man.

It was a stupefying discovery, and for a moment I felt panic that he might see in my eyes what I felt in my heart, but he was busy chalking my cue for me, then his own, before setting up the red ivory ball for us to begin play.

I lost the game by a wide margin, but at least the playing of it gave me time to recover something of the natural easiness I had always known with Henry. When the game ended he wanted us to have high tea together but I declined, saying I did not want to be late returning to Stanford Square, which was true. Henry made no protest but took me in a carriage to the station and saw me off on the train, as he had done months before, again giving me a good-bye kiss on the cheek, never dreaming how it made my pulse race.

I felt more exhausted than I had ever felt since the day I brought Caspar Galliard unconscious to Herat after a journey of half a thousand miles. The ordeals of telling Henry the truth about Anne Melanie Galliard, then facing his mother and recounting the story of Sandru, had been exacting enough; but on top of all had come the shock of being smitten suddenly and deeply by a love so strong that I had only to picture his dear, kind, comical face for my heart to begin pounding as if I had just run up a hill.

"You'd better get control of yourself, Jemimah Lawley," I told myself sternly as the train rattled through Hampshire. "He's fond of you, but he's not in love with you and never will be, and if you show what you feel he might think you've decided that you'd like to marry a rich lord. Oh dear . . . when Caspar goes away, I'd so much love to go with Henry on his ridiculous trip down the Mississippi, but I daren't, I daren't. I could never hide what I feel if we were together day after day like that."

It was a relief to find, when I reached the house at Stanford Square, that Caspar Galliard had not yet returned from whatever business he was about. According to Edge, he had left the house at noon without saying when he expected to return.

"I'm rather tired, Edge," I said, "and I shan't be wanting dinner. Will you have some brown bread and butter and a pot of tea sent to my room, please?"

"Certainly, Miss Jemimah."

"And perhaps you will explain to Mr. Galliard, asking him to excuse me from joining him at dinner. I shan't be coming down again this evening unless he wants me for something, or unless Mrs. Galliard returns earlier than usual and wishes to see me."

"Very well, miss."

By nine o'clock I was in bed, reading a chapter from *Our Mutual Friend*, but time and again finding that my mind had wandered far away to memories of my days on the road with Henry, reliving moments now precious to me, small and unimportant moments when he had laughed, or dropped a puppet and cursed, or played the fool, or expressed ecstasy at a meal I had cooked; or even remembering, without jealousy, the occasion when he had fled from Paloma's wrath and returned from the woods walking hand in hand with her, a little circlet of flowers on her head.

I made myself keep reading, even though I was taking very little in, and by ten o'clock my eyes were so tired that it was easy for me to fall asleep. Next morning, after my usual walk before breakfast, I learned from Edge that neither Mr. nor Mrs. Galliard had returned to the house the night before. "Nothing to worry about, miss," he said, watching Daisy set out chafing dishes on the sideboard. "The master sometimes has to go off on confidential business very unexpected, like."

I sat down at the table and said, "Yes, but Mrs. Galliard was supposed to return from the Sanctuary yesterday evening. She was only going there for the day, so I understood."

"Quite so, miss, but I expect she changed her mind. She's done so before."

"I see. Well, thank you, Edge, that will be all for now."

I had barely finished breakfast when he entered again, making no attempt to hide his anxiety. "There's two policemen here, miss," he said in a hushed voice. "Well, they say they're policemen and they've got special cards they showed me, but they're just in ordinary clothes. They say they're detectives from this newfangled Criminal Department."

Startled, I said, "Why are they here?"

"Well, they asked for the master, and when I told them he wasn't at home they asked for a member of the family. I said there wasn't anyone else apart from Mrs. Galliard, and she was away, so they asked for the senior member of the staff, and that's you, really, miss."

I tried to sound calm as I said, "Very well, Edge. Show them into the drawing room and I'll be there directly."

"Thank you, miss."

I drank the last of my coffee, dabbed my mouth with a napkin, glanced in the looking glass to see that my hair was tidy, then made my way to the drawing room. Two men stood waiting, one heavily built with a square face and square mustache, the other younger and slighter, clean shaven with sandy hair.

"Sergeant Perry, miss," said the older man, holding out a card for me to examine. "Criminal Investigation Department. Here's my warrant card, for identification purposes, and this is my colleague and assistant, Detective Constable Wooderson."

I said, "Good morning gentlemen, I am Jemimah Lawley, companion to Mrs. Galliard. Would you care to sit down?"

"Thank you, miss." They seated themselves rather stiffly on the edge of the upright chairs. The younger man took out a notebook and pencil, and Sergeant Perry said, "We're advised that Mr. Caspar Galliard is not at home. Can you say when he was last here, miss?"

I said, "I last saw him myself yesterday morning at about half past nine o'clock. I understand from the butler that he left the house later in the morning, and he has not yet returned. We were not alarmed because he is sometimes called away suddenly on private business, but I now feel very anxious, Sergeant. What has happened to bring you here? Is something wrong? An accident of some kind?"

"I'd rather come to that when I've asked a few more questions, if you don't mind, miss," the sergeant said politely but firmly. "Did you see Mrs. Galliard yesterday?"

"I saw her at breakfast, as usual, and at nine o'clock she left for a small house she owns in Southwark."

"Would that be what's called the Sanctuary, miss?"

"Yes."

"And you've seen neither party since?"

"That is correct." I was in a fever of anxiety to know what was behind all this, but in Sergeant Perry I recognized a ponderous man who would not be hurried. The quicker I dealt with his questions, the sooner I would discover why he was asking them.

"Were you present in this house all day yesterday, miss?"

"No, I left here at about ten o'clock and took the train down to Granger, in Hampshire. I returned at about seven o'clock."

Sergeant Perry sucked in air through his nose and nodded solemnly, darting a glance at his colleague. "Can anyone confirm that you spent the day in Hampshire, miss?"

I stared at him, suddenly angry. "You may inquire of the Most Honorable the Marchioness of Whitchurch, and of her son, Lord Henry Boot, if you so wish, Sergeant."

He swallowed, and ran a finger around his collar. "Ah, quite so, miss."

I decided to follow up my advantage and said, "I think it is now time you told me the reason for your inquiries. Mr. and Mrs. Galliard will certainly wish to know when I advise them of your visit on their return."

The sergeant looked down at his boots and turned his hat around in his hands. "I'm afraid I have a shock for you, miss," he said gravely. "I don't know about Mr. Galliard, but Mrs. Galliard will not be returning. She was murdered in that place called the Sanctuary sometime yesterday evening."

I gripped the arms of my chair and felt the skin of my face creep with horror. *"Murdered?"* I whispered at last, and with the word I recalled the stress in Caspar Galliard's eyes when I had last seen him.

"I fear there's no doubt of it, miss," said the sergeant. "She was killed by two very violent blows to the head with a blunt instrument, said instrument being missing from the scene of the crime and suspected of being deep in the Thames mud now. Would you like me to call the butler, miss? I realize this is very nasty for you."

"No. No, thank you, Sergeant." I sat up straight in my chair. "I've been trained in nursing and I've dealt with very ugly injuries, so I won't have hysterics or faint, I promise you."

"Ah, well, that's a help, miss." Sergeant Perry nodded approvingly. "I'm at liberty to tell you that the body was discovered early this morning by one Alfred Cromer, who seems to be a sort of caretaker there, though he's known to us as a man with a criminal record. Both he and his wife have identified the body." Sergeant Perry paused and stroked his mustache. "There are certain aspects we find highly peculiar in respect of this place the Sanctuary. Indications that it might have been used for immoral purposes. However, we've been able to eliminate Cromer and his missus as suspects. The police doctor says Mrs. G. was killed not later than nine o'clock last evening. He can tell that from the state of the body, rigor mortis and suchlike. You'd understand about that, being a nurse, miss. It so happens that some folk in a house opposite saw the lady at the front door having a word with Cromer himself at seven o'clock, so that means the foul play took place between seven and nine. These folk say Cromer came away from the house, picked up his missus, and they both went up the road to a pub, where the landlord and several others vouch for them being there till closing time at eleven."

He got to his feet. "Well, thank you for your help, miss. I don't think we need trouble you further."

His colleague rose, and I stood up at the same time. "Then at present you have no idea who was responsible?" I said.

Sergeant Perry surveyed his hat and brushed a speck of dust from it with his sleeve. "No idea at all, miss," he agreed. "But in view of the highly peculiar aspects we observed at the Sanctuary, we're very anxious to interview Mr. Caspar Galliard."

*   *   *

As soon as I had given Edge the brief facts and told him to pass them on to the other servants I walked to the post office and sent a telegram to Lord Henry. It reached him in little more than an hour, and he was at the house before one o'clock.

"Dear God," he said as he sat with me on the chesterfield, holding my ice-cold hands, "do you think the police believe Caspar did it?"

I nodded, clenching my teeth to stop them chattering.

He said, "And do *you* believe so?"

"It . . . it's possible. He told me he was afraid of himself, afraid of what he might do. I know he's made of iron, but there's always a breaking point, and it was so dreadful that day, seeing her go off to the Sanctuary, still in full mourning for her mother, and knowing what she would be doing there. It could have been the last straw. Do *you* think he could have done it?"

Henry sighed, then nodded slowly. "His profession has required him to kill from time to time," he said with reluctance, "and God knows there was enough provocation. I'll tell you something, Mim. Yesterday at the White Hart there came a moment when I had to accept that Anne Galliard, my perfect woman, whom I'd always admired and adored, was rotten to the core, a cruel and pitiless destroyer. In that moment I felt so betrayed, so deceived and cheated, I would have been afraid of what I might do if she had been within reach of my hands."

I whispered, "And Caspar Galliard has endured for all these years."

"There's one thing," Henry said bleakly. "He's out of the country by now, if I'm any judge. He'll be traveling in his own clandestine ways, and nobody will recognize him as Caspar Galliard. They'll never catch him, Mim."

"But if he just disappears . . . disappears forever, it means he gives up everything."

"Perhaps," said Henry thoughtfully, "he considers that a small price."

"Price for what?" I jumped with shock as a new light dawned. "Oh, dear God in heaven, could he have done this terrible thing to protect me?"

Henry pressed my hands. "I don't know, Mim," he said. "I just don't know. He loves you, he feared for you, and he is a man of action. But don't indulge in the foolishness of blaming yourself in the slightest degree. Now let's be practical. What have you done about informing Anne's father?"

I drew my hands away and went to stand by the fire, trying to pull myself together and think calmly. "I was going to send him a telegram," I said, "but there was no way to phrase it that didn't seem brutal, so I sent a message to Sergeant Perry asking if he would make contact with the local police at Saxmundham, so they could send an officer round to break the news. The reply said that this would be done."

"Good girl. What do you plan to do now?"

"I have no authority in this house, Henry. I sent a message to Mr. Galliard's solicitors in Lincoln's Inn, and the senior partner called here at eleven o'clock. He holds something called power of attorney in Mr. Galliard's absence, so he will take responsibility for the house and the staff. He asked if I would remain for a while, but I said no. I'm sure Caspar Galliard won't return, so there's nothing for me to do here now."

"You haven't done badly in the last few hours, my little paleface with bruised eyes," said Henry. "When can you come down to Torringtons?"

I hesitated. "Will that be all right? I don't want you to feel obliged in any way."

"I won't allow anything else," he said simply. "When can you come?"

"In two days, I think. That will give me time to sort out Mr. Galliard's notes and manuscripts in case . . . well, I don't know why, but I must do it. Two days will also allow time for Mrs. Galliard's father to come down from Suffolk—if he decides to do so."

Henry nodded. "Let's make it so, then. I shall stay at my club and call here daily to lend a hand in any way you need, but particularly in dealing with police, lawyers, reporters, or sundry busybodies."

I managed to force a smile and said, "God bless you, Lord Henry Boot."

During the next two days the newspapers made considerable play over the brutal murder of what they termed a well-known society beauty, and there were oblique hints concerning "surprising discoveries" at the Sanctuary; but, strangely, all references to Caspar Galliard's absence were very cautious.

I traveled down thankfully to Torringtons with Henry and was made welcome by his mother. "I think it best that we neither discuss nor speculate upon this dreadful murder of Anne Galliard," she said at dinner that evening. "If the police make any significant discovery we shall no doubt read of it in the press, and if not, then the matter will remain in limbo, as it were. For myself, I have urgent matters to attend to and shall be spending a few days in London for that purpose. It is quite possible to register surprise without showing so much of the whites of your eyes, Henry."

"I tend toward exaggerated facial expressions, Mamma," said Henry. "May one ask why you are visiting London again after so many years, and where you propose to stay?"

"You may not ask why," Lady Whitchurch replied amiably. "That I shall explain in my own good time. As for where, I have arranged to stay with my cousin Matilda."

"Mamma's cousin Matilda," said Henry, "is the Duchess of Selbrook, whose London pied à terre occupies a large part of Belgravia. I've heard they do you quite a decent breakfast there, Mamma."

Lady Whitchurch frowned. "I almost laughed at that comment, Henry," she said. "I do hope your incorrigible vulgarity is not beginning to rub off on me."

In the following few days I suffered a seesaw of emotion. I scanned *The Times* each morning, fearful of reading that the police had found and arrested Caspar Galliard. I went to church and prayed for him. I also prayed for the soul of Anne Melanie Galliard but felt a hypocrite, knowing that I only did it because I hoped it might reinforce my prayers for Caspar.

At other times I was joyously happy at simply being in the company of the familiar friend and companion I had always found lovable and with whom I now knew myself to be in love. I schooled myself rigorously to avoid showing my feelings by any word or look or touch and found this not too difficult since we had always been affectionate with each other.

Surprisingly, I felt only a tinge of sorrow at the knowledge that there could be no more between us than already existed. Henry liked me well, but he was not in love with me, and even if he had been, no outcome was possible. I was no chaste English maiden suitable to be wife to the son of a marquess; I was an unfortunate creature who had been ravaged and defiled by a barbarian *pacha* in a primitive land, and this put me beyond consideration for marriage.

The thought crossed my mind that Henry might be glad to take me as his mistress for a while, and it would have pleased me greatly to please him, for I had nothing else to give, but I quickly put the notion aside. To become his bedfellow would inevitably change our friendship and could never be a lasting situation. Far better for me to hold to what I had. Perhaps better for him, also.

Lady Whitchurch returned after six days, arriving by the noon train and looking more energetic and alert than I had ever seen her. That afternoon she summoned us both to the drawing room and told Jackson we were not to be disturbed. "I hope you have something exciting to impart, Mamma," said Henry, leaning back in his chair and stretching out his legs. "Perhaps your cousin Matilda, who once called me a horrid little boy, has made a flight in a hot air balloon—" He sat up straight and banged his fist on his knee. "Mim! There's an idea! Gas rather than hot air, perhaps, but nobody has yet beaten the record set up by those chaps fifty years ago. Almost five hundred miles nonstop from London to somewhere in Germany—"

Lady Whitchurch broke in. "I have a more useful suggestion to make, Henry, if you will be so good as to listen. I don't think you will find the venture I have in mind boring."

He blinked in surprise. "By all means tell us about it, Mamma."

Lady Whitchurch looked at me. "For the first time in many years I have a purpose in life, Jemimah, and it is you who have given me that purpose. I am determined to bring Georgios Alexandrou—or Sandru, as you call him—out of Shul and safely home to England."

I was unable to speak and had to force myself not to look at Henry. If I had, my expression would have asked if his mother had taken leave of her senses. She went on with a small tremor in her voice. "I have no illusions. I know Georgios is an old man now, and probably very different from the young man I knew and loved. Nevertheless, he is the man I have always loved in my heart, and if it is humanly possible I will *not* allow him to die in poverty and degradation, unwanted and unloved, among barbarians he has spent his life in serving. If my love for him has any meaning at all, then I shall gladly care for him with every tenderness through his declining years."

When she stopped speaking there was silence for long seconds. Henry looked at me as if inviting me to reply first, but I said no with my eyes. I could only think this was madness, but I could not bring myself to utter such words. Henry looked at his mother and said, "Mamma, I love and respect you as never before for what you have just said. It is . . . it is truly a wonderful purpose and desire. But, oh, my dear Mamma, it is *not* humanly possible. Mim knows better than anyone, and she will tell you so."

I said unhappily, "It's true, Lady Whitchurch. I had Sandru's help to escape from Shul, and I made that journey through mountain snows and parched plains with . . . with a man called Kassim who spoke the language and knew the country and its customs. Even so, we barely survived. Oh, please believe me, I would give anything to bring Sandru to safety, for I owe him my very life, but truly it cannot be done."

Henry said, "You spoke of a venture for me, Mamma, and I would attempt this for you if I thought there was any hope of success. I've traveled in far places, it's true, but I don't know Afghanistan, and I doubt if I would ever reach Shul alive. Besides, who would guide me? Who would speak to Sandru and persuade him to leave? Oh no—don't look at Jemimah! You can't possibly ask such a thing of her!"

"I am not in the habit," said Lady Whitchurch, "of asking young women of whom I am fond to risk their lives on my behalf, Henry. Do you imagine I have been wasting my time in London?"

Henry looked baffled. "I have no idea what you were doing in London, Mamma, but I don't see how you could make possible the impossible."

"Then I shall tell you, Henry. I have had several discussions with Hugh Childers and certain military persons to whom he commended me."

"Childers? He's the fellow Gladstone appointed as Secretary of State for War, isn't he?"

"Yes, and he is also an old friend of mine."

Henry said slowly, "Mamma, what have you been up to?"

"I have been using influence, Henry. I laid the matter before Hugh Childers and told him it was a disgrace that the government had never sought the release of a gallant soldier who had been a prisoner of war for almost forty years. At first he felt unable to help, but then it occurred to him to wonder how the British public would react if Jemimah's story of this captive British soldier were to appear in the *Morning Post.*"

Henry said, "It occurred to him?"

"Yes, after I had pointed out that I had more than sufficient influence with the editor of that newspaper to arrange for her story to appear."

Henry smiled at his mother, who smiled back at him, and I felt the seed of strange excitement beginning to burgeon within me. Lady Whitchurch said, "Hugh Childers then consulted his military advisers and found several who were surprisingly keen to support my request. It would, of course, be a splendid thing for the Army's reputation to bring home a soldier believed dead since the Kabul disaster of '42. They would also be pleased to show the flag in the wilds of Kafiristan, as a warning to the Russians."

I felt a pain and found my hands were clenched so tightly that the nails were digging into the flesh. It seemed that something like a miracle was in prospect, but I dared not let myself believe or hope too much yet. Henry was saying, "God save us all, have you got the British Army on your side now, Mamma?"

"I believe the military authorities have been able to see the wisdom of giving favorable consideration to my suggestion," she said in a mild voice. "Nothing can be done before spring, of course, since the passes will be blocked, but a certain Lieutenant General Hardiman in White-hall is anxious to have a discussion with Jemimah concerning the terrain and traveling conditions on the approaches to Shul, to confirm information from other sources."

Henry said, "Do they believe Mim is Jemimah Lawley now?"

Lady Whitchurch pursed her lips. "At the moment they are not concerned with that. They are simply concerned with the fact that she escaped from Shul after spending two years there with Captain Georgios Alexandrou of the 44th Regiment of Foot."

I said, "Henry, it doesn't matter what they think about my identity. All that matters is bringing my master home, my poor dear Sandru. Lady Whitchurch, what are they proposing to do?"

"They will send a company of light infantry into Kafiristan along the camel trails," she replied. "Apparently there is peace in Afghanistan at the moment, so the force should meet no more than the occasional sniping from Pathans in the hills. I am told that considerable advances in methods of transport have been made in the last year or two, and the British force will have the benefit of a troop of artillery to deal with any form of organized attack from Shul itself."

I said, "Deenbur won't fight a force like that, Lady Whitchurch. In Kafiristan the *pachas* only attack other tribes when they are sure of winning."

"Very sensible," said Lady Whitchurch. "The general will wish to question you on that aspect also, no doubt, but it was made clear to me that the success of the expedition must depend on the soldiers being able to find this place in the wilds of the Hindu Kush, and then being able to seek out Captain Georgios Alexandrou himself."

I said quickly, "They must be very careful. Shul is a rambling little kingdom, and the capital is Kuttar. If they question local people, the news will travel like lightning, and if it becomes known that they're seeking Sandru, he could well be hidden away or killed before they find him."

Henry said quietly, "So that's the venture you have in mind, Mamma." He looked at me. "It won't work unless you can be our guide for the final part of the journey, Mim. You could lead the soldiers straight to Kuttar and straight to Sandru, and you alone could speak with him, and reassure him, and"—he glanced at his mother—"and tell him who has sent you to bring him home. I'll be there with you, but can you do it, Mim? Can you make yourself go back?"

I expected to feel the clutch of deep cold fear as his words hung on the air, for even with three hundred and more soldiers to protect me, the land of Shul remained for me a land of shame and misery and terror. But strangely I felt no fear. I felt gladness to know that I would be leaving England soon, leaving memories of Caspar Galliard, who loved me, and of Anne Galliard . . . Stormswift, devourer of human prey, who now lay dead; and I was unafraid because the man I loved, the man with the funny bent nose and the gentle heart and the wild outlandish notions, would be with me.

I looked at Lady Whitchurch and smiled. "I long to go and bring Sandru home," I said. "Thank you for making it possible."

XVII

We sailed from Southampton two weeks later, after spending a full day in London ordering suitable clothes and luggage for our expedition. I told Henry that on reaching India I planned to equip myself with native clothes for the journey from Peshawar onward.

Remembering how Sandru had marveled at the stupidity of putting British soldiers in unsuitable uniforms, I had no intention of suffering the discomfort of English dresses, skirts, stockings, and petticoats. In the heat of the plains I would wear a loose robe; in the cold of the mountains I would wear sheepskin, and I did not care if it was smelly. I was used to that.

Our voyage down to Gibraltar and across the Mediterranean was uneventful, and I counted this a blessing. There had been enough events in my life of late, and I was glad to be in the small isolated world of the ship, where nothing from the outside could penetrate and disturb. The *Windermere* was a new vessel, well equipped and with a good turn of speed. We were traveling first class, and no doubt because Henry was a peer we sat at the captain's table. To prevent curiosity and speculation, Henry gave out that I was his ward, the orphaned child of old friends of his family.

Throughout the voyage I came to love him ever more deeply as I saw how the kindness in him was given freely to all. There was nothing solemn about it. He was always the happy-go-lucky person I had first known as a traveling Punch and Judy man, infectiously cheerful, and talking as easily with a seaman swabbing the deck as with any of the ladies or gentlemen at the captain's table.

Both being early risers, we walked the deck each morning before most people were awake but never talked of the events we had left behind us in England or of what lay before us in the weeks to come. We played

deck games, draughts, chess, and in the company of two pleasant gentlemen at our table Henry taught me whist, never showing a hint of irrita-
tion when my blunders lost us game after game, but simply chuckling
and explaining patiently how I might deduce the position of hidden
cards by the run of the play.

I did not grieve or pine over the fact that he was not in love with me. I
had learned in a hard school to be truly thankful for good health and
small blessings. My health was excellent, and to have Henry's affection
was a large blessing indeed; I would have been frightened to yearn for
more.

We came to Port Said in thirteen days, and there a telegram from
England awaited Henry. I stood beside him at the rail as he opened it,
looking out over the busy dock as coal and provisions were brought
aboard and some of the passengers disembarked. "Doubtless from
Mamma," said Henry, "exhorting me to achievements beyond my reach,
such as behaving like a gentleman, for example, or—"

He stopped short with a quick intake of breath, and I turned to look at
him as he stood very still, reading the message on the buff-colored paper,
his eyes growing bright with pleasure. "My God, Mim, here's news! *He
didn't do it!*"

I stared. "Didn't what? Who didn't do what?"

"Caspar!" He handed me the telegram. It read:

CHARLES HUTTON MADE FULL CONFESSION FOLLOWING HIS ARREST
FOR MURDER OF ANNE GALLIARD STOP MY LOVE TO YOU BOTH
AND I PRAY FOR YOUR SUCCESS STOP ELIZABETH WHITCHURCH.

My heart leapt with relief and joy, followed by a stab of pity for the
man I had seen with Anne Melanie Galliard in her boudoir at the Sanctuary. In him she had claimed a last victim.

"Hutton?" said Henry wonderingly. "The fashionable Harley Street
doctor?"

"Yes." I handed back the telegram. "That was the man I saw with her.
I didn't tell you his name. I expect he was frantic with worry, knowing I
had seen him. She would have enjoyed that, I suppose, being sure I
would never speak, but she must have gone too far in frightening him. I
remember Caspar calling him a poor devil and wondering what torment
she planned for him . . . but she made a mistake at last."

"Then why did Caspar disappear?" Henry said slowly. "And where on earth is he now?"

"I think he will be wherever his masters have sent him," I said, "perhaps on his way to Herat now, to report to Mr. Arthur Renwick."

"Mad as a hatter," said Henry with a sigh. "It's not for the money he does it, in fact I doubt if he's paid a penny by our grateful government, so in heaven's name why does he keep risking his neck like this?"

I said, "Because he believes it to be his duty."

Henry nodded and gave me a wry smile. "I know, Mim. It was just a rhetorical question."

We disembarked at Karachi fifteen days later, and there I relearned a lesson I had learned in childhood, that the ways of an army are as ponderous as those of a tortoise. From this point, our travel and accommodation arrangements were in the hands of the military, and so it took us ten days of waiting and false starts to get to Peshawar by train. Here we were received as guests in the comfortable bungalow of a Major White of the Army Veterinary Service and his wife, and here we remained for five days while awaiting the arrival of a company of Highland Light Infantry to escort us to Shul.

On the second day I was on the veranda playing a game of draughts with Henry when Mrs. White came to say that a gentleman had called to see me on official business, a Mr. Arthur Renwick. I thanked her, trying not to show surprise, asked Henry to accompany me, and went through the bungalow to the drawing room.

The small man, with bright eyes like a squirrel, rose to greet me with a bow. "Good morning, Miss Lawley."

"Good morning, Mr. Renwick. Are you sure you are addressing me by my correct name?"

He shrugged the thrust aside. "That is not a matter that concerns me, madam, but having been advised of the reason for your arrival here, I have come to ask you some questions." He glanced at Lord Henry. "Privately, if you please."

Henry said without heat, "Miss Lawley doesn't please, Renwick. All that you have in common with her is mutual acquaintance with a man you would wish us to refer to as Kassim. I have been Kassim's friend since boyhood, and I know the nature of his activities, so you can ask your questions in my presence or not at all. Whether or not Miss Lawley will answer them is another matter."

Arthur Renwick looked at me steadily and said, "I well understand that you resent my failure to support you in establishing your identity,

Miss Lawley, but my wider responsibilities prevented me from doing so. I accept Lord Henry's presence, and I shall be most grateful if you will help me."

Henry raised an eyebrow at me and said, "Mim?"

I nodded, and moved to take a chair. "Please sit down, Mr. Renwick. I have very vivid memories of the shame I felt when Captain John Selby pointed out to me the supreme importance of the work done by men like Kassim, men despised by their own countrymen, who owe them so much. I realize that your work is also of supreme importance, since you receive reports from such men, and you are therefore bound to put these concerns before the welfare of any individual."

Mr. Renwick looked down at the pith helmet in his hands. "I can assure you that I put these concerns before my own life and welfare, Miss Lawley."

"I don't doubt it, Mr. Renwick," I said. "Please ask your questions."

"They are very simple, Miss Lawley. We know that Kassim's wife was brutally murdered on the thirteenth of February and that the murderer has since been arrested. We know that Kassim vanished from London on the very day of the murder. Do you know where he is? Do you know what he is doing? Can you help me to make contact with him?"

I stared in surprise. "I thought he was in Afghanistan by now, under your orders, Mr. Renwick. I imagined he was making his annual journey from Herat out to Badakhshan, then down through the Hindu Kush to Kafiristan, and back along the east-west trails to Herat."

Mr. Renwick shook his head. "There is no trace of him," he said. "Clearly Kassim does not want to be found, and he has long experience of traveling as unobserved as a ghost, when he so wishes. The man could be anywhere from Khartoum to Calcutta, or right under our noses at this moment." He stood up with a shrug. "Well, I must make the best of what resources I have. I won't trouble you further."

I rose and gave him my hand. "I'm sorry I haven't been able to help you, Mr. Renwick, but to be honest I would not do so if I thought it was against Kassim's wishes."

He smiled. "I know, Miss Lawley. That is why I did not mention such possibility until after it was clear that you could not help me. Thank you for your time, and I'll wish you good day. Good day, Lord Henry."

When he had left I looked at Henry and said, "Where on earth can Kassim be?"

"Lord knows, Mim. It looks as if he's just gone into hiding somewhere, maybe in a cottage in the Grampians for all we know, but I've no idea why. If he's in the wilds and away from all sources of news, he may not even know that Anne is dead."

"Oh dear, I hadn't thought of that." I took Henry's arm as we moved through to the veranda. "All we can do is hope he's safe and well, wherever he is."

"That's all, Mim."

Three days later we left Peshawar with a company of Highland Light Infantry, a troop of artillery, and three men of the Army Hospital Corps to provide medical attention. I thought ruefully how little had changed since Sandru's day. There were no officers in the Army Hospital Corps, and qualified doctors were still engaged haphazardly on a regimental basis, as Sandru had been, and as John Selby had been almost forty years later.

The whole of this force was under command of a Colonel Rafford, and the baggage train for it extended well over a mile. I had chosen to ride a horse rather than be jolted interminably in one of the wagons, and Henry had secured a good mount for me. We rode together between the main force and the advance guard, thereby avoiding much of the dust raised by the column's passage.

Colonel Rafford seemed a sharp and efficient soldier, but he clearly had no time for me or for Henry—or perhaps for any civilian. However, he was under strict orders from his commander-in-chief to accept my guidance as soon as we reached territory I recognized, and to heed my advice in the matter of extricating Sandru safely from Kuttar. Lord Henry did not enhance his popularity with Colonel Rafford by remarking that it was amazing to realize there was a high-ranking officer in the British Army with sufficient intelligence to issue such a sensible order.

Our route was to take us through the Khyber Pass to Jalalabad, where we would leave the road to Kabul and take to the camel track running north into Kafiristan. The plan was to cover fifteen miles each day as far as Jalalabad, which would take four days, then eight miles each day on the more difficult trail that climbed steadily into the mountains. This was a shorter distance than the way through Kabul and would bring us to the approaches of Shul in a further eight days if all went well.

One of the baggage wagons that carried tents during the day provided sleeping quarters for me when it was unloaded at night. "Just like when you were a world-famous Punch and Judy performer, Mim," said Lord Henry. He was provided with a bivouac tent of his own, and since it was out of the question for a woman to eat in the large tent with high walls that was the officers' mess, Henry and I drew rations for two which I cooked over an open fire, as I had once cooked for Kassim and myself throughout the long weeks of our journeying a year before.

In the foothills it was already hot, and I knew that by now the snows in the mountains would be melting. I rode as I had ridden with Kassim, my mind still and remote, hardly touched by awareness of heat or thirst or weariness. I thought I might have to explain to Henry that my quiet-ness was not because I was annoyed or unfriendly, but I found no expla-nation was needed. After the first day he said, "You're right, Mim. It keeps the dust out of your throat, the tiredness out of your bones, and makes the day pass quickly. Evening is the time to talk."

This was strange, for I had not said as much to him, yet he under-stood. "I picked up the way of it when I was with Kassim," I said. "Except that we didn't even talk when the day's march was done."

After the soldiers had made camp for the night we were often visited by some of the young officers, who would vie with each other in trying to impress me. "My word, Mim," said Henry, "you're the toast of the Khyber Pass. You could take your pick from scions of some of the best families in Great Britain."

That made me smile. "I'm neither flattered nor deceived, Henry," I said. "When you happen to be the only white woman for two hundred miles, your beauty of appearance and qualities of mind increase by leaps and bounds. But if they knew I'd been despoiled for almost a year by a barbarous native *pacha*, they wouldn't come calling again."

He took the bowl of goat's-meat stew I handed him and said, "Kassim doesn't think that way."

"Kassim is different," I said.

We always used that name if we spoke of him. Where he was, heaven alone knew, but we were both very much aware that he followed a profession in which his life depended on secrecy, and we were careful to guard our tongues.

On the second day after Jalalabad the advance guard was fired on from the hills shortly before noon. There were no more than half a dozen shots from *jezails* carried by the Pathan tribesmen, and our only casualty was a soldier wounded by a bullet cutting a deep groove in his thigh. I offered my services to tend the wound but was curtly told by Colonel Rafford that it would be dealt with by military personnel. A small patrol was sent up into the hills to rout out the attackers but returned after an hour without having made contact.

That evening the adjutant called to visit us as we sat outside my sleeping wagon after dinner. "The C.O.'s compliments, Miss Lawley," he said with a strong Scottish accent, "and he has told me to say that, although we may expect occasional incidents of the kind that occurred today, he anticipates no organized attack on the column. Today was just a matter of a handful of goatherds spotting a column of soldiers and taking a few shots by force of habit. As I believe you know, there are various tribes here, each divided into clans and subclans, and they spend most of their time scrapping with each other. It's only when they get together that they become a wee bit dangerous."

I smiled up at the young man and said, "Please thank Colonel Rafford for his reassurance, Captain Howard. Would you care to join us for a mug of coffee?"

He hesitated, tugging at his long chin. "Most kind of you, ma'am, but I'd best get back now."

Henry grinned and said, "Did Rafford really tell you to bring that message, Captain?"

The young Scot pulled even harder at his chin and looked uncomfortable. "It is the duty of an adjutant to anticipate his commanding officer's wishes, Lord Henry," he said at last, "and to carry them out as if he had expressed them."

I suppressed a smile and said, "This was a most kindly anticipation of yours, Captain Howard, and we much appreciate it."

"My pleasure, ma'am." He saluted and marched briskly away.

On the fourth day we again received some scattered shots from the high ground, this time against the main force, but the only casualty was a mule. Once more a patrol was sent to deal with these skirmishers, but the tribesmen melted away into the hills. By now we were climbing steadily and the track was becoming narrower and more difficult. To cover eight miles in a day's march was hard work, for if a wagon wheel stuck fast in a rut or crevice it was often necessary to unload the wagon before it could be heaved free by manpower.

The terrain was now beginning to resemble the kind I had known during the final days of being brought captive to Shul, and from time to time I was shaken by powerful emotions. When I recalled the nightmare journey I had made with my band of Hindu captors by another and much longer route out of Kabul after the massacre, I was sometimes swept by fear and agitation.

This was foolish, for I now had the protection of three hundred well-armed and disciplined soldiers, but the fear was too instinctive to be wiped away by logic. When I could make myself believe the astonishing fact that I was now within a few days' march of Kuttar, where I had endured so much at Deenbur's hands, and where, God willing, I would find Sandru, who had saved my sanity and my life, then I was torn between revulsion and eager anticipation.

On the fifth day, in the afternoon, as Henry and I rode around a bend in the track, we saw that the advance guard was halted some two hundred yards ahead. There had been no shooting, and at this point the rocky walls rising on either side of us were too steep to conceal any tribesmen, but Henry and I drew rein, for it was a standing order that we should remain at least at this distance from the advance guard.

A few moments later we saw some of the uniformed figures move aside, then the lieutenant in command began to ride back toward us at a slow walk, accompanied by two natives, each mounted on a sturdy Afghan pony. One man sat rather slumped in the saddle. He wore a hat with a drooping brim and a leather jacket over a woolen robe. The other was tall and long-legged, in a thigh-length coat and a round leather hat, a *jezail* slung across his back.

Beside me Henry said, "It makes a change to meet a couple of natives who aren't unfriendly. You're our interpreter, Mim, perhaps you can have a chat with them."

I sat staring at the two approaching figures, and as they drew closer I felt my heart begin to thump and my flesh to tingle with shock and excitement. For long seconds I did not dare to believe what my eyes and my memory were urging upon me, but at last, when the riders were no more than fifty paces away, I knew the truth.

"There won't be need for an interpreter," I said in a voice I barely recognized. "That's Kassim . . . *and Sandru!*"

I slid to the ground and ran forward, arms outstretched. My robe had a hood that I wore for protection against the sun, and as I ran it fell back, leaving my head bare. Without even reining to a halt, Caspar Galliard swung down from his mount, bright blue eyes staring incredulously as he came striding to meet me. Then I was in his arms, and he was holding me close, murmuring my name over and over again, and I was weeping tears of joy to find him safe, with my old master, Sandru, whom I had come thousands of miles to find.

"Wait . . . wait, Kassim," I panted at last, leaning back to look up into his lean brown face, "we thought . . . oh, I don't know what we thought, but never that you had gone to fetch Sandru! Oh, please let me greet him."

He released me with the first smile I had ever seen on the face of

Kassim, and I turned to find Sandru standing before me. He looked older, rather drawn and frail, but his eyes were alert as he reached out his hands and said, "Can this really be my Lalla?"

"Oh yes, master, *yes!*" I found I was putting my palms together and bowing, as I had in the days when I was his servant, and I half laughed though I was still weeping for joy. "Yes, it's Lalla, and I've come back for you, master. Oh, thank God you're safe and well." I reached out to take his hands, then kissed him on the cheek, as I had done on the night of my departure.

After a moment he drew back his head and frowned at me in mock anger as he said, "Whatever has got into you, girl? You send Kassim to bring me out of Shul, then come yourself with half an army to do the same thing!"

I shook my head, still holding his hands. "I didn't send him, master. I don't know why Kassim came, I only know that I came myself for the sake of a lady who . . . no, wait, I'll show you." I unfastened the tightly buttoned pocket inside my robe and took out a small pouch of soft leather. Unfastening the flap, I slid the locket into my hand, opened it carefully, and held it out so that Sandru could see the miniatures within. "This is the lady," I said. "Her name is Elizabeth Whitchurch, and she is longing for you to come home to her at last."

His hands trembled so violently that he had difficulty in grasping the locket. Then he simply stood gazing down at the portraits while tears ran unheeded down his cheeks. I turned away to give him some small measure of privacy and saw that Kassim was speaking with Lord Henry, both men smiling and animated.

The lieutenant in charge of the advance guard was not smiling but tugging uneasily at his mustache and clearing his throat loudly. "Miss Lawley, gentlemen," he said, "I must ask you all to accompany me to company headquarters with the main column at once. It seems I have to report to Colonel Rafford that the purpose of this expedition no longer exists, since it has already been achieved." He ran a finger around his collar and looked distinctly unhappy. "I fear Colonel Rafford will be none too pleased about this."

*　　*　　*

Two hours later we were encamped a mile short of where we had met Kassim and Sandru, at a point where the rock walls became hills and the

track widened briefly into a flat valley of sufficient size to make a good
site for the company of soldiers to pitch their tents.

I sat on a straw mat beside Sandru, our backs against a wheel of my
sleeping wagon. One of his hands rested in mine, and in the other he
held the open locket, gazing into it with unceasing wonder.

Colonel Rafford had indeed been less than pleased to find that his
men no longer had a mission to perform and that all their efforts had
been wasted. He had wanted to press on into Kafiristan and make a show
of force there, since this had been a minor part of his mission. Kassim
was violently opposed to the notion, saying that it would cause the Russians to mount a similar mission and create unrest throughout the whole
area. He and Lord Henry had been at company headquarters ever since
we had made camp, and I suspected that a bitter argument was in
progress. I was not greatly concerned about the outcome, for I knew
that, whatever Colonel Rafford decided, the four of us would turn back
now. Being unprotected, we would travel differently, as natives; but we
would travel a great deal faster and would be as safe in Kassim's charge as
with the soldiers.

I had heard Sandru's story now, and I again thanked God that he was
safely out of Shul, for his position there had changed greatly in the past
year. After my escape, and despite the drug Sandru took to divert suspicion, Deenbur had become terrifyingly angry and had blamed him for
failing to keep me chained at night.

"A few days later Deenbur managed to strike a fresh bargain with
Akbah the Mad for the Lohstan girl he wanted to take as wife," Sandru
had told me as I warmed a bowl of soup for him soon after we stopped to
make camp. He fanned some flies away with his limp-brimmed hat and
gave a wry smile. "Of course she failed to conceive, as you and the others
had failed, because the fault lies with Deenbur. One of the *deshtayu* who
was jealous of me gave Deenbur the notion that I was casting spells to
prevent him siring a child. I don't think Deenbur believed it, but it gave
him the chance to vent his spleen upon me. I was lucky not to lose my
head under the ax, but he contented himself with having me flogged and
then imprisoned, from full moon to full moon, to drive the wicked
demons out of me, he said."

I felt almost sick with pity and anger, and made Sandru show me his
back but was thankful to find no scars. The flogging, he assured me, had
been a token affair, perhaps because a severe flogging would have killed
him, and Deenbur was reluctant to lose his services entirely; but the
whole incident gravely damaged Sandru's reputation and standing in

Shul. Much of his success had resided in the trust and confidence the people placed in his powers to heal them. A doctor in disgrace with the *pacha*, one who had been flogged and imprisoned, no longer inspired such confidence.

"Also I had no reliable nurse," he said ruefully. "I did not realize how much I had come to rely upon you, Lalla." He took a few spoonfuls of soup, gazing thoughtfully into the little cooking fire I had made. "The future for me was very dark, and I was becoming afraid. You know what it would be like in Shul for an old man without family, who was no longer of use."

I did indeed know, and it had distressed me greatly for many months past. Sandru chuckled and gestured with his spoon. "But then the miracle happened. With the first melting of snows, Kassim came and said that, whether I wished it or not, he would take me back to England so that I could identify Miss Jemimah Lawley, whose name and birthright had been usurped by an impostor. He said that this was the only way he could pay his debt to Lalla of Shul, who had saved his life."

So here was the answer to the mystery of Caspar Galliard's sudden disappearance from England. He had traveled secretly and in his own devious ways to India, and there he had become Kassim once more, to penetrate the primitive kingdoms of Kafiristan, not for Mr. Arthur Renwick and his masters in Whitehall, but for me, Jemimah Lawley, who had once been Lalla of Shul.

Sandru's story was quickly told, but mine took longer, for there was more to tell and he would not let me omit any part of it, eyes bright with interest in his wrinkled brown face, and full of laughter when I told of my days with the Punch and Judy show; full of compassion when I spoke of Anne Melanie Galliard's faithlessness, cruelty, and death.

He did not hurry me to reach the time when I had recognized him in my dream as the young man whose portrait lay in a locket worn by the woman he had loved forty years before, the woman whose arranged marriage had later made her Lady Whitchurch; but when I told how I had revealed to her that he had not been killed in action, but still lived in the distant land I had escaped from, when I told of her response, and how in all those years she had never ceased to love him, then tears crept down his cheeks and he begged me to tell him this part of the story again.

Now we sat by the wagon, waiting for Kassim and Lord Henry to return. Sandru gazed at the pictures in the locket and I kept silence, not wanting to break in upon the dreamy happiness that possessed him. At last he said wonderingly, "You believe Elizabeth will take me into her house? A useless old man like me?"

"I know she will, master. When she has you to love and cherish it will give her the happiness she has always lacked."

He pressed my hand. "Call me Sandru now, child. We are no longer master and servant, thank God. In Shul I dared not treat you otherwise without angering Deenbur and bringing danger upon you, but if I was ever unkind to you, I hope you can forgive me."

In my youth I had never truly known what it was to love another person, but I loved Sandru, and now I knelt up and put my arms about him, saying without words all that lay in my heart. He patted my arm and whispered, "Thank you, Lalla, my dear."

As I sat down beside him again he said, "You have problems to face, I think, for I perceive that you have lost your heart to Elizabeth's son, Lord Henry, have you not?"

I jumped in alarm. "Oh, master! I mean, Sandru. Does it show so clearly?"

His cheeks crinkled in a smile. "Only to me, and only when you were telling me of the days you spent with him on the road and at Torringtons. Then it was in your eyes. But you will not be telling that tale to him, so you need not fear that he will learn your secret, though I see no cause to hide it, Lalla."

I let out a sigh of relief and said, "We're good friends, but he isn't in love with me, and if he suspected the truth it would make him feel awkward. Then the friendship we have might be lost."

"You are sure he is not in love with you?"

"Oh yes. I'm sure I would know if he were. Besides, it would be quite impossible. Henry is a peer, his brother is an earl, and his father a marquess. He could never marry a girl whose body was at the disposal of a savage like Deenbur for months on end."

Sandru nodded slowly, sorrow in his eyes. "You are very much a realist, Lalla."

I smiled, though with something of an effort. "If I hadn't learned to be a realist in Shul I would never have survived. It must have been the same for you, Sandru."

"Well . . . we do what we must, I suppose." He looked down at the open locket in his hands, and his eyes grew misty with dreams once again.

A few minutes later Kassim and Henry appeared, weaving their way between the tents and bivouacs that now spread over half the small valley. Henry was smiling. His companion's face—I was careful to think of him as Kassim still—held as little expression as usual, yet I was aware of a profound inner difference in him.

As the two men reached us I was getting knives and forks, enamel plates and mugs from our baggage. "Mim, my grubby brown angel," said Henry, "have you food for two famished fellows? Ah, I see a welcome dixie simmering on the fire. A casserole of nightingale's tongues, I'll wager."

I said, "It's goat's-meat stew, Henry, and there's some chupatty bread to go with it. Sandru and I have already eaten, so sit down and I'll serve you. I've also coaxed a bottle of claret from Lieutenant McDougal, the mess president, so you can drink a toast of celebration."

Lord Henry let his mouth fall open, spread his arms wide, threw back his head, and rolled up his eyes. "God save us all, is this how she looked after you before, Kassim, you fortunate fellow?" he demanded.

Kassim's eyes rested on me warmly. "She looked after me well enough," he said.

They sat cross-legged on straw mats, and I brought water and a towel for them to wash their hands, served them each with a plate of stew, then poured wine into four glasses. These I had borrowed from Lieutenant McDougal by dint of some outrageous flirting, of which I ought to have been heartily ashamed but was not.

We drank to Sandru, to each other, and, at Henry's exhortation, to all Punch and Judy men on land and sea. Then, as the two men began to eat, Henry said, "All credit to old Rafford. He was very starchy, and obviously filled with loathing and contempt for anyone of Kassim's profession, but in the end he did have the sense to yield to inexorable logic. The whole column will begin marching back tomorrow."

"I've agreed that we shall remain with them," said Kassim. "Since bringing Sandru home was the main purpose of their mission, it would make Rafford look foolish if we returned ahead of them, and I've no wish for that. There are enough problems here without squabbles between military and civilian services to make them worse."

I sat gazing at the embers of the fire, very much aware of his eyes upon me, and after a while I looked up and said, "Has Henry told you about . . . about your wife?"

He nodded, his eyes bleak for a moment. "Yes, he's filled in some details of the affair for me, though I knew she had been murdered before I went north into Afghanistan."

I stared. "You knew?"

"There's no mystery, Lalla." It was strange how the old name came so naturally to him. "I didn't travel in India as myself or by official routes, and when I was preparing for the journey from Peshawar I spent some days in the house of an Indian friend of mine on the outskirts of the town. He belongs to the Indian civil service, and through him I learned that a request had been telegraphed from Scotland Yard, asking that I be detained for questioning concerning my wife's murder if I entered the country. Since nobody knew I had entered, I hadn't been detained."

Sandru said, "You did not tell me of this, my friend."

Kassim shrugged. "There was no point." He looked at me, and his mouth twisted as if with sudden pain. "I knew it must be one of her lovers who killed her, probably Charles Hutton, and Henry tells me that was the case. She must have pushed him just too far, poor devil. Strange . . . for she was a clever judge of such things."

I said awkwardly, "I . . . I hardly know what to say. It was such an abnormal situation."

Kassim said quietly, "I cannot grieve for her, I cannot mourn her. When I first decided to bring Sandru out of Shul, I knew the risk was high and I might not return. That was why I asked you to tell Henry the truth about Melanie. I knew he was in love with her, as so many men were, and I knew he was a challenge to her. I feared that if I died she might in time entrap him as her husband and her victim, as she entrapped me, and that I could not allow." He shook his head slowly. "I cannot pretend to sorrow I do not feel. I can truly say I never wished her dead despite all she was and did, but I would be a hypocrite to deny the relief I feel at being delivered from constant shame and torment. God forgive me, but I am a different man." He looked at me again, and the blue eyes suddenly smiled into mine. "And when I can discard once more the name and the role of Kassim, I shall be still more different, Lalla."

Lord Henry reached for the bottle of wine. "Let's drink to that," he said cheerfully.

Dusk was falling as the two men finished their dinner with goat's-milk cheese and chupatties. Kassim rose and said, "I would like to talk with Lalla. Will you gentlemen excuse us if I ask her to stroll a little way with me?"

A faint snore was Sandru's answer. Henry said, "I'll finish the claret; there's still a glass left."

I was full of unease as I walked with Kassim toward the camp perimeter, for I felt sure I was about to face an awkward situation, yet I could not imagine its precise nature. It was out of the question that he might ask me to be his wife, even though he loved me, for no man would want the leavings of a creature such as Deenbur. It was barely possible that he might want me as a mistress, but this I doubted, partly for the same reason and partly because I believed his very rigid sense of honor would prevent him.

We began to walk the picket line, where a sentry was posted to patrol each fifty yards of the perimeter, but after a minute or so of walking in silence we moved beyond the pickets to be out of earshot. Kassim held my arm, and I sensed that he kept nerving himself to speak but could not quite summon the courage. At last, simply to break the silence, I said, "I'm deeply grateful to you for bringing Sandru safely out of Shul. Will you excuse me for calling you Kassim? I thought it best to do so while you are playing your present role."

"Yes, of course." My words seemed to have freed his tongue, and his hand tightened on my arm as he said, "I call you Lalla now because it was with Lalla of Shul that I fell in love. In other circumstances it would seem a shocking thing for me to say what I am about to say now, at a time when my wife has been murdered only a few weeks ago, but you above all people will understand, Lalla. I can perhaps feel pity for her dreadful death, and I shall conform to all the necessary conventions of mourning, but I can only be thankful that I am free at last."

We passed another sentry, thirty yards away, and I kept my voice low as I said, "Yes, I understand. There's no need to explain."

He stopped and turned me to face him in the dusk. "I want you to be my wife, Lalla," he said gently. "I know I must wait awhile, and I only speak now because I fear that if I wait out the proper time following Melanie's death I may lose you."

I said, startled, "Oh, but you can't want me as a wife. You know Deenbur owned me for almost a year."

"That's past, Lalla. It means nothing to me, except as a part of all that has made you the woman I admire, respect, and love." He took both my hands. "I have an honorable name, Lalla. You will bring it yet more honor if you will take it as your own. You have only ever seen me as an aloof, austere man, but that is not my real nature. I have so much to give of kindness and affection, and I would never wittingly cause you a moment's distress."

I saw him smile in the half-darkness. "Kassim will cease to exist, and so will other roles I have played for Arthur Renwick and his ilk. You need not fear that I would give you cause to worry about my safety. Will you be my wife, Lalla? Will you?"

XVIII

I turned to walk on, taking his arm, and said, "Don't speak for a little while, Kassim."

Many thoughts were crowding through my mind in confused fashion. The man I loved was Henry, but even if he had been in love with me he could never have asked me to be his wife, my defilement by Deenbur surely precluded that. I was grateful enough that Henry liked me and was my friend. I was almost stunned by the fact that Caspar Galliard, an English gentleman, wished to marry me in spite of Deenbur, and I was sure he must be unique in this. It seemed ironic that, though I liked and respected the man at my side, I was not in love with him.

I found it hard to envisage what my life would be like when I returned to England. Perhaps I would live again in Witchwood Hall, if Sandru's words carried sufficient weight, but I was none too sure of this, even though I kept my doubts to myself. However that might be, I did not want to live out my life as a lonely spinster, whether rich or poor, growing older and more solitary with the passing years, and I felt in my heart that I could bring happiness to Caspar Galliard with my friendship and affection.

But . . . but . . . oh, how I yearned to be with Henry, whether sailing down the Mississippi for two thousand miles or following his latest wild notion of trying to set a record for a balloon flight; to be anywhere with him, and to be anything to him if he so wished.

Was such yearning selfish? Foolish? Or merely shocking?

At this moment I could agree to marry Caspar Galliard, or I could decline to marry him, or I could say that I would decide after we returned to England. I knew at once that I could not bring myself to take the third option. To shilly-shally would be unkind and unfair. I wondered how badly hurt he would be, and what effect it might have upon him, if

I declined. Would he plunge into the work of his profession again, becoming the withdrawn man I had first known, a man constantly putting his life at risk, and not averse to losing it?

To accept would be the kindest and easiest choice; and no doubt the best and most sensible choice for me.

But . . . but . . .

Something plucked viciously at the shoulder of the sheepskin jacket I had put on against the evening's chill, and in the same instant I heard the whipcrack sound of the passing bullet and the distant report of a *jezail*. We were moving across a slight rise of ground and must have been silhouetted against the glow of lanterns and campfires of the soldiers, making a target for a man looking down from the slope of the hills—no, more than one man, for the first shot was followed instantly by another.

Kassim's arm coiled about my waist. He swung me around to shield me with his body and at the same time pulled me to the ground. As he did so there came a burst of three shots, so close together they sounded almost as one, and I felt Kassim's body jerk unnaturally as we fell, a gasping grunt breaking from his lips.

Next moment came a great medley of noises from all around. Several of the picket sentries were firing up into the hills, a bugle was sounding, orders were being shouted. I lay dazed for a second or two with Kassim sprawled over me, then heard him whisper in a strange wavering voice, "Lalla? You're not hit?"

"No." I was breathless under his weight, shivering with fear and shock, and my own voice came gaspingly as I said, "But I felt . . . oh, Kassim, are you . . . ?"

"Like before," he muttered thickly, then made a sound that might have been a laugh. "The moment I turn my back . . ."

His voice failed and his body went limp. Struggling to control panic, I eased him gently aside and got to my knees. Then, cupping my hands about my mouth to make myself heard above the clamor of sound from the camp, I shrieked for help.

*   *   *

Several lamps had been hung in the Army Hospital Corps tent to give a good light. The senior of the three A.H.C. men, a corporal, tended a stove on which an iron bucket of water was kept at the boil. Kassim lay face down on a palliasse set on a broad trestle table, stripped to the waist and still unconscious. Sandru was swabbing blood from the second of two bullet wounds in his back. I stood ready with a bowl of disinfectant and fresh swabs, trying to prevent my teeth from chattering.

In theory Captain Georgios Alexandrou of the 44th Regiment of Foot still held the Queen's commission, and nobody had objected to his taking charge of the wounded Kassim. The Army Hospital Corps men were glad to be relieved of the responsibility, for they had no medical qualifications.

Lord Henry stood by the wall of the tent, arms folded, head bowed a little, watching with somber eyes. Sandru gestured, and I passed him a fresh swab. Another gesture, and I unfolded the dressing I had prepared, then held it over the wound while Sandru strapped it in place, using strips of plaster.

With a sigh he straightened from his task and began to wash his hands in a bowl of hot soapy water on a side table. "One of the bullets must have struck a nerve center to render him unconscious," he said. "The loss of blood is insufficient to have done so. I could wish there was more external bleeding."

Henry said, "More?"

Sandru nodded. "He is bleeding internally, and that I cannot prevent."

I began to wash my own hands and fought to keep my voice steady as I said, "Will you try to remove the bullets, Doctor? If they remain in him, he will die."

"I am sorry, child," Sandru said heavily. "God alone knows where those bullets lie, for they have been deflected by bone, and he would die by the knife long before I could find them."

Henry took a step forward. "Then what will you do, Sandru?" he asked with quiet urgency.

Sandru looked at me, knowing that I knew what he must answer. "I can do nothing, young man," he said bleakly. "The best of surgeons working under the best of conditions would be equally helpless. The drug I gave him will save him from pain if he wakes, but Kassim is dying, and I think the end will come well before morning."

I wanted to weep, to be alone and weep, but for the time being I was Sandru's nurse again. The corporal said, "Sir, will there be aught else you're wanting?"

Sandru shook his head. "Not until it is ended. You may dismiss till then."

As I dried my hands, Kassim stirred and mumbled. I was beside him in a moment, crouching to see his face. An eye was half open, and I saw recognition come into it. "Lalla," he said, indistinctly but with troubled urgency, "who shot . . . ?"

I rested a hand on his brow, knowing his half-waking thoughts, and said, "It wasn't a Russian. You needn't worry, Kassim, we're with the Army now, remember? It was just a handful of Pathans, picking out a random target in a camp of English soldiers. Our men killed one of them when they returned fire."

"Ah." His eye closed for a moment, then opened again, and in it there was a misty glint of humor. "Sorry I keep . . . doing this to you."

I forced a smile and said, "The wound isn't so bad this time, and you have a real doctor to look after you now."

"Good . . . please turn me over . . . on back, Lalla. Can't see you properly."

I looked beyond him to Sandru, who gave a nod. Lord Henry came forward and both men helped me turn Kassim on his back, though he seemed quite unaware of them and kept his eyes fixed on me. For a few moments he lay panting, then screwed up his eyes and muttered, "Light . . . too much light."

Sandru and Lord Henry moved about the tent, putting out the lamps until at last only one was left, its glow barely encompassing the table where Kassim lay. I was holding his hand now, and Henry came quietly up with a chair for me to sit on. Again Kassim seemed unaware of any other presence but mine. He lay with eyes closed for a while, his breathing ragged, hand feebly gripping my own, then he said, "You . . . didn't answer, Lalla."

I thought he was rambling and said, "Oh, I'm sorry. What was it that I didn't answer?"

His eyes opened. "The question . . . the important question." His voice was slurred but there was no mistaking the words. "I asked you . . . to be my wife. Most important question . . . in the world."

I drew in a long deep breath and made myself try to believe every word I spoke as I said slowly, "I long to be your wife, dearest Kassim. I could never tell you before, but I love you with all my heart. Somewhere on that long journey we made together, it happened to me. . . ."

I went on speaking, trying to make my voice low and soothing, gentle and comforting, holding his hand, stroking his brow, saying whatever came into my head that would make my lies seem truth, and overwhelmingly thankful that the words came smoothly and unstumbling to my lips, as if from some source beyond me. ". . . It was before that day when you were shot that I came to love you, dearest Kassim. Perhaps it was when I hurt my ankle fetching water from the river, and you bandaged it for me. Do you remember? In the days after that moment I found it so hard to hide my feelings from you. Often I pretended to be angry or sullen so that you wouldn't see the truth, my darling. Yes, I will be your loving wife, Kassim, and we will cherish each other always. . . ."

His eyes had closed again, and his breathing was slower and deeper, but I went on talking, letting the words come as they would, making a spoken lullaby for my dying friend. There came a time when Sandru emerged from the shadows beyond the light of the single lamp, lifted one of Kassim's eyelids for a brief moment, and said, "He sleeps, Lalla. You can rest now, child."

I moistened my parched lips and looked up. "Is it over, Doctor?"

"Not yet, but he sleeps, and you have given him peace and joy at the last. There is no more for you to do now."

I shook my head. "I shall stay to the end, holding his hand."

"As you wish, Lalla."

Even in the dim light I could see the weariness in his eyes, and I said, "Your work as doctor is done now, Sandru, and it has been a hard day for you. Please go and rest so that you are restored for tomorrow's journey."

He hesitated, and Henry's voice from the darkness said, "I will stay with her, Sandru."

In the time that followed we did not speak, Henry and I, and he remained somewhere in the darkness beyond the lamplight, leaving me alone with Kassim. My mind was empty now. I was aware of no coherent thought and had no idea how long had passed when the hand I held tightened for a moment on mine, then became limp, and one last exhalation of breath was followed by silence.

As Sandru would have done, I felt for a pulse in wrist and neck but there was none. When I held my small handbag mirror to Kassim's mouth, there was no misting. I bent to kiss his cheek and carefully drew a blanket up over his face.

Henry was beside me, saying in a low voice, "Has he gone, Mim?"

"Yes." I knelt by the table and said a silent, stumbling prayer. When I rose I said, "I must fetch the Army Hospital Corps men, and have them prepare a coffin for carrying him when we move on tomorrow."

I heard Henry catch his breath; then he put his arm about my shoulders and said quietly, "I'll see to that and everything else, but first I'll take you back to your sleeping wagon. No arguments, Mim."

There was no strength left in me to resist. Together we left the tent

and made our way to where my wagon stood. Halfway there I stopped
and turned to Henry, weeping against his chest as he held me, then we
moved on again.

"My poor Mim," he said sadly. "My poor little Mim."

                              *   *   *

We made forced marches on our return journey and reached Peshawar
seven days later. Accompanied by Lord Henry, I took some notes I had
found hidden in Kassim's coat to Mr. Arthur Renwick and reported
what had happened.

"So," he said, leaning back behind his desk and looking at us with his
small bright eyes, "for the second and last time you are Kassim's faithful
messenger, Miss Lawley. I am grateful to you, and I deeply regret his
death. It is a loss to our country, I assure you. May I ask what funeral
arrangements have been made?"

Lord Henry leaned forward. "We are in dispute with Colonel Rafford
on that subject," he said. "To my certain knowledge Caspar Galliard
held the rank of captain in the Grenadier Guards and should therefore
be buried in the military cemetery here with military honors, but Rafford
won't have it so. This is an insult to my friend, and I intend to call
Rafford out—"

I jumped and said, "No, Henry! No!"

Mr. Arthur Renwick raised a hand and showed his small white teeth
in a smile without humor. "You may leave Colonel Rafford to me," he
said. "Captain Galliard was permanently seconded from the Guards to
the service I represent some six years ago. He is entitled to military
honors, and they will be given. In my view he would be so entitled even
though he held no military rank. I am sick at heart when I think of the
way the men in my service endure so much of hardship and danger,
working alone, often dying alone, only to be treated with contempt by
soldiers and civilians alike, whose lives they do so much to save. Fortunately I have authority over Colonel Rafford, and you may rest assured
that Caspar Galliard shall have his due."

I said, "Thank you very much, Mr. Renwick. There is just one more
thing. Captain Georgios Alexandrou still holds the Queen's commission.
When he reaches England, we wish him to do so as the soldier who left
that country so many years ago. Can you authorize the making of a
uniform for him to wear?"

Mr. Arthur Renwick drummed fingers on his desk and gazed into

space. "Let me have his measurements, and I will send them by telegraph to a military tailor in Karachi," he said. "A suitable wardrobe will
be ready by the time you reach there, and it may even be possible to
provide the appropriate badges of the Royal Berkshire Regiment."

I rose and said, "You are a kind man, Mr. Renwick. I apologize for
being rude to you in Herat."

He smiled, but for a moment his bright eyes were somber with regret.
"I am of necessity a very ruthless man, Miss Lawley," he said. "It is quite
a relief for me to step out of character, however briefly."

Caspar Galliard was buried next morning, in the military cemetery
and with military honors, and on the same day a telegram was sent to
Lady Whitchurch, telling her that Sandru was safe with us in Peshawar.
Three days later we were in Karachi, and within an hour of our arrival a
military tailor presented himself at the hotel where we were to stay while
awaiting passage home. With him he brought both dress and undress
uniforms for Sandru, together with a complete wardrobe of western gar-
ments including two civilian suits. The suits and uniforms had been
made up ready for final fitting and in another twenty-four hours were
completed.

This was the same hotel Henry and I had used on the outward journey, and four days after our return to it with Sandru a bulky letter
arrived from England, dispatched a month earlier and addressed to me in
Lady Whitchurch's hand. I read it through with growing astonishment,
read the newspaper cuttings that accompanied it, then went along the
passage to Sandru's room and tapped on the door. He and Henry were
on the veranda playing a game of chess, Sandru looking younger and very
strange to my eyes in his white shirt and white flannel trousers. Henry
brought a chair for me and poured me a glass of cool lemonade from a
chatty. I longed to watch his every movement but made myself talk
brightly to Sandru until Henry was seated again, then I showed the
letter.

"It's from Lady Whitchurch," I said. "Shall I read it all through or
tell you what it says?"

"Tell us, Lalla," said Sandru, leaning back comfortably and closing his
eyes. "I like to hear your voice, child." He still called me Lalla, as Henry
still called me Mim, and I was happy to answer to both names.

I looked at Henry. "Well, it seems that soon after you first brought me
to Torringtons your mother decided to make some inquiries about the
people at Witchwood Hall, even though it seemed impossible that they
could be frauds. She obtained photographs of them from one of the

society magazines and sent them to your brother George, in Cape Province, asking him to look up any records available of Arthur Lawley, the black sheep who emigrated to southern Africa, and his son, James Lawley, whose existence was unknown to the family in England."

Sandru murmured, "Brother George, you said?"

I smiled. "Yes. Henry's mother called her firstborn after you."

"My dear Elizabeth." He rubbed his eyes with finger and thumb. "Forgive me, Lalla. Please continue."

I said, "George engaged a good lawyer, and after some time it was discovered that Arthur Lawley had in fact married, and there had been a son called James, an only child. Arthur and his wife died of drink, and so did James when he was still in his early thirties."

Henry said, "So it isn't only the girl who's an impostor? I thought perhaps James Lawley had hired her."

I shook my head and looked at the letter again. "Your brother George made a discovery by way of the police in Cape Province. They don't know the true name of the man in the photograph, because he has used different names at different times, but he is a professional swindler. They know him because of swindles he perpetrated in selling a diamond mine he didn't own in Kimberley, and a great deal of land he didn't own in Natal. The newspaper report in England refers to him as a confidence trickster."

"God save us all," said Henry, "you mean it's already been reported in the English newspapers?"

"Yes. Your mother gave out all details of the story as soon as she received them from George, and she has sent cuttings for us to see."

"But who is the girl? And how did they contrive the whole thing, Mim?"

I picked up a cutting from *The Times*. "Cape Province police say the girl works in partnership with this man. She is believed to be his wife or mistress and is older than she looks. They both disappeared from Witchwood Hall shortly before the Surrey police arrived there to question them, and it's thought they have now fled the country. The newspapers say this trickster must have met the real James Lawley at some time, heard something of his story, and decided there was an opening for a clever fraud when he read that my father was a wealthy, titled man on government business in Afghanistan. Perhaps the trickster planned to present himself as James Lawley, who was dead by then. The Cape Province police know that he and the girl, using the name Lawley, left

Cape Town for Bombay in July that year, which would have brought him to India shortly before the Kabul massacre."

Henry tugged at his bent nose, and I looked away so that he should not see how much I wanted to go to him and put my arms around his neck and kiss him. I was grateful that there would be no long battle to establish my identity when we reached England, but I was unable to feel any great excitement at the knowledge that I was now a rich young woman with a name and fine estate.

I looked at the newspaper cutting again, and read aloud:

"We may surmise that when news reached India that Sir George and Lady Lawley, together with their daughter, Jemimah, had died in the Kabul massacre, the trickster decided on a new plan which he put into operation as soon as it was known that British forces were again in control of the Afghan capital.

"By traveling in disguise, and by bribery of a few natives, it would not have been difficult to arrange a sequence of events which provided that 'Mr. James Lawley,' a cousin of Sir George, should arrive in Kabul seeking news of his relatives, and that a day or two later 'Miss Jemimah Lawley' should be brought into the city by natives purporting to have helped her escape the massacre.

"In this way the miscreant of many names, together with his female accomplice, succeeded in a far greater fraud than they can ever have dared to hope when they first set out on their criminal enterprise. Instead of possibly swindling Sir George out of a sum of money, large or small, on one pretext or another, they were able to lay hands on the whole of the Lawley estate and fortune."

I looked up and said, "There's quite a lot more, but nothing important. I'll leave the letter and cuttings for you to read at leisure."

Henry leaned forward to touch my hand. "Congratulations, Mim. I'm so glad for you."

I wished he would leave his hand on mine, but it was gone in a moment. "I must send your mother a telegram of thanks," I said. "I'm so grateful to her."

"Good girl. Yes, do that." Henry leaned back in his chair and smiled. "I must say, when Mamma sets her mind to something, she doesn't let go easily."

"No," said Sandru softly. "No, indeed, or I would not be here." He looked at me with a whimsical smile. "And you no longer need my testimony now, Lalla. I am just a useless old man."

I shook my head and got up to put my arm about his shoulders and press my cheek to his. "The lady in the locket needs you," I said. "Your Elizabeth needs you."

XIX

At seven o'clock on a warm August afternoon, shocked and ashamed of myself, I took an atlas from the library, gave Hardwick the butler my orders for dinner, then made my way across the lawns of Witchwood Hall to the walled garden beyond a small copse, to sit in a hammock chair near the gazebo.

Several weeks had passed since the ship from Karachi brought me to the Royal Albert Dock. There I had stood by the rail with Lord Henry, watching Sandru make his way ahead of us down the gangway, very upright in his fine uniform. Lady Whitchurch waited below, and we had watched them take each other's hands, embrace gently, then stand holding hands again, looking at each other.

I had seen no more, for tears blurred my vision, and there had been little time later for me to greet Lady Whitchurch, or to say my farewells to her and to Henry and Sandru, for no sooner had I set foot on the dock than I was confronted by two very grave and worried gentlemen, Mr. Wingate and Mr. Stroud, the two senior partners of Messrs. Cossey and Wingate, solicitors. This was the firm that had been deceived by the false James and Jemimah Lawley and, as Henry had predicted with a grin, their toes were curling from anxiety that I might take legal action against them.

I had no such intention and wanted as little fuss as possible, but there were many legal and household matters to be attended to, and for the next two or three weeks I was caught up in a great confusion of affairs. To my relief all this was over at last. I was now well established in the home I had inherited, with the Oakhurst folk falling over themselves to make much of the new lady of the manor, telling one another, and me, that they had always thought there was something not at all right about those wicked creatures who had taken my place for so long. Today I had received a call from the vicar's wife and daughter; yesterday from Dr. Ingram and his wife; and on other days from various of the local gentry.

I was shocked and ashamed of myself, and had felt so for some time, because although my birthright and fortune had been restored, although I lived in the kind of safety and luxury that in Shul would have seemed the fulfillment of impossible dreams, I was miserable. I sat in the hammock chair now with the atlas open on my lap, telling myself I must accept that I could never belong to the man I loved, or indeed to any man unless I concealed what had been done to me in Shul, and that I would not do. Surely, I told myself, this was little enough cause for misery compared with the ordeals and fears of my long sojourn in captivity.

I started suddenly as the quietness of the garden was broken by a voice, a small squeaky voice I knew well.

"Judy," it called rather diffidently. "Ju-u-u-udy."

My heart turned over with pleasure and I looked to my right. There, showing just above the low wall, was the little figure with his tall curving red cap and hooked nose, clutching a stick in his arms. I laughed and said, "Hallo, Mr. Punch. How are you today?"

"Very well, thank you, Judy."

"And how are my friends at Torringtons?"

"Oh, they're well too. You should see Henry's mother and Sandru. They never stop fussing over each other. It's very touching. I couldn't stand another minute of it."

"For shame on you, Mr. Punch!"

The puppet banged his stick on the wall and said, "Well, never mind about them. I want to talk to you, Judy. Seriously, I mean."

"Oh? That's not like you, Mr. Punch. Is something wrong?"

"Not really. The thing is this, Judy. A friend of mine wants to know if you think you might settle for second best. He realizes that Caspar was the love of your life and doesn't expect to replace him, but—"

"No, wait!" I said sharply. "Caspar was never the love of my life. Why do you think that?"

"*What?*" The head of Lord Henry Boot popped up beside the puppet, his eyes wide, eyebrows raised almost to the brim of the familiar and battered top hat he wore. Hastily he extracted the swazzle from his mouth, then: "You *weren't* in love with Caspar?" he said incredulously. "But I took it for granted! After all, he was in love with you, and he was the *sort* of man I thought you were bound to be in love with, Mim. Then there were all those things you said that night when he was shot, about loving him and wanting to be his wife. I heard you myself . . ." His voice trailed away uncertainly.

"Henry dear, he was dying," I said, closing the atlas and laying it on the grass beside me. "Caspar was a fine, brave, honorable man, and I'm proud to know he loved me, but I was never in love with him. I lied most lavishly to him during his last few minutes of life in the hope that he would die happy, and I'm not ashamed of what I did. If it means a black mark against me in heaven, so be it. I owed Caspar much more than that, and I would do the same again. Now . . . what did you mean when you said a friend wanted to know if I might settle for second best? What friend, anyway?"

Henry came scrambling over the wall, leaving Punch on top of it as he dropped down on my side, and I saw he was wearing the ancient frock coat and trousers he had worn during his days as a Punch and Judy man. "I meant me, Mim," he said in a puzzled way, taking off his hat and tossing it to the ground. "Surely you guessed? I'm the friend and the second best."

There was a long, long silence as we simply looked at each other. From the village came the sound of the church clock striking the quarter hour, and the single mellow note seemed to mark for me a moment when my life began anew. If Henry wanted me, nothing else mattered, and I found myself close to both tears and laughter at the same time.

"No, you're not second best," I said at last, and reached out to take his hands, drawing him down to kneel beside me on the grass, then taking his face between my palms. "Pay attention, Henry Boot, if you please. What I'm about to say is quite unmaidenly, but as you well know, I'm neither maidenly nor a maiden. The truth is, I've loved you as a dear friend almost from the beginning, but I'm also deeply in love with you, and I discovered it quite suddenly that day at Torringtons, when I came down to tell your mother about Sandru. It was in the moment when you patted my hand in the billiards room."

"In the *billiards*—"

I gave his head a small shake. "No, don't gape at me and don't say anything yet. The only woman you have ever been seriously in love with was Anne Melanie Galliard, but she was Caspar's wife and not for you, thank God. In a less serious way there was Paloma, and I don't doubt one or two others before her. Well, I have no family and nobody to please but myself, and I simply want you to know that I shall be available in that less serious way if you want me, Henry dear. If not, please don't feel you have to be polite about it, we're much too good friends for that. I won't be hurt if—"

"Mim!" he burst out indignantly. "Oh, Mim, that's an outrageously improper suggestion!"

I smiled and smoothed back his tousled hair. "That's the only kind of suggestion I can make, Henry. Why are you so upset about it?"

"Why? Because I love you and I came here to ask if you would marry me, that's why!"

"Marry you?" I echoed, then frowned. "Don't be foolish now, Henry. I know Caspar wished to, but that was different. You're a lord from a very high family, and I'm spoiled goods. You can't possibly marry me."

He took my wrists, drew my hands from his face, then held my own face firmly as he said, "Now you listen to *me*, Jemimah Lawley. Once upon a time I was in love with a woman who didn't exist, and probably never could exist, the woman I imagined Anne Galliard to be. That was more than foolish, but it's long over now. What's even more foolish is this obsession of yours that because of what happened in Shul you're debarred from marriage. That is *rubbish!*"

"But—"

He shook my head to silence me, as I had silenced him. "Pay attention, Mim! I'm flabbergasted to hear that you love a funny sort of chap like me, and I've barely managed to grasp it yet, but it makes me want to dance and sing and . . . and push houses over. I don't think there was a particular moment when I suddenly realized I loved you. It came to me gradually, I suppose, during these past weeks at Torringtons without you. I get up in the morning and the day is empty because you're not there. I'm restless because there's nobody I can talk to as I talk to you. Nobody laughs with me as you do, nobody makes me feel happy and at peace as you do. Without you, I've no sense of purpose because I have nobody to share the day with, as you and I have shared so many days together. You've spoiled me for anything else, Mim. I want you to marry me and be with me always, and I promise I'll settle down and stop going in for wild ventures. I'll be a good husband—and father, I hope, and will you please, please agree to marry me without any more argument?"

I could not find words to tell him of the happiness I felt, but for answer I drew him toward me and kissed him on the lips with a long loving kiss, feeling weak with joy as we stood up together, his arms about me, holding me very close. At last, with my head resting on his chest, I whispered, "Don't settle down too much, my darling. When I was small

I would have loved to have a nice funny father who did outrageous things and made me laugh. Please always be yourself, Henry."

"And you, Mim. Oh, Lord, but I love you so."

I kissed him again, then moved reluctantly from his arms to pick up the atlas, while Henry collected Punch from the wall where he lay. As we came together again I said, "Do you know what I would really like to do, my lord?"

He grinned, screwed up his eyes in thought for a moment, then shook his head. "Pray tell me, Miss Lawley."

"Well, these past few weeks I've been imagining you might already be in America, on the Mississippi, and I've been poring over an atlas so I could be with you in spirit, because that was the best I could hope for. But it's different now. If you really want me, Henry—no, don't glare at me, I'll withdraw that. *Since* you really want me, dearest Henry, I would like us to be married very quietly from Torringtons. Not here, I have no feeling for Witchwood Hall. Then, for our honeymoon, I would like you to take me to Minneapolis so we can sail all the way down the Mississippi to the Gulf of Mexico. Not in luxury, just the two of us alone, as if we were on the road again. I don't know if they have Punch and Judy in America, but we can take the booth and puppets and see what the people there think of them. Would you like that?"

He scooped up his hat, threw it in the air, caught it again, clapped it on his head with a flourish, then stood with hands on hips, gazing at me with warm loving eyes. "Mim, you're an extraordinarily wonderful girl," he said.

"I'm an extraordinarily lucky girl," I replied, taking his arm. "All the bad things that happened to me have combined in the end to offer me a new kind of life . . . a life I could never otherwise have dreamed of, and I'm so thankful. Come along, let's go up to the house."

"All right. And what about after the honeymoon, Mim?"

"Well . . . it will be quite a long one. Shall we wait till we reach New Orleans before deciding where we wish to live and have our family?"

He nodded vigorously. "That's a splendid idea. I love the way you manage to be calmly outrageous and sturdily sensible at the same time. I need you so much, Mim. How soon can we marry?"

"As soon as you can arrange it."

"A perfect answer. Why are we going up to the house now? I'm P08 hardly dressed for a formal visit."

I said, "There's something I would very much like to suggest we do this evening, if you agree."

We were walking across the main lawn now, each with an arm about the other. I did not care a jot what the servants or anybody else might think. Henry shot me a sideways glance. "What's the suggestion, Mim? Remember I'm now a respectably affianced gentleman."

I laughed and rested my head against his shoulder. "No, I'm not repeating my earlier offer. I'm going to change into the clothes I wore when we were on the road, to make us more of a match. I still have them, you know. Then I would like you to drive us through to the King's Head at Little Farrington, so we can dine there just as we did with Paloma that first day we met."

His arm tightened about my waist. "There's nothing I'd love more. And this time you won't have to save me from choking on a swazzle first."

I smiled and said, "Since I discovered I love you, I've often remembered the first words you ever said to me."

"You have? What on earth were they?"

"You said, 'God help us all, I thought I was a goner for sure.' It wasn't very romantic, Henry."

He gave a shout of laughter, then kissed my cheek. "I'll make up for it," he said. "From now on I'll make up for it, Mim, my love."

I seemed to be walking without feeling the ground beneath my feet. The westering sun at my back was still warm, the arm about me was strong, the future unknown but agleam with promise, and I knew a thankfulness and a sense of completion beyond all words as we moved on together.